Sovereign or Slave?

"Don't you know what you've done to me these past months? I can't work, I can't sleep, I can't function for thinking of you."

When his mouth touched hers, he felt her heart race in perfect concert with his. He was acutely aware of the texture of her mouth, soft and pliant, against his. He felt her arms go around him, felt her fingers in his hair. His ardent kiss deepened. He felt both powerless and strong, at the mercy of the woman he held prisoner in his arms. As he sought to possess her, she possessed him completely. Her submission was a victory, and he, her physical conqueror, was most willingly hers to command.

* * *

"Jean Nash cleverly leads readers into a delicious maze, compelling them to eagerly turn the pages."

—*Romantic Times*

SAND CASTLES

Jean Nash

PAGEANT BOOKS

PAGEANT BOOKS
225 Park Avenue South
New York, New York 10003

Copyright © 1988 by Jean Nash

Cover artwork by Franco Accornero

Printed in the U.S.A.

First Pageant Books printing: September, 1988

10 9 8 7 6 5 4 3 2 1

FOR SUSAN
my daughter, my best friend

Acknowledgments

To my agent, Adele Leone, for her wisdom and perseverance. And to my editor, Carrie Feron, for her insight, her sensitivity and her delicious sense of humor.

As is the mother, so is her daughter.
—EZEKIEL 16:44

Prologue
◆ ◆ ◆ ◆ ◆

Newport, 1893

LAURA'S DAUGHTER WAS spoiled; there were no two ways about it. Whitney Sheridan was fourteen years old, looked seventeen, and sometimes behaved like an intractable two-year-old. And yet, as much as Laura deplored the situation, she had to admit that she herself was largely responsible for spoiling her. Whitney was her only child, and she was so loving, so endearing, that it was nearly impossible to deny even her smallest wish. Her smile was irresistible; it could melt a heart of stone. Had Raphael tried to paint her, he could not have captured her radiance. Dusky-dark curls enhanced a luminous fair face; a thick brush of lashes framed impudent dark eyes. Whitney's coloring was her father's, but her stubborn chin, offset by a charmingly upturned mouth, was dangerously identical to her mother's.

1

"But I *want* to go away to school," she repeated, plaguing Laura on the last day of the season at Bailey's Beach in Newport. "Marcella is going, and you know how strict Mr. MacKenzie is. Mama, it's not the Middle Ages, for heaven's sake; it's 1893. Girls *do* leave home to be educated nowadays. Besides, it's only a three-year course. And you have your decorating assignments to keep you busy; you won't even miss me."

Laura, on a lawn chair, sighed and looked out to sea. Sailboats bobbed in the distance. A great saffron sun shed hazy light on the spitting surf and silvery sand. On shore, colorful umbrellas shaded fashionably dressed ladies taking the last days of summer sun. Children raced to and fro, shouting, laughing, and eluding harried nursemaids, who pursued their rowdy charges in vain. Younger children, more docile, sat contentedly at water's edge building castles of sand with the help of doting papas.

How wonderful it had been when Whitney was younger, Laura thought wistfully. She could picture her at the age of five or six, a budding beauty in white dotted swiss, a pink sash at her waist, a pink ribbon in her hair. She'd been a perfect angel at that age: chubby, cherubic, sweet, and obedient. In fact, now that Laura thought about it, Whitney had been an ideal daughter even as recently as the summer before last. But Steven had been alive then, and Whitney had worshiped her father.

"Laura, why not let her go?" said the gentleman lounging beside her beneath the blue and green umbrella. "The Parker School is the finest girls' school on the entire Eastern Seaboard. And Connecticut is not the end of the earth, you know. We could go up to visit her occasionally; she'd be home for Christmas and Easter vacations—and of course all summer. To be educated by the Parker sisters is a splendid opportunity for a young lady. Several of my patients' daughters were schooled there, and they have nothing but the highest praise for Eudora and Vivian Parker."

Whitney, kneeling on the sand at Laura's feet, glanced at him gratefully. "Mama, see?" she said pleadingly. "Even Uncle Avery agrees with me."

Laura sighed again, outflanked and outwitted by the two she loved best. Avery Sheridan, her brother-in-law, had seen her through the difficult time following Steven's death. A widower himself, Avery had experienced firsthand the anguish of losing a life mate too soon. Three years ago his wife had died in childbirth after only fifteen months of marriage. At that time Laura had been his strength and support, never dreaming that a year later their roles would be reversed.

Avery was forty-one years old, nine years older than Laura. He differed physically from his brother, who had been ten years his senior. Fair-haired and gray-eyed, he had the look of a dreamy poet about him. He was anything but, however. At Saint Luke's Hospital he fought a never-ending and most times losing battle to improve sanitary conditions. He was one of the few physicians who scrubbed before surgery and operated in a clean surgical gown rather than street clothes. Though his colleagues sometimes mocked him, they feared him, for in his position as chief of staff he had dismissed many a slovenly practitioner. At home, though, he was another man: a compassionate friend to Laura, a loving uncle to Whitney. And Laura's gratitude for his concern for her knew no bounds.

"Very well," she agreed, causing Whitney to leap to her feet and whoop with joy. "When must you be there?"

"On September eleventh, a week before classes start. Uncle Avery enrolled me in May—"

"Avery!" Laura said, shocked.

He smiled lazily. "Come now, Laura," he said. "We knew you'd say yes. You always do."

"But—"

Whitney planted a lopsided kiss on her mother's cheek, cutting off any further protest, then she flung her arms around Avery's neck. "Uncle, I knew you could convince her!" she said triumphantly. "Mama, I'm going home to write to Marcella. She'll be thrilled to pieces when she hears I'm going to Connecticut with her."

She tore off across the beach, as graceful as a gazelle and as innocently uninhibited. Laura turned with a frown to her brother-in-law. "Avery, I'm terribly annoyed with you for enrolling her without telling me."

"Laura, forgive me," he said with a penitent moue. "It *was* an underhanded thing to do, but

I knew you'd change your mind about letting her go. If I had waited till now to enroll her, it would have been too late for her to start the term with Marcella."

"That's no excuse," she persisted.

"Laura, Laura." He reached over and gave her hand a persuasive squeeze. "You know how much Whitney wants this. It'll be good for her to get away, to have new interests. She broods too much about Steven. A change like this will benefit her immensely. And she did have a point before: You, at least, have your business to keep you occupied."

He had pronounced the word "business" with an undertone of irony that would have escaped Laura's notice had she not known him so well. "You disapprove of what I'm doing."

He leaned back in his chair and tipped his straw boater lower over his brow, obscuring his eyes and the expression therein. "It's not that I disapprove," he said carefully. "When you were decorating for a hobby, it was all well and good. But now that you've gone into business . . . well, it's simply that so many working women are feminists, and you know how I deplore those radicals. Besides," he added, "it's not as if you needed the money."

"Oh, but Avery, I don't do it for the money," she said at once. "I enjoy decorating houses. So many of our friends have neither the knack nor the patience to do it on their own. Those who rely on architects or furniture dealers are often disappointed in the results. Steven always said that the interior of a house needs a woman's touch. That's what gave me the idea in the first place."

"Laura," he said sternly, "I doubt Steven was suggesting you should do such a thing for a living."

"Perhaps not," she admitted. "But this is something I want to do. Social calls and charity work are no longer enough to fill my time. If Steven were alive, I would be more than happy to devote myself to him. But . . ." She trailed off and said nothing more. It was almost two full years since her husband had died, and she still found it difficult to speak of him.

Avery watched her surreptitiously from beneath the brim of his boater. He was used to these sudden silences. But he wasn't thinking of his brother at the moment. He was thinking how lovely Laura looked in her white voile frock and of how hard it had been for him to convince her to shed those awful mourning clothes. He was also thinking that never in his life had he seen skin as delicately ivory-colored as hers, or brown hair more lustrous, or blue eyes more celestially beautiful.

"It might be a good idea," he said presently, "if we were to accompany Whitney to Connecticut a few days earlier than scheduled. You could look around the place, get acquainted with the Parkers—I know you'll like them. And this way, having seen where she'll be spending her time, you won't be so lonely while she's away from you."

"Yes," Laura said softly. "I'd like to do that."

She gave him a smile that did not quite reach her eyes. He was right, of course: Boarding school would be the best thing in the world for Whitney. The girl missed her father; his death had been a blow from which she had still not recovered. But it wouldn't be easy letting her go—losing her—for that was what Laura felt the separation was going to be: a loss almost as irrevocable as that of Steven.

Laura Whitney Sheridan had been Steven Sheridan's wife for thirteen years, the greater part of a lifetime when one is married at seventeen, as she was. She had known him from childhood; he had been her father's partner in the architectural firm of Whitney & Sheridan. Although he was nineteen years older than she, it was her father's wish—and therefore hers—that she should marry him. She had been content as his wife, for she had loved and respected him, and he in turn had loved and cosseted her as thoroughly as her father had done before him.

It had been an easy transition from pampered daughter to pampered wife. Laura had had the conventional rearing of well-to-do girls in New York: a German governess, an Italian tutor, classes in dancing and art, occasional trips to Europe to broaden her cultural horizons. The only child of Laurence and Amelia Whitney, she had been blessed with the best traits of both parents: her mother's beauty and captivating charm and her father's sense of humor and his well-ordered, logical mind.

Laura's fondest childhood memories were of tiptoeing into her mother's boudoir and watching her dress for an evening at the Academy of Music. The room itself was an enchanted place to Laura. Pink damask paper covered the walls, and the furnishings were fragile Empire pieces with tapestried or damask seats. Amelia, at her dressing table, was likewise enchanting with her abundant dark hair, her dark-lashed blue eyes, and satin-smooth skin no less lustrous than her ivory satin gown.

Catching sight of her pretty daughter at the door, Amelia would beckon, smiling, *"Entrez, ma petite!"*

Happily Laura would patter into the room and fling her arms about her mother's neck. The most delicate of Parisian scents clung to that satin skin, a perfect floral tribute to the exquisite flower who wore it. Amelia would scold her daughter in her native French for being awake so late. In the same breath she would tell her, "Sit down and be as quiet as a little mouse, else Fraulein Gunther will hear you and whisk you off to bed."

Laura would watch, enraptured, while her mother completed her evening toilette. Diamond earrings graced tiny lobes; a diamond necklace spanned the whitest of swanlike necks. To Laura her mother seemed a brilliantly plumed exotic bird, dazzlingly beautiful in her gilded cage, and only a little bit tamed.

Later, her father would join them, handsome and dignified in his impeccable evening clothes. "Well!" he would exclaim with his irresistible smile. "Which one of you stunning creatures am I to escort to the opera tonight?"

Against the jewel-bright brilliance of Amelia's beauty Laurence Whitney's dark good looks were the perfect backdrop. Where she glowed with vivacity, he glimmered with quiet elegance. He was the quintessential Eastern Seaboard Yankee to her delightful Gallic coquette. They had met in Paris in 1860. Amelia was the eighteen-year-old daughter of an impoverished marquis, and Laurence was a twenty-year-old architectural student, the heir to a fortune in shipping and trade. A short courtship and swift marriage filled the marquis's empty coffers and cost him a daughter. The newlyweds sailed to America, conceiving their only child aboard ship. Laura often asked her mother if she ever regretted leaving home and family for the man she loved. Amelia, her superb eyes flashing, invariably answered, "I would have left heaven itself to be with your papa!"

Perhaps that was one of the reasons Laura found it so easy to fall in love with Steven Sheridan. He was very much like Laurence with his polished good looks and his good-humored aristocratic urbanity. He was a few years younger than Laurence, but no less sagacious. When he proposed to Laura, he told her sensibly, "I know I'm much older than you, but I love you very much and I think I can make you happy. If you want a younger man, though, I shall quite understand."

But Laura wanted *him*. He was the man her father wanted for her, and she wholeheartedly concurred in his choice. Not once during all her years with him did she regret her decision.

They lived in a showpiece of a Georgian mansion on Fifth Avenue, which Steven himself had designed for his delighted wife. They took frequent trips abroad to collect antiques and bric-a-brac for their stately house. Within a year of their marriage Laura presented Steven with a daughter, who bore his dusky-dark looks. When Laura's mother first saw the child, she said to her, *"Alors, ma petite,* you have brought forth life; the chain continues. The child is descended from my forebears, who fought with Du Guesclin and Jeanne d'Arc, and from your papa's people, who served the Plantagenets. Guard well the sacred life you have created."

Laura, weary from the birth but awed and exhilarated by her mother's pronouncement, nodded solemnly. In her mind's eye she saw a parade of progenitors: soldiers, saints, and scholars; intimates and enemies of chieftains and kings. From this magnificent lineage the infant in her arms had come to light. Laura was both exalted and humbled by the tiny miracle who nuzzled hungrily at her breast. No mother, she thought fiercely, could love a daughter as much as she loved this precious link between the past and the future.

As a young child, Whitney was partial to her father, but she was in awe of her beautiful mother. She would often wander into Laura's boudoir and watch her dress for an evening at the newly opened Metropolitan Opera House. To Whitney the shining beauty of the room was but a reflection of the woman who inhabited it. She would watch Laura, mesmerized, as she pinned up her lustrous hair or touched a bit of scent to the graceful line of her throat. Shyly she would press her cheek next to Laura's and gaze into the mirror, admiring the exquisite portrait that gazed back at them. "Mama, I look like you, don't I?" she would ask earnestly, hopefully. "Oh, no!" Laura would say and hug her close to her heart. "You're a hundred times prettier than I am."

They were the happiest of families, leading the happiest of charmed lives. When Laurence and Amelia were killed in a boating accident nine years after Laura's marriage, her grief was tempered by the belief that neither of her parents could have survived without the other and that their deaths, although untimely and tragic, were in reality a blessing. But when Steven died four years later after a fall from his horse, Laura's outlook was not nearly so pragmatic. When her husband died, taking with him all the loving security she had always taken for granted, all the comforting illusions of her pampered, sheltered youth died with him.

Whitney was brimming with excitement on the morning she was to leave for Connecticut. She kept darting between her bedroom and Laura's, rechecking the luggage, asking Laura a dozen times if everything had been packed, if she had the train tickets, if Uncle Avery would be at the house in plenty of time to get them to the station. Laura, dressing with the help of Rachel, her maid, had to laugh to keep from crying.

"Whitney, *please*," she said as Rachel fastened the buttons of her rust-colored traveling costume. "Everything is in order. Calm yourself, I beg you, or Uncle Avery will have to give you a sedative when he gets here."

"But, Mama, what if we forget something?" Whitney danced impatiently between the pier mirror and her mother, trying to capture her attention. "Marcella said the Parker sisters demand absolute adherence to their every rule. Did you remember to check their list and pack everything on it?"

Whitney was wearing a new garnet suit and a pink shirtwaist with a high lace collar. She had already put on her hat, an English straw trimmed with a spray of pink roses. She looked twenty years old except for her adolescent fidgeting. Again Laura laughed to stem a flood of maudlin tears.

"Darling, I packed *everything*," she assured her as Rachel finished buttoning her dress and turned to some last-minute tasks. "Now stop bobbing up and down. You're making me woozy."

Whitney pulled herself together and eyed her mother askance. "Mama, I don't think you realize the significance of this day," she said, annoyed. "Why, it's a turning point in my life. From here on in, I'm no longer a child. I'll be living on my own for the first time—"

"With two hundred other girls," Laura interjected.

"—and I'll be making my own decisions."

"Provided the Parker sisters permit you to do so."

"*You* didn't leave home until the day you were married," Whitney pointed out with self-importance. "At fourteen, I shall achieve a level of maturity that you didn't achieve until you were seventeen."

"I'm impressed," Laura said.

Whitney frowned at her mother's refusal to take her seriously, then, aware of her own absurdity, she giggled. "I sounded like a pompous fool just then, didn't I?"

"A little," Laura said wryly. "Now stop your chattering and come give me a hug."

The girl went readily into her arms. They hugged each other so tightly that both of them were breathless, but neither made a move to break the embrace. Laura's throat swelled; her eyes grew hot. The dreaded moment was almost at hand. She was losing her, losing her baby. In an hour or so they would be boarding a train, together still, but the breach of separation had already begun. Laura had known it would be difficult to see her fledgling leave the nest, but she hadn't expected the loneliness to start this soon.

"You will be careful?" she whispered, stroking Whitney's silky hair.

"Yes, Mama." Her voice, too, was subdued.

"And you'll be a good girl, respectful and obedient?"

"Yes, Mama."

"If you need anything, darling, *anything*—"

"Mrs. Sheridan," Rachel interrupted, "I just heard the doorbell. It must be Dr. Sheridan come to fetch you."

Whitney wrenched herself out of Laura's arms and went dashing out the door. Laura, feeling slightly stunned and greatly abandoned, looked bleakly about the room that only a moment ago had shone with the radiance of Whitney's youthful ebullience. It seemed dark now, and barren, a desolate cell no less empty and lonely for its elegance.

Chapter One

✦ ✦ ✦ ✦

New York City, 1895

CHRISTOPHER WARREN WAS late for his appointment,
but worse than that, he felt he wasn't prepared.
He had been up all night putting finishing
touches on his plans for the Tylers' new house
on Fifth Avenue. A dozen times this morning he
had gone over the specifications to assure himself of the perfection of his design. The house,
for the most part, was a masterpiece of Palladian
classicism. But instead of sporting porticoes as
he had originally planned, and most other architects would have drawn, he had featured Diocletian windows, giving the house a dramatic
effect. This inspiration had struck him midway
through the design. It was that deviation from
the original concept that bothered him now, because it was too late to change it, and he suspected the Tylers would dislike it.

15

With an impatient sigh he wrapped the rolled plans in a length of oilcloth, then tucked them under his arm and gave himself a final inspection before leaving his flat. In the cracked pier mirror he saw a lean, hard face; curling dark hair; fierce, dark eyes; and a strong, slender frame as graceful as an athlete's despite the threadbare suit and frayed linen shirt that covered it. He was poor; he wasn't ashamed of it. At the age of thirty-two Christopher knew who he was and what he was. Sixteen years in an orphanage had matured him early, had taught him that a man gets nothing from life but what he puts into it.

He envisioned the architects against whom he would be competing for the Tyler house. They would all be superbly dressed, expertly barbered, wearing boots of the finest leather buffed to a mirror shine by fastidious valets. Behind all of them would be years of formal schooling, at Harvard perhaps, or at L'École des Beaux-Arts. The most successful architects were all aristocrats. They designed great mansions in which they themselves could afford to live—unlike Christopher, who could barely afford the rent on his one-room flat on the lower East Side.

It was raining when he left the building, a cold autumn rain that sent him dashing to the corner to take shelter beneath a store awning, where he waited, shivering, for the Houston Street streetcar. His appointment was for ten o'clock; it was already five minutes past. With luck he would arrive at the Tyler house near Washington Square at half past ten.

His employer and mentor, Henry Carlisle, had warned him: "Whatever you do, be on time for the presentation. The Tylers are sticklers for punctuality. Don't take the chance of losing your first commission simply because of tardiness."

"I won't be late, sir," Christopher promised him. He would have promised to give up his life if Henry had requested it.

Years earlier, Henry, an architect of great repute, had been appointed chairman of the board of trustees of Saint Peter's Presbyterian Orphanage. Silver-haired, with a sweeping white mustache and keen gray eyes, he was a Jovian figure, an imperious tyrant when dealing with contractors and builders, but beneath his fearsome exterior beat the most tender of hearts. When he discovered the cruelty that prevailed at Saint Peter's, the insufficient meals, the corporal punishment meted out by sadistic men of the cloth, he summarily dismissed every last member of the staff. Upon interviewing the older boys, Henry was impressed by Christopher's tight-lipped refusal to discuss his tormentors. "They're gone and good riddance to them," was all the boy would say.

Taking Christopher under his wing, Henry installed the boy as an apprentice in his offices and taught him architecture by day and engineering by night. And how Christopher loved architecture! How he gloried in the precision and romance of its art. Christopher owed much to Henry Carlisle, who had expanded the scope of his world, offering vistas undreamed of. Now, as he sighted the Houston Street streetcar and

prepared to board en route to Washington
Square, he hoped he would be able to justify his
mentor's faith in him.

The Tyler house was a Gothic horror of
pointed arches, flying buttresses, and ribbed
vaults. As Christopher mounted the front steps,
he shuddered with distaste and with renewed
doubt of the success of his design. The Tylers
would disdain the classic simplicity of his house,
he was now sure of it. This was a garish age,
paying homage to flamboyance and ostentation,
and the Tylers' house was a reflection of that.
People lived in French "chateaux," worshiped
on Sundays in Gothic Revival churches, caught
trains in railway terminals reminiscent of Roman
baths. Christopher knocked at the door and felt
suddenly sick. He shouldn't have come; he
wasn't ready for public presentation. He had
neither the stomach nor the desire to compromise his principles, to conform to the standards
of this gaudy gilded age.

A butler answered the door, portly and pompous in funereal black and spotless white
gloves. "Yes?" he said, casting a scornful look
on Christopher's rain-soaked hat and well-worn
attire.

"I'm Christopher Warren." His tone was defensive. He had not missed the significance of
that look. "I'm an architect. The Tylers are expecting me."

The butler sniffed. "The interviews are over."

He started to close the door, but Christopher
leaned a shoulder against it. "I have an appointment," he said.

"Listen here, young man, you had better—"

"Who is it, Collins?" said a voice from the foyer.

The butler turned, still barring the door. "It is another architect, madam."

"Let him in." The voice was soft, feminine, but unmistakably authoritative.

"Very good, madam."

Collins opened the door with ill-concealed resentment, stepping aside to let Christopher enter. A woman stood in the foyer, her features indistinguishable in the gloom, but wealth and good breeding were evident in her carriage and in the exquisite draping of her blue cashmere dress.

"Mrs. Tyler," Christopher said, removing his hat, "I'm sorry I'm late."

"I'm not Mrs. Tyler," the woman said. "I'm Laura Sheridan. I'll be decorating the interior of the Tylers' new house. You're Christopher Warren, aren't you? I had almost given you up for lost. How do you do?" She held out her hand, and when Christopher took it, he was surprised by both the softness of her skin and the firmness of her grip. "Come into the study; we can talk in there. Collins, take Mr. Warren's hat, if you please."

The butler complied, handling the hat as if it were a section of decomposed carcass.

The woman laughed softly as she preceded Christopher to the study. "Don't mind him," she said in a confidential tone. "He even intimidates the Tylers. They've wanted to discharge him for years, but they're too afraid to do so!"

Christopher smiled, slightly more at ease as he entered the study. The room was brightly lit, and there was a good fire on the grate. He was dimly aware of dark draperies and heavy rococo furnishings, but his attention was riveted on the graceful woman as she sat behind the desk and motioned for him to be seated.

He could not tell her age. She was one of those fortunate women whose perfect bone structure supports silk-fine flawless skin from brow to jawline. Her hair was a rich shade of brown, expertly coiffed in the current Gibson Girl mode. Her nose was straight and narrow, saved from severity by a soft, charming mouth naturally upturned at the corners. But her most arresting feature was her eyes—a deep, pure blue fringed by long, dark lashes, from which Christopher found he could not tear his gaze.

"May I see your design, Mr. Warren?"

His hands tightened on the plans. She was watching him, *studying* him it seemed. Christopher was suddenly aware of what he must look like to her: his trousers soaked at the cuffs, his hair curling untidily on his brow. "Miss Sheridan, I—"

"It's Mrs. Sheridan."

She was married. The news surprised him. And, inexplicably, it annoyed him. "Mrs. Sheridan," he said more sharply than he intended, "it was my understanding that the Tylers would be looking at my design."

She did not answer. She continued to watch him, apparently taken aback by the forcefulness of his tone. After a moment she said evenly, "The

Tylers are not here, Mr. Warren, but they have given me full authority to choose a house that will best suit their needs. Of course, if you have some objection to showing me your plans—"

"I have no objection!" he said at once, regretting his harshness and silently cursing himself. He was unused to dealing with women. For the first sixteen years of his life he had seldom seen one. And even after he left the orphanage, he had devoted himself so fully to his work that he had not had the time to make social contacts, either female or male. The few women he did know, however, could in no way be compared with the lady now facing him, whose arresting blue gaze dwelt so intently upon him.

"Mrs. Sheridan, please forgive my bad manners. To be perfectly frank, this is my first presentation, and I'm a little short-tempered today."

She smiled unexpectedly, which put him somewhat at ease. It was a lovely smile, oddly tentative, as if she feared he might think she was making sport of him. To Christopher it seemed the essence of femininity.

"Mr. Warren, how different you are from the men I've been talking to all morning."

He returned her smile wryly. "I've been told that before, Mrs. Sheridan."

"I'm anxious to see your design," she reminded him tactfully.

"Yes, of course."

He rose with alacrity, unwrapped the plans, and spread them out before her on the desk for her to study. He could not see her eyes, but from

the curve of her cheek and the lift of her mouth,
he could tell she was very much impressed.

She said, still looking at the plans, "I see you
are an admirer of Andrea Palladio."

"Why, yes," he said, surprised, resuming his
seat and leaning forward, elbows on knees.
"You're familiar with his work?"

She looked up at him and smiled again. "Yes,
I am. My husband was an architect; he, too, was
partial to Palladian design."

" 'Was'?"

"He died four years ago."

Christopher chose not to comment. He had
the sudden, insane desire to say, "I'm delighted
to hear that." Instead he leaned back in his chair
and folded his arms. He wasn't himself today.
He had been agonizing too long over this presentation. But as he regarded the woman who
held his fate in her hands, he realized dimly that
his present agitation had little or nothing to do
with his work.

She returned her attention to the plans. "I'm
going to be very candid with you," she said
slowly. "I like your design, but I'm a little uncertain as to what the Tylers will think of it."

A swift rage assailed him. She looked up at
that moment and caught the look on his face.
"Mr. Warren," she hastened to say, "there's
nothing wrong with your work, I assure you. It's
simply that the Tylers' taste runs to the more . . .
ornate."

"I see."

His tone was leaden. He rose abruptly and

reached for the plans. He should have known better than to . . .

"No, please!" Her hand closed on his—so soft a hand and yet so steely a grip. "Mr. Warren, I didn't say the answer was no."

He pulled his hand from hers with a roughness that startled her. "Mrs. Sheridan, let's not waste each other's time. The Tylers obviously want a house with battlements and turrets and stained-glass windows, am I right? I don't design such houses; I would sooner dig ditches for a living than put my name to one of those atrocities."

"Mr. Warren, please sit down." Her unruffled demeanor tempered his anger but did not abolish it. With none too good grace, he sat. "No one's asking you to design such a house. You're not far wrong in your assessment of the Tylers' preferences, but in this instance they have told me they will rely entirely on my judgment. That's not to say that their taste can be completely disregarded. Do you understand me?"

"Yes," he said shortly. "You mean that if they do choose my house, I shall have to alter the design to resemble a nightmare of a gingerbread Gothic."

"I mean nothing of the kind." She paused, then said carefully, "Mr. Warren, forgive my impertinence, but you're far too defensive about your work. You'll garner precious few commissions with that attitude."

His face grew hot. He knew she was right, but before he could stop himself, he snapped, "What concern is that of yours?"

He regretted his words the instant he spoke them, for a look of astonished injury leaped into her eyes. The look vanished at once, and she answered simply, "It concerns me a great deal to see talent like yours go to waste."

Again his anger was tempered in the face of her cool control. He had never known a woman like her; he had never known anyone quite like her. She was attractive, intelligent, supremely self-possessed, yet in her straightforward gaze and her soft, upturned mouth he sensed a core of vulnerability that was totally at variance with his impression of her.

"I'm sorry," he apologized. "I had no call to speak to you that way. Keep the plans; show them to the Tylers—that is, if you still want them."

"I do want them," she said evenly. "I should very much like the Tylers to accept your house. You see," she added quietly, her long lashes lowering to conceal her fine blue eyes, "it's exactly the sort of house my husband would have designed."

Chapter Two

✦✦✦✦✦

AFTER CHRISTOPHER LEFT the Tyler house, Laura remained at the desk and looked at his presentation for a very long time. In the ground plans, elevations, and traverse sections she saw not a pen-and-ink rendering of a Palladian-style house, but the architect's lean face, his hard, handsome mouth, and those brilliant, disturbing dark eyes.

She lifted a sheet of the plans to examine it more closely and was astonished to discover that her hand was trembling. What a tempestuous man he was! Never in her quiet, well-ordered, sheltered life had she met anyone like him. He seemed an untamed force of nature, volatile and dangerous, with the breathtaking beauty of a violent storm. She tried to concentrate on his work, but all she could see was his dark curling hair framing that strong, arresting face: the high brow, the straight nose, the elegant curve of his jaw.

She could not tell how old he was. Having spent most of her life in the company of people so much older than herself, she found it difficult to pinpoint the age of a contemporary. Surrounded by men in their forties, fifties, and sixties, she was surprised that someone as young as Christopher appeared could have attained such a degree of excellence in his work. She also wondered how an architect so gifted could be in such obviously straitened circumstances. Despite his well-worn attire, he had the look of a warrior prince about him: tall, fierce, regal, and commanding. Laura could picture him on horseback, a shield in one hand, a gleaming sword in the other, vanquishing all foes, surmounting all obstacles, taking everything he wanted just by the force of his will.

Collins entered the study with his unobtrusive, light-footed tread. He cleared his throat. Laura looked up from the plans with a start.

"Yes, Collins?"

"Will you be staying for lunch, madam?"

"Thank you, no, Collins. If you'll get my things, I'll be leaving now."

"Have you made a decision as to the new house, Mrs. Sheridan?"

Laura rose and rolled up the plans. "Yes, I have," she said. "When the Tylers return, you may tell them I'll call on them tomorrow morning to discuss my choice."

It was still raining hard when she left the Tyler house and traveled to her own. As the carriage approached Fifth Avenue and Fifty-fifth Street, Laura looked out the window past the nondescript brownstones to the white Georgian house that stood in solitary splendor. The sight of her house's artistry never failed to thrill her. Three stories rose majestically within a single order of Corinthian pilasters. Tall leaded windows lent a gracious, mellow air to the utter simplicity of the structure. As the coachman handed her down from the carriage, an umbrella held high, the thought occurred to Laura that Christopher Warren, with his fierce insistence on architectural purity, would approve of this design without reserve.

When she entered the house, the lovely arpeggio of a Scarlatti sonata reached her ears. She recognized Avery's piano technique. As her butler took her things, she asked, "How long has Dr. Sheridan been here, Thompson?"

"Not long, Mrs. Sheridan. Perhaps a quarter hour or so."

"Set another place for lunch, please."

"Yes, madam."

Carrying Christopher's plans, Laura crossed the long hall to the music room and drew open the double doors. Avery, at the piano, stopped playing and rose.

"My dear," he said, smiling, "forgive the intrusion. I was in the neighborhood visiting a patient, and I thought I'd stop by to see you."

She dropped the plans on a table, went to him, and gave him a brief kiss. "I forgive you," she said dryly. Avery, it seemed, was forever "in the neighborhood," especially since Whitney had gone away to school. "Sit down," she said, taking a seat by the fireplace. "You'll stay for lunch, of course?"

"Thank you, I will." He swished aside his coattails and sat opposite her. "How are you, Laura? I haven't seen you in a while."

She suppressed a smile. He had seen her only last week. "I'm well as always, Avery. And I'm happy to report that my 'little business venture,' as you call it, is keeping me quite busy."

"Now, Laura," he said sternly, "I've told you straight out that I'm not belittling what you do.

You know what my reservations are about your working for money. It's a little . . . degrading, if you'll permit me to be blunt. If Steven were alive, he'd be the first one to protest."

"I think you're wrong," she said quietly. "I think he'd . . ." She trailed off and lowered her gaze. She didn't want to talk about Steven. He'd been strong in her thoughts today, ever since that curious young man had presented his design to her.

Avery watched her for a moment with an intensity that would have troubled her had she seen it. Presently he said, "What do you hear from Whitney? How is she enjoying her final year at school?"

Laura's thoughts of her husband were replaced by even more troublesome thoughts of his daughter. "I've only had one letter from her since she left in September," she said unhappily. "Despite the fact that we parted on good terms, I think she's still angry that I refused to allow her to go abroad with her friends next summer. Avery, I just don't understand modern girls. When I was her age, I wouldn't have dreamed of going to Europe without my parents."

"This is a different time," he pointed out, "an era of change. In a few more years we'll be entering a new century."

"I suppose you're right," she had to agree. "Perhaps I think differently because I'm from another generation." Or, she thought, because I am so much in the company of people who are two or three generations removed from Whitney. "That reminds me," she said suddenly, her thoughts turning to someone who was very much of her generation. She rose and went to the table where she had left Christopher Warren's plans. "Avery, I want to show you something extraordinary."

He rose and joined her as she unrolled the plans. "Take a look at this design," she said, casually covering Christopher's signature with a paperweight.

"It's very handsome," Avery remarked. "I've never seen this one. When did Steven do it?"

"It's in his style, isn't it?" Laura said.

"Yes." Avery gazed pensively at the exquisite fluid lines of the house. "Steven's style was unique."

"This isn't his work, Avery."

"What?" He looked at her in disbelief. "Whose is it?"

"It was done by a young man named Christopher Warren. He's Henry Carlisle's protégé. Henry asked the Tylers to consider his design for their new house."

"But that's astonishing!" Avery looked again at the plans. "Did Steven train him? No, of course not. You just said he was Henry's protégé. Laura, the similarity of style is incredible."

"It is, isn't it?" she said softly.

Avery shot her a keen look, but Laura didn't see it. Her attention was on the classic lines of the design that was almost painful in its familiarity.

"Laura, you did say this house was for the Tylers?"

"Yes." Her attention remained rooted to the plans.

"Have they seen it yet?"

She looked up at last. "No, they haven't."

Avery shook his head reprovingly. "I can't imagine why you're even contemplating this house for those people. You know very well what Nina and Jeremy will think of it. I hope you haven't been so rash as to have raised that young man's hopes."

A pang of conscience brought a flush of color to her cheeks. Reluctantly she admitted, "I did tell him that the Tylers would rely on my judgment."

"For heaven's sake, Laura. Whatever possessed you to do such a thing?"

Her soft mouth hardened stubbornly. "I want this house."

"*You* want it? That's not your decision to make."

"I can persuade the Tylers—"

"No you can't, and you know it. Think about the house they now own. Only a mad Bavarian nobleman would have chosen such a design. Do you honestly believe the Tylers will even look twice at this house?"

"Avery, they must!" she said with a fervent intensity. "This house is—"

"This house is not yours," he said flatly. "Please bear that in mind, Laura."

But she was unable to make that distinction in her mind. Those bold strokes on paper spoke to her. The purity of design was Steven Sheridan's hallmark. Every line, every curve, was as familiar to her as the contours of his face—she saw them still. She missed him so much; she wanted him back, and she wanted this house.

Or, she thought suddenly—and the thought brought her up short—was it something else she wanted, something else that was moving her so deeply? Something, perhaps, that she had never really had?

The next morning, Laura, in a trim walking suit of navy blue broadcloth, set out for the Tyler house near Washington Square. Her tailored white blouse featured a high stock collar; her shallow-brimmed felt hat gave the final no-nonsense touch to her businesslike attire. The Tylers were Laura's friends, but it was important that she impress upon them that this meeting was not a social one. Although most of the people she knew accepted her work as a serious endeavor, there were still those few who considered it a lark, the amusing diversion of an idle-rich widow.

As the carriage rolled south, Laura's thoughts kept returning to her uncharacteristic outburst at Avery the day before. What was it she saw in that strange young man? Surely, on the surface, it was the similarity of his style to Steven's. But it was more than that, much more. There was a vigor—no, a drive—in Christopher Warren that had never existed in Steven Sheridan. Steven had taken his work seriously, but he had never had to struggle to succeed as Laura imagined Christopher Warren did. Christopher's work, unlike Steven's, seemed his very essence, his life-force. Laura had actually felt currents of energy emanate from his person as he watched her across the desk and waited for her verdict. The feeling had been disturbing, yet not unpleasantly so. Even now, simply thinking of him, she felt invigorated by the memory of his contagious vitality.

When she reached the Tyler house, she alighted from the carriage, mounted the front steps, and tucked Christopher's plans more firmly under her arm. Their proximity reassured her at the same time that they strengthened her purpose. She knocked at the door. Nina herself answered, bright-eyed, apple-cheeked, wearing a fussy pink frock that defiantly called attention to her overly plump form.

"Dearest Laura!" she greeted her, ushering her eagerly into the house. "Collins tells me you've chosen a house for us. I can't wait to see it!"

In the study, Jeremy, a lean rail of a man with thinning dark hair, rose with alacrity as the two women entered. "Laura!" he said, directing her to his chair behind the desk. "Sit down. Nina and I have been waiting on pins and needles to see our new house."

Laura sat down and placed the plans on the desk but did not unroll them. She looked up at the Tylers, who beamed down at her expectantly, and a momentary qualm held her silent. These were her friends, she was fond of them, and they trusted her completely. Yet all she

could think of was that fierce young man she
hardly knew.

"Before I show you the house," she finally
said, "I want you to prepare yourselves for
something different."

"Different?" echoed Nina, who thrived on
stylish conformity. "In what way different,
dear?"

"I have here," Laura said in a hushed, important tone, "a design so revolutionary that it
promises to be the vanguard of twentieth-
century architecture."

"My word!" said Jeremy, hastily drawing up a
chair for himself and his hesitant wife. "Let us
see it at once, Laura."

"I must warn you again," she said gravely.
"This is a design so unique that the unpracticed
eye may fail to grasp its momentous significance."

"Yes, yes," Jeremy said, bursting with curiosity. "Let's have a look at it."

With great ceremony, Laura unrolled the
plans. The Tylers stared at the house while
Laura, outwardly calm, inwardly anxious,
looked from Jeremy's blank face to Nina's.

"Laura," Nina said, raising bewildered eyes to
hers, "are you sure you've brought us the correct plans? This building looks like . . . like a
library in rural New England."

"One moment, my pet," said Jeremy, equally
bewildered but more open to innovation than
his slavishly conventional wife. "As Laura said,
this design is unique, revolutionary. Naturally,

at first glance, one would be apt to disregard or condemn it."

"But, my love," Nina said uncomfortably, loath to insult or injure, "it is so very *plain*."

"I was afraid of this," said Laura, affecting a tone of regret. "A design as exceptional as this one is often misunderstood." She rose with a sigh. "I so much wanted you two to be the first in our set to have this house, but I see now that it's not at all the right thing for you."

"Hold on there, Laura," Jeremy said as she leaned over to retrieve the plans. "Let *me* decide if the house is right or wrong for us."

"Jeremy . . ." Nina said pleadingly.

"Now, now, my pet." He patted her hand. "Do you remember how much you disliked Mr. Sargent's portrait of Lady Agnew? Yet it was that very same painting that won him election to the Royal Academy last year. You must not be so quick to judge, Nina. Come, look at the house. You hardly glanced at it before."

"Jeremy," said Laura with a regret now that was genuine, "I think Nina's reservations may be valid. This *isn't* the right house for you. Let me have the plans. I'll telephone one of the other architects I spoke with. I'm sure I can find something more suited to your needs."

"Nonsense," he said brusquely. "I want to give this house my full consideration. Leave the plans here, and I'll let you know in a day or two what I've decided."

He rose and went to the bellpull that hung alongside the mantel. "Will you stay and have lunch with us? I know it's early, but we rushed through breakfast in anticipation of your visit, and now I am absolutely famished!"

"Thank you, no," Laura murmured, glancing guiltily at the plans.

Having artfully piqued Jeremy's interest, there was now no way for her to dissuade him. She was certain he would accept Christopher Warren's design despite Nina's aversion to it. Laura had done what she had set out to do. For the first time, she had deliberately advised a friend, not with his ends in mind, but with her own.

Chapter Three
✦✦✦✦

CHRISTOPHER WARREN WAS ravenously hungry, though only an hour before he had lunched at Delmonico's as a co-worker's guest, consuming so large a meal that the stout young draftsman had growled enviously, "Where the devil do you put it all? You eat like a vulture, yet you never gain an ounce."

Lavishly buttering his fourth hot roll, Christopher had laughed. "If you worked a little harder," he had joked, "you might lose some of that excess weight."

"Hard work?" The draftsman had shuddered. "I'll leave that to you."

Christopher shook his head and laughed

again. "You always do, Ned. You always do."

Christopher was seated in his alcove at the architectural firm of Carlisle & Hastings, quietly segregated from the busy conglomeration of drafting tables, drawing racks, print rooms, and general offices. He was listlessly sketching a holy-water stoup for a Catholic cathedral Henry had designed for the archdiocese of Baltimore. This was Christopher's principal function in the firm. He was Henry's junior assistant, but all he did in that capacity was add ornament and decoration to the churches, libraries, and learning institutions that Carlisle & Hastings was renowned for designing.

For years Christopher had been pleading with Henry to allow him to design on his own. "I'm ready," he constantly told his mentor. "Let me show you what I can do; I won't disappoint you."

"Not yet," Henry kept saying.

"When?" Christopher would demand. "When I'm old and gray and too feeble to hold a pencil?"

Henry would smile at his protégé's impatience. "It won't be that long, I give you my promise."

But it had seemed at least an eon until Henry finally relented and gave Christopher the Tyler house to design. And the ten days Christopher had been waiting for an answer from Laura Sheridan seemed even longer than that. He couldn't work, couldn't sleep; he thought of nothing but his design and of the woman who held his future in her beautiful and aristocratic hands. He kept seeing her face, the flawless skin, the curve of cheek, the upturned mouth, the brilliant color blue of her extraordinary eyes. He kept hearing the intonations of her soft cultured voice. Over and over again he imagined that voice saying, "I'm so sorry, Mr. Warren. I did my best to try to convince them, but the Tylers have decided that they don't want your house."

"Christopher," said a voice, interrupting that dismal thought, "Henry wants you in his office."

Christopher looked up from his drawing board to see Ned Bailey, the co-worker who had treated him to lunch. At the age of twenty-seven, Ned was five years younger than Christopher, but with his roguish green eyes and often tousled ginger hair, he looked even younger. He was wealthy and well connected, a competent but uninspired architect who cheerfully accepted the fact that he would never be anything but a drafts-man at Carlisle & Hastings. Good-natured and unambitious, he greatly admired Christopher's talent and was a good friend to him, despite their differences of class and temperament.

"What does he want, Ned?"

"I think it's about your design. Laura Sheridan is with him."

"Laura Sheridan?" Christopher leaped to his feet, upsetting a bottle of ink, which sent a splash across the detail of the stoup. "Christ," he muttered, hastily grabbing a cloth and dab-bing at the mess.

Ink stained his fingertips as he blotted the spill. "Damn, *damn!*" He threw down the cloth and stared fiercely at his hands. "I'll never get this off."

"Go to the lavatory," Ned suggested help-
fully. "Some oxalic acid will banish those stains.
Don't forget to rinse thoroughly with water afterward."

"Yes," Christopher said distractedly. "Oxalic
acid. That'll do the trick. Ned, tell Henry I'll be
with him in a moment."

He swept past his friend and made haste toward the lavatory, oblivious to the heads that
turned his way as he sped by. He was wringing
his hands, much in the manner of Lady Macbeth. A waggish architect, catching sight of this,
quipped loudly, "Out, damned spot! out, I say!"
But Christopher heard nothing; his thoughts
were bent solely on the lady in Henry's office
and on the design that he feared had been rejected absolutely.

Once in the lavatory he snatched a bottle of
oxalic acid from the shelf, ripped out the cork, and
poured a generous measure on his hands. He
took a stiff brush from the sink stand and
scrubbed till his flesh burned. The ink stains vanished, but beneath his fingernails and around his
cuticles a telltale trace of black remained.

Turning on the tap and holding his hands under running water, he glanced up into the mirror
and was appalled by what he saw. His hair was
disheveled; beads of perspiration dotted his face.

Ned Bailey poked his head in the doorway.
"Shake a leg, Christopher! Henry's waiting."

Christopher jumped. One hand jerked up and
hit the spigot with a painful rap. "Damn it,
Ned!" He whirled on him angrily. "I'll be there
directly, for God's sake."

Ned tactfully withdrew. Christopher turned
back to the mirror, clumsily attempting to smooth
his hair with damp hands. It was hopeless, hopeless; he looked like a tramp. Never before in his
life had he wished he were sleekly prosperous
like most of the smug young men with whom he
worked, but he fervently wished it now.

With a grimace of disgust, he turned off the
tap, dried his hands on the coarse linen towel,
and left the room. Henry's private office was at
the front of the building, looking out across
Broadway onto Trinity Churchyard. From the
tall double windows could be seen the impressive monument to Alexander Hamilton, as well
as the stone marking James Leeson's grave with
its lugubrious epitaph: REMEMBER DEATH.

No less somber was Christopher as he entered
the office. The smart appointments of the wood-
paneled room failed to catch his notice and lift
his spirits as they normally did in times of stress.
His entire attention was on the woman who
turned in her chair as he entered, whose lovely,
aristocratic, unsmiling face told him all he had
been dreading to hear.

"There you are at last!" said Henry from behind his desk. "Come in, Christopher; sit down.
Mrs. Sheridan has been waiting to talk to you."

Christopher sat on a straightback chair opposite Laura, his eyes never leaving her face. She
was wearing a Persian lamb jacket with a camel-
colored wool skirt. Her hat was a Persian pillbox,
the black veil lending mystery to her fine dark-
lashed eyes. On her lap was a small muff upon
which her slender white hands were gracefully

crossed. She looked even more beautiful than when Christopher had last seen her.

"Mrs. Sheridan," he said, "good afternoon."

"Mr. Warren," she said, "how nice to see you again."

Those simple courteous words and the low tone of her voice put him somewhat at ease despite the paralyzing tension that held him in its grip. "I take it you've brought me bad news," he said and was astonished that he could speak so lightly about a disappointment he felt so profoundly.

"On the contrary," Laura said, astonishing him further. "The news is good, Mr. Warren. The Tylers want your house."

For a moment he could not breathe, nor indeed could he speak. His shirt collar was a strangling constriction about his throat; his hand moved unconsciously to the knot of his tie. "They want it?" he said blankly.

"They want it," Laura said, and she finally smiled.

He had forgotten her smile, the charming tentative upcurving of mouth, the glimpse of ivory teeth, the hint of a dimple in her gardenia-smooth cheek. He wished she were not wearing a veil. He wished suddenly, feverishly, that he could touch that soft mouth, that he could feel it, warm and pliant, against his throat, against his cheek, and then yielding submissively beneath the hard demanding onslaught of his own.

He gave himself an abrupt mental shake, wondering what in God's name had come over him. This was not one of those women at the brothel on Sixth Avenue. Laura Sheridan was a lady, a well-bred, respectable widow, and to even think of her in that manner was an insult of the vilest kind. He stared at her silently, aroused and rendered speechless by his erotic thoughts. She returned his gaze in that quiet, searching way that so disconcerted him, and again he became acutely aware of how he must look to her.

"Laura," Henry commented, "I strongly suspect that you had to use the most skillful of salesmanship tactics to convince the Tylers to accept Christopher's design."

Now Laura was the one who appeared disconcerted. She fidgeted with her muff then looked up at Henry. "Not really," she said. "The Tylers perhaps did not have a house such as Mr. Warren's in mind, but after they saw it and thought about it, they were most enthusiastic."

Henry leaned back in his chair and tugged thoughtfully at his mustache. "I think you're being too modest, Laura."

"Henry, no," she said softly. "I had very little to do with it, I assure you. Nina and Jeremy love the house; they're anxious to begin construction." She paused, and looked to Christopher. "They're also anxious to meet with you, Mr. Warren, to discuss certain aspects of the design. Would you be free to dine with the three of us tomorrow night at my house?"

"Dine with you?" he echoed. He glanced down at his shabby broadcloth and at his hands clenched on his knees, the fingernails and cuticles still distinctly traced with ink. "Very well," he said reluctantly. "What time shall I be there?"

"At eight," she said, rising and giving him the address. The two men rose also. "I must be going now. Good day, Mr. Warren." She reached out to shake his hand, and again he was surprised by the firmness of her grip.

"Mrs. Sheridan," he said, holding on to her hand, unwilling and quite unable to release it, "I cannot tell you how much I appreciate . . ." He trailed off and stared at her, unaware that his hand was crushing hers, unaware that Henry was watching him, his keen gray eyes taking in the situation with comprehension and concern.

"Let me escort you to your carriage, Laura," Henry said, moving toward her. "Christopher, please wait here for me. I'd like a word with you."

Christopher dropped Laura's hand and stepped back from her. "Yes, of course, sir. Good day, Mrs. Sheridan. I'll see you tomorrow night."

She smiled and nodded, then turned to Henry and left the room with him. The instant they were gone, Christopher began pacing, no longer able to contain his excitement. He had won his first commission; he could scarcely believe it. His joy was a great bubble in his breast, on the point of exploding and sending showers of sensation through every fiber of his being. He wanted to freeze this moment in time, to hold on to it, to savor it, for even in the midst of his elation, he dimly realized the transitory nature of such a breathtaking triumph. "Happiness is fleeting; sorrow endures." Where had he read that? And why did he think of it now when his joy was so overpowering he could barely endure it?

"Christopher, what's the verdict?" Ned Bailey

was at the door, his eyes alight with the contagion of Christopher's evident excitement. "She said yes, didn't she?"

"Yes!" Christopher loped over to him and grasped both his arms in a painful grip. "Ned, I can't believe it; the Tylers want my house. My God, I'm numb!"

"Ouch!" Ned said, twisting out of Christopher's hold. "You're not so numb that you can't break my arms. Relax, won't you? So you've sold your first design. I told you you had nothing to worry about. Sit down," he said, leading him to the chair. "Tell me all the details. Have they accepted it as is, or are they going to want changes?"

Christopher ignored the chair and took up his restless pacing again. "I don't know. I'm meeting with the Tylers and Mrs. Sheridan tomorrow night to discuss—" He stopped suddenly as an unpleasant thought struck him. "Jesus, Ned."

"What's the matter?"

"I'm having dinner with them," he said, running a hand through his hair, "and I haven't the proper clothes."

Ned's eyes scanned Christopher's ancient suit. "Hmm, I see what you mean." He slipped his hands into his trouser pockets and thought for a moment. "I've got it!" he said, brightening. "My brother Todd is just about your size. Come home with me tonight and you can try on some of his things."

"Won't he mind?" Christopher asked dubiously.

"No, why should he? Anyway," Ned added,

grinning, "he's in Canada on a hunting trip. What he doesn't know won't hurt him."

Henry came back into the office and strode to his desk. "Mr. Bailey," he said curtly, "have you nothing to do this afternoon?"

"Yes, sir," Ned said at once, moving to the door with an alacrity surprising for one of his heft. "I was just taking a moment to congratulate Christopher."

Henry eyed him severely from behind his desk. "Do that on your own time, Mr. Bailey. Carlisle and Hastings does not pay you to while away your afternoons chatting with your co-workers."

"Yes, sir." Ned nodded. "Thank you, Mr. Carlisle. It won't happen again, sir."

As soon as he was gone, Christopher turned on Henry and said testily, "Why do you always treat him like that?"

"Because he needs it," Henry said coolly. "Ned's a good boy, but he's lazy; he needs a firm hand. Remember that, Christopher, when you're in charge of your own architectural firm and dealing with a recalcitrant employee. Now, sit down. I want to talk to you."

Christopher obeyed, his thoughts neatly diverted by the idea of heading his own firm. But before he had time to ponder that delicious possibility, Henry said briskly, "First off, I want to offer you my own congratulations. I'm extremely proud of you, Christopher . . . and a little surprised by your success."

"Surprised, sir?"

"I must confess," Henry admitted, "that when

I considered asking you to design for the Tylers, I was reasonably certain they would reject anything you submitted."

"But . . ." Christopher was puzzled. "If you thought that, then why did you let me design for them?"

"I almost didn't." Henry flipped open the humidor on his desk, extracted a cigar, and rolled it between his fingers. "But then I learned that Laura Sheridan was choosing the house for them. I knew Laura's husband," he remarked, gazing pensively at the cigar. "A fine gentleman, a superior architect." He looked up at Christopher with penetrating gray eyes. "Your style is very much like his."

Christopher's puzzlement increased. There was an undertone in Henry's voice he could not quite grasp. "Yes," he said warily. "She mentioned that to me."

"Did she now?" Henry studied him a moment, then busied himself with lighting his cigar. "Tell me," he said, brusquely changing the subject, "how does it feel to have sold your first design?"

"I can't believe it," Christopher answered, feeling again the bubble of excitement in his breast. He was fully aware now of the elegant appointments of the room: the radiant light, the blue silken curtains, the gleaming paperweight with its exquisite store of flowers. He could hear the cheerful ticking of the Tiffany clock; it echoed the tempo of his rapidly beating heart. He gripped the sides of the chair to restrain himself from leaping to his feet and cutting a caper. His body felt hot and restless; he wanted to run, he wanted to fly.

Henry drew on his cigar and watched his protégé with an affectionate smile. "Don't ever play poker, Christopher."

"Sir?"

"You wear your every emotion like a banner. What an expressive face you have! You might have made quite a skillful actor."

"Maybe my parents were actors," Christopher suggested.

"No," Henry said, regarding him thoughtfully. "Your parents, I think, were of the Italian nobility, dark-haired and handsome, possibly descended from the Borgias or the Medicis. There were painters and sculptors among your ancestors—and architects, of course . . . perhaps even your favorite, Palladio . . . speaking of which . . ." Henry's thoughtful look faded, and his face turned rather stern. "I have a bone to pick with you, Christopher."

"A bone, sir?"

"I don't think you realize how fortunate you are to have won the Tyler commission. You designed that house to your own taste despite what I told you the Tylers had in mind. I'm afraid I won't be suggesting you for any future presentations. I cannot risk the firm's reputation again because of your blatant disregard for your client's wishes."

Stunned but not daunted by this unexpected attack, Christopher argued, "What risk are you talking about? The Tylers accepted the house, didn't they?"

"If it hadn't been for Laura Sheridan," Henry pointed out, "they would have tossed your plans in the trash heap."

"Why are you doing this?" Christopher asked with some heat. "You just said you were proud of me. Why this sudden turnabout?"

"I am proud of you," Henry snapped. "Your talent approaches genius; I've told you that repeatedly. I have also told you time and time again that your first responsibility is to your client. If the Tylers had wanted a replica of the Worms Cathedral, round towers and all, it would have been your job to provide it for them. When you understand that and accept it, Christopher, I will ask you to design again—and not before."

Christopher glared at him in a rage, unable to refute the truth. An architect's first duty *was* to please his client, which in this age of vulgarity meant designing imitation castles and pseudo-chateaux that were as crass as they were ostentatious. That was not what Christopher wanted to do; it was not, he often thought, what he was capable of doing. He yearned to create open spaces, lofty ceilings, pristine white walls, and floor-to-ceiling windows that allowed blazes of brilliant sun to illuminate every corner of the house. It filled his hungry heart just to think of such havens of beauty and warmth. Henry's refusal to let him design them drove him mad with frustration.

"Doesn't it matter to you," he said bitterly, "that the most successful architects in this firm are the least talented?"

"It should matter," Henry said grimly, "but it doesn't."

"Why did you encourage me to excellence all these years?" Christopher cried. "You know I'm the best man you have. Why in God's name won't you let me design as I please?"

"It's not that simple," Henry muttered. "There are other considerations—"

"Considerations be damned!" Christopher said. "All that ought to matter is the quality of a man's work."

Henry regarded his protégé with both compassion and regret. "I wish that were so," he said. "But in this world, it isn't."

Chapter Four

❖ ❖ ❖ ❖

AT EXACTLY EIGHT o'clock the following evening, Laura Sheridan descended the marble staircase in a simple black dress and went into the drawing room to await her guests. The Tylers were always punctual, but she did not expect them yet, for she had issued their invitation for half past eight. Impulsively, she had invited Christopher Warren for a half hour earlier.

In Henry's office the day before, Laura had sensed Christopher's reluctance to accept her invitation, thus her impulse to invite him earlier. His reason for reluctance had been obvious. Laura had not missed his quick glance at his well-worn attire, and because of that she had telephoned the Tylers this morning and had suggested plain dress for dinner. Her own gown, a black bengaline with white lace jabot, was one she wore often for quiet evenings alone at home.

As she went to a corner table and gave a final touch to the arrangement of fragrant bouvardia in the cameo vase, she felt, as always, that faint sense of trepidation that preceded any social event. But more than that, she felt a tingling anticipation, the same inexplicable exhilaration she felt whenever she thought of Christopher Warren these past days. His frankness, his fervor, his undisguised ambition, were such a startling change from the ambiguous, jaded, lackadaisical society of which she was a member. How she longed to speak her mind as he did. He had been so right when he talked about the perverted tastes of the elite, of the "nightmare of gingerbread Gothics." How Laura admired his honesty! How she envied his courage!

With a sigh she turned away from the flowers and looked about the gracious drawing room. Soft light glimmered on a pale-green sofa and pretty tapestried chairs in pale green and pink. An ormolu clock ticked gently on the Carrara marble fireplace; still lifes by Roesen and Rubens Peale graced the ivory-painted walls. But the room always seemed empty without Whitney's ebullient presence. Laura missed her daughter terribly. She missed her husband, too, but it had been four years since Steven's death, and sometimes his memory was so dim that she actually felt guilty for not actively mourning him. Recently, in the past year or so, the only truly vivid moments of her life were when Whitney was home with her. During those brief but happy periods Laura felt content and fulfilled. Once she even thought, *I don't live when Whitney's away; I only exist.* And then, as that thought had taken form in her mind, a dart of disquiet had shuddered through her. There was something not quite right about living one's life through another. Laura wanted a life of her own.

"Madam, the Tylers are here," announced Thompson from the doorway.

"They're here?" Laura said, disappointment in her tone. Then, collecting herself: "Please show them in, Thompson. And you may bring in the sherry now."

"Very good, madam."

The Tylers were shown in, as pink-cheeked and bright-eyed as children.

"Laura!" said Jeremy, sweeping into the room and bending to kiss her cheek. "I know we're early, but you must forgive us. We're bursting to meet your new genius!"

Laura embraced him warmly and did the same to his wife. "Nina, how pretty you look. Is that a new gown?"

"Yes," Nina said, preening plumply in her peacock-blue faille. "Since we weren't dressing for dinner, I thought I'd wear this. Madame Borel made it up for me. Isn't it a love?"

"It's perfect," Laura smiled. "Thompson," she

said as the butler entered with the sherry, "just leave the tray on the table. We'll help ourselves, thank you."

The Tylers sat on the sofa; Laura poured sherry, served her guests and herself, then settled on a chair opposite them. "I'm afraid my 'genius' isn't here yet," she said, glancing at the clock, which just then chimed the quarter hour, and she worried whether he would come at all. "He's awfully talented, as you must know from his design. I daresay he's so busy that—"

"Mr. Warren, madam," announced Thompson from the door. Behind him stood Christopher in full evening attire.

Laura turned and stared at him, so stunned by his appearance that she momentarily forgot her manners. He looked elegantly regal, like a prince of the realm. His curling hair gleamed, his eyes were a lucent darkness in his lean, handsome face. It did not immediately strike Laura that, unlike herself and the Tylers, he was formally dressed. But when she saw him catch sight of Jeremy's suit and his cheeks turned ruddy, she realized the discrepancy, and she rose abruptly with a soft sound of dismay.

"Mr. Warren," she said, approaching him with a smile that she hoped hid her chagrin, "welcome to my home."

He did not return her smile, nor did he look at her. His eyes were on Jeremy, who had risen with Laura and whose casual attire seemed to mock the formality of Christopher's own.

"Come meet your clients," Laura said brightly, acutely aware of the embarrassment she had caused him. "Jeremy, Nina, may I present Christopher Warren, your architect? Mr. Warren, this is Jeremy Tyler and his wife, Nina."

Jeremy looked at Christopher's clothes, gave Laura a puzzled glance, then held out a hand to Christopher and said cordially, "Mr. Warren, it's a pleasure to meet you at last."

"How do you do?" Christopher said, recovering smoothly.

Laura, flustered, poured another glass of sherry. As she turned and handed it to Christopher, the glass tipped and spilled on his waistcoat. "Oh, I'm sorry!" she cried, pulling a handkerchief from her sleeve and dabbing at the stain. "Mr. Warren, how clumsy of me!"

Christopher looked down aghast at the ruined waistcoat. Laura said distractedly, "Jeremy, would you ring for Thompson? Mr. Warren, please come upstairs with me. You can wear one of my husband's waistcoats while Thompson cleans yours."

Nina remarked in an effort to be helpful; "He'll never get out that stain, my dear. Wine is calamity on moire."

"Nina, please!" Laura snapped. Then, seeing the startled look on her face, said, "I'm sorry, dear; I didn't mean to bark at you." She turned to Christopher and took his arm. "Come, Mr. Warren. Thompson will have your waistcoat as good as new in no time."

Christopher accompanied her to the door in a

tight-lipped silence that increased her agitation. Thompson met them in the hall, and after Laura explained the situation, he nodded and followed. As the three climbed the stairs, Laura still held Christopher's arm. She kept glancing up remorsefully at his lean, hard face.

"Mr. Warren, please don't worry," she said as they neared Steven's bedroom. "My husband once spilled half a decanter of brandy on his waistcoat, and when Thompson was through with it, no one was the wiser. Do you remember, Thompson?"

Thompson, who recalled no such incident, replied loyally, "I do indeed, madam."

Laura opened the door and switched on the electric light. She had not been in Steven's room for almost a year. The sight of the tester bed, the Italian writing table, and the handsome Nanteuil prints on the wall froze her for a moment. The room seemed bathed in an unnatural light that hurt her eyes. She felt oddly disoriented, poised on the brink of a strange, precipitous path. As she stared at the room and its appointments, she swayed dizzily, not even realizing it until Christopher's hand closed firmly on her arm.

"Mrs. Sheridan . . ."

She stared at that hand, at the long, slender, artistic fingers, then she looked up slowly into eyes so brilliantly dark that she felt drawn into the vortex of a violent storm.

"Mrs. Sheridan, are you all right?"

The words jolted and restored her, bringing

her back to reality. Christopher had released her
arm, and that, too, broke the eerie spell that had
taken her in its grip.

"Yes, I'm fine," she murmured, walking to
the wardrobe.

She could feel Christopher's eyes on her as
she opened the doors. A faint smell of camphor
emerged. Steven's clothes hung on padded
hangers, his shirts lay folded on shelves, and on
the floor of the wardrobe his shoes were neatly
lined up, along with the riding boots he had
worn on the day he died.

Laura deliberately ignored the boots and
searched through the hangers until she found
what she was looking for. "Ah, here it is," she
said, extracting a slim white waistcoat embroidered with white leaves and buds. "I think it will
be a perfect fit, Mr. Warren."

Christopher glanced at the waistcoat, then
raised his dark gaze to hers. Laura's breath
caught in her throat. Again she felt the beginning of that dizzy disorientation. With a supreme effort of will she tore her eyes from his
and looked to the steadying influence of her butler's impassive face. "Thompson, assist Mr. Warren with his coat, if you please."

Thompson took Christopher's coat and laid it
neatly on the bed. Then he took the wine-stained
waistcoat and, at a nod from his mistress, left the
room. In shirtsleeves and suspenders, Christopher's aura of untamed strength was even more
evident to Laura. Though he stood very still, she
felt currents of energy emanating from his per-

son, a contagious vitality that was both pleasurable and dangerous.

"Try this on," she said, distracted, handing him the waistcoat. Then, gathering her wits about her, said, "I can't tell you how embarrassed I am."

"Embarrassed?" Christopher paused in midmotion, his hands on the buttons. "You? Why?"

"I ought to have told you the dinner was informal. Your lovely waistcoat has been spoiled because of my clumsiness, and also because of my negligence."

"It's not my waistcoat," he said with honesty that renewed her admiration. "It belongs to the brother of a friend."

"Then I am all the more embarrassed," Laura admitted. "But you needn't worry, Mr. Warren. If Thompson is unable to remove the stain, I'll gladly replace the garment."

Christopher shook his head as he looped Ned's watch chain through a buttonhole. "I couldn't allow you to do that, Mrs. Sheridan."

"I insist, Mr. Warren."

"No."

"But I—"

"I'm sorry"—his tone was adamant—"but no."

His stubborn pride touched her, as did the aspect of dignity in his hard, unsmiling face. Laura watched him in silence as he slipped on the coat and adjusted his shirt cuffs. She was impressed anew by his effortless grace of movement and by the look of regal elegance in his tall, slender form. It was difficult to believe that the clothes he wore so well did not belong to him. The waistcoat fit him as perfectly as if it had been made for him.

Christopher had often eaten fine food—at Delmonico's and the Hotel Brunswick as Ned or Henry's guest, or at their homes—but nothing in his experience had prepared him for the cuisine at the home of Laura Sheridan. The shrimp bisque was delicious, the sole fillet melted in the mouth. Duckling à la Bourguignonne followed a saddle of venison with a hot entremets of chestnut croquettes. The dessert was ambrosia: Venetian sherbet so heady with brandy and champagne that more than two or three spoonfuls could induce intoxication. Christopher had to consciously restrain himself from wolfing down each mouthwatering course.

With every forkful of food, he felt his discomfiture fading. He forgot Todd's ruined waistcoat, he even forgot that he stuck out like a sore thumb amid his less formally attired tablemates. The Tylers were kind and congenial; they praised Christopher's work. Jeremy said he was "the architect of the future," and Nina kept saying that her friends were green with envy. Laura Sheridan was more admirable a lady than any Christopher had ever met. The house in which she lived was an extension of her classic beauty. The fluid lines, the flawlessly proportioned rooms, were but a reflection of her refinement and taste. It was a house such as this one, all gracious warmth and elegance, that Christopher would have liked to call his own.

As he ate, as the conversation flowed about him, he looked often at his hostess when her face was turned away from him. He kept thinking of the stricken remorse in her eyes when she had spilled the wine on him and of the gentle pressure of her hand on his arm as they climbed the stairs to her husband's bedroom. He kept thinking, with a trancelike intensity, of her delectably curved form standing close to the bed and of how the glow of the electric light threw subtle shadows across the exquisite planes of her face . . .

"Could that be done, Mr. Warren?"

Christopher hastily swallowed a mouthful of mushroom patty. "I beg your pardon, Mr. Tyler. I didn't hear what you said."

"I was discussing the central hallway," Jeremy told him. "If you pull in the circumference, the rooms abutting it could be made larger."

A fine line creased Christopher's brow. "I'm afraid that's impossible, sir. To change the dimensions of the central hall would throw off the symmetry of the entire three floors."

"But, Mr. Warren," Nina interjected, "the ballroom and the dining room could use the extra footage. Is symmetry so important?"

"To the layman, perhaps not," Christopher said. "To the architect it is essential."

"Well, I do see your point," Nina conceded, "but I definitely want a larger ballroom. We have so many friends, Mr. Warren. I should hate to have to limit my guest list because of a room of inadequate size."

"You needn't ever do that, Mrs. Tyler," he pointed out. "If you will recall the details of my plans, I put folding doors at either end of the ballroom so that it opens up to both adjoining rooms. The overall area of the three rooms will easily accommodate more than four hundred people."

"Oh," Nina said sheepishly. "I hadn't noticed. How very clever of you to have thought of that."

"Not at all," Christopher said. "I'm well aware that no Society home is complete without a ballroom the size of the Roman Colosseum."

"Quite so," Nina agreed, oblivious to the irony in his tone. But from the corner of his eye Christopher saw Laura suppress a smile. Expansively, he speared another mushroom patty and popped it into his mouth.

"Now about the outside decoration, Mr. Warren."

Christopher lowered his fork. "The outside decoration, Mrs. Tyler?"

"On the portico," Nina specified. "I was thinking of having a stone Minerva atop the peak. She is the goddess who protects the home, you know. And on either side of her, I should like to have rearing griffins. Griffins are supporters on the Tyler escutcheon, and I thought it would be ever so cunning to have them displayed on the portico. Don't you agree, Mr. Warren?"

Christopher started to answer. But Laura, noting the ominous look on his face, said quickly, "Nina dear, the house is of Greek design, and Minerva is a Roman goddess. Surely you don't want to mix the two cultures and risk the derision of your friends?"

"Oh . . . really?" Nina wavered. "A Roman goddess? I can never remember which are Roman and which are Greek."

"As for the griffins on the portico," Laura went on, "don't you think it would be more dramatic to have a pair of them flanking the fireplace in Jeremy's study?"

"Oh, Laura, what a splendid idea! Why didn't I think of that?"

"It's not your job to think of those things," Laura said diplomatically. "Why don't you tell me the changes you desire tomorrow, and Mr. Warren and I will meet some time this week and do our best to try to accommodate you."

Christopher looked gratefully at Laura. For a brief instant her gaze locked with his in silent communication, then she turned to Jeremy and began discussing Donizetti's *La Favorita*, which was scheduled to premiere the following Friday at the Met. As Christopher watched her cameo-clean profile, the pure line of her brow and nose, the soft curve of her mouth, his throat suddenly went dry. He picked up his wineglass and, despite Ned's admonition, he drained the entire contents in one swallow.

A footman refilled his glass; Christopher drained it again. Laura was saying to Jeremy,

"I'm afraid Avery is going to miss the opening. He's speaking that night at a medical conference in Albany."

"Dash it, Laura!" said Jeremy. "I was looking forward to the four of us making an occasion of it. I've even engaged a table for after the performance at the Beer Garden. I thought it would be amusing to follow an evening of Italian tragedy with an hour of German *Frivolität*."

"Mr. Warren," Laura said as Christopher drank off his third straight glass of wine, "are you an admirer of Signore Donizetti?"

Christopher put down the glass but kept his hand on the stem. "I'm not much of an authority on grand opera, Mrs. Sheridan."

"Donizetti is one of my favorites," she said with that tentative smile he found so charming. "He dramatized the lives of ordinary people rather than the heroic and legendary figures used by so many of his fellow composers. I think you'd like his work. If you're free next Friday night, perhaps you'd consider joining us?"

"Yes, why don't you?" Jeremy urged. "We always have a marvelous time at the premieres, Mr. Warren. Everybody who is anybody will be there. I guarantee you'll enjoy yourself."

Christopher had once seen the crowd exiting from the Metropolitan Opera House at Broadway and Thirty-ninth Street. The gentlemen in silk-lined opera capes and tall silk hats had been no less resplendent than the ladies in satin gowns, diamond dog collars, and ruby stomachers. Now, in his mind's eye, he pictured himself among them, a discordant duckling shattering the perfect harmony of a symphony of swans. But then, amused by the comic image, he laughed aloud at his uncharacteristic self-indulgence.

"What?" said Jeremy, startled.

"Forgive me," Christopher said smoothly. "I was thinking of something else. Thank you kindly for your invitation, but I am engaged next Friday night."

When dinner was over, Laura set aside the convention of leaving the gentlemen to their port and asked them instead to join the ladies in the drawing room. Christopher was relieved. He was already muddleheaded from all the wine he had drunk; even one glass of port would have put him under the table.

In the drawing room he settled on a chair and watched in a disembodied daze as Laura poured coffee. The evening had taken on the quality of a queer sensate dream. The room seemed bathed in a champagne-golden mist; the glow of the firelight was a dancing luminescence; the tinkle of silver on china was melodious and sweet.

"Your coffee, Mr. Warren."

Laura's voice, to Christopher, had a lovely bell-like quality that resounded through the chambers of his wine-sodden brain. She was standing over him, a cup and saucer in her hand, and that was odd, because he had not seen her rise from her chair. He took the cup and saucer in both hands and lowered it slowly to his knee. "Take care," she said softly, the words a fragile chime. "You don't want to burn yourself; the coffee is very hot."

She returned to her chair, gracefully arranging a fold of her skirt as she sat. Christopher watched as she poured more coffee, thinking dimly that she resembled nothing less than a statue of alabaster and ebony, a classic Galatea, needing only Pygmalion's touch to become mortal and attainable. He wished he were alone with her. He had the sudden strong urge to stroke her soft cheek and her sweet rounded neck. He could imagine the feel of her pulse beneath his hand. He imagined further undoing the buttons of her black frock, baring her white flesh, loosening her hair and letting it fall about her shoulders, and then lifting a fragrant tendril and drawing it gently across his mouth.

He felt a tightening in his groin. The cup and saucer rattled on his knee. Very carefully he set them on the table at his side, unable to control the surge of physical desire that was as fierce as it was unexpected.

"I almost forgot!" Jeremy exclaimed suddenly, rising from the sofa and pulling an envelope from his inside coat pocket. "Here's the draft for your commission payment, Mr. Warren."

Christopher took the envelope and opened it, his thoughts of Laura temporarily suspended. "Hanover National Bank of New York," the draft read. "Pay to the order of Christopher Warren four thousand five hundred dollars."

At first, the figure was meaningless to him. His mind, dulled by wine, absorbed the words but failed to translate them into currency. And then it struck him. Four thousand five hundred dollars!

Pin money, perhaps, to people like the Tylers, but to Christopher it was a fortune beyond belief.

This sum meant funds at his disposal to be spent as he chose: a flat in a better neighborhood; furnishings of his own; two or three new suits of clothing; linen shirts; pure-silk ties; boots of buttery leather that would buff to a mirror shine. He stared at the draft as if it contained all the treasures of the universe, then he looked up at Jeremy with brilliant dark eyes.

"Thank you," he said with a quiet intensity, then he looked over at Laura, who was watching him with a smile.

She seemed bathed in the radiant mist that shimmered sensuously about the room. No—she *was* the radiant mist; she was the fire and the light. All else dimmed in his vision, he saw nothing but her; his every need, his every dream coalesced into one. She was warmth and gratification, the source of all things good. Beauty and wisdom, wealth and success, emanated from her exquisite being and integrated the plain cloth of Christopher's aspirations with gossamer threads of gold.

Chapter Five

✦✦✦✦

WHEN LAURA LOOKED back on the evening with Christopher and the Tylers, she, too, remembered the atmosphere to be bathed in a lovely golden mist. The drawing room and dining room had seemed to shimmer with light and warmth, thanks primarily to Christopher's presence. And, oddly, as the days passed, Whitney's absence no longer plagued her with the sense of empty loss. She felt young and lighthearted, optimistic and spirited, in a way she had not felt in years.

She did not meet with Christopher that same week, as she had planned to do. It took her longer than she anticipated to convince the Tylers that the dozen or so changes they wanted would destroy the classic simplicity of the house.

"Would you redesign the Parthenon?" she argued. "Or any building on the Acropolis?"

"Certainly not," Nina said. "But we're not living in ancient Greece, Laura."

"Neither are you living in thirteenth-century Bavaria, Nina, but your present house is almost an exact duplication of those in the Rhenish Palatinate."

She fought harder to preserve the architectural purity of Christopher's house than she had ever in her life fought for anything. She employed logic, appeals to reason, cajolery, and when all else failed, she threw up her hands and resigned from the job.

"No!" Nina cried. "I won't let you do that! Have the house built as you wish. I want *you* to do the decorating."

Laura capitulated grudgingly; she knew her battles were not yet over. And indeed they were not, for Nina made a last-minute, adamant decision to change the location of her bedroom and boudoir from the rear of the house to the front. Laura consented on this point; she was tired of arguing. Moreover, the change in no way threatened the integrity of the design.

When she finally telephoned Christopher at Henry's offices to arrange a meeting, he said in his forthright way, "I thought when I didn't hear from you that the Tylers had changed their minds. After meeting them, I realized that Henry was probably right when he said you had to use the most skillful of salesmanship tactics to convince them to accept my design."

"Not really," Laura said, ignoring a twinge of guilt. "The Tylers sometimes get a little confused about what they want. I merely pointed them in the right direction."

"Do they want many changes?" Christopher asked, and in his voice Laura detected both resistance and apprehension.

"Only a minor one," she assured him. "When can we meet to discuss it?"

"At your convenience, Mrs. Sheridan." His relief was audible. "Shall we meet here?"

Henry's offices, of course, would have been the ideal place for them to talk over any changes in the plans. But for some inexplicable reason, Laura said, "Could you come to my house tonight? I know it's an imposition to ask you, but I've been so—"

"It's no imposition at all," he answered smoothly. "What time shall I be there?"

She was strongly tempted to ask him to dine with her—she kept picturing his dark eyes, the fine line of his jaw, the innate grace with which he moved—but she said instead, "Is nine too late?"

"Nine is perfect," he said. "I look forward to seeing you."

Laura felt the same way, but she merely said good-bye. It would be nice having an architect in the house again.

She dressed with great care that evening and with more anticipation than the situation warranted. Her dress was an ivory cashmere house gown with a black velvet yoke and high collar. The bodice was crisscrossed with black velvet ribbon, the pattern repeated on the slightly trained skirt. As her maid dressed her hair, Laura stared at her reflection in the mirror, wondering why her eyes were so alive and her cheeks such a glowing shade of rose. She knew she was excited about the house, she knew she was happy that no real change would mar its perfection; but she couldn't help thinking, as incredible as it seemed, that she hadn't looked so radiant since her wedding day.

Christopher was punctual this time, which pleased her inordinately. When Thompson showed him into the drawing room, Laura rose with a smile of welcome and gave him her hand. The instant her flesh touched his, she experienced again that charge of electrical energy, that surge of revitalization that had coursed through her on the day she first met him.

"I'm so glad you could come," she said and was somewhat embarrassed to hear a tremor in her voice. "Won't you sit down?" she said, flustered, then gave some instructions to Thompson, who nodded and left.

Christopher waited for her to be seated before taking a chair opposite her in front of the fireplace. Laura sat on the sofa and adjusted the folds of her skirt, attempting to regain her composure. When she finally looked up at him, she noticed he looked different; she couldn't think why. And then she suddenly realized he was wearing new clothes.

"You're looking very prosperous this evening," she said, admiring the handsome blue broadcloth and his fine linen shirt and silk tie. "I see you've started to make use of your commission payment."

"Too much use, I fear," he said with a laugh. "I paid off a longstanding debt to Henry, bought an entire new wardrobe, and leased a house on Patchin Place the day after I received the Tylers' draft. I spent more money that day than has ever been in my possession the whole of my life. I'll tell you truthfully the extravagance frightened me, but at the same time it exhilarated me as nothing has ever done. I suppose that's how the rich live: buying at will, never counting the cost. It was an unsettling experience; I doubt I'll ever do it again."

"I think you will," she contradicted, watching him curiously. He was such an unusual man, so completely without guile, so totally different from the people she knew. "I think in time you're going to be so successful that spending money extravagantly will become second nature to you."

"I doubt that." He shook his head. "My nature is already formed, Mrs. Sheridan. Spending money like water will never come easily to me."

"Was your family poor?" she asked gently.

"I have no family," he answered. "I was raised in an orphanage."

"Oh." This information took her slightly aback. "I'm sorry; I didn't mean to intrude on your private life. You needn't talk about it if you don't want to."

"There's nothing to talk about, Mrs. Sheridan. I was left on the orphanage doorstep with only a note stating my name and birthdate. I don't even know if Warren is my middle name or my surname. That must seem odd to you," he said pointedly. "I daresay you can trace your ancestry back to Noah and the ark."

She gave an uneasy laugh. Despite the casual manner in which he spoke of his background, she sensed an underlying defensiveness about him. "Not that far, Mr. Warren. In any case, one doesn't live on one's ancestors' accomplishments. We all have to make a life that is solely our own."

Her answer appeared to meet with his approval. He leaned back in his chair and crossed his legs comfortably. "Did I mention to you, when I was here last, how much I admire your house?"

"No." She relaxed. "But I knew you'd like it. My husband designed it. Your style, you know, is remarkably like his."

Thompson entered the room bearing a tray of cakes and coffee.

"Ah, good," Laura said as he set it down on the low table. "I hope you like French pastry, Mr. Warren. My chef is an absolute genius. Thank you, Thompson; that will be all."

The servant left. Laura filled a dish for Christopher, remembering with an inward smile his hearty appetite the week before. "These are especially good." She indicated the vanilla Chantilly éclairs. "And the rum babas are delicious. They're small; I'll give you two of them."

"Mrs. Sheridan . . ." Christopher accepted the heaping dish and placed it on the coffee table. "Don't you think we should start working on the plans?"

She was pouring a cup of coffee. She put down the pot. "Oh," she said, disappointed. "Have you another appointment later tonight?"

"No, it's not that," he said. "But I *am* anxious to see what changes the Tylers have in mind."

"How thoughtless of me!" She rose at once. "Come along, then, Mr. Warren. We can have our coffee later."

She directed him to a console table beneath the windows where the plans were spread out in a professional manner. Christopher glanced at them, then said with a smile, "It's easy to tell you were an architect's wife."

The remark gave Laura pleasure, and to her chagrin it made her blush. She bent over the plans to hide her embarrassment.

"Mrs. Tyler wants her bedroom and boudoir in the front of the house," she said, wondering what had come over her. "If you put the three-room guest suite in its place, it should pose no great problem, because the square footage is the same. The only change will be the location of the windows, but that, too, should pose no problem, as you can see."

Christopher bent over the plans to have a better look. He was standing so close to her that she could smell the clean scent of his shaving soap. She could even see a tiny cut above his lip; he must have shaved a second time tonight, and done so in a hurry.

Her gaze traveled upward to his straight nose, to the thick brush of lashes shading his eyes, to the smooth line of his brow under curling dark hair. Studying the plans, his hands braced against the edge of the desk, he looked like a Michelangelo sculpture, all lean bone and muscle, hard and graceful and strong.

Laura suddenly found she couldn't tear her eyes from him. She felt numb, helpless, captive to a force she neither recognized nor understood. She felt hot, then cold, then hot again. She had the strongest urge to brush the hair back from his brow, to take his lean face in her hands, to see those cool, intense, compelling dark eyes growing warm with an emotion to which she could not give a name.

"What's the matter?" He had noticed her scrutiny. He straightened up and eyed her questioningly. "Is something wrong?"

"No . . . nothing," she said, and again that curious tremor was in her voice. "I was just thinking . . . I mean, I was just wondering if you agree with me about the change."

"Yes, I do." He stared down at her intently with those penetrating eyes.

With a supreme effort of will she tore her gaze from his and moved away from him. She was trembling—what was wrong with her—and her throat felt parchment-dry.

"Are you all right?" she heard him ask.

"Yes," she said, gathering her wits about her. "I'm fine." She sat down on the sofa and gestured for him to resume his seat. When he did, she explained, "I'm a little tired, though. I'm afraid I've been concentrating all my energies on this house, and tonight . . . well, it seems to have caught up with me all of a sudden."

"Shall I leave?" he asked, concerned.

"No, of course not," she said at once. "Let's have our cake and coffee, and then . . ." She picked up the pot and was relieved to see that her hand was steady. "And then let's talk about the construction of your beautiful house. I'm really anxious to see it built. Aren't you?"

Christopher watched her a moment with those disturbing dark eyes. "More anxious," he said quietly, "than I could ever convey to you."

*   *   *

They met again the following week—at
Laura's suggestion—and this time she asked him
to dinner. She needed to spend more time with
him; she didn't know why. She only felt, she
knew, that she wanted to get to know him better.
He was so different from everyone she knew:
alien, but in the most fascinating way. He
seemed untouched and unbounded by the conventions that had ruled Laura all her life. He was
a man unto himself, an individual, unique.
When they had had their coffee and cake that
first night, Laura had questioned him about his
days at Saint Peter's. His answers had been brief,
to the point, and utterly without self-pity. Laura
had tried to imagine such an existence and had
failed. When he spoke of Henry Carlisle, his
loyalty to his mentor and his profound esteem
for him had been evident. When he had talked
about architecture, his cheeks had colored with
enthusiasm, his dark eyes had glowed. No man
of Laura's acquaintance—not even Steven—had
ever openly exhibited such passionate fervor
about his work—or about his life. For hours after
Christopher left that night, Laura had lain
awake, hearing the sound of his voice, recalling
in vivid detail his every word and intonation.

Again, like the week before, she dressed with
great care to entertain her special guest. Her
gown was a changeable blue-green silk, very dé-
colleté, with a frothing of ivory lace at the bodice, that deepened the color of her eyes and
enhanced the creamy luster of her skin. When

Christopher arrived on the stroke of eight o'clock, Laura received him in the drawing room. He was wearing another new suit, black, very smart, with a fine gray silk tie pierced by a single pearl. As always, Laura was struck by his regal bearing, so at odds with his humble background. He carries himself like Vulcan the fire god, she thought in a moment of whimsy. And aloud she said, "How nice to see you again, Mr. Warren."

"Mrs. Sheridan." He shook her hand and immediately released it. His eyes, she couldn't help noting, lingered a moment at her daring neckline. "It's good to see you, too." His gaze met hers. Laura's breath caught in her throat. In the depths of his eyes she saw an emotion deeply restrained, an emotion she shared, but one she told herself she couldn't possibly be feeling.

"Won't you sit down?" she said as Thompson entered, placed a tray on the low table, and left. "Sherry?" she asked as Christopher sat on the sofa.

He raised a dark eyebrow, causing Laura instantly to recall the evening with the Tylers. "I'd rather not," he said politely, then unexpectedly he smiled.

"I promise you," Laura said with a laugh, "I shall not ruin your handsome clothes."

"Very well, then," he said, leaning an arm on the back of the sofa. "I'll trust you this time, but I warn you: If you spill wine on my vest, I'm going to demand that you buy me a new one."

He looked totally at ease and at one with his elegant surroundings. Laura marveled at the fact that he was not "to the manner born." Yet despite his air of composure, she sensed in him a carefully controlled tension. Or was the tension, she wondered suddenly, her own?

"Did you bring the plans?" she asked, distracted, handing him a glass and filling another for herself.

"Why, yes, of course," he said, surprised at the question. "Thompson put them in the study. He said you had instructed him to do so, that we would look at them after dinner."

Laura laughed again, chagrined. Why did this man fluster her so? "You'll have to forgive me," she said. "I've been a little at loose ends of late. Nina—Mrs. Tyler—has been bedeviling me day and night about the house. I'm abashed to have to tell you that she wanted another change—"

"What change?" He sat upright and put down his glass.

"No, no, don't worry," she said at once. "I talked her out of it. She wanted a porch running across the entire second story, with jigsaw work."

"Are you joking?"

"Unfortunately, no." Laura looked rueful. "In any case, when I pointed out the unsuitability of such an addition, Mrs. Tyler soon changed her mind."

Christopher regarded her curiously. "It's a good thing I have you to intercede for me," he said.

Laura said nothing. She only watched him, momentarily mesmerized by his steady, dark gaze.

"I imagine," he said further, "that you were a great help to your husband in his work."

"Why, no, I wasn't," Laura said, the realization somewhat stunning her. Steven had never needed her help, nor, indeed, had he ever asked for it. And she had never known that had bothered her—till now.

Dinner was a delight: puree of partridge soup, imperial timbales, lamb cutlets Giralda, and fruit mousse for dessert, all of which Laura consumed with as hearty an appetite as her appreciative guest. Christopher drank no wine this time; Laura, on the other hand, drank more than she should have. She was having a marvelous time. The conversation was lively, so much more enjoyable than her usual dinner parties, where the talk generally revolved around the genteel and accepted topics of the weather, the latest fashions, and horticulture.

Christopher Warren followed no such convention. To Laura's delight, he spoke of his work and questioned her about hers (business was never discussed at society tables!). He told her of Richard Canfield's gambling rooms, which no lady had ever been permitted to enter. She had asked Avery about them once, and he had said, rather sternly, "I'm sure you couldn't have the slightest interest in such an establishment." Laura had been mildly annoyed by his patronizing attitude.

Christopher mentioned Arthur Conan Doyle's latest effort, *Memoirs of Sherlock Holmes*—Laura was a secret afficionado of the sagacious sleuth—and he spoke of Richard Harding Davis, another of Laura's secret favorites.

"My husband disliked popular fiction," she told Christopher, "and while he was alive, I never read any. But in the past few years I've read all of Conan Doyle's books, and I loved Mr. Davis's *Gallegher and Other Stories*."

"Try *Van Bibber and Others*," Christopher suggested. "It's about—"

"I've read it!" Laura exclaimed, delighted. "Wasn't it exciting?"

And as they exchanged remembered episodes of the dashing modern Robin Hood, Cortland Van Bibber, Laura felt gayer and more light-hearted than she had since she was a girl.

When they retired to the study to look over the changes Christopher had made in the Tyler house, Laura's excessive consumption of wine had all but anesthetized her. Her lips were numb, but there was the most pleasant tingling sensation in her fingertips and toes. As Christopher spread out the plans, she watched him, bemused. And when she bent over the desk to view the changes, she swayed dizzily and would have fallen had he not caught her in his arms to steady her.

For a long, electric moment she lay full-length against him, feeling every bone and muscle in his long, slender frame. From the depths of her being stirred sensations long forgotten, along with feelings new and strong that left her breathless and giddy.

"Oh," she whispered and looked up at him dizzily. How strong his mouth looked, how inflexible and hard, but she knew that if she touched it, it would be velvety warm.

"Mrs. Sheridan." His low voice shook. "Are you all right?"

"Yes . . . yes." Embarrassed, she moved away from him, but not before she felt his trembling. She, too, was trembling; she could barely stand upright. She moved to the armchair and sat down abruptly. "I think," she said faintly, "that I've had too much to drink."

He didn't answer, he didn't move, but she was intensely aware of him. When she looked up reluctantly into his brilliant dark eyes, she knew that the source of her giddiness was not the wine.

The weather that autumn was unseasonably stormy. October rain turned into November sleet. Hardly a day passed without precipitation, so that the earth of the Tyler lot was sodden and unstable. When the snows started, it was understood that construction would have to wait until spring. Christopher was disappointed, but no more so than Laura, for she was desperate to see him again, to speak to him, to touch him—and now there was no excuse for her to do so.

As Christmastime neared, Laura's thoughts, of necessity, turned elsewhere. On the nineteenth of December, Whitney came home from school; and on the twenty-first, the Sheridans attended a gala annual Christmas ball at the home of Cynthia and John Barnes, two of Laura's dearest friends.

The ball was Whitney's first "grown-up" affair. Although her official debut was still a year away, she had pleaded so desperately to be allowed to attend that Laura had been unable to refuse her. And how beautiful she looked when she presented herself for her mother's inspection! Her gown, a modest white silk, was trimmed at the sleeves and hem with fluffy ruffles. The bodice was plain and fitted, delineating the curve of her youthful breast. Her hair, upswept for the first time, was a dusky-dark aureole accentuating her ivory skin and her enchanting dark eyes.

"Mama, look at me!" she cried. "I'm a woman!"

"You certainly are, darling," Laura agreed with a tremulous smile.

Where had the years gone? Surely this bewitching young lady in lovely flounced silk was not the scamp of a daughter who not so long ago had lisped her prayers at night with angelic sweetness and had awakened every morning with the devil in her eyes. Laura's heart swelled with love as Whitney pirouetted before her, her pretty face pink with excitement.

The Barneses' ballroom was ablaze with the light of countless candles as Avery Sheridan escorted his sister-in-law and niece into the room. Twin chandeliers hung from a serpentine plaster ceiling. At one end of the room a fragrant fir tree towered toward the ceiling, its graceful branches decorated with twinkling lights, golden stars, downy angels, and colorful elves. At the opposite end of the room, four linen-covered tables groaned beneath the weight of a hundred different delicacies and a choice selection of wines.

As Laura moved into the room on Avery's arm, the orchestra broke into a Viennese waltz, and couples filled the floor and began to whirl around the room. Flashes of bare white shoulders, glittering gems, and colorful silks dazzled Laura's eye. The effect was dizzying.

"There are the Barneses," Avery said, spotting a couple at the buffet. "Cynthia! John!" he called, approaching them. "Happy Christmas!"

Cynthia, a statuesque brunette in holly green velvet, greeted Laura and Whitney with embraces and a kiss. "My, my," she said, chucking Whitney under the chin. "And who, may I ask, is this delectable young siren?"

The husband, a great bear of a man with a fierce, dark beard and playful brown eyes behind a sparkling pince-nez, crushed Avery's knuckles with his paw of a hand and said jovially, "Happy Christmas, Avery, Happy Christmas, ladies. Isn't it a wonderful turnout?"

"Why, yes," Avery said, scanning the merry crowd. "It looks like everyone in town is here, along with a dozen or so representatives from every state in the union."

"John *does* get carried away when he's making out a guest list," Cynthia commented. "We saw *La Favorita* last month at the Met and went backstage after the performance. John wanted to invite the entire cast here tonight, but that's where I put my foot down."

"Mama, there are the MacKenzies," Whitney said. "May I go over and say hello?"

"Yes, darling," Laura said absently. "Tell them we'll be over to see them in a moment."

Whitney bounded off. Laura said to John, "Did you actually want to invite the entire cast?"

"Only the tenor, the soprano, the baritone, and the chorus," John said sheepishly. "I didn't care for the basso's performance."

Laura laughed. Cynthia said with exaggerated casualness, "There *is* someone coming tonight whom I think will interest you."

"Who is that?" Laura asked.

"Your architectural genius, Mr. Warren."

Laura's heart skipped a beat. Avery said with a frown, "Why do you call him that, Cynthia?"

"I can think of no other phrase to describe him," she said dryly. "Laura has been bending my ear about him for months. 'Mr. Warren is so gifted.' 'Mr. Warren this; Mr. Warren that.' Let me tell you frankly that when I meet him, I expect him to be wearing a pair of gilt-edged wings, at the very least."

"He *is* gifted," Laura said, disconcerted. "But you're exaggerating, Cynthia; I don't talk about him that much."

Cynthia glanced at Avery, who was studying Laura. The expression on his face was quite easy to read. Cynthia wondered, as she always did, why Laura was sometimes less than perceptive about the people with whom she was most closely involved.

"My mistake, Laura," she said. "It's Nina who's always gabbing about him. You can relax now, Avery," she added sardonically.

Avery's eyes darted to hers. "I don't know what you're talking about."

"No, of course you don't," she drawled. "And neither does Laura."

Later in the evening, Laura was doing the polka with Avery, who was an accomplished and enthusiastic dancer. When the orchestra concluded the lively number with a flourish, Laura, pretty as a picture in dove-gray silk threaded with silver, snapped open her fan and plied it vigorously to cool her flushed and burning cheeks.

"Avery!" she said breathlessly as he escorted her to a window seat. "One more turn about the floor and I'd surely have collapsed at your feet. I wish you'd be less energetic when you dance. I feel as if I've been dragged down Fifth Avenue by a team of runaway horses."

"That's a fine thing to say!" he said in mock insult. "Don't you know that there are a dozen women here tonight who would *kill* for the honor of being my dance partner?"

"And be killed for the honor," Laura said, sinking gratefully onto the window seat. "Avery, I'm parched. Could you fetch me a glass of wine, please?"

He went off at once, and Laura looked about the crowded room, hoping to spot Christopher. It was almost midnight, but he still hadn't put in an appearance. Laura's nerves had been tingling ever since Cynthia mentioned he would be here. In fact, she had been thinking about him for months, hearing his voice, visualizing his face and the unexpected grace of his form. It puzzled her, this almost obsessive interest in him, and a vague guilt often accompanied her thoughts of him; yet it was curiously pleasurable to re-create in her mind every word, every action that had passed between them.

Avery returned with two glasses of champagne. Laura drank thirstily, still looking about the room. "Do you see the baby?" she asked, pressing the cool glass to her cheek.

"Whitney has just turned seventeen," Avery reminded her. "I doubt she takes kindly to being referred to as 'the baby.' "

Laura answered with a laugh. "When Whitney has babies of her own, she will still be 'the baby' to me. Where *is* she, Avery? I haven't seen her for the past hour."

"The last time I saw her," Avery said, "she was whispering in a corner with the MacKenzie girl. It seems they both have their eye on Jamie Olmsted, and they were conspiring to attract his attention. What they see in that boy I'll never know. His father may be the shrewdest operator on Wall Street, but Jamie's dumb as a post, and unattractive besides."

"That's unkind," Laura admonished him. "Jamie may not be an intellectual, but he's the sweetest boy. Still," she added worriedly, setting down her empty glass, "I do wish Whitney were less preoccupied with young men."

"She's not 'preoccupied' with them," Avery said, defending his niece. "It's merely a healthy interest."

"I don't know," Laura said dubiously. "She's such a romantic, forever imagining herself in love with someone. Whitney's far too young for that."

Avery's mouth curved ironically. "You were *married* at her age, Laura."

Laura did not answer. Could it be possible, she wondered incredulously, that she had been married to Steven at Whitney's tender age? Seventeen was only a step away from childhood, yet at that age Laura had not only been a wife, she was also soon to become a mother. It was not inconceivable, therefore, that in the not-too-distant future Whitney might marry, have children, and permanently move away from her mother into a home and life of her own.

"Oh, Avery," she said, staring down at her lap, "I can't bear the thought of losing her."

"Come now," he said softly, lifting her chin with a finger. "Whitney's not getting married tomorrow, is she? Why start torturing yourself now about something that may not happen for years and years?"

She covered his hand with hers and gave him a wistful smile. She was so fond of Avery and so profoundly grateful. What would she have done without him these past four years? No brother of blood could have been kinder or more con-

cerned. In so many ways he had filled the void
left by Steven's death. To Whitney he was a
loving surrogate father; to Laura he was the most
devoted friend. She pressed her cheek against
his palm, silently expressing all her gratitude
and affection. As she did so, a shadow fell across
her face, and she looked up with a start into
Christopher Warren's intensely dark eyes.

Standing beside him was Cynthia's cousin,
Ned Bailey. Ned was smiling; Christopher was
not. Laura's heart leaped unaccountably as she
released Avery's hand and rose in a rustle of silk
from the window seat. "Mr. Warren," she said,
her breath catching in her throat, "what a pleasant surprise to see you here."

"The pleasure is mine, Mrs. Sheridan." His
gaze turned to Avery, and still he did not smile.

"Ned, good evening," Laura said, correcting
her oversight. "Mr. Warren, I don't believe you
know my brother-in-law, Dr. Avery Sheridan.
Avery, this is Christopher Warren, the architect
I told you about."

Laura watched them shake hands, her heart
beating rapidly, unaware of the keen look that
Avery gave Christopher.

"Mr. Warren," he said, "I've heard a great
deal about you from my sister-in-law. If only half
of what she says is true, you have a spectacular
future ahead of you."

"Mrs. Sheridan has been very generous,"
Christopher said, "with both her assistance and
her encouragement of my work."

"You're too modest," Avery said. "I've seen
your work, Mr. Warren. I can think of no greater

compliment than to say that your style is almost identical to my late brother's."

"So I've been told," Christopher said.

"Perhaps," Avery suggested, "you were similarly trained. Did you attend L'École des Beaux-Arts?"

"No," Christopher said. "I did not."

A fleeting look of anger crossed his face. It seemed to Laura that he had detected in Avery's casual question an insinuation that was not clear to her. Fearing a quarrel, though none seemed to be forthcoming, she said, to change the subject, "The Tylers are most eager to begin construction, Mr. Warren. I've no doubt that when the house is finally built, you'll be offered more commissions than you can handle."

Christopher turned his gaze to hers. "I hope so," he said and stared down at her so intently that her heart gave a thump.

He looked away first, and for that she was grateful. The most unsettling emotions were stirring in her breast. To her relief, Avery picked up the conversation and mentioned the Supreme Court's decision to declare the income tax unconstitutional. As he declaimed at length about the wisdom of the decision, Laura's eyes and her thoughts remained on Christopher. He seemed different tonight, although she couldn't think how. Or was it she, she wondered dimly, who had changed in some way?

"Mama, there you are! I've been looking all over for you."

Whitney, flushed and pretty, descended on the group with a puppyish exuberance that brought a smile to Laura's lips. The girl slipped a hand through Laura's arm, greeted Ned and her uncle, then looked inquiringly to Christopher, who had turned and was watching her in puzzled surprise.

"This is your daughter?" he said to Laura. And, when she nodded: "But that's impossible."

"I assure you it isn't," Laura said with a soft laugh. "May I present my daughter, Whitney? Whitney, Mr. Warren is the architect who designed the Tylers' new house."

Whitney released Laura's arm and offered Christopher her hand. He took it in his and said in amazement, "I cannot believe it." And when Whitney answered teasingly, "My mother wouldn't lie to you," Laura saw Christopher smile for the first time that night.

"I wouldn't dream of doubting your mother's word," Christopher bantered. "It was just something of a shock to learn she has such a grown-up daughter, when I wasn't aware she had a daughter at all."

"Mama, I'm surprised at you!" Whitney said in mock reproach. "I thought you boasted about me to everyone you knew. And now Mr. Warren tells me he wasn't even aware of my existence."

"My apologies," Laura said with another laugh, but she was looking at Christopher, wondering why he had never used that bantering tone with her.

"I know all about *you*," the girl declared, turning back to Christopher. "Mama has talked of nothing else since I returned home from school.

She said your house is a masterpiece and that when my father died, she had thought never to see again such gifted work as his. That's an extraordinary compliment, you know, Mr. Warren. My father was the best architect in the country."

"I've no doubt of it, Miss Sheridan." He smiled again, amused. "And I'm fully aware of the honor your mother does me by comparing me to your father. I only hope that I live up to her expectations."

"You needn't worry about that," Whitney said smartly. "My mother is never wrong about anything!"

"Whitney," said Ned with an appreciative glint in his eye, "is there room on your dance card for me?"

The girl smiled prettily at her old family friend. "It just so happens," she said, taking his arm, "that this very dance is free. And the next waltz," she said to Christopher, "is yours, Mr. Warren."

"I'm afraid I don't dance," he responded.

"You don't? But why not?" she asked ingenuously. "It isn't an injury, is it?" And then, realizing the impropriety of the question: "Oh, I do beg your pardon."

"No," Christopher said, his dark eyes gleaming, "it's not an injury, Miss Sheridan."

"I've never met anyone who didn't dance." The girl was astounded. "Is it against your religion?"

"Whitney," Laura cautioned, "perhaps Mr. Warren would rather not discuss that."

"Yes, come along, Whitney," Ned chimed in impatiently. "You can interrogate Christopher later. This waltz will be over before we know it."

"Very well," she said, chastened. But as Ned urged her toward the dance floor, she said to Christopher over her shoulder, "Mr. Warren, I didn't mean to be rude. You will forgive me, won't you?"

"There's nothing to forgive," he said with yet another amused smile.

Laura watched him in silence, thinking how different he looked when he smiled. His cheeks were faintly colored. His dark eyes, as they followed Whitney, were alive with animation. His entire face was changed; it was handsomer, charming. Laura was also wondering, with an inexplicable feeling of despondency, why not once during the evening had he chosen to smile at her.

Chapter Six

✦✦✦✦

"MAMA, ISN'T Mr. Warren the *nicest* gentleman?" exclaimed Whitney to her mother the evening following the Barneses' Christmas gala.

They were having a light supper in the family dining room. Avery sat at the head of the table, Laura on his right, Whitney on his left.

"Indeed he is," Laura agreed as Thompson served the chicken sauté. "I don't know Mr. Warren well, but he seems quite an admirable young man."

"And isn't he *handsome?*" Whitney said rapturously, her eyes aglow.

Laura smiled at her daughter's ebullience. "He *is* good-looking, darling, but I'm afraid he's too old for you to start having ideas about him."

"Mama, he isn't!" Whitney protested. "Ned told me he's thirty-two. There's only fifteen years between us. Papa was nineteen years older than you."

"That's different," Laura answered, her voice suddenly distant.

"Why?" the girl insisted. "*Why* is that different?"

"Whitney," interjected Avery, "when your mother married your father, life was not as it is now. A girl of seventeen in those days was a mature and responsible woman. Moreover, your mother knew your father from her earliest years. You know nothing about this Mr. Warren."

"Oh, but I do!" Whitney said. "Ned told me he was raised in an orphanage and that Henry Carlisle took him under his wing and taught him everything about architecture. Ned also agrees with Mama: He said that Mr. Warren is a genius, and that in a few more years he's going to be the most sought-after architect in the city."

"That's all well and good for Mr. Warren," Avery said, "but it has nothing to do with you, Whitney. Mr. Warren seems a decent sort, but at the risk of my sounding like an insufferable snob, the gap between his world and yours is incapable of being bridged."

"Uncle Avery!" the girl said, stunned. "I can't believe you said that. Mama taught me to judge people on individual merit, not on basis of class. You *are* a snob if you look down on Mr. Warren just because he has no family."

"Whitney!" said Laura sharply.

"But, Mama, it's true! You taught me—"

"I believe I also taught you to respect your elders, did I not?"

"Yes, but—"

"Kindly apologize to your uncle. And then you may be excused from table, Whitney."

The girl's face flushed scarlet; she looked contritely to Avery. Laura, despite her anger, regretted her harshness. Whitney's rudeness to her uncle was inexcusable, but Laura herself had instilled in her daughter the principle of fairness that had prompted it.

"Uncle Avery," Whitney said softly, rising, "please forgive me for speaking to you like that."

Avery looked embarrassed. "Yes. Well . . . no harm done. Come, kiss me good night, my dear."

The girl complied, hugging her uncle tightly, then she pressed her cheek against his. "I love you," she whispered. "I love you very much."

Avery's arm tightened around her; Laura saw him swallow hard. "I love you too, funny face."

Whitney straightened and turned to her mother. "Good night, Mama," she said penitently. "I apologize to you too for upsetting you."

Laura's heart melted against her daughter's distress, but she only said quietly, "I accept your apology, Whitney. Good night."

Head bowed, shoulders drooping, the girl left the room. Avery, discomfited, picked up his wineglass, then put it down without drinking.

"Really, Laura," he said mildly, "need you have banished her from the table? She was quite right, you know. I *am* a snob—in certain circumstances, that is."

Laura picked up her fork, but found she had suddenly lost her appetite. She rarely reprimanded her daughter, but whenever she did, it left her shaken and remorseful. Nevertheless she answered firmly, "Being right is no excuse for discourtesy, Avery. I'm sorry I ever sent her to school. She's become far too bold to suit me. The next thing I know, she'll be powdering her face and smoking cigarettes."

Avery burst into laughter. Laura frowned at him fiercely. "What's so amusing?" she demanded.

"Powdering her face?" His voice shook with mirth. "Smoking cigarettes? Come now, Laura, aren't you blowing this incident out of all proportion? You'll have that poor child a hardened criminal before you're through with her."

"I suppose you're right," she admitted, her expression softening. "I *am* being a little hard on her. But, Avery"—her tone was adamant—"I won't have Whitney acting disrespectfully, no matter what the provocation."

The laughter disappeared from Avery's eyes. "Then you agree with her, Laura?" he said quietly. "You think I was wrong to say what I did about Mr. Warren?"

Laura's long lashes lowered, concealing her eyes and her suddenly unsettled emotions. For the most part she did agree with Whitney, but she also saw clearly the validity of Avery's objection. Despite Christopher Warren's unfortunate background, he was a true gentleman, courteous, well spoken, and undeniably gifted; but as a suitor for Whitney he was entirely out of the question. The very thought of such an arrangement was disturbing to Laura, more disturbing, she dimly realized, than it should have been.

"Avery," she evaded, "let's have our coffee and dessert in the music room. I'd like to hear you play tonight."

Later, in the music room, as Avery played a selection from Schumann's *Carnaval*, Laura sat tensely on the Carlin settee, totally oblivious to her brother-in-law's artistry. She felt restless and unsettled, at loose ends and vaguely dissatisfied. She could not pinpoint the cause of her discontent. Except for the fact that she was a widow, she had everything in life that anyone could want: a lovely daughter, a considerate brother-in-law, wonderful friends, a fine home. And yet all she could think of now—all she had been thinking of for the past few months—was, *I want, I want, I want.* But what she wanted was impossible for her to determine.

"Laura, what are you thinking about?"

She turned with a start and looked over at

Avery, who was half-turned on the piano bench, watching her with a smile. She had not even been aware that he had stopped playing. She said apologetically, "What a dreadful hostess I am. I ask you to play for me, then my thoughts start to wander. You'll have to forgive me, Avery. I'm afraid I haven't been myself lately."

Avery's smile was replaced by a look of searching concern. He rose from the piano bench and sat opposite her on the bergère chair in front of the fireplace. "I know that," he said, leaning forward, elbows on knees. "I've been worried about you for months."

His gravity surprised her and brought her out of herself. "Have you?" she said gratefully. "You needn't be, dear. I'm just being foolish and self-indulgent."

"What do you mean?" he pressed. "Tell me what's been bothering you."

"I . . ." She faltered and paused. How does one articulate such nebulous thoughts? "Avery, I really don't know what's bothering me. I've been feeling so restless lately, so . . . unfinished. I don't even know if that's the right word." She shook her head helplessly. "It's probably some nuisance of a female maladjustment. I don't expect you to understand it. Women are different from men."

"Really?" His voice was droll. "I didn't know that." And when she didn't answer but only glumly pleated a fold of her skirt, Avery rose from the chair, sat beside her on the settee, and took her hand firmly in his.

"Listen to me," he said, "you must stop fretting. You haven't been yourself since—well, you haven't been the same for quite a while. I think you've been brooding about Steven—"

"No," she said quickly, and the answer surprised her, because she suddenly realized she hadn't thought of Steven in a very long time. Guiltily, she amended, "I mean, that's not what's bothering me."

"My sweet girl," Avery said fervently, "whatever is bothering you, I give you my word I'll make it better."

The warmth of his hand and the concern in his eyes brought a measure of comfort to Laura. She gave him a tender smile. "You always know the right thing to say. What would I do without you?"

His hand tightened on hers. "I hope you mean that, Laura."

"Of course I mean it." She reached over impulsively and brushed his lips with hers. "I wonder sometimes why you put up with me."

For a moment he watched her with a sudden breathless stillness. Then: "Do you?" he said quietly. "Don't you know I 'put up with you' because I love you?"

"I love you too," she said warmly, unaware of his full meaning. "But I honestly don't know if I could tolerate in you all that you tolerate in me."

"I don't think you understand me." His tone was deliberate. "I love you, Laura."

His steady gaze held hers like an inescapable bond. His hold on her hand became a lover's urgent plea. So stunned was Laura by his unexpected confession that she could neither think nor speak. Not for one moment had it ever occurred to her that the affection Avery felt for her was other than brotherly.

"Perhaps I shouldn't have spoken yet," he said. "But I've been worried about you lately. I think I know what's really troubling you . . ."

A thrill of alarm darted through her. For a reason unclear to her she thought of Christopher Warren, and every nerve in her body tensed as she awaited Avery's next words. But to her relief he only said, "You can't bear the thought of being alone, just as I couldn't bear it after Rosalind died. If it weren't for your kindness after her death, I don't know that I could have survived. And then when Steven died, when you needed me, it was the most natural thing in the world that I should try to fill the breach in your life, as you had done with mine."

She found her tongue at last. "Avery," she said faintly, "please don't . . ."

"Wait," he insisted. "Hear me out. I've been keeping this inside for years, and now that I've spoken, I must—" He stopped, took a breath, then went on resolutely, "Laura, I love you; I want you to marry me. I know I can make you happy. And as for Whitney, why, I love her as completely as if she were mine. Whitney needs a father; you as much as said so tonight. I'd make her the best of fathers, and you the most devoted of husbands. Please say yes," he beseeched her, pressing her hand to his lips. "You'll never regret it, I promise you."

Tears stung Laura's eyes as she gazed into the hopeful questioning in his. Of all the people in the world, Avery was the one whom she least wished to hurt. And yet the answer she must give him would do nothing but hurt him. She loved him dearly, deeply, but he was a brother to her; she would never be able to think of him as anything else.

"Avery," she said as gently as she could, "you must know how much I care for you, but I couldn't possibly—"

"Laura, don't answer me now," he urged. "I know this comes as a shock. Think about it for a few days."

"No," she said softly, unwilling to prolong his agony. "I won't change my mind."

"Laura—"

"No, Avery."

Her voice was low, but her decision rang clear. Avery stared at her, his hand crushing hers, his aching disappointment like a knife in Laura's breast.

"Perhaps," he said heavily, "there's someone else you'd rather marry."

Again her nerves tensed as she inexplicably thought of Christopher. "Avery, no. There's no one else."

"Are you sure?"

His voice shook with an emotion Laura saw clearly as rage. Why was he so angry, and why did she keep thinking of that disturbing young man?

"I give you my word," she whispered guiltily, "there's no one else. Avery, I'm so sorry. If I had known the way you felt, I would have—"

His face flushed a fiery red. He released her

hand abruptly and rose to his feet like a shot. "I'd better leave."

"Avery!" She jumped up and caught his arm.

"Let me go, Laura!"

"No, wait. Please stay. Don't leave like this. Let's talk this out."

He shrugged off her hand and started for the door. "I can't stay," he said hoarsely. "I can't talk. I'll telephone you tomorrow."

"Avery, don't—"

But he was out the door before she had a chance to stop him. She stood there uncertainly, considered going after him, then realized the futility of it. There was nothing more to say. In refusing his proposal of marriage, Laura had said it all.

Avery did not telephone her the next day, nor did he come to the house on Christmas Eve as had been his custom for as long as she had known him. Worried and upset, Laura telephoned him on Christmas morning, only to be told by his butler that he had left two days earlier for Palm Beach, Florida.

"Palm Beach?" she said, stunned. "But, Briggs, the last time I saw him, he never mentioned anything about . . ." She trailed off into silence, staring blindly at the holly-festooned hall. She had known she had hurt him, but she had never imagined that the hurt had gone so deep.

Briggs said tactfully, "It's quite possible, madam, that when Dr. Sheridan last saw you, he had no idea of the trip. You see, Mr. Henry Flagler telephoned a few days ago and asked Dr. Sheridan if he would be his guest over the holidays at his new hotel . . . I cannot recall the name of it."

"The Royal Poinciana," Laura said bleakly.

"Yes. Thank you, madam. In any case, Dr. Sheridan accepted the invitation and told me he plans to be in Florida until the sixth of January. May I give him a message when he returns?"

"Only that I telephoned," Laura murmured, then bade him a soft good-bye.

Whitney, who was impatiently waiting in the drawing room for news of her uncle, said to Laura when she entered, "Mama, where *is* he? He never keeps us waiting."

"I'm afraid he's not coming, darling." She went to the fireplace and numbly extended her chilled hands over the fire. "You may as well open your gifts now."

"Not coming?" Whitney's smooth brow furrowed. She rose from her kneeling position beneath the Christmas tree and went to her mother. "Mama, why? And why wasn't he here last night?"

"Whitney, I told you," Laura said, aching, her eyes on the blaze. "He must have had an emergency at the hospital."

"And today?" the girl persisted, clearly unconvinced.

"Well, he . . ." Laura paused, then looked at her daughter. "He has decided to spend the holidays in Palm Beach."

"Palm Beach?" the girl repeated in surprise.

"Why did he go there? He always spends Christmas with us. Why, he was even with us the year Aunt Rosalind died. I remember it so well because when I opened the gift she had bought for me, he had tears in his eyes."

"Yes." Laura was close to tears herself as she thought guiltily of the reason for Avery's absence this holiday. "I remember that too, darling."

"Mama, what's happened?" Whitney demanded. "Uncle Avery didn't up and decide to go to Florida for no reason. You and he had a quarrel, didn't you?"

It would have been easy to lie, to say, "No, of course we didn't quarrel." But Whitney was no longer a child who must be protected against life's harsh realities. She was a woman now—much as Laura tended to resist that fact—she was a woman who both demanded and deserved the truth.

"Whitney, sit with me," Laura said, urging her daughter to settle alongside her on the pale-green silk sofa. "Uncle Avery," she began hesitantly when they were seated, "is upset because of something that happened last week."

Whitney looked backward in time for a clue. "Mama," she said suddenly, "is he still angry because I called him a snob? But I apologized to him, and I meant it. I could have sworn he'd forgiven me."

"Darling, no, it's not that," Laura quickly assured her. "He did forgive you. In fact," she added in a wistful tone, "he scolded me later that evening for being so harsh with you."

"Then, what . . . ?" the girl asked, puzzled.

"It was something that happened between your uncle and me," Laura admitted with reluctance. "You see . . ." She paused again, then went on in a low voice, "He asked me to marry him."

Whitney's eyes widened; she stared at her mother as if seeing a familiar object suddenly take on an alien shape. "He asked you to *marry* him?"

Despite her distress, Laura could not help smiling. "Does that shock you, Whitney?"

"No . . . no," the girl said slowly. "It's . . . I mean, I love Uncle Avery almost as much as I loved Papa, but I'm not sure how I'd feel if you married him."

"How do you mean, darling?" Laura asked gently.

"Well . . ." Whitney's young face reflected her conflicting emotions. Her dark eyes were baffled as she struggled to bring order to her unruly thoughts. "Mama, I think I'd be jealous of anyone you married. I'd feel he was taking you away from me." She shook her head, and her cheeks colored slightly. "I know that sounds childish," she murmured, "but that's the way I feel."

Laura's eyes warmed with love. "Whitney, you needn't worry about that," she said softly. "I told Uncle Avery I couldn't marry him."

The girl sighed with relief, then instantly looked remorseful. "Is that why he's not here?"

"Yes, darling, I think so."

"Is he *never* coming back?" she asked, alarmed.

"Oh, Whitney, no," Laura said swiftly. "He'll come back to us."

"Mama," Whitney blurted, grasping her mother's hands, "I couldn't bear it if I never saw him again. I do love him, despite what I said about your marrying him. And now I really feel dreadful that I called him a snob. He must think we both don't love him anymore."

"Whitney, I'm sure he doesn't think that," Laura soothed. But in her heart she was wondering what indeed Avery was thinking. "When he comes home, when he's had time to get over his . . . disappointment, he'll come back to us; you'll see."

She took hold of her daughter's chin and gave her an encouraging smile. Whitney returned her smile, but her eyes were very bright. With a ragged sigh she laid her head on Laura's breast as she used to do when she was little. "I hope so," she whispered shakily. "I don't want to lose him."

"You won't lose him," Laura promised, her arm going protectively around her. "Do you think Uncle Avery would ever abandon his little 'funny face'?"

The girl did not answer. Laura gently stroked her hair. The house was very quiet; only the crackle of the cedar fire could be heard, and from the dining room the soft clatter of cutlery and china as Thompson laid the table for Christmas dinner. It seemed such a long time since Laura had held her daughter in this way. No more did a sleepy touslehead curl up on her mother's lap; no more did dimpled arms encircle Laura's neck.

How good it felt to hold her baby again, how natural and right. But how sad that the fear of losing her uncle was what had caused Whitney to seek solace in her mother's arms.

The holiday was a subdued one, and not very merry. Whitney opened a mountain of gifts: pretty shirtwaists; the latest novels; garnet earrings; a shellwork glove box; a beaded purse; and from Avery, in a gaily wrapped package he had left at the house several weeks earlier, an exquisite coral brooch in the shape of a bell-flower, with small buds and leaves on a stem of chased gold. Although dinner was a sumptuous feast of roast goose à la Thieblin, watercress and apple salad, Parisian style peas, and burnt almond Angelica ice cream for dessert, neither Laura nor Whitney was feeling very festive.

When they returned to the pine-fragrant drawing room and were having their coffee, Laura finally said, "Whitney, you mustn't brood. Uncle Avery will come back to us; you have my assurance on that."

The girl put down her coffee cup and looked up, rather sheepishly. "Mama, I wasn't thinking of Uncle Avery. The truth is . . ." She gave a nervous laugh. "I invited Ned Bailey to stop by tonight. I hope you don't mind."

"Darling, of course I don't mind." Laura was puzzled by her daughter's uneasiness. "But why did you wait until now to tell me?"

"I don't know." Whitney lowered her gaze. "I was going to tell you this morning, but when you told me about Uncle Avery . . ." She looked up then, and said abruptly, "Mama, I *was* thinking about him while we ate. You said you refused his proposal, but you didn't say why. It wasn't because of me, was it? I know what I said about being jealous and all that. But if you wanted to marry him, I wouldn't object; honestly I wouldn't."

"I appreciate that," Laura said with a smile, "but my decision has nothing to do with you, Whitney. It's simply that I could never think of Avery as my husband." And, inexplicably, strongly, Laura thought of Christopher Warren.

Whitney was silent for a time, her eyes very dark in a curiously blank face. At last she said slowly, "Mama, I forgot to tell you something."

"Yes, darling?"

"I asked Ned to bring Mr. Warren with him tonight."

"Mr. Warren?" Laura's heartbeat accelerated. Her tone, when she spoke again, was sharper than intended. "Whitney, why did you do that? I specifically told you he was too old for you."

"Mama, please don't be angry," the girl implored. "I like him; I want to see him again. You like him too, I know you do. Why do you keep harping on his age when Papa was so many years older than you? It's not his background you object to, is it? He can't help it if he's an orphan."

"Of course I don't object to his background." Laura's hands began to shake; she placed her cup on the table. "But I do object to the age

difference, Whitney, and I'm afraid you're going
to have to trust my judgment in this matter and
abide by what I say."

"Mama—"

"I refuse to argue the point," she said sternly,
and wondered why her heart kept beating at
such an alarming rate. "Mr. Warren is welcome
here tonight since he's already been invited, but
I must urge you strongly never to do such a
thing again without first asking my permission."

Whitney started to plead again, but Laura silenced her at once. "That will do!" she commanded. "I don't want to hear another word
from you about Mr. Warren. Is that understood,
Whitney?"

The girl stared at her with startled eyes. Laura
finally became aware of the same breathtaking
anger that had gripped her the last time Whitney
had spoken of Christopher Warren. Dimly Laura
realized that the fear of someday losing her
daughter to marriage lay at the root of her excessive ire. But that was surely no reason to
object so strenuously to a relationship that did
not and might not ever exist. Whitney had been
in and out of love a dozen times in the past year.
Whatever she now felt for Christopher Warren
would eventually fade into obscurity as had every last one of her previous "grand passions."
Laura knew that her anger was senseless, out of
all proportion to the cause. But she couldn't, for
the life of her, think why.

Chapter Seven

◆◆◆◆◆

"GET A MOVE on, Christopher," said Ned Bailey as they walked the four blocks from Henry Carlisle's house to the Sheridan house on Fifty-fifth Street.

The night was crisply cold; a panoply of stars lit an ebony sky. Traffic was light on Fifth Avenue this evening. Most people were home celebrating the holiday, enjoying the company of family and friends.

Christopher and Ned had had Christmas dinner with Henry and his family. Christopher's pace was sluggish due to a grinding headache acquired at the Carlisle house. His temples pounded with the echo of the squabbling and screeching of Henry's seven grandchildren. Moreover, he was both anxious and reluctant to see Laura Sheridan. He knew how she affected him. And at this moment, with his head aching from too much noise and too much drink, he knew he hadn't the strength to control himself.

Over the past several days Christopher had come to the conclusion that he wanted Laura Sheridan, wanted her in a way he had never wanted anything else. She was the epitome of all he esteemed: ethereal beauty, dignity, and grace. She was the classic purity he fiercely revered, a vivid substantiation of his every nebulous dream. Having never had anything, he wanted this woman, who had and was everything on which he placed value. But most of all he wanted her because he knew that beneath her seemingly serene exterior beat a heart as vibrant, as passionate, and as hungry for life as his own.

"Will you hurry up?" Ned broke into his thoughts. "You're walking at the pace of a century-old tortoise. I told Whitney we'd be there at eight o'clock, and it's a quarter past, for God's sake!"

"Pipe down, Ned," Christopher said testily. "My head's splitting. What's the difference if we're late? Didn't you once tell me that being on time for a social engagement is the ultimate faux pas?"

"Not when one is seeing the young lady of one's affections," Ned retorted.

They stopped at the corner of Fifty-second Street as a long line of carriages filled with boisterous holiday revelers clattered by. Christopher winced at the noise, then eyed Ned askance. "Are you referring to Whitney? You're rather old for her, aren't you?"

"Old?" Ned said indignantly. "I'll have you know I'm in the prime of life! In any case, the Sheridan women prefer older men. Whitney's father was some twenty years older than his wife."

A gust of icy wind chilled Christopher. He shivered and pulled up his coat collar to cover his ears.

"I haven't expressed my intentions yet," Ned chattered on as they crossed the street, "but I'm fairly confident that Whitney feels something for me. You saw how she danced almost every dance with me at my cousin's gala. And she was most insistent that evening that I should spend Christmas night with her. I'm sure she asked me to bring you along so that it wouldn't look like she was being too forward. You know how women are."

The truth was that Christopher knew little about women. Reared exclusively by men in an orphanage filled with boys, he was less than an expert about the opposite sex. The women he knew at Madame Beverly's bawdy house were an entirely different species. For the most part they were deliciously feminine, clad in their filmy negligees with precious little on underneath, ardent and artful when he took one to bed. But otherwise, they were very much like the men he knew: They enjoyed an off-color joke; they drank whiskey without a grimace; and some of them even smoked an occasional cigar.

"Does her mother know we're coming?" Christopher asked.

"Why, yes, I suppose so." Ned turned and looked at him. "What's the matter with you? You're as jumpy as a cat tonight."

Christopher shrugged. "Nothing's the matter. Do you think the brother-in-law will be there?"

"Who, Avery? Most likely he will. Since his brother died, he's been Laura's shadow. If you ask me, I think he's in love with her."

"What about her?" Christopher asked, dreading the answer. "Is she in love with him?"

"Who knows? I would guess that she is. They have an awful lot in common, you know."

"I know," Christopher said, and he shivered again with cold. Ned, at his side, was impervious to the weather, buoyant and warm at the prospect of seeing Whitney.

When they finally reached the Sheridan house, they were ushered inside by Thompson, who wore a sprig of holly in his lapel and whose cherry-red nose bespoke holiday imbibing.

"Good evening, sirs," he slurred, taking their things. "If you'll please follow me, the ladies await you in the drawing room."

As they followed him down the hall, Ned whispered to Christopher, "Thompson's drunk as a skunk. This house definitely needs a man in residence."

Christopher bristled with indignation, but said nothing. Just because Thompson was a servant, was he not allowed the simple pleasures enjoyed by his moneyed masters? For a moment Christopher hated Ned; hated him for his carelessly brutal snobbery. But then Ned squeezed his arm and leaned over to say encouragingly, "Buck up, Christopher. I know you don't like these social commitments, but Laura thinks you're God's gift to architecture. With her connections and your talent, you'll soon be giving Stanford White a run for his money."

"Mr. Bailey and Mr. Warren," announced Thompson, stepping aside to permit the gentlemen entry.

"Ned! Mr. Warren! Happy Christmas."

Whitney leaped up from her chair and greeted both men with an exuberant handshake. "Come in, come in. Mama, Ned and Mr. Warren are here."

"So I see," Laura said with a smile from the sofa. "Happy Christmas, gentlemen. I'm glad you could be with us tonight."

Ned went to her, took her extended hand, and bowed in his best courtly manner. "So good of you to have us, Laura. Christopher was especially looking forward to seeing you again. You and he could almost be considered soul mates, you know."

"Oh?" Laura's smile froze. "How do you mean that, Ned?"

"You're united in a common cause," he explained. "You're both fervently dedicated to eradicating the blight of Gothic architecture in the city."

"Ah, yes." Laura relaxed and looked over at Christopher. "Let's hope our cause is successful, Mr. Warren."

"By all means, Mrs. Sheridan."

She looked more beautiful to Christopher than she ever had before. The cheery color of her dress gave her cheeks a silky glow. Her luminous blue eyes touched his heart, warmed his soul. How he wanted this woman; how he ached to make her his own. His need for her was a hunger he would never be able to sate.

"Look here, you two," Ned suggested. "Seeing that you have formed a holy alliance, don't you think it's time you dropped the formalities?"

For just the briefest moment Christopher thought he detected resistance on Laura's part. But she said pleasantly, "Why, yes, you're right,

Ned. Is that agreeable to you . . . Christopher?"

"Yes," he said quietly. "Of course it's agreeable."

"Splendid!" Whitney interjected, joining her mother on the sofa. "It's so much nicer being on a first-name basis. I dislike stuffy, old-fashioned formalities. Don't you, Christopher?"

He turned to her and smiled. What a delightful little girl she was. On the first night he met her he had admired her charming loveliness. And Laura seemed justly proud of her gem of a daughter. But to Christopher, Whitney was but a dim facsimile of the resplendent beauty and grace that was her mother.

Before he could think of an appropriate answer to her question, Laura reminded her daughter, "Formalities sometimes serve a purpose, Whitney. For example, our guests are still standing. And Thompson is waiting for instructions."

"Oh!" Whitney said, chagrined. "How stupid of me. Please sit down, Christopher. You too, Ned. Thompson, you may bring in the mulled wine and cakes now."

The gentlemen sat opposite the ladies. Thompson left the room and returned a few moments later with a great silver tray bearing a cut-glass punch bowl and wine cups and a colorful assortment of small holiday cakes.

Christopher groaned inwardly as the smell of spiced wine reached his nostrils. His head began to ache again. If he so much as tasted another drop of holiday cheer, he knew his skull would explode into a thousand fragments.

After Thompson withdrew, Ned extracted a small box from his inside coat pocket and handed it to Whitney. "Laura, I hope you don't mind. I've brought Whitney a small token in honor of the season."

"How nice, Ned," Laura said as she ladled out cups of wine. "I don't mind at all. That was very thoughtful of you."

Whitney opened the package to reveal a Tiffany scent bottle, overlaid with platinum and studded with enamel hearts and tiny diamonds. The gift, despite its small size, was unquestionably costly.

"Ned, how stunning!" Whitney exclaimed.

"Ned, you shouldn't have," Laura frowned.

"Oh, Mama, please don't scold him. It's the most beautiful thing I've ever seen. Ned, thank you; you're a darling." She rose impulsively and bent to kiss his cheek. Ned reddened with pleasure; his chest expanded visibly.

"Honestly, Ned!" Laura's tone was stern, but her frown had vanished in the face of her daughter's enthusiastic delight. "You know perfectly well that such a gift is unsuitable."

"Laura, you're absolutely correct," Ned said with his most winning smile. "But in light of the season, and because our families have been friends for eons, I took the liberty of overstepping the bounds of propriety just this once. You *will* forgive me, won't you?"

Laura laughed, defeated by his puckish charm. "Between you and Whitney I haven't much choice, have I? Very well, I forgive you. But I'll not permit a repetition of this, Ned."

"You have my oath," Ned said solemnly, placing a hand on his heart, "that I'll never buy a scent bottle again."

Laura sighed and shook her head, then handed a cup of wine to Christopher. "How do you put up with this rogue?" she asked him.

"I mostly ignore him," Christopher said, setting his cup on the table.

"Aren't you drinking?" Laura said, passing cups to the others. "We must toast the season, Mr. War— I mean, Christopher."

Christopher swallowed hard and picked up the wine cup. His head throbbed.

"Happy Christmas to all!" Ned said, raising his cup. "And to the dawn of a new year."

Christopher brought the cup to his lips. The sweet, spicy smell of the wine invaded his nostrils and struck at his skull with the force of a sledgehammer. He put down the cup abruptly and covered his eyes with a hand.

"What the deuce?" Ned said.

"Christopher!" Whitney exclaimed. "What's wrong?"

"It's nothing," he said while waves of pain attacked his brain. "It's a headache; it's nothing."

Laura rose at once and went to him. "Come with me," she said. "I have some headache powders upstairs in the lavatory."

"No," he said, rising, "I'll go up on my own. I don't want to inconvenience you. Where is the lavatory? You stay here with your guest."

Laura looked at him dubiously, then relented. "Turn right at the top of the stairs," she said.

"It's the last door down the hall. The powders are in the medicine chest, marked 'citrate of caffeine.' "

He left the room and climbed the stairs with pulsating temples. In the lavatory he mixed the citrate of caffeine with some water, took a generous swallow, then rinsed his face with cool water and dried it vigorously with a towel. For ten minutes or so he sat on the edge of the sink thinking of Laura, which had the effect of banishing his headache and causing discomfort in a more erotic part of his anatomy.

Presently, he left the lavatory and walked down the hall toward the staircase. An open bedroom door caught his eye. He stopped and looked in, knowing instinctively that the room was Laura's. Without a second thought, he stepped inside.

A small lamp burned atop the bedside table, and a low fire on the grate further lighted the high-ceilinged room. Over the headboard was a gilt-framed painting of a madonna and child. The bed, with tall posters, was covered with a pale-blue spread, and the leaded windows were hung with the same delicate silk. An Aubusson rug in shades of pale blue and rose covered a floor of golden oak. Objets d'art and personal mementoes reposed on burr yew tables and a mirrored vanity, and on a satinwood bureau with silver-handled drawers stately white roses in a silver vase filled the lovely room with subtle fragrance.

The room was exquisite, flawless; it was Laura in microcosm. It had her beauty and her grace, and her irresistible charm. A great calm descended on Christopher, a serenity of spirit he had never before experienced. In this dim, quiet room he felt a curious peace, a sense of warmth and well-being that no place in his memory had ever afforded him.

He heard a sound behind him; he turned with a start. Laura stood at the door. The light from the hallway cast a halolike radiance about the angelic perfection of her form.

"Mr. Warren . . . Christopher . . . are you all right?"

Her voice was worried; her face, in dim shadow, clearly showed her concern.

"Yes, I'm fine, thank you." He did not move. "I apologize for—"

"No, please." She came into the room. "Don't apologize. I was worried when you were up here so long. Are you sure you're all right? You're very pale."

"Yes. I'm all right."

He still did not move. Laura slowly moved closer. If she thought it strange that he was in her bedroom, it was not evident. She merely said, "Ned told me you would rather not have come here tonight. He said you dislike socializing, and that that, probably, was what had caused your headache."

She had come up so close to him that Christopher could have reached out and spanned her waist without taking a step. He looked down into her eyes. He could feel the rise and fall of her breast as she breathed. His own breathing became labored; his chest ached and burned.

"That's not entirely accurate." He found it difficult to speak.

"I didn't think so," she said softly. "I think it had to do with Ned and Whitney."

"Ned and Whitney?" His brow creased in puzzlement.

"Yes." She lowered her gaze. "It occurred to me that you might see Ned as a rival for Whitney's affections."

"I don't understand," he said.

"I am aware," Laura said slowly, her eyes still down, "that you're interested in my daughter. At the Barneses' gala it was obvious to me that you were . . . that you found her appealing. And then tonight, the way you looked at her, the way you smiled at her. . . . Well, it confirmed my belief that your interest in her is serious."

"My 'interest' in her?" he repeated slowly, grasping her meaning. "You think I want your daughter?"

"Yes," she said in a whisper, then raised her gaze to his. "And, you see," she went on haltingly, "a relationship between the two of you is something I cannot allow. Whitney is barely seventeen. As womanly as she may seem to you, she is still a child. And you . . ." She faltered and paused. "You are a man."

He stared down at her intently, rendered breathless by her nearness. There was a tightening in his throat and a roaring in his ears, so that his voice, when he spoke, sounded foreign and unreal. "Listen to me," he said. "I haven't the slightest interest in your daughter. You couldn't be more mistaken."

"I am mistaken?"

Laura's voice, too, sounded strange. There was a strangeness, in fact, about her entire lovely person. Her body seemed softly pliant, and in her splendid blue eyes there was a joyous but fearful emotion Christopher could not quite identify.

"Then that wasn't the reason?" she asked faintly.

"The reason for what?"

He had forgotten what they were talking about. When Laura did not respond, he did not find it odd; her mouth, slightly trembling, held all his attention. He thought it neither odd that her mouth should be trembling nor that her face, upturned to his, unmistakably reflected the turbulent emotions he himself could no longer hold in check.

"Laura." He spoke her name for the first time, savoring it on his lips, caressing it with his voice. "Laura."

He raised a hand and touched her soft cheek. Her skin was warm, hot. A tremor shot through Christopher, an electric current that sent both pleasure and pain to the very core of his being. Laura neither moved nor spoke. She, too, seemed captive to the incandescent charge that crackled between them.

"It's not your daughter I want," he said in a voice that shook. "It's you. Don't you know that? Don't you know what you've done to me these past months? I can't work, I can't sleep, I can't function for thinking of you. I have wanted you since almost the first day I saw you. I've wanted to touch you, to hold you, to feel my arms around you—"

"Please, no, you mustn't," she whispered faintly, but his arms, firm and urgent, had already encircled her waist.

He drew her close, disregarding her feeble protest. He heard nothing, knew nothing but his own hungry need. She was fulfillment in his arms, an exquisite gratification that supplanted the barren emptiness of his past. Her body against his made him whole and entire. When his mouth touched hers, he felt her tremble in his arms, he felt her heart race and pound in perfect concert with his. And when his lips parted hers and she submitted with a moan to the seduction of his kiss, he felt a thrill more intense than the fierce consummation of physical love.

All rational thought deserted him; only sensation remained. He was acutely aware of the texture of her mouth, soft and pliant, against his; of the smooth feel of cashmere beneath his hands; of the faint but beguiling fragrance of her warm, silken skin. He felt her arms go around him, felt her fingers in his hair. His arms pressed her closer, his ardent kiss deepened. He felt both powerless and strong, at the mercy of the woman he held prisoner in his arms. As he sought to possess her, she possessed him completely. Her submission was a victory, and he, her physical conqueror, was most willingly hers to command.

"Please, no," she whispered at last against his mouth. But even as she protested his sensuous persuasion, he felt her arms tighten around him as if she would never let him go. "Christopher, don't. We mustn't . . ."

He lifted his mouth from hers, but he still held her fast. "Mustn't what?" he said hoarsely. "Give in to our feelings? Laura, I love you, I want you. And can you deny that you want me?"

"Yes, I deny it," she said wretchedly, unable to meet his gaze.

"Look at me!" he demanded. "Look at me and deny it. Kiss me again, and then deny it."

"No, no; let me go." She twisted helplessly in his hold.

"Never!" he said, his arms crushing her ribs. "I'll never let you go. Laura, don't fight me; don't deny me. Tell me only that you feel as I do. That's all I ask of you now."

"I feel nothing for you," she whispered miserably, and still she would not look at him. "You must stop this. What you're saying is madness."

"Madness?" he said roughly and took hold of her chin and forced her to face him. "Yes, it is a kind of madness, what I feel for you. But don't try to tell me you don't share that feeling. I won't believe you."

"I *don't* share the feeling!"

She broke free of his hold and backed away from him, breathing hard. Christopher took a step forward. Laura held up a hand, fending him off. "Stop it!" she said, but though her voice was hard, her soft mouth shook, and she was quivering visibly with an emotion that was clearly not anger.

"Laura—"

"Christopher, don't!" Her breast rose and fell with the effort to control herself. "Don't come near me, don't touch me. What you want is impossible. For one thing, I'm older than you—"

"Older? How much older?"

"Two years."

"Laura—" He laughed shortly, partly from tension, partly from relief. "Two years doesn't matter."

"It matters to me," she said sharply. "What you feel for me—or what you think you feel for me—can come to nothing. You must put me out of your thoughts; you must forget what happened here tonight."

"Forget it?" he echoed, aching to hold her again, yearning to stem her protests with his mouth hard on hers. "I can't forget what I feel for you. I can't switch off my emotions like an electric light just because you tell me to do so. I want you, I tell you, and by God I'm going to have you. And if you think I can forget that, you're very much mistaken."

For a moment she said nothing. On her face Christopher saw pain and confusion, fear and indecision, and another emotion more profound than the rest. She was still quivering slightly; her hands were clenched together as if grasping desperately for the control that had deserted her.

She finally said in a quiet, deliberate voice,

"You have no choice in the matter. You see, I'm going to be married soon."

"Married?" A blast of rage and jealousy exploded on his brain. "To whom?"

"To Avery Sheridan. You met him at the Barneses' gala. He is my—"

"I know who he is," he said hotly. "Why didn't you tell me sooner? Why did you let me—?"

He broke off, so furious that Laura's face blurred momentarily before his eyes. Married—to her brother-in-law. No, it wasn't possible. Not when she had kissed Christopher the way she had, not when she had trembled in his arms, not when she had held him so close that he could hardly endure the joy of it.

"I don't believe you," he said harshly.

"Believe me."

But to Christopher her sudden composure was suspect. "If that's true, then why isn't he here tonight?"

"He is out of town . . . on business."

"Laura, you're lying to me."

Her gaze flickered and fell. She stared at the floor as if seeking there the solution to her dilemma. "No," she said. "I'm not lying. We're to be married in the spring. All the arrangements have been made."

Christopher went to her swiftly and violently grasped her arms. Laura's head flew up; she stared at him in a panic.

"Then why did you let me kiss you?" he demanded fiercely. "Why did you return my kisses? Were you playing some perverted game with me? Is that what you aristocrats do? Marry old men and seek pleasure from the young?"

Laura gasped and wrenched away from him. Christopher reached out again for her, but she eluded his grasp and ran from the room. He stood motionless for a time, paralyzed with rage and with the dim realization that Laura had indeed lied in an attempt not to hurt him. In turn, he had hurt her in the vilest of ways. With a few brutal words he had hatefully shamed the only woman he would ever love.

Chapter Eight

✦✦✦✦

A SHRILL, PERSISTENT ringing woke Christopher the next morning. He opened one eye to an overcast day. The windows rattled against a blustery wind. That sound, and the continual ringing, sent saber-sharp peals of pain through his already pounding head.

He sat up with a groan, wondering for a moment where the ringing was coming from. Then he remembered. A week ago, at Ned's suggestion, he had had a telephone installed in the house. The monthly rate, Ned had assured him, was well worth the convenience. "Think of it!" Ned had said with his infectious exuberance.

"Whenever you want to talk to someone, no matter the time of day or night, you can pick up the telephone instead of racing around town in a hack or on a streetcar."

"I don't know," Christopher had said, worried about the expense.

"Christopher, you *must* have a telephone! How will your clients be able to reach you?"

"What clients?"

"The ones who'll be clamoring for your services the instant the Tyler house is erected!"

So Christopher had had the gadget installed, much against his better judgment. And now, as he padded downstairs, belting his dressing gown, his head jarring at every step, he was strongly tempted to rip the wire from its connection.

He reached the jangling instrument, slumped grumpily onto the hall chair, and snatched the receiver from the switch hook. "Yes?" he snapped. "Who is this?"

Ned's voice snapped back, "What the devil did you think you were doing last night, leaving like that?"

"Ned, for the love of— What time is it? Can't you let a body sleep? I told you I had a headache last night."

"Headache, my foot! You just didn't want to be there, so you left. I know how you hate social calls, but I never dreamed you'd humiliate me that way. How do you think I felt, having to make excuses for you? Laura was devastated by your bad manners. She never spoke a word after you left. You ruined my evening, Christopher, and you may have ruined my chances with Whitney. Even she had little to say after you left."

Christopher's nerves tightened. "What did Laura say?" he asked swiftly. "Did she—"

"I just told you she said nothing!" Ned raged. "What did you expect her to say? I know she thinks she offended you in some way. Before I left, I apologized for you again. Do you know what she said? She said, 'Don't be angry with him, Ned. It's my fault he didn't stay.' "

"What did she mean by that?"

"How the devil do *I* know? Her saying that, though, just proves that she's ten times more a lady than you are a gentleman."

Christopher's hand clenched the receiver as he recalled with regret his cruel words to Laura. "You're right about that," he said bitterly. "I proved to her last night that I'm no gentleman at all."

"What are you saying?" Ned's anger was arrested as he detected in Christopher's tone something more serious than a social blunder. "Did something happen last night that I don't know about?"

Too distressed to dissemble, Christopher told Ned everything that had happened in Laura's bedroom. Not knowing what reaction to expect, he was stunned when Ned chuckled. "You old dog, you. I didn't think you had it in you. You and Laura, eh? Despite the obvious obstacles, I approve the match."

"What match?" Christopher muttered. "She rejected me. Didn't you hear me?"

"I heard you," Ned said lazily. "But, my hot-headed friend, Laura lied to you. While you were upstairs with her, Whitney told me that Avery had proposed to Laura and that she'd turned him down. Don't you see, Christopher? If Laura found it necessary to lie to you, it means she cares for you and is afraid to admit it."

Christopher sighed impatiently. "Ned, even if that were true, she couldn't possibly want anything to do with me after what I said to her."

"That *was* rather tactless of you," Ned conceded. "But I think Laura's perceptive enough to know that your heightened emotional state prompted your outburst. In any case, the thing for you to do now is to be patient and let her alone for a while. After a suitable amount of time has passed, you can begin to press your suit—but in an entirely different manner. When construction begins on the Tyler house, you're bound to be thrown into contact with Laura again. When you are, be as courteous as you can be, but be distant. No woman—not even Laura—can resist a challenge."

"Ned, is that wise?" Christopher asked worriedly. "Wouldn't it be better if I apologized to her and told her that I—"

"Christopher, I can't talk anymore," Ned said, cutting him off. "By the way, the reason I telephoned is that it's half past nine and Henry wants to know why you're not at your drawing board. You'd better get down here as fast as you can. And you'd best be prepared to have your head handed to you."

*   *   *

Eighteen ninety-five had been a banner year for the architectural firm of Carlisle & Hastings. Their shingle-style villas, with twin front gables, bell-shaped roofs, and arcaded verandas, abounded on Long Island. In Newport their touch was everywhere, from romantic casinos and restaurants of rough stone to baronial dwellings overlooking the sea, topped by the turrets and spires of Old World chateaux. In New York, too, in every corner of the city, the hand of Carlisle & Hastings was evident: on Wall Street their banks; on Fifty-seventh Street their brownstones; and on Fifth Avenue their magnificent mansions of marble and limestone.

Any architect in the country would have been honored to be a member of such a prestigious organization. Christopher Warren was well aware of his exceptional good fortune in being the favored protégé of the firm's senior partner. This distinction, however, was not without cost. If Henry favored Christopher, he likewise demanded of him ten times more than he demanded of any other employee. "Discipline" was Henry's watchword where Christopher was concerned, discipline and a hawklike vigilance that sometimes drove the younger man to distraction.

In March 1896, Henry said to him, "I've been giving this a lot of thought lately, and I've finally decided that it's time you were working on a project of your own."

They were at the Greenwood Cemetery, in Brooklyn, where Henry was inspecting a mausoleum he had designed. It was almost spring, but winter's chill still lingered in the air.

"A project?" Christopher said, turning his attention from the stately monument to stare incredulously at Henry. "Are you joking?"

"I don't know why you're so surprised," Henry said dryly. "You've been badgering me for a project for years."

"And you've been refusing me for years," Christopher reminded him. "What changed your mind?"

Henry took his time answering as he tried to light a cigar against the gusty blasts of wind. Abandoning the attempt, he took Christopher's arm and walked with him to the coach waiting in the roadway.

"You've just celebrated your thirty-third birthday," Henry said, climbing into the coach. "When I was your age, I had already designed my first house in Newport. I remember it well," he said pensively as Christopher climbed in after him and the coachman flicked his whip, sending the horses off with a jolt. "It was an unholy conglomeration of pavilions, porches, and dormers. You would have hated that house, Christopher! But I could not have been prouder of it."

Christopher smiled at his mentor's unlikely lapse into nostalgia. "I daresay I would have hated it," he agreed. "It sounds like an absolute horror."

"Oh, it was, I assure you." Henry finally got

his cigar lighted. "As time passed, whenever I was in Newport and happened to see the house, I would get the cold shudders. I thanked the Fates when it was razed fifteen years ago. It's curious how one's values change as one grows older." He gave Christopher a sidelong glance. "When I was in my thirties, I thought I knew everything."

Christopher bristled at Henry's obvious innuendo. But then, observing the jocular glint in the older man's eyes, he laughed. "I take your meaning, you sly fox. Now tell me about the project."

Henry looked out the window at the small lakes and picturesque trees that followed the contours of the winding road leading out of the cemetery. "It's an interesting challenge," he said. "I hope you're equal to the task."

"Yes, go on," Christopher urged, eager to hear the details.

"The job entails renovations on an existing library, plus a new gymnasium and an academic building, additions to a girls' school in Hadlyme, Connecticut."

"What's the budget?"

"One hundred fifty thousand dollars. There's a ten percent commission; forty percent of it is the firm's, the rest is yours."

"My God!" Christopher exclaimed. "That's nine thousand dollars!"

"You'll more than earn it," Henry said pointedly. "You'll be dealing with two sisters in their sixties—they own and operate the school—and they have very definite ideas as to what they want. This is not your typical girls' school, run on a shoestring by genteel but indigent spinsters. Eudora and Vivian Parker inherited one of Boston's oldest merchant fortunes. Moreover, Charles Bulfinch was their great-uncle. And I don't have to tell you, do I, that Bulfinch's Tontine Crescent project was the most civilized example of city architecture in the last century."

Christopher was impressed. Bulfinch's Federal style was one he greatly admired. "What exactly do the ladies have in mind, do you know?"

"I know only this much," Henry said. "The school building was built in 1840. It's a castellated Gothic design of dressed granite. The library is adjacent, a smaller structure of coursed rubble masonry, with a bracketed cornice topped by battlements."

"It sounds like a military post," Christopher said scornfully.

"I believe it once was." Henry frowned at his tone. "You had best change that attitude if you're to work on this project. The Parker sisters want the new buildings in strict keeping with the existing ones. If they want a gymnasium in the style of William Burges, don't give them something that might have been designed by Inigo Jones."

"Don't worry about it," Christopher said confidently. "I'll give the Parker sisters exactly what they want."

"I know you will," Henry said ominously. "Because if you don't, this project will be your first and your last."

Henry's threat bounced right off Christopher;

his spirits were too high. This project, a renovation and two buildings with a more than generous budget, would challenge his creativity and hopefully establish him as an architect of great distinction. Once he was established, there would be no more obstacles to his pursuit of Laura Sheridan. Laura . . . just the thought of her could start his heart to pounding furiously. He had taken Ned's advice and let her alone. But these past few months without seeing her had been hard. He loved her, he wanted her, and by God he was going to have her. Nothing in heaven or on earth was going to stop him!

When he told Ned the good news about his project, Ned said excitedly, "The Parker sisters? That's Whitney's school! If you see her while you're there, you must put in a good word for me. We've been corresponding since she returned to Connecticut, but I don't want her to forget my numerous charms. Christopher, you *will* remind her how intelligent, witty, and attractive I am?"

"As if she could ever forget!" Christopher laughed.

A week after his conversation with Henry Carlisle, Christopher packed his bags and took the morning train to Chester, Connecticut, where he boarded a ferryboat that transported him across the Connecticut River to Hadlyme.

It was a mild day in March, a warm, spectacular day with blinding blue skies and a radiant sun that cast diamond-bright light on the rushing river's surface.

Christopher was met at the landing by an el-

derly coachman who, in spite of the mild day,
wore a caped greatcoat and a peaked cap secured by a muffler tied under his chin.

"You the archy-teck?" the man inquired. And
when Christopher nodded: "Climb in, then."
Indicating an open victoria fronted by a handsome chestnut mare.

It was a fifteen-minute ride up oak-lined
slopes overlooking the river. The view was
breathtaking. Christopher could well understand why the Parker sisters had chosen this site
for their school.

"Here we be!" announced the coachman,
stopping the horse on the graveled driveway in
front of the school.

Up close, the building was even more imposing. The twin towers were separated by an
arched portico, giving the structure the look of a
medieval castle. Christopher almost expected to
see a band of Crusaders, clad in chain mail and
cross-emblazoned surcoats, emerge from the
archway brandishing bloodied swords.

The coachman interrupted this flight of fancy.
"Go on inside," he said. "Miss Eudora's office is
on the first floor, in the left tower. I'll bring your
luggage to your room."

"My room?" Christopher said, alighting from
the victoria. "It was my understanding that I
would be staying at the inn in town."

"Don't know about that," the man shrugged.
"Miss Eudora said you was staying here. I'll
bring your bags to your room, like I was told.
You fight it out with Miss Eudora as to where
you're going to lodge."

The coachman took the bags and shuffled away. Christopher dusted himself off, straightened his tie, and walked toward the tower.

There was a thick oaken door within the archway. Christopher knocked and entered a small antechamber where a bespectacled secretary, after taking his name, motioned to the door behind her and said, "Miss Eudora is expecting you. Please go right in."

He knocked at that door and entered a circular room with rough stone walls, a high ceiling, and embrasured windows. In the center of the room was a Hepplewhite desk, incongruous to its surroundings, behind which sat a silver-haired woman with a heroic figure and formidable dark eyes in an exceptionally handsome face.

"Mr. Warren?" she said as Christopher removed his hat and approached the desk.

"Yes, ma'am."

"You're rather young," she said bluntly.

"Yes, ma'am," he said again.

She was wearing a plain black dress with a white pleated yoke that gave her the look of a twelfth-century abbess. Her eyes bore into Christopher's as if testing his mettle by sheer intimidation. When he returned her gaze unflinchingly, she nodded, satisfied, then bade him sit.

"Henry tells me you have a mind of your own," she said straight out. "I like that in a person, provided . . ." She paused, then went on pointedly, "Provided that person's convictions concur with mine."

Christopher did not reply. He was dimly reminded of the first time he met Henry. Henry's bark, Christopher had learned, was far more fearsome than his bite.

"You haven't much experience," the woman continued. "Henry also told me that you've had only one commission before this one."

"Yes, Miss Parker," Christopher said. "Construction is to begin in May on that house. But I have every confidence that I can handle your project to your complete satisfaction."

"*I'll* be the judge of that," she said. "And you will call me Miss Eudora," she added imperiously. "My sister, whom you will meet later, you will address as Miss Vivian."

"Yes, Miss Eudora."

The meekness of Christopher's reply was at variance with the wryness of his tone. Eudora shot him a quick look, but his expression betrayed nothing but the utmost respect.

"Let me make absolutely clear what's expected of you," she said, drumming her fingers on the desk. "This building was erected more than a half century ago, its purpose to house and instruct military trainees. It outgrew its usefulness some twenty years ago, at which time my sister and I purchased it and started our school. The Parker School is the finest institution of its kind on the entire East Coast. Our enrollment has quadrupled in the past ten years, necessitating additional facilities, which is the reason you're here."

"Yes, ma'am," said Christopher, merely punctuating her soliloquy.

"When you design the new buildings, Mr.

Warren, you are not to deviate one iota from the guidelines my sister and I will set forth to you."

"Understood," he said gravely.

"You will spend several days here as our guest, touring the building and the grounds, absorbing the very essence of what the Parker School is. You will take all your meals with my sister and me in our private dining room. And at no time, Mr. Warren—at *no* time, do you understand me?—will you have intercourse of any kind with my girls."

Christopher smiled inwardly at her choice of words. "Yes, ma'am," he said. "I understand perfectly."

"Good," she said briskly. "Now, come with me." She rose and took a cape from the coat tree near the door. "I want to show you the library."

Christopher left his hat on the desk and followed her outdoors. The afternoon had warmed, and in the air there was a pleasant scent of wallflowers and pine and of new, sun-kissed grass.

"It's beautiful up here," he commented, keeping pace with Eudora's long stride. When she gave no answer, he went on conversationally, "I was reared in the city. I never saw the countryside until I was seventeen years old and spent a month at Mr. Carlisle's hunting lodge in upstate New York. This place has a wilder look, though, a feeling of precivilization, if you know what I mean."

She stopped walking, looked over at him, and unexpectedly she smiled. "Yes," she said. "I know what you mean. That's precisely the reason I chose this spot to school my girls. I wanted them to learn that a beauty exists in the world that is far superior to the transitory glitter of wealth and social position."

Christopher nodded agreement, but he couldn't help thinking that Miss Eudora might not be so quick to disparage wealth and position had she not spent her whole life enjoying the same.

They reached the library and went inside. Freestanding bookshelves stood chockablock with study tables occupied by fifteen or so uniformed girls. Further crowding the room were large glass cabinets displaying stratified and metamorphic rock, a dazzling collection of butterflies, and several remarkably lifelike stuffed birds, including a stately owl, a fierce marsh hawk, and a colorful fire weaver with a puffed face and breast.

Despite the great size of the room and a twenty-foot ceiling, Christopher suddenly felt claustrophobic. "This room needs improvement," he said uncomfortably.

Coolly, Eudora answered, "That's why you're here, Mr. Warren."

He spent five busy days in Connecticut—successful days too, for his association with Henry Carlisle had prepared him well to deal with the likes of the redoubtable Parker sisters.

Vivian Parker, though not as outspoken as her older sister, was likewise demanding. She was a slim wraith of a woman with soft brown eyes and gray-streaked brown hair, whose sweet voice and gentle aspect concealed a will of iron. It had been her idea to build a gymnasium for her girls. *"Mens sana in corpore sano,"* she said to Christopher, reminding him that a healthy body was indispensable to a sound mind. And he, thankful at least to Saint Peter's for a respectable education in languages, replied, *"Sic itur ad astra."* Such is the way to immortality!

Christopher made an important decision while he was in Connecticut, a decision based partly on his desire to win Laura. Although totally absorbed now with his work, he had never for a moment stopped thinking of her. After the incident on Christmas night, Christopher had come to the conclusion that it was not the two-year age difference between them that Laura objected to, but rather his poverty. *How could a woman like her even consider marrying a man without means?* It was understandable that she, widow of one of the city's finest architects, wealthy and successful in her own right, should want a man equal to her status.

Christopher's goal, thus reinforced, was to succeed. But to do that, it was absolutely essential that he compromise his principles and design in certain styles he thought abhorrent. Left to his own devices, he would have created a gymnasium and academic building reminiscent of the Greek temples of Athena and Zeus. As it was, with his newfound resolution, he acceded to the Parker sisters' every demand, showing them preliminary sketches so contrary to his taste, so loaded with sally ports and parapets and basket arches, that Eudora, who had been

warned of his preference for Palladian purity,
said, surprised, "Henry was wrong about you,
young man. You're not the least bit difficult to
work with."

The ladies were especially pleased with
Christopher's proposed changes for the library.
In this one instance he chose the clean classic
lines he favored, and because his choice greatly
improved the library's utility, the Parker sisters
approved his decision.

On his last day in Hadlyme he encountered
Whitney Sheridan. He had previously been too
busy to seek her out; indeed, he had almost
forgotten she was a student at the school.

It was a Sunday morning. Christopher was at
the proposed site of the academic building, making sketches of the area, so that when he was
ready to work, he would have the setting for his
design fresh in his mind. It was a bright sunny
morning. He was sitting on the grass, leaning
against a tree stump, sketchpad on his knees. He
had removed his hat and coat, and the sun shed
welcome warmth on his bare head and shirt-
sleeved arms.

"Why, Christopher Warren, there you are! I've
been hoping to see you for days."

He looked up. The sun was at Whitney's back,
throwing her lovely features into shadow. Her
hair was down; he had never before seen it that
way. One shining lock lay charmingly over her
breast; the rest, a mass of curls, hung down her
back to her waist. She wore the Parker School
uniform, a white shirtwaist with high-necked
collar, and a navy blue skirt. She was pink-

cheeked and vivacious, as pretty as a Gainsborough. Christopher put aside his sketchpad and rose eagerly to greet her.

"Whitney, how wonderful to see you!" He reached for his coat, but she gestured for him to discard it. "You're a sight for sore eyes after days of those two old tyrants."

She laughed, delighted, and perched on the tree stump. "They *are* awfully bossy, aren't they? It took me a long time to get used to them. They're the finest teachers, though," she said in defense. "I'll miss them when I leave here. I'm graduating in June, you know. I hope you'll attend the ceremony."

"In June?" He settled on the grass at her feet. "Yes, I think I'll be able to come. My designs should be ready by then. Ned will be coming too, won't he? I know he's looking forward to seeing you again."

"Ned?" she said, as if considering that thought for the first time. "Yes. Of course he's welcome to come . . . if he wants to."

"If he wants to? Whitney, there's nothing Ned wants more than to see you. You feel the same way about him, don't you?"

The girl colored and lowered her gaze. Christopher, attributing her silence to maidenly modesty, said, "Well, in any case, you'll be seeing each other for Easter. You're going home next week, aren't you?"

"No," she said regretfully, looking up at him. "I'm staying at school. You see," she confessed, "my French grade is low, and I hope to make it up by studying hard all that week. It's ironic, you know. My mother and grandmother spoke nothing but French to me when I was a child. But after my grandmother died, Mama never spoke a word of it again. I think she couldn't bear to hear the language because it reminded her so much of her mother. As the years passed then, I forgot every word of it."

Christopher looked down at the grass, warm and soft beneath his hand. "How is your mother?" he asked quietly.

"She's fine," Whitney said. "She been very busy, choosing fabrics and furnishings for when the Tyler house is built. She . . ." Whitney paused, then said slowly, "She's also been seeing a lot of my uncle lately."

"Oh?" Christopher raised his gaze to hers.

"I wonder . . ." Whitney mused.

"What do you wonder?"

"I wonder if she's going to marry him. It's the most curious thing. My uncle proposed to her at Christmastime, but my mother refused him, and they had a big row, and then my uncle ran off to Palm Beach—" She broke off suddenly, realizing her indiscretion. "Christopher," she said abruptly, "this is in the strictest confidence. You won't say anything to anyone, will you?"

"I won't tell a soul," he said evenly.

"Well, when I returned to school after the holidays," Whitney continued, "Mama wrote to me and said that she had made up the quarrel with Uncle Avery. She assured me she wasn't going to marry him and that my uncle had accepted that fact. But from her recent letters I gather she's been spending a great deal of time with him. I just wonder if that means he's starting to change her mind."

"Could he do that, do you think?" Christopher's low voice was steady.

"I don't know," the girl said dubiously. "My mother loved my father so much. I simply can't imagine her being married to anyone else. I wish I were going home for Easter. Then I could see firsthand how she feels."

Christopher's hand crushed a clump of grass. Damn Laura's brother-in-law! He had everything in his favor: wealth, social position, and, most important, he had probably known Laura for years and years. On the other hand, though, Avery Sheridan had no conception of what it meant to do battle for what he really wanted. On that score, Christopher thought, I am surely the good doctor's superior.

In an attempt to conceal his racing thoughts, Christopher said lightly in French, "If you had studied your lessons, you wouldn't be in this unhappy predicament."

"Christopher!" she cried. "Your French is perfect! Where did you learn to speak it so beautifully?"

"At the orphanage where I was reared," he said in English. "Afterward, while I lived in Henry Carlisle's house, he insisted I keep it up. He made me read all the architectural theories of Cochin and Laugier in the original French. Henry was trying to make a gentleman of me," he added with a laugh.

"*Trying?*" Whitney exclaimed. "How can you say that? You're one of the finest gentlemen I know."

Christopher stared at her silently, his eyes hard, his thoughts elsewhere. He *had* to finish this job quickly and get back to New York—to Laura. He needed to see her, to hear her voice, to touch her skin—as much as he needed the very air he breathed.

"And you're establishing yourself as a superlative architect," Whitney went on.

"Superlative?" She had caught his attention; he regarded her with some amusement. "Is that what you think?"

"Yes, yes!" she said fervently. "I think you're the most admirable man I've ever met."

His amusement increased. "Do you?" he said. "You're rather admirable yourself, Whitney. You always say exactly what you're thinking. I like that in a woman."

"Really?" She leaned suddenly forward, laid a hand on his shoulder, and regarded him searchingly.

"Yes, really." He patted her hand as if she were seven years old. "If women were always honest about their feelings . . ." He paused and thought of Laura, looked into her daughter's face, and saw the elusive but unmistakable resemblance there: the flawless skin, the determined chin, the upturned mouth he longed to kiss. He remembered the feel of Laura's lips beneath his, soft and warm and utterly compliant. . . . He shook his head suddenly to clear it.

"Life would be a lot less complicated," he finished bitterly.

Whitney's eyes widened. She opened her mouth to speak, then quickly clamped it shut. Her hand was still on Christopher's shoulder, grasping it so tightly that he winced.

"Whitney, what's the matter?" He took her hand from his shoulder and held it in his.

"Christopher . . ." Her voice was soft yet urgent. Urgent, too, was the tenseness of her posture and the look in her dusky-dark eyes. "Christopher, I want to tell you something."

"Yes?"

"I . . ."

The sound of approaching footsteps stilled her words. "So there you are, Miss Sheridan. May I ask why you were not at chapel this morning?"

Whitney jumped and pulled her hand from Christopher's. Eudora Parker, in all her black-and-white authority, stood several feet away, glowering at her truant student.

"M-miss Eudora," Whitney stammered, "the reason I wasn't at chapel is . . . well, I . . . I felt ill this morning, so I took a walk to clear my head."

"Indeed?" Eudora turned to Christopher, who had risen to his feet and was pulling on his coat. "Mr. Warren, did I not mention to you at the beginning of your stay here that there was to be no fraternization between you and my girls?"

"Yes, you did," Christopher said with all respect, "but, you see, ma'am, Whitney and I know each other—"

"And that gave you call to arrange a tryst with her?"

"Miss Eudora!" the girl cried. "It's not like that at all. I happened upon Christopher by accident. This wasn't a tryst; I promise you!"

"Be still, miss! Mr. Warren, I believe you had planned to leave today. If you've nothing further to do here, I'll have Walter drive you to the ferry landing."

"Yes, ma'am," Christopher muttered, bending to collect his sketchpad and hat. The indignity of his position infuriated him. He wanted to tell the old dragon to go to the devil, but there was too much at stake here to speak his mind.

Eudora returned her attention to Whitney. "Young lady, go back to the school and remain in your room until otherwise advised. We'll discuss this matter further after I've written to your mother."

"My mother? Miss Eudora, please don't do that! This meeting was entirely innocent!"

Christopher froze. If Laura should receive a letter saying that he had had an assignation with her daughter—

"Miss Eudora," he said rapidly, "I beg you not to write to Mrs. Sheridan. I give you my solemn word of honor that this meeting was not prearranged."

"Good-bye, Mr. Warren. I'll expect to look at your designs in June."

"Miss Eudora, please—"

"*Good-bye*, Mr. Warren," she repeated emphatically, then took Whitney's arm and started back to the school.

The hapless girl stumbled away alongside her merciless headmistress, looking back at Christopher with a wretched white face, her eyes bright with tears of humiliation. Christopher watched her leave, unable to move or speak. Laura, he could only think in a torment. *Laura.*

Chapter Nine
❖❖❖❖

PREVIOUS TO WHITNEY's starting school, she and Laura had been closer than most mothers and daughters. Perhaps this closeness stemmed from the fact that after Steven Sheridan's death they had had no one but each other. More likely, though, it was because Laura and Whitney were very much alike: strong-willed, decisive, and, in certain circumstances, single-minded to the point of obsessiveness.

When Steven died at the age of forty-nine, Laura felt at the time that the light of her life had been extinguished. When she buried him, she felt certain that she had buried all earthly joys with him. Never, she thought, would she love another man as she had loved Steven—until she met Christopher, that is—and then, every certainty she had ever known irrevocably changed.

Christopher Warren. His very name warmed her blood. She loved him, she could no longer deny it, in a way she had never loved Steven Sheridan. Steven had been the best of husbands, she could not deny that, but her relationship with him had been based more on respect and youthful admiration, the love of a diligent pupil for a much revered mentor. Steven had been almost a second father to her, kind, wise, and utterly predictable. Whereas Christopher, with his volatile temperament and his passionate dedication to his work, was a continual source of excitement to Laura.

How vividly she remembered the first time she had seen him. How magnetic he was, how irresistibly attractive with those compelling dark eyes and that innate air of dignity that even his well-worn attire could not fully disguise. And then later, when they worked together on the Tyler house, Laura had seen in him the same fervor for his work that she had for hers, a fervor that Steven had regarded with amused paternalistic indulgence and that Avery regarded with barely concealed contempt.

Laura was no longer able to lie to herself about the man who for months now had been obsessing her thoughts. She had lied to Christopher on Christmas night—not very convincingly, she feared—but to herself the truth was undeniable. She loved him, she wanted him, surely as much as he wanted her; and to her mingled shame and disbelief, she had very nearly permitted him to make love to her.

Try though she might, it was impossible for her to forget that night, to forget the touch of his hands, the strength of his body, the knee-weakening passion of his fierce, possessive kisses. She would have submitted to him then, there, had not a momentary flash of lucidity brought her back to sanity. And afterward—dear God, how she cringed at the thought! All the while she was telling him that their actions were madness, she had wanted to go back into his arms, to experience again the blissful madness she so strenuously denied. She had wanted to touch his hair, his brow, his cheeks, his mouth; she had wanted to feel the hard male urgency of his young, of his oh so young, body pressing hotly, erotically against hers. . . .

"Laura, what in the world are you thinking about?" asked Avery Sheridan as they strolled up Fifth Avenue on Good Friday morning. "You're miles away!"

They had just attended early services at Saint Thomas's church and were walking the two blocks to Laura's house. Avery was handsomely turned out in black broadcloth, a sober striped tie, and pearl-gray waistcoat. Laura looked lovely but subdued in a *demi-saison* dress of checked wool with chic velvet embroidery on the bodice and hem. She turned to him slowly when he spoke, expecting to see the lean, dark face in her thoughts. It was somewhat of a shock to see Avery watching her.

She laughed self-consciously and looked guiltily away from him. "I *was* in a brown study, wasn't I? To be perfectly honest," she lied, "I was thinking of Whitney. I'm disappointed she won't be here for the holiday. Easter won't be the same without her."

"I know what you mean," Avery said, and the genuine regret in his voice increased Laura's guilt. "I'll miss her too. But, cheer up," he added, his tone brightening. "She'll be graduating soon. Why don't you open the house in Newport, and we'll spend the month of July there with her. How does that sound to you, Laura?"

"It sounds wonderful."

Laura had been seeing a great deal of Avery lately, not, as her daughter feared, pursuant to marrying him, but only to make amends for having so adamantly refused him. She wondered if Avery was as reconciled to her rejection as he appeared to be. When he had returned from Palm Beach, he had actually apologized to *her*. "I'm sorry about the way I acted that night," he had said sincerely. "I shouldn't have left the way I did, and I should never have said what I did about . . . What I mean to say is, I know what you and Steven had together. It was foolish of me to think you might consider marriage with anyone else. You will forgive me, won't you? Let's be friends once again; let's forget what happened that night."

And Laura, who blamed herself for Avery's hasty flight to Florida, had readily agreed to bury the past.

"But, Avery," she said now, "surely you can't leave your practice for an entire month just to go to Newport. What would your patients say?"

"I'm due for a long vacation," he said, taking her arm as they crossed Fifty-fourth Street. "I can direct all my patients to Hal Weber while I'm gone. July is generally slow anyway; everyone is away for the summer."

"Let's discuss it when Whitney comes home," Laura suggested, evading a definite commitment. "She may have made plans with her friends as she did last year."

"Yes, all right," he said agreeably. "We'll wait for Whitney."

When they reached her house, Avery saw her to the door, confirmed their engagement for Easter dinner together, then went on to his offices on Madison Avenue. Laura let herself into the house, removed her hat and gloves, and laid them on the hall table, where the morning post awaited her on a silver tray.

She picked up the stack of letters. There was little of interest—several bills, appeals for local charities—but at the bottom of the stack there was a vellum envelope embossed with the Parker School crest. Mildly curious, Laura slit the envelope with an ivory paper knife and drew out the letter.

My dear Mrs. Sheridan, the letter began. *It is always distressful when a student's conduct necessitates my writing to her parent. On the whole, Whitney's record at this school has been exemplary, although her French, as you know, bears improvement. Her academic standing, however, is not at issue here. My concern is her obedience and her sense of decorum, which, like her French, appears to warrant considerable improvement.*

On the date of this letter, your daughter deliberately missed Sunday services in order to meet with a young man on school grounds. Though I am convinced that

*no improprieties were committed at this meeting,
Whitney will nonetheless be disciplined for her actions. My purpose in writing is neither to alarm nor
to anger you. Whitney's infraction of the rules was not
a grave one, but you may rest assured that my sister
and I do not take lightly the responsibility with which
the parents of our girls have entrusted us.*

*To further set your mind at rest, the young man in
question is not unknown to you. His name is Christopher Warren, and he is under architectural commission to the school at the behest of Henry Carlisle, with
whom I believe you are also acquainted. Be that as it
may, I wish to doubly assure you that Whitney's lapse
will be dealt with equitably but firmly and that an
incident of this kind will not reoccur.*

The letter was signed: *Yours most sincerely, Eudora Parker*.

Laura sat down abruptly on the hall chair and
reread the letter, attempting to glean a particle of
relevance from the mountainous heap of Eudora's stilted verbiage. Her mind was spinning;
it was difficult to think. A meeting? What kind of
meeting? Whitney and Christopher? It was impossible. Christopher had assured Laura that he
had no interest in her daughter. "It's you I
want," he had said. But then why had they met?
How could Eudora Parker be certain that no "improprieties" had been committed? If the meeting
had been innocent, why had that long-winded
woman found it necessary to write to Laura?

With a rush of anger, Laura crumpled the letter, threw it to the floor, and reached for the
telephone.

"Hello, Central?" she said curtly. "Connect me with Broadway five-three-nine."

The connection was made. A man's voice answered, "Good morning. Carlisle and Hastings."

"Good morning," Laura said. Her own voice was shaking; her hands on the telephone were damp with perspiration. "I'd like to speak to Christopher Warren. Is he available?"

"May I ask who's calling?"

Laura gave her name.

"One moment, please, Mrs. Sheridan. I'll see if I can locate him."

A few minutes went by that to Laura seemed an hour. The ticking of the hall clock was a cacophony in her ears. Her throat had gone dry; she swallowed convulsively. Her anger was being replaced by a feeling twice as fierce, an emotion she was unable at the moment to identify.

"Laura?"

His voice startled her. She tried to speak and failed.

"Laura, are you there? It's Christopher."

"Yes . . . yes," she said with difficulty. "I'm here. I need to see you, to talk to you."

"Yes, of course. When? Where?" His voice sounded odd, half-eager, half-apprehensive.

"As soon as possible. Could we meet at lunch-time?"

"Yes," he said at once. "Where would you like to eat? Delmonico's? The Hoffman House?"

"No." Her tone hardened. "I don't want to take lunch with you. I don't want to meet in public. What I have to say to you is of a personal nature."

He was silent for a moment. Then: "You've heard from Eudora Parker, haven't you?"

"Christopher," she said tightly, "I won't discuss this on the telephone. I want to see you immediately—in private."

"Your house?" he suggested.

"No. I don't want you here."

He fell silent again, a long, palpable silence. Laura could hear his soft breathing, could almost feel it on her lips. She closed her eyes; her throat ached and burned. "Well?" she said in a cold voice that was at variance with the heat of her emotions.

Christopher said warily, "Would you want to meet at my house?"

"Where do you live?"

He told her, then added, "I can be there at noon."

"Good. I'll see you then."

Without waiting for an answer, without a good-bye, Laura hung up the receiver, rose stiffly to her feet, then stared blindly at the letter that lay crumpled on the floor.

At exactly twelve noon Laura alighted from her carriage in front of Christopher's house and instructed her coachman to wait for her.

She was somewhat more controlled now than she had been an hour earlier. Her anger remained, but it was less erratic, more focused and in hand. Her purpose was clear: She would tell

Christopher that he must never, under any circumstances, see Whitney again. Laura was not interested in the details of their meeting in Hadlyme. All that concerned her was that this man, who had awakened certain unmentionable feelings in her, must never be alone with her daughter.

The heat of her emotions was now an icy calm that numbed her perception. Had she had her wits about her she would never have chosen to meet, alone, with Christopher. A woman—a lady—never went to a gentleman's house unless properly chaperoned. No matter that she was a widow; certain rules must be adhered to. In this case, however, Laura was making an exception. Certain rules, she thought grimly, had already been broken.

She knocked at the door. Christopher opened it at once as if he had been waiting just behind it for her knock.

"Come in," he said tensely. He ushered her into the foyer and closed the door.

The house was very quiet. It smelled pleasantly of soap and beeswax; and from another room Laura detected the faint aroma of freshly brewed coffee. She looked at Christopher, but before she could speak, he took her arm and directed her to a small parlor, simply furnished and neatly kept.

Laura's purpose was temporarily diverted by the cozy warmth of the room. Books filled the wall shelves, their worn covers giving evidence of much use. A tweedy armchair was companion to a brown plush sofa, made cunningly more attractive by a colorful patchwork quilt thrown over the backrest. Cheerful scatter rugs lay on the shiny pine floor; and in a small copper bowl on the mantel was a spray of yellow-and-white narcissus. Laura guessed that Christopher had bought the flowers on his way home. The gesture touched her heart. With a great deal of effort she summoned the anger that had brought her to this charming place.

"Sit down," Christopher said. "I've made some coffee. I'll get you a cup."

"Thank you, no," she said stiffly. "What I have to say to you will take just a moment. As you suspected, I did hear from Eudora Parker. She wrote and told me what happened last Sunday, and I am only here to tell you that you are never to see my daughter again."

He took a step toward her; she instinctively backed away. Despite Laura's purpose, being in the room with Christopher further threatened to weaken her resolve.

"Laura, if you'll please let me explain—"

"I'm not interested in your explanations. I'm not interested in anything you have to say to me. It's very curious . . ." She paused, then went on bitterly. "You once accused me of playing a perverted game with you—"

"Laura, for God's sake, let me—"

"But it seems that you are the one who plays games, Christopher. On Christmas night you tried to force your attentions on me, insisting all the while that you felt nothing for Whitney. The next thing I know you're arranging secret meetings and maybe forcing your attentions on *her*."

"That's not true!" he said sharply. "What did that old witch tell you? Laura, I never touched your daughter. Our meeting was accidental; all we did was talk."

"Somehow," she said coldly, "I find that difficult to believe. I happen to know what kind of man you are. I know firsthand, don't I, that your attitude toward women is less than honorable."

"That's not true!" he said again, and again he moved toward her.

"Stay away from me, Christopher!" She raised her hand defensively and took a step backward. "Don't you ever touch me again. How could you?" she said sharply, and her icy calm thawed as that emotion she could not name surged hotly to the fore. "How could you have the gall to do what you did in my bedroom and then turn around and try the same thing with my daughter?"

"Jesus Christ, I told you I never touched her. Why won't you believe me?"

"Why should I believe you?"

"Because I love you!" he flung back at her, his indignation turning to rage. "Because Whitney means nothing to me, and you know it." He closed the gap between them in two rapid strides. His hands grasped her arms and he shook her once, hard. "You must believe me. If Eudora Parker said that something happened between Whitney and me, she lied. You're the only woman I want, the only woman I shall ever want."

His hands were bruising her flesh; his face, white and furious, was inches from hers. Laura

felt his angry trembling, felt his breath on her
lips, as she had felt it, hot and dizzying, on that
night in her bedroom.

"Let me go!" she cried in a panic.

She wrenched free of his hold and turned
wildly to escape him, to escape the shameful
longing to go shamelessly into his arms. Her foot
caught on a scatter rug; she tripped and fell to
the floor with a painful thud. Her hat pulled
loose from her head; her purse flew from her
hand. Christopher was with her in an instant,
kneeling beside her, his face wretched with fear
and remorse.

"Laura . . ."

She lashed out at him blindly, afraid of his
nearness, afraid of the driving emotion that
had nothing to do with maternal protectiveness. The jet buttons on her sleeve raked his
temple, slashed the skin. Christopher started
in pain and surprise, rocked back on one knee.
A trickle of blood traced a trail down his cheek.
He touched the open wound and looked incredulously at his bloodstained fingers, then he
looked up at Laura in a stunned aching silence
that broke her heart.

"I'm sorry!" she cried softly, and raised herself to a sitting position. "I didn't mean to hurt
you." She groped for the purse, pulled out a
handkerchief, and pressed it to his temple.
"Christopher, I'm sorry; I truly am."

He said nothing, he only watched her as she
dabbed at the wound. Laura avoided his gaze,
too filled with regret and confusion to face him.
He hadn't behaved improperly with Whitney.

Laura knew that now; she had known it even while she reviled him with her infamous accusations.

The bleeding stopped. Laura dropped her hands to her lap and stared at the handkerchief, stained red with Christopher's blood. "I'm sorry," she said miserably, "for hurting you . . . and for everything I said to you today."

For a time he did not answer; his silence shamed her further. Then, she felt his finger under her chin. "Look at me," he said, and sat beside her, facing her. "Laura, look at me; I want to ask you something."

"What is it?" she said, but she would not raise her head.

"I want you to look at me." His voice was gently insistent. "I want to see your face when you answer me."

She looked up reluctantly. His temple was reddened and beginning to discolor into an ugly bruise. Laura's breast ached as she looked into his eyes. No reproach was in his gaze, only concern and understanding and a deep, restrained emotion that stopped her breath in her throat.

"Do you believe me about Whitney?" he asked quietly.

"Yes," she said in a whisper and tried to look away, but his hand cupped her chin so that she could not escape his scrutiny.

"Do you believe that I love you—truly and honorably?"

"Yes," she whispered. "Yes."

"And will you admit that you feel something for me?"

She could not answer. His hand tightened gently on her chin. "Laura?"

She wanted to speak, but she dared not. She wanted to tell him that not a day had gone by in the past few months that she hadn't thought of him, longed for him. She wanted to go into his arms, to lay her head on his chest, to feel the warmth of his body and the comfort of his embrace. But she said and did nothing. And he, sensing the fearful reticence that kept her silent, said softly, "I do love you, you know. I have never loved another woman before you. I daresay I've done all the wrong things: angered you, insulted you, scared you. If circumstances were different, I should know how to treat you, but as things are, I can only be guided by my love for you."

"Christopher, don't," she implored him, touched and rendered defenseless by his earnest admission. "You mustn't say those things. There's no future for us; can't you understand that?"

"No," he said firmly. "I refuse to accept that. I love you. That's all I know or want to know. And I think you love me— Look at me; don't turn away from me. Laura, I love you so much," he said with a quiet intensity. "If I were offered all of life's treasures but couldn't have you, I would say, 'Keep it; deny me everything; I want nothing but her.' "

She was captive to his gaze and to the truth of the emotions she could no longer deny. She did love him, utterly, profoundly. She loved him so totally that nothing mattered now save the joy of his nearness, nothing else was of importance but that he loved her as much as she loved him.

"Christopher," she whispered, and reached up to embrace him.

His arms went around her. He bent his head to kiss her, and when his lips touched hers, she surrendered absolutely to the all-encompassing sovereignty of her love for him. Logic and discretion held no place now in her mind. She wanted him, only him. She wanted his heart, his soul, his essence; she wanted to hold him so close that nothing and no one could come between them.

He eased her down to the floor and kissed her deeply, his mouth moving on hers with deliberate design. He was wooing her, seducing her, but Laura's desire was such that she needed no inducement to submit to his will. She knew he wanted to make love to her. She didn't care; she wanted it too. She had been moving toward this end, it seemed, from almost the moment she set eyes on him. All rational thought receded in the wake of her love for him, and in the tide of his persuasive and loving passion.

His hands, his lips, his body became an extension of hers. She was part of him, one with him; they kissed and touched and moved in exquisite accord. His mouth was hot and demanding; it seared her flesh, scorched her senses. His hands, those artist's hands, sketched a sensual portrait on the canvas of her skin. His body, hard and strong, molded urgently to hers, bringing to light the fever of the flesh that had lain for too long a time in the darkness of disuse.

When they physically joined, it was but a reaffirmation of the unity they had already achieved. Inside her, he became her, and she, enveloping him, became all that he was. His ecstasy in possessing her was her joy in receiving him. When he kissed her, caressed her, whispered urgent words of passion, his name on her lips was a passionate pledge of love. When he drove deep inside her, again and again, it was his pleasure that fueled hers. When he reached culmination, crushing her close to his heart, it was his shuddering satisfaction that gave rapture and completion to her own.

Afterward, for a long time, they neither moved nor spoke. Christopher did not withdraw; he remained inside her, his arms tight about her. Laura could feel the violent pounding of his heart against hers. Her own heart was racing, sending waves of warm sensation through her pleasantly tingling nerves. She lay quietly beneath him, deliciously drowsy yet intensely aware of his arms around her and of the silky-rough feel of the hairs that covered his chest. There was a pleasurable languor in her limbs and in her mind. She could only feel, not think. Her consciousness floated beyond words, beyond thought. Her senses were sharpened, honed to such a fine pitch, that when he stirred slightly and she felt the smoothness of his flesh against hers, it was as exquisite a sensation as the sweet consummation of love.

"Christopher," she whispered, "Christopher." She spoke his name as if for the first time; she turned her head and her lips touched his shoulder and lingered there, lingered there against the smooth, fragrant warmth of his skin.

"My God, I love you so much," he said in a shaking low voice. "Laura, it's never been like this for me, never."

"Nor for me," she murmured, kissing his cheek, his chin, his sensuous mouth, and she quivered with the memory of his love.

She had been loved before, but never like this. Never had her emotions been so heightened, never had she felt as one with another as she felt now with this man. Nor had she known she was capable of such uninhibited emotion. With Steven, the act of love had not been unpleasant but neither had it ever stirred a response in her. With Christopher she had been all warmth and giving. As he had pleasured her, so it was her desire to cleave to his flesh, to meld to his heart, to become one with the very essence and soul of him.

Her arms tightened around him. She loved him so intensely it was an agony in her breast. She could hear his ragged breathing; she could feel the beat of his heart, strong and steady, against hers. The floor beneath her back was hard and slightly cold, but she felt no discomfort; she felt protected and warm. When he shifted above her and tried to rise, she pressed him close. She would not—she could not bear to—let him go.

He kissed her brow briefly and disentangled

himself from her hold. "I'll be right back," he assured her. "I just want to get the quilt; you're trembling with cold."

"Not with cold," she said softly, watching him as he adjusted his disarranged clothes and fetched the quilt.

"With what, then?" he asked, pulling her to a sitting position and draping the cover about her shoulders.

He sat down beside her, rested his back against the armchair and drew her into his arms. Laura leaned close against him and laid her head on his shoulder. His body was hard, all lean bone and muscle, but to Laura it was a luxury of comfort.

"With wonder, I think," she said, moving aside his unbuttoned shirt and lightly touching the dark hairs on his chest. "I came here today with quite a different purpose in mind."

Christopher smiled. "I'm happy your plans went awry."

"So am I," she said pensively, her hand moving downward to his slim middle.

"Laura," he said, his low voice vibrating pleasantly in her ears, "if you continue in that vein, I will not be responsible for my actions."

She looked up at him, surprised, and spoke from the innocent reservoir of her marital experience. "But you couldn't, could you? Not again. Not so soon."

"Oh, no?" He took her hand and pressed it against his body.

Pleasure replaced surprise. Laura's hand lingered sensuously on the proof of his potency.

"When we're married," Christopher said, moving lazily beneath her exploration, "I shall demonstrate how readily and often I am able to make love to you."

"Married?" She drew back and stared at him.

He stared back at her with a frown. "Of course we must marry. And we must do so at once. I've just made love to you, Laura. What if I've given you a child?"

A child. Laura's heart thumped, and her eyes went soft and luminous. A strong healthy boy, with Christopher's dark hair and his intensely dark eyes. Hungrily, yearningly, she pictured his son, first as an infant with rosy cheeks and rosebud mouth, and then as a toddler, a solemn-eyed cherub in a sailor suit. She envisioned him growing up: a schoolboy in knickerbockers, a youth in long trousers. She saw him as a man, as irresistible as his father, with Christopher's tall, slender form; his long, artistic hands; and the hard, handsome face she so loved.

And then, with a sigh, she returned to reality.

"Christopher . . ." She moved out of his arms, dropped the quilt from her shoulders, and put her clothing in order, as if suddenly embarrassed that he should see her half-undressed. "It's impossible for us to marry."

She picked up her hat and purse and rose to her feet. Christopher shot up after her like an uncoiled spring.

"What the devil are you saying? We *must* marry. You've just proved you love me."

"I . . . I do love you," she said, looking down

at her purse, which was tightly clenched in her hands. "But there are other considerations."

"What considerations?" he pressed her. "If it's a question of money, I'm well on my way to earning a good living. Laura, it's not what you're used to, but I know I could support you."

She smiled bleakly and forced herself to face him. "It's not that," she said. "I know you're going to be very rich and successful one day. But, Christopher, I have a daughter who . . ." She started to say, "who has taken a fancy to you," but she said instead, "who is almost an adult."

"Laura, for God's sake, what has that got to do with anything?"

"And most of my friends," she continued with some reluctance, "are old enough to be your parents."

"What difference does that make?" he snapped. "I wouldn't care if they were old enough to be my grandparents."

"Some of them are," she said dismally. "Christopher, don't you see. My life is immutably fixed. I can't change it now. And my brother-in-law . . ." She paused and lowered her gaze. "He would never understand."

"Why should you care what he thinks?" Christopher said stubbornly. "*We're* all that matters, you and I and what we feel for each other."

"If you were older," she said softly, "you would know that's not true."

"Older?" he said. "Like your husband, do you mean? A man old enough to be your father? Laura, look at me," he demanded, grasping her hands in his. "We're the same, you and I. We're contemporaries, equals. You'll have a better, happier, more complete marriage with me than you ever had with him."

If only that were true, she thought wistfully. But they weren't equals, not in the eyes of her family and friends, at any rate. If only she *could* marry him, not caring about anyone's outraged objections. To be a wife again, to live with Christopher, to be his helpmeet and support, to share his bed, to bear his children—oh, what she wouldn't give to be free and unencumbered, free to marry and live with this very special man she loved.

"Christopher, I'm sorry," she said wretchedly, "I can't marry you. It's out of the question."

And before he could stop her, before she weakened and changed her mind, she pushed past him and fled from his house and, regretfully, from his love.

Chapter Ten
✦ ✦ ✦ ✦

IN MAY, CONSTRUCTION was begun on the Tyler house on Fifth Avenue. The location of the property was on the corner of Fifty-sixth Street, one block north of Laura Sheridan's house. Despite her proximity to the building site, Laura chose not to visit it. When the Tylers chided her for this, Laura assured them that she was busy day and night coordinating the interiors of the house and that for her to observe the construction in progress would serve no purpose.

The fact of the matter was, Laura very much feared she might see Christopher at the building site, so she stayed away from it. She was in truth busy with her work, choosing fabrics and furnishings, onyx lampstands, ormolu clocks, painted fire screens, and sundry other decorations for the Tylers' new house; but under other circumstances she would have enjoyed, and probably benefited from, watching the construction. As it was, she avoided the site like the plague, immersing herself in her work; yet never once during her labors was Christopher out of her thoughts. Her rejection of his marriage proposal had in no way lessened her interest and her faith in his work. It was her intention that Christopher's first commission should be a showpiece of grace and elegance, its understated interiors a perfect complement to the Palladian purity of its exterior.

New Yorkers, Laura knew, might not readily embrace the classic simplicity of Christopher's design. Never in the city's history had architectural tastes been so ludicrously opulent. A firehouse on Lafayette Street was designed in the style of a Loire Valley chateau circa the reign of Francis I. The already baroque Grand Central Depot was enlarged by the addition of three flamboyant floors and copper-clad cupolas. There were, of course, architects who resisted the highly ornamental Gothic and Romanesque styles, but they were few and far between. Charles McKim was one, along with John Merven Carrère; the excellent Stanford White was another. And now Christopher numbered among that elite group. Laura often thought grimly that in that respect, at least, her family and most of her friends would approve of him.

It was a bitter disappointment when she discovered she was not going to have Christopher's child. If she had been pregnant, Laura would have had no recourse but to marry him. There was no question in her mind about wanting to marry him. She did want it—desperately. She had been born to be a wife. Her years with Steven, instead of filling her with guilt when she considered her love for Christopher, only increased her desire to marry him.

But she hadn't the courage to defy convention, nor could she forget the fact that when she married Steven, Christopher had been only fifteen years old. She also kept thinking that when she reached forty Christopher would be thirty-eight, at the height of his physical attractiveness. Laura's love for him was strong, but her fears seemed stronger. Hence, she avoided him. And he, to her combined gratitude and despair, made no effort to contact her.

In June, Laura took a much-needed hiatus from her work and from her thoughts and traveled with Avery to Hadlyme to attend Whitney's commencement. Avery made the travel arrangements. Instead of the train he booked passage on the *City of Hartford*, the graceful steel side-wheeler that steamed up Long Island Sound and then into the Connecticut River, affording a stunning view of riverside rocky slopes dotted with bluebells and hyacinths and lovely mountain laurel.

As Laura stood at the steamer's rail, her linen collar flaring and bonnet ribbons snapping, she took deep breaths of the freshening wind, turning up her face to the rays of the morning sun.

"Ah, Avery," she said, "this is incredible. How did you know it was just what I needed?"

Avery's gray eyes were thoughtful. His dreamy poet's face, so unlike his brother's, was grave and thoughtful as he watched her pink cheeks and bright eyes. "Who knows you better than I do, Laura?"

She looked over at him and smiled. Yes, he knew her so well, sometimes better than she knew herself. They were cut from one cloth: They shared the same life, the same faith, the same friends; and most important, they were both bound by blood to Steven's daughter. If only Laura could have loved him, this man who was so like her, instead of a man so totally different from everyone she knew.

In Hadlyme, on the grounds of the Parker School, a platform had been erected for teachers and guest speakers, among which was the dauntless feminist Anna Howard Shaw. Rows of chairs flanked a rose-covered arch, through which the happy graduates passed to collect their diplomas. The girls looked lovely in their white dresses of organdy and muslin and dotted swiss. Not one of them, though, looked lovelier to Laura than her darling, who wore a dress of China silk with leg-of-mutton sleeves, lace yoke, and a lace-bordered skirt. In her hair Whitney wore a garland of lily of the valley, fragile and fragrant. In her ears were lustrous white pearls, a gift from her doting uncle.

When Whitney received her diploma, Laura's eyes grew misty, and she clutched Avery's hand. "Isn't she beautiful?" she whispered. "I'm so proud of her."

Avery covered her hand with his. "No prouder than I am," he said softly.

After the ceremony, there was an outdoor buffet at the rear of the school building on the edge of the fragrant woodland that bordered the grounds. Linen-covered tables were heaped with lobster and crab canapés. A delicious Victoria punch, spicy with fruit and cider and Angelica wine, was served by white-coated waiters. Laura had greeted and spoken with several other parents and was just sampling the punch when Whitney bounded across the lawn, dark eyes aglow, skirts swirling, her diploma clutched triumphantly in an upraised hand.

"Mama, Uncle Avery, I've done it; I've graduated!"

She kissed her mother and uncle, then snatched a crab canapé from the table and popped it into her mouth. "I'm famished!" she said. "Is this all the food there is? With all the Parkers' millions, you'd think they'd have a proper spread instead of these tidbits." She took another canapé and quickly dispatched it.

"Whitney, don't gobble," Laura admonished her. She picked up a napkin and dabbed at her daughter's mouth. "I think it was very thought-

ful of the Parkers to have this buffet. Where are
they, by the way? I'd like to pay my respects."

Whitney scanned the well-dressed crowd.
"They're somewhere about, Mama. I don't see
them now." She turned to her uncle. "What did
you think of Dr. Shaw's speech, Uncle Avery?
Aside from being a leading feminist, she is an
ordained minister and a medical doctor."

"Yes, I know," Avery said scornfully. "Dr.
Shaw might have more success stamping out the
injustices she preaches against if she actively
practiced either of her professions, rather than
gadding about on the lecture circuit."

"You shouldn't have asked him that," Laura
told her daughter wryly. "Your uncle deplores
the cause of feminism."

"Do you, Uncle Avery? Why?"

"Because it's all a lot of nonsense," Avery said
crossly. "If a woman is married to the right man,
she has all the freedom she needs."

"But what if she isn't married to the right man?
What if she isn't married at all?"

"Then she should marry posthaste. That's the
trouble with all those feminist radicals. They're
frustrated old maids who need a good—"

"Avery!" Laura stopped him.

"Really, Laura!" he said, scandalized. "I was
only going to say, 'a good husband.' "

Whitney giggled. Avery frowned. Laura's face
flushed with color, and she murmured, embarrassed, "Forgive me. I thought—"

"I know what you thought," Avery said
sternly. "I'm surprised at you, Laura."

"Mama, look!" Whitney exclaimed, spotting a

familiar figure across the lawn. "There's Christopher Warren."

Laura's flushed face blanched. She followed the direction of Whitney's gaze and saw Christopher approaching. At his side was Ned Bailey, whose presence Whitney had notably failed to observe.

"Whitney, did you invite him here?" Laura asked severely.

"Not exactly," the girl evaded, taken aback by her mother's tone. "Christopher told me he had to submit his designs to the Parker sisters in June, and I said maybe his visit would coincide with the commencement. Mama, please don't be—"

"We'll speak of this later," Laura said curtly as Christopher and Ned came into earshot.

"Whitney, congratulations!" Ned said merrily, grasping her hands and kissing her on both cheeks.

He greeted Laura and Avery. Christopher shook Whitney's hand. The girl said softly, glancing sheepishly at her mother, "I'm so glad you could come."

"I'm happy to be here, Whitney. Congratulations." He turned to the others. "Laura," he said coolly, "Dr. Sheridan, it's good to see you both."

Laura's anger with her daughter was heightened by Christopher's chilly greeting. Logically, she knew he was merely reacting to her deliberate avoidance of him these past weeks, but emotionally she could only wonder in rage how he had the arrogance barely to glance at her now, when that day in his house he had so thoroughly and so possessively made love to her.

Her face was a frozen mask as Christopher returned his attention to Whitney. "I see you were successful in improving your French grade," he said with a smile that did nothing to warm his eyes.

"Why, yes." Whitney's smile was genuine. "I think I was inspired by your beautiful fluency. Mama, Christopher speaks perfect French."

"Does he?" Laura said tightly.

"Whitney," said Ned, extracting a small box from his coat pocket, "I have something for you—a small token of my esteem for the honored graduate."

Whitney took the box with thanks and opened it to reveal an exquisite lapel pin in the shape of a dove, worked in diamonds and platinum, with a sapphire eye.

"Ned, it's magnificent," she said, awed. "But you shouldn't have."

"You shouldn't have, indeed," Laura said shortly. "Ned, I believe I cautioned you once before about gifts of that nature. Is it the fashion with the gentlemen of this age to make a mockery of convention? I'm afraid I cannot permit Whitney to accept—"

"Mama, don't!" Whitney pleaded, humiliated for Ned, who was staring at Laura in open-mouthed disbelief.

Avery, astonished by Laura's words and by the hard set of her mouth, laid a hand on her arm. "Laura," he said carefully, "perhaps, in light of the occasion, you could make an exception this time."

Laura shrugged off his hand and glared at

him. "I'll thank you not to interfere, Avery. Whitney is my daughter. I think I know best how to handle her. Whitney, return that article to Ned, if you please."

Avery drew back, stung. Ned still stared at Laura as Whitney clumsily pressed the box into his hands. Laura was not aware of anyone's shock, anyone's embarrassment; she looked only at Christopher, who returned her defiant gaze with unreadable dark eyes.

"Mama, how could you?" Whitney whispered, her face a fiery red.

Laura turned to her sharply. "That will do, Whitney. Your graduation from this school does not entitle you to insolent behavior."

"Mama, with all due respect," the girl said, shaking, "it is your behavior today that does both of us no credit."

"That will do," Laura repeated coldly. She turned to Ned, unable to control the rage that, she dimly realized, had nothing to do with the hapless young man's gift. "I expected more from you, Ned. You're years older than Whitney; you ought to have known better."

Ned said rigidly, "I humbly beg your pardon, Laura. Let me assure you that I have only the highest regard for your daughter, and I meant no disrespect in so gifting her. Now, if you'll excuse me . . ."

His amiable face was grim. He bowed stiffly to the group and strode rapidly away. Christopher looked at Laura, a look she could not interpret, then he, too, bowed and left.

Whitney stared after them, on the verge of

mortified tears. She turned suddenly to her
mother, whose eyes were riveted on Christopher. "Mama, I'll never forgive you for this!"
she cried with all the youthful passion of
wounded dignity. Then, choking back a sob,
she picked up her skirts and ran off into the
woods.

"I'll never forgive her," Ned kept repeating to
Christopher during the train trip back to New
York. "I've never been so humiliated in my life.
She's known me for years, for God's sake. It's
not as if she were dealing with some bum off the
street."

Ned's body was tiger-tense as he stalked about
the parlor car, which was empty save for Christopher and himself. Christopher sat in a faded
maroon armchair, gazing out the window at the
countryside. The clickety-clack cadence of the
train's wheels on the track was hypnotic.
Christopher heard Ned's complaints, and occasionally he answered him, but his thoughts were
exclusively on Laura.

Christopher knew the reason for Laura's mis-
directed anger. She loved him but was afraid to
marry him, and it was causing her great anguish. He fully understood her dilemma. Laura
wanted, and deserved, a man of wealth and position. It was therefore all the more important
that Christopher set aside his principles and
strive for success in a manner he had previously
scorned and abhorred. If people wanted houses

that looked like thirteenth-century nightmares, by God, he would accommodate them.

"She *must* know how I feel about Whitney," Ned droned on. "A blind man could see I love her. Christopher, what the devil am I going to do? She'll be away all summer; I won't even get to see her. She'll be all the way up in Bar Harbor, Maine, for God's sake, with Marcella MacKenzie and her family."

"MacKenzie?" Christopher said. "Malcolm MacKenzie and his family?"

"Yes, that's right." Ned was puzzled by Christopher's interest. "I didn't know you knew him."

"I don't, Ned. But I'll be spending some time at his place in August. Henry asked me to go up there to discuss the design of a new house he wants. Don't you see? This is perfect. If Whitney's going to be there, I can remind her—subtly, of course—of your numerous charms. When I get through singing your praises to her, she'll fly down to New York on wings of love, in a fever to change her name to yours."

"What if she doesn't?" Ned said dejectedly. "What if she thinks I'm an ineffectual fool because of what happened today?"

"She won't," Christopher said gently, genuinely concerned for his broken-spirited friend. "Ned, you have my solemn promise that I'll do everything in my power to set matters right between you and Whitney."

Chapter Eleven

❖❖❖❖❖

BAR HARBOR, MAINE, situated on the northeastern shore of Mount Desert Island, is five hundred miles from New York. It took Christopher an entire day to travel that distance, first by train to Boston and on to Rockland, Maine, and then by steamer across Penobscot Bay to North Haven, Northeast Harbor, and at last to Bar Harbor.

At Henry's suggestion, Christopher stayed at Rodick's, the poshest of all Bar Harbor's hotels. On the morning following his arrival, he engaged an open surrey and asked the driver to show him around the area before taking him to the MacKenzie oceanfront cottage. It was a soft, hazy August morning. The sky was a liquid blue, the sun saffron yellow. The air was velvety warm and tangy with the smell of the sea. As they turned onto Ocean Drive, old Amos Zachary, the coachman, pointed out all the hallowed landmarks of Bar Harbor: Cliffs of Otter, Sand Beach, Schooner Head, and the whimsically named Anemone Cave. There was a wild, exciting beauty to the place that fired Christopher's imagination. Here on the rugged shore, facing a turbulent sea, he would design a great fortress of a house of sand-colored stone, which would be part of the very landscape, rising as cleanly and as majestically as the Green Mountains in the distance.

"Here's the MacKenzie place," Amos announced, reining in the horse in front of a three-story white clapboard house. He added as Christopher alighted, "Malcolm's a dour Scot from Aberdeen who came to this country when he was just a lad. He quick made his fortune in coal; but, more's the pity, he has no male heir, only seven little girls. If you're fixing to marry one of them, son, you'd best be penurious. Malcolm don't hold with extravagant young men. Frugality, he says, is the key to achieving and maintaining great wealth."

Christopher smiled and shook the road dust from his handsome new straw boater. "Thank you for the tour and for your help, Mr. Zachary. I'm not planning to marry one of Mr. MacKenzie's daughters, but I do want to make a good impression on him. With the information you've given me, I consider myself well armed."

Amos clicked to the horse and drove off. Christopher mounted the porch steps and knocked at the door.

A young maid, somewhat harried, answered.

"Yes?" She darted a look over her shoulder as a large beach ball bounced by, followed by four shouting girls in yellow pinafores and hair ribbons, and an immense barking dog with a shaggy coat and the muzzle of a wolf.

"Stop that now!" the maid said vainly.

One of the girls kicked the ball into a room adjoining the hallway. The youngsters and the dog scrambled after it. There was a crash and the sound of breaking glass, followed by more shouts of glee and furious barking.

"Yes, what is it?" the maid asked Christopher as if he were personally responsible for the ruckus.

"I'm Christopher Warren," he said, suppressing a smile. "I have an appointment to see Mr. MacKenzie."

"Why didn't you say so? Come in. I'll fetch him."

She ushered him inside with none too good grace, then disappeared into the room where the girls were playing. Christopher heard harsh words, then a chorus of indignant wails and a pleading whine. A moment later the maid emerged, beach ball in one hand, the collar of the cowering dog in the other, and went upstairs.

The girls tumbled out into the hall, hot on the trail of their property. Catching sight of Christopher, they stopped dead in their tracks and stared at him.

"Who're you?" asked the tallest of the group.

All four of them approached him, a quartet of perky blue-eyed redheads, ranging in approximate age from five to eight.

"My name is Christopher," he said as they clustered curiously about him. "I'm going to design a new house for your father. And," he added with a grin, "I'm going to include a huge room in the basement where you girls can play ball to your hearts' content."

"Papa has a hat like yours," said the youngest, reaching for the boater in Christopher's hand.

"Does he?" he said, placing the hat on the coat

tree, safe from the probability of instant destruction.

"Ah, Mr. Warren, I see you're acquainting yourself with some of my brood."

A tall gentleman, casually dressed in gray flannel trousers and a tweed sweater descended the stairs and approached Christopher with an outstretched hand. He was perhaps forty-five years old, with the same sky-blue eyes as his daughters, and auburn hair several shades darker than theirs.

Christopher shook his hand. "They're lovely girls, Mr. MacKenzie."

"They're perfect hellions," MacKenzie retorted.

"Papa, Papa!" the children clamored, winding demanding arms about his waist and legs. "Mitzi took Homer and our beach ball. Make her give them back to us."

MacKenzie detached himself from his clinging daughters. "Girls," he said sternly, "go upstairs and have your lunch. After you've eaten, you will all help Mitzi clean up the debris in the parlor."

"Oh, Papa," they pouted in unison, but nonetheless obeyed him.

As the girls straggled up the stairs, MacKenzie said to Christopher, "Come along. Let's talk on the front porch. I never tire of looking at the sea. It reminds me of my home in Aberdeen. Have you ever been to Scotland, Mr. Warren?"

"No, sir," Christopher said regretfully, following his host out the door. "I've never been out of the country."

"Haven't you?" said MacKenzie as the two men settled on cushioned rattan chairs. "That surprises me. I thought all American young men took a Grand Tour following graduation from university."

"I didn't," Christopher said, looking out to the restless sea, which was shimmering with sunlight as it drove ceaselessly toward shore.

MacKenzie watched him a moment and saw in his strong profile a mingling of pride and burning determination, emotions that he, MacKenzie, had been well acquainted with in his youth.

"Shall we talk about the house, then, Mr. Warren?"

Christopher came to immediate attention. "Yes, sir."

"I have something specific in mind," MacKenzie said, leaning back in his chair and crossing his legs. "In Scotland, in Campbell country, there is a fifteenth-century castle inhabited by the present thane of Cawdor."

"The thane of Cawdor?" Christopher's interest was piqued. "Like Macbeth?"

"Indeed," MacKenzie answered. "Macbeth was not a figment of William Shakespeare's imagination, Mr. Warren. He actually lived, and he did murder King Duncan and take over his reign. In any case, the present thane lives in Cawdor Castle, complete with moat and drawbridge. There's even a fortified garden wall with a small bastion, loopholed for muskets, defense against possible invaders."

MacKenzie paused. His eyes grew pensive, and when he spoke again, his voice was very low. "I saw that castle once when I was a boy. I had nothing then. My family were dirt-poor, and I never expected I would be anything else, for in Scotland, as you're born, you die. But I wanted that castle, Mr. Warren, or one like it. I vowed to myself that if I died trying, I would one day live in a house worthy of a Highland laird."

MacKenzie paused again and looked out toward the sea, as if seeing in the sunlit waters a bright realization of a fathomless dream. "Do you understand what I'm saying, Mr. Warren?" he asked quietly. "Do you think you can give me what I want?"

Christopher nodded, feeling a kinship with this man, a kinship forged in memories of deprivation and despair. "Yes," he said as quietly. "I do know what you're saying. And I'm sure I can give you exactly what you want."

That evening Christopher was invited to dine at the MacKenzie cottage, with Malcolm's instruction: "Dress informally, if you please, Mr. Warren. I like to relax at Bar Harbor."

This mandate suited Christopher very well. He had packed his evening clothes, but he felt far more comfortable in his blue or brown broadcloth. He chose brown for dinner—suitably earthy, he thought, for his down-to-earth host—and with it he wore a sporty rep tie. At the hotel shops he bought a bouquet of tiger lilies and a box of bonbons for Mrs. MacKenzie. In remarkably good spirits he set off for Ocean Drive.

Mitzi, the harried maid, answered the door.

She was more cordial than she had been earlier. Evidently, the four young MacKenzie terrors had been put to bed for the night.

"Go right into the parlor, Mr. Warren," she said pleasantly, indicating the room where the beach ball debacle had taken place.

But before he had taken two steps, Whitney Sheridan rushed into the hall, followed by yet another redhead with sparkling blue eyes.

"Christopher!" Whitney said. "I thought I heard your voice." She took firm hold of his arm, nearly causing him to drop the flowers and candy. "Marcella," she said excitedly to the other girl, "here he is! Christopher, this is my very best friend, Marcella MacKenzie."

Christopher shifted his burden to shake Marcella's hand. He knew she must be close to Whitney's age, but her snub nose and dancing eyes were as mischievous as her little sisters'.

"I feel I already know you, Mr. Warren," she said with an impish grin. "Ever since Papa mentioned you were coming here, Whitney has talked of nothing else."

Whitney gave Marcella a surreptitious poke in the ribs, then said to Christopher with a proprietary air, "Come into the parlor, Christopher. The MacKenzies will be down directly."

The parlor was large and casual, with every window open to the balmy night air. The worn chintz-covered furnishings gave testimony to the rough-and-tumble abuse of the younger Mac-Kenzies. Christopher placed the flowers and bonbons on a scarred mahogany coffee table.

Marcella, he noticed when all three were seated, kept looking him over as if he were a prized piece of horseflesh.

"Miss MacKenzie," he said politely, hoping to divert her disconcerting scrutiny, "I met four of your sisters earlier today, but I understand there are seven girls in the family."

"My sisters Jane and Delia are in Newport," Marcella explained. "Frankly, I prefer Newport to Bar Harbor. To be even more frank, I prefer to be anyplace where my little sisters are not present."

Christopher said discreetly, "They're high-spirited girls."

"High-spirited? My dear Mr. Warren, a stampeding herd of deranged elephants would be easier to control."

He laughed and looked over at Whitney, who was watching him quietly, her hands folded neatly on her lap. She looked especially lovely this evening in a white dress of crocheted lace, with a demure high neck and long sleeves. Her hair, piled high on her head, was a mass of ebony curls. Her lips and cheeks were rosebud pink; her eyes, dusky dark and shaded by thick lashes, were intriguingly full of thought. In her sweet, upturned mouth and her silky, flawless skin Christopher saw again, as he had seen in Hadlyme, her unmistakable resemblance to Laura.

Without thinking, he said softly, "How like your mother you look."

Her eyes changed almost imperceptibly. The finest of lines marred the perfection of her brow.

"Everyone says I look like my father," she said.

"That may be," Christopher said. "But you are definitely your mother's daughter."

She said nothing; she lowered her gaze. It occurred to Christopher that she might still be at odds with Laura. In an attempt to ameliorate the situation he said, "I very much admire the relationship you and your mother share. Having no kin of my own, it especially pleases me to see close family ties."

Whitney looked up then, her mouth slightly parted, her eyes softly luminous. She was about to speak when Marcella commented, "If my sisters were yours, Mr. Warren, you'd sing a different tune about family ties."

"Marcella, hush," Whitney said with a frown. "What a tactless remark."

"Tactless? Why?" Marcella asked. Then, remembering, "Oh, Mr. Warren, I'm sorry. I forgot that Whitney told me you were an orphan."

"There's no need for an apology, Miss Mac-Kenzie." Christopher's tone was sardonic. Though he addressed Marcella, his eyes were on Whitney, and his thoughts, tinged with bitterness, were hard-set on Laura. "The fact that I have no family seems to bother other people more than it does me."

"Christopher, you don't mean me, do you?" Whitney said in a rush. "It doesn't matter to me that you're an orphan. I've told you before that I think you're one of the finest—"

She broke off in a fluster. Her pink cheeks flushed scarlet; her dark eyes were brilliant with fervor and chagrin.

Christopher stared at her in astonishment. "No, of course I don't mean you."

"Oh, thank goodness," she said with a sigh.

Christopher's forbidding gaze softened, and he gave her a sober smile. How lovely she was and how touchingly sweet. Although she was blessed with wealth and social position, those worldly endowments meant little to her. Christopher felt certain that if Ned Bailey were a pauper, it wouldn't matter in the least to Whitney. How lucky Ned was to have the love and support of a loyal girl like her.

When Christopher set out to design Malcolm MacKenzie's house, he did so from a new perspective and with a dawning realization of needs other than his own. How glibly he had previously mocked the pretentious houses he hated; how smug had been his scorn of ribbed arches, flying buttresses, and other ornamentation he found not to his taste. But when MacKenzie confided his lifelong dream, Christopher saw past the wealthy coal magnate to the penniless boy who had yearned for a castle. In everyone, Christopher then realized, be he plebeian or patrician, there burned hopes, dreams, disappointments, and sorrows that were universally shared. It was this commonplace conclusion that fired Christopher's design for MacKenzie's new house with extraordinary brilliance.

He spent a pleasant two weeks in Bar Harbor: working, exploring the island with Whitney and Marcella, sailboating, and riding—his first experience on a horse, which he fervently hoped would be his last. He dined every night at the MacKenzie cottage. The meals there were as forthrightly unpretentious as was his unaffected host. Mrs. MacKenzie, too, was delightfully natural—a slim, energetic carrot-top with an impudent snub nose, who Christopher found hard to believe was the mother of seven daughters.

When he mentioned this to Whitney, she said wistfully, "I wish *I* had a large family."

They were walking on the beach beneath a glorious full moon. It was the first time they had been alone together since Christopher's arrival in Bar Harbor. The MacKenzies were visiting neighbors, and Marcella had declined Christopher's invitation for a stroll by the sea. "You and Whitney go on," she had said, her devilish eyes dancing. "I have a headache. I'll just stay here and rest until it goes away."

"Then we'll stay with you," Christopher had said.

"Don't be silly." Marcella had glanced at Whitney. "I need to be alone for a while. You two go for your walk. I'll see you later."

Christopher admired Marcella's graciousness. He said to Whitney later on the moonlit beach, "Yes, it must be wonderful having a large family. As much as Marcella complains about her sisters, I think having them is what makes her such a considerate person. She's been extremely good to me this past week."

Whitney looked up at him through her lashes. "It's easy to be good to you, Christopher."

He laughed shortly. "My masters at Saint Peter's didn't think so."

Whitney stopped walking abruptly and laid a hand on his arm. "Was it terrible for you at the orphanage?" she asked with a degree of concern that was touching in its urgency. "Did they mistreat you? Did they . . . beat you?"

Christopher looked down at her, his eyes very dark in the silvery moonlight. "No," he said evenly. "They didn't."

"Oh, I'm so glad," she said, relieved, taking his arm and walking on. "I've heard such dreadful stories about orphanages, about how the poor children are worked nearly to death, how they're clothed in rags and eat the most revolting food."

"Exaggerations, I'm sure," Christopher said.

"Really?" she pursued, her hand tightening on his arm. "You ate well and were treated decently?"

"Like a little prince," he said.

"Thank goodness," she said, as if a great weight had been lifted from her shoulders. "Christopher, I can't tell you how happy I am to hear you say that. Whenever I think of you being in one of those places, I get goose bumps."

He patted her hand. "That's sweet of you, Whitney, but you may set your mind at rest. My years at Saint Peter's are a part of my life I'll never forget."

They walked on in silence for a time, Whitney dreamily content, her arm snug through Christopher's, and he wrapped in memories of his unforgettable past.

His time spent with the MacKenzies, though thoroughly enjoyable, had made him suddenly aware of his own lack of family. He wondered vaguely if his mother and father were living, and if they were, if they ever thought about him, if they regretted the circumstances that had caused them to abandon him. Christopher seldom thought about his parents, but he did wonder sometimes about the woman who had borne him, if she had loved him, if it had been difficult for her to give him up. He couldn't begin to imagine giving away a child of his own. If he had a son, or even a rascally daughter like one of the MacKenzie girls, he would do anything, anything in the world, to hold on to his own flesh and blood.

"Christopher, what are you thinking about?"

Whitney's soft voice broke into his thoughts. He looked down at her and smiled; and at the sight of her face, charmingly upturned to his, he remembered a solemn promise he had not as yet kept.

"I was thinking about Ned," he said, "slaving away at Carlisle and Hastings. I wish he were here with us. I rather miss him."

"Oh."

Oblivious to the disappointment in her tone, Christopher went on. "Ned's the best friend I have. He has never let me down in all the years I've known him. He's a gentleman in the purest sense of the word. He's sensitive and caring, honorable and true. I've never met a finer man, nor do I think I ever shall."

"Yes," Whitney said softly. "Ned's awfully nice."

They came to the end of the beach, to a jagged rock formation that jutted out into the sea, where waves crested and broke against the immovable barrier. Whitney stepped up on a rock ledge and sat down. Christopher rested an elbow beside her.

"Do you like the seashore?" he asked, looking out to the pounding waves.

"Oh, yes," she said, "very much."

"Ned does too. His parents have houses in Oyster Bay and in the Berkshires, but he rarely goes to either place. He usually vacations with friends or relatives who have houses in Newport or Long Branch. The sea air renews him, he says. Is that the way you feel about it, Whitney?"

"Yes," she said. "I suppose so."

Her voice was curiously toneless. Christopher eyed her questioningly. "What's wrong?" he asked. "You've gone quiet all of a sudden."

"Nothing's wrong." She looked down at her hands in her lap.

"Whitney." He regarded her skeptically. "You've been brimming with conversation all evening, till now. Don't tell me nothing's wrong. What is it? Is it something I said? Is it—?" He stopped and thought, then came to what he felt was a logical conclusion. "You miss Ned too, don't you?" And when she didn't answer, he urged gently, "Come now, you can confide in me. I know you miss him; you may as well admit it. When you care for someone, Whitney, you oughtn't to be afraid to say so."

He had taken her hand in his as he spoke. When he said the last, Whitney raised her head and stared at him, and her fingernails dug into his palm. "Christopher, I do care," she said swiftly, fervently.

He smiled at her ardor. "I knew you did."

"But . . . but not for Ned," she said.

"Not Ned?" His smile disappeared. "I hope you're joking."

"It's not a joke," she said wretchedly. "Ned's not the one I care for; it's someone else. Don't you know who it is? Haven't you guessed?"

"No," he said, watching her warily as an alarming suspicion took form in his mind, "I haven't any idea who it could be."

"Oh, Christopher . . ." She seemed on the verge of tears. Her mouth was quivering, and her fingernails dug so deeply into his hand that they hurt him. "You must know," she whispered. "You must know how I feel."

"Whitney—"

"Please don't silence me," she begged him. "You just said that a woman should admit when she cares for a man. I do care for you; I love you."

The hairs rose on the back of Christopher's neck. He stepped back abruptly, breaking her hold on his hand. "Whitney," he said hoarsely, "you don't mean that."

"Oh, I do, I do!" She scrambled down from the rock ledge and plucked pleadingly at his sleeve. "Christopher, listen to me," she implored him. "I know you're thinking I'm too young for you, but I'm not. My mother married at my age, and my father was years older, and they were the two happiest people I've ever known."

It was the worst argument she could have employed. Christopher thought of Laura, of what she would do if she learned of her daughter's rash words. And Ned . . . if Christopher were to tell him that Whitney didn't love him—

"Jesus," he uttered.

"Christopher, talk to me," she said miserably. "Tell me you care . . . or that you will in time. I'll wait forever if you ask me to. But please say there's a chance."

"There isn't a chance," he said more sharply than he intended. "I don't feel that way about you; I never will."

"Oh," she whispered, and the word was a sob. She gazed up at him despairingly. Tears welled in her eyes and spilled unchecked down her cheeks.

Christopher had never seen a woman cry. In all his years he had never before been placed in the untenable position produced by a woman's tears. The shock of it paralyzed him. He stared down at her helplessly; he opened his mouth to speak, but words would not come. That he had caused this girl to weep was a horror outside his experience.

"Whitney, don't." He found his tongue at last. He reached out tentatively and touched her cheek. As if it were a signal, the girl threw herself, sobbing, into his arms.

Instinctively Christopher embraced her, his

mind in a turmoil, his emotions chaotic. Whitney was a trembling broken blossom in his arms, weeping mournfully, desolately.

"Please," he said anxiously, stroking her back, smoothing her tumbled hair. "Whitney, please stop crying. I didn't mean to make you sad."

"Sad?" She looked up at him with tear-drenched eyes. "My life is over, Christopher. I'm never going to love anyone but you."

His hands at her waist tightened impotently. Ned had spoken almost the same words to him.

"Yes you will," he said, attempting to banish her woe. "You'll love again, Whitney. Someday, when you're married and have a dozen children, you'll look back on this night and laugh, you'll see."

"Never!" she cried. "I'll never marry anyone else. I want to be *your* wife; I want to have *your* children!"

She flung her arms about his neck and pressed an urgent mouth to his. Christopher was unprepared for her onslaught. He was likewise unprepared for the swift surge of passion that sent a tremor through his frame, so intense and so thorough it almost buckled his knees.

She was a hot wind in his arms, moving feverishly against him, as if to kindle in his body the desperate flame that raged in hers. He tried to move away, but her arms clung fast to his neck, and she molded herself against him, unleashing the desire he strove vainly to keep in check. His heart beat furiously, his thoughts were a turbulence of sensuality and fear. Laura was on his mind; her daughter was in his arms.

For one frightening, rapturous, bewildering moment they became one and the same woman.

His arms tightened around her; his mouth crushed the mouth pressed so dizzyingly to his. His legs went weak beneath him. He leaned back against the rock ledge, pulling the girl half atop him, then he grasped her hips and pressed her hard to his body and groaned low in his throat when she arched herself erotically closer. There was a roaring in his ears and a pounding in his blood. It was Laura he kissed, Laura who returned his kisses. It was the woman he loved whose arms clung to him, whose body answered him, whose hot, ardent mouth stoked the fire of his passion until it blazed uncontrollably, consuming every last vestige of reality and reason.

He was never to know what finally brought him to his senses. One moment he was kissing her, devouring her, on the very brink of taking her. Then, like a flash of heat lightning that illuminates a pitch-black night, he was clearly, startlingly aware of what he was doing—and to whom he was doing it.

He tore his mouth from hers. His hands at her hips bit so deeply into her flesh that she cried out softly. "Whitney," he said hoarsely, "I'm sorry. I . . ."

He could barely speak, could hardly breathe. His legs shook so violently that it took a superhuman effort to stand upright. The ache of unrelieved desire was a torment in his body. He slumped back against the rock ledge, breathing hard, and stared at the quivering girl before him with burning dark eyes.

"I'm sorry," he said again, his voice a ragged whisper. "I don't know what came over me. I never meant to—"

"Don't apologize," she said, her own voice unsteady, her body trembling, too, with her first taste of passion. "I'm glad it happened. I've been wanting you to do that for the longest time. If you only knew how many times I've envisioned you kissing me, touching me—"

"My God, don't talk of it," he uttered, cringing.

But she went on unheedingly, "Since that night at the Barneses' house I've been thinking about you and wondering if you could ever return the love I have for you. I knew from the moment we met that you were the man I wanted to marry. I was afraid at first that you might think me too young, but then I thought of my mother and father, and I realized my fears were baseless."

"Whitney, please don't go on with this," he implored. "You're imagining something that simply isn't true."

For a moment she was silenced, regarding him quietly with dark eyes that burned as fiercely as his own. Then she smiled and said, "Christopher, you do care for me, I know you do. Otherwise, you wouldn't have kissed me as you did."

"You don't understand," he said tersely, but the fact of the matter was that Christopher himself did not fully understand what had motivated his disgraceful conduct.

"What don't I understand?" she asked. "The

situation couldn't be clearer. I know now by your actions that your feelings for me are the same as mine for you.''

He shook his head impatiently. ''Men are different from women,'' he said shortly. ''Men have physical urges that they sometimes can't control. It has nothing to do with love. It has only to do with . . . carnal needs.''

The instant those words were out of his mouth he could have bitten his tongue. *Physical urges. Carnal needs.* What if Whitney repeated this conversation to her mother? What if—dear God, no!—what if she were to tell Laura what had happened here this night?

''Whitney, listen to me,'' he said swiftly, grasping her arm, ''you must never tell anyone about tonight. Not anyone, do you hear me?''

''Why?'' she asked. ''I'm not ashamed of what we did.''

''Jesus Christ!'' he cried in a panic, thinking of Ned and Laura. ''You don't *know* what we did.''

''Yes, I do,'' she said tranquilly. ''You wanted to make love to me. I've been waiting for this for months, waiting for a sign that you cared for me.''

''I *don't* care for you!'' he snapped, fear roughening his tone, ''and I never will.''

''Oh, no?'' she said. ''We'll see about that.''

Then, with a serene confidence that further panicked him, she kissed him lightly on the lips and walked calmly away.

* * *

He left Bar Harbor without seeing her again. The next morning, prior to leaving the hotel, he sent a message to Malcolm MacKenzie thanking him for his hospitality and saying that he would have the design for his new house ready in September when MacKenzie returned to New York. If the manner of his departure was improper, Christopher neither knew nor cared. His need to flee the scene of his infamy was far greater than his concern for the social amenities.

All the way back to the city he thought incessantly, guiltily, of the night before. He spared himself nothing. Although Whitney was the one who had initiated their physical encounter, Christopher blamed only himself.

Laura's daughter. God Almighty! He wasn't an inexperienced boy, for Christ's sake. He was thirty-three years old, old enough to know better than to have taken such inexcusable liberties with an innocent girl.

And yet, as Christopher stared blindly at the New England countryside that flashed past the train window, his thoughts of Whitney were displaced by the thought of Laura in his arms, Laura's ardent mouth on his, her silky skin beneath his hands, her flesh enclosing his, filling his mind and heart with ecstasy, as he filled her with his passion . . .

Dear God. Laura! He sat bolt upright. What if she learned what he had done? No, no. She must never learn of it. He uttered a choked sound and pressed his burning forehead against the window. How could he defend himself?

There *was* no defense for what he had done; there were no words in the world to either mitigate or excuse what he had done to the daughter of the woman he loved.

And Ned—would Christopher ever be able to look him in the eye again? Ned was his dearest friend, as cherished as a brother. Was this how Christopher repaid his many kindnesses to him in past years, by nearly making love to the girl he adored?

As soon as he arrived in New York, he went home, shed his clothes, crawled into bed, and sought the blessed escape of sleep. But that blessing was denied him. He tossed and turned the entire night through. Finally, toward dawn, he fell asleep and dreamed of Laura.

In the dream she was lying in his arms, on the grass, on the school grounds at Hadlyme, Connecticut. She was wearing a white dress of crocheted lace. Her hair was unbound; he had never seen it that way. He buried his face in the fragrant mass, then kissed her throat, her cheek, her sweet upturned mouth. She returned his kisses hungrily, pressed ardently close to him. He was unendurably aroused. His need for her was stronger than it had ever been before.

He began to undress her, quickly, feverishly, then just as quickly he tore off his own clothes and pulled her hard against his naked form. In one urgent motion he turned her, mounted her, and pushed deep inside her. So vivid was the dream that he could feel her breasts hot against his chest, her legs wrapped on his, and the heat of her passion enveloping him, drawing him deeper, achingly deeper, until he could no longer bear the rapture of possessing her.

His climax, when it came, was violent, almost painful. He groaned aloud and clutched her close to his heart, but as he embraced her, she vanished, leaving him trembling, chilled, and empty. He woke with a start, sat bolt upright, and whispered her name, but, of course, she wasn't there; she had never been there.

He slumped back against the pillows and kicked aside the covers, then lay very still, watching the room brighten with daylight. His heart thudded dully, his skin prickled with cold. The sheet beneath his body was tangled and damp. In his mind's eye he saw Laura—lovely, elusive, ephemeral—like the memory of his fast-fading dream.

Chapter Twelve
◆ ◆ ◆ ◆

SUMMER'S END WAS always a sad time for Laura Sheridan. There was something so poignantly heartrending about fading leaves, wilting flowers, and that melancholy early chill in the late-summer air. And, too, her husband had died at summer's end. While riding one early morning in Central Park, Steven's mare had stepped in a deep rut and stumbled, unbalancing him and causing him to fall to the ground, where he struck his head on a boulder and lay undiscovered for hours. Avery had assured Laura that Steven had died instantaneously, that he had not, as she painfully suspected, lain dying for hours, vainly calling for help. She was thankful for that, at least, a quick end without suffering; she couldn't have borne to see Steven suffer. But whenever autumn approached, laying its dark hand on the brilliant summer landscape, Laura would find herself thinking how Death had snuffed out too soon the warm light of her dear husband's life.

This summer, however, Laura felt differently. She did not think of Steven; she was anxious to have the season end, anxious to see Whitney, who had left for Maine in early July with only the briefest of kisses and so perfunctory an embrace that it would have been better not given. Laura had brooded for weeks over her daughter's coolness, brooded so much, in fact, that Avery and the Tylers, her guests in Newport, had done everything in their power to cheer her up—but to no avail. For Laura knew she was in the wrong, knew she had hurt Whitney and poor, innocent Ned. She'd hurt them both because of Christopher, because she loved him so intensely, because she knew that even though she loved him, she would never have the courage to marry him.

When Whitney finally came home the second week of September, Avery was with Laura—at her express invitation—for she was fearful of

facing her daughter alone. It was one of those
flawless late-summer days. A regal golden sun
shone in a sapphire sky, and the air shimmered
with languorous heat, gently tempered by an
occasional breeze. Laura and Avery were sitting
in the garden when Whitney appeared. The girl
stepped through the open French doors, still
wearing her hat and gloves. Her two-piece traveling costume made her look older, more
worldly. She seemed a stranger to Laura, this
woman-child in crimson cashmere, a young
phoenix emerging from the fire of her newborn
independence.

"Darling!" Laura said, rising from her chair.
"You're home at last. How I've missed you!"

For a fraction of an instant, Whitney hesitated,
her dusky-dark eyes a disturbing enigma. Then,
perhaps, responding to a bond that transcended
all else, her darksome gaze brightened, a smile
curved her lips, and like the child she still was,
she threw herself with a happy cry into her
mother's open arms.

"Oh, Mama, I've missed you too," she confessed, holding on to Laura for dear life. "I was
an awful brat before I left. Please say you forgive
me. I can't bear it when we're at odds with each
other."

"Dearest child," Laura whispered, hardly able
to speak for the emotion that tightened her
throat, "it is you who must forgive me."

Avery interposed, taking his niece by the arm.
"Everyone forgives everyone," he said. "There,
that's settled. Now how about a hug for your
much-neglected uncle?"

"Oh, Uncle Avery, I missed you too!"

The girl threw her arms about Avery's neck, nearly strangling him in the process. He submitted willingly to her ardent assault, while Laura looked on with misting eyes.

Thompson appeared with the tea tray, bringing order to the helter-skelter scene. "Shall I serve, madam?" he asked in a voice so studiedly unemotional that Laura had to laugh.

"Thank you, no," she said. "I'll do it." And after he placed the tray on a table and withdrew, she said to her family, "Thank goodness he came out here when he did. I would have been in tears in another minute."

"So would I," Whitney said ruefully, removing her hat and gloves and joining her uncle on the wrought-iron bench. "Mama, I'm truly sorry for the way I acted before I left. I didn't realize until I saw you just how much I had hurt you."

"Darling, don't give it another thought," Laura said, limp with relief, for the sentiments Whitney had voiced were doubly her own.

"I agree," Avery chimed in. "Let's all forget this entire past summer. Your mother, young lady, was impossible to live with in Newport. She quite ruined Jeremy and Nina's vacation, not to mention mine. If you love me, Whitney, promise me you'll spend next summer with her."

The girl accepted the cup of tea Laura handed to her and said readily, "Of course I will. And I must return Marcella's hospitality. Mama, you don't mind if I invite her to stay with us in Newport?"

"Not at all," Laura said, passing a cup to Avery and then filling her own. "How was everyone at Bar Harbor, Whitney? Did you give the MacKenzies my best wishes?"

"Yes, Mama. They send their best to you, too."

"You must remember to write a note thanking them, darling. And I think I'll pick up that cunning Saly caviar pail for them. I remember Janet admiring it the last time we shopped together."

"Mrs. MacKenzie will like that," Whitney said, looking down at her cup. "How was Newport this season, Mama?"

Laura laughed softly. "I believe your uncle covered that subject rather thoroughly. I would have preferred to have had you with me, Whitney, but it was pleasant enough. I had a good rest. By the way, I saw Ned Bailey at a ball at the Barneses' cottage while we were there. I'm afraid he hasn't forgiven me for scolding him at your commencement. We talked, but he was decidedly cool."

"He'll get over it, Laura," Avery said.

Laura shook her head regretfully. "Not if I don't make a special effort to make amends. I should have apologized when I saw him, but I simply couldn't bring myself to do so. He looked so angry and so . . . hurt."

"Mama," Whitney suggested, "why don't I telephone him and invite him to dinner? We'll have Florence snow soup and Richmond mousseline, all his favorite dishes. You know what an old softy Ned is after he's dined well."

"Darling, that's a splendid idea!" said Laura,

brightening. "Let's make it for Saturday after next. It should be cooler by then."

"Very well," the girl agreed. "And, Mama . . ." She smiled appealingly. "Shall I ask him to bring Christopher? It might be less awkward for Ned if his friend were here with him."

Laura bit back a quick refusal. To quarrel now with Whitney about Christopher Warren would certainly weaken their truce. She glanced over at Avery, who was watching her with a look that was oddly unsettling. "Yes," she said to Whitney, her eyes on her brother-in-law, "by all means invite Christopher. Avery, you'll join us, won't you?"

"I think not," he said distantly.

"Please come," Laura pressed him, unnerved by his attitude.

Before he could answer, Thompson appeared at the French doors. "Madam," he said, "there's a telephone call for you."

Laura turned to him impatiently. "Who is it, Thompson?"

"Mrs. Tyler, madam. It's something about the new house. She says it's urgent."

"Oh, bother," Laura said, rising. "Avery, I'll probably be awhile on the telephone. Nina has been impossible about this house. You saw how she was in Newport, bedeviling me day and night about one change or another. Please don't leave before I can talk to you."

"I'll wait for you," he said in that same remote tone.

When Laura left, Whitney set down her teacup and said to Avery, "What's wrong, Uncle? You and Mama haven't had a tiff, have you?"

Avery, too, set down his cup. Then he leaned back and folded his arms across his chest. "Now, what makes you think that?"

"Uncle Avery," she said, annoyed, "I'm getting a little tired of people treating me like a child. If something's wrong between you and Mama, I wish you'd tell me straight out instead of trying to protect my 'tender sensibilities.' "

Avery smiled unexpectedly and reached over to pinch her cheek. "How formidable you look when you frown, my dear! I apologize if you feel I've patronized you. In answer to your question: no. Your mother and I are on the best of terms."

"Then why were you looking at her so oddly before? And why did you refuse to come to dinner?"

The odd look Whitney had mentioned crossed Avery's face once more. It appeared he was not going to answer, but then he said bluntly, "I prefer not to socialize with Christopher Warren."

"But why?" the girl exclaimed. "Uncle, how can you hold his unfortunate background against him? He's—"

Avery rose abruptly from the bench and thrust his hands into his trouser pockets. "Mr. Warren's background is the least of my concerns." His voice was low; he stared at the open French doors. "It is his . . . undue effect on your mother that bothers me."

Whitney let out a sigh of relief. "So that's it," she said. "Uncle Avery, I quite agree that Mama is unreasonable where Christopher is concerned.

I gave it a lot of thought this summer, and I came to the conclusion that she refuses to admit to herself that I've grown up. Mama's always been overprotective of me, even more so since Papa died. Why do you think she got so angry when Ned gave me that pin? She can't bear the thought that I'm old enough now to receive such gifts, that I'm old enough, in fact, to marry and have a life of my own."

"There's more to it than that," Avery muttered.

"Yes, I know," Whitney said sagely, basking in the luxury of being addressed as a peer by her uncle. "As much as I know Mama likes Christopher, she is still reluctant to accept him as a son-in-law."

Avery shot her a penetrating look. "Son-in-law? What are you talking about? I thought you and Ned—"

"Honestly!" she said irritably. "Why is everyone trying to cram Ned Bailey down my throat? It's Christopher I love. And I'm sure he loves me."

"What makes you say that, Whitney?" Avery's words were deliberate. He waited in fixed attention for her response.

"I . . . I just know it," she faltered, uneasy beneath his steady gaze.

"Tell me why."

"He . . ." She looked away nervously. "Christopher spent two weeks in Bar Harbor, and we—"

"What was he doing in Bar Harbor, Whitney?"

She explained the reason, then went on. "We

talked while he was there. I think he cares for me."

"Did he say so?"

The girl looked down at her lap. "Not in so many words. But . . ." She raised her head and said rapidly, hopefully, "But a woman knows those things, Uncle."

"I sincerely hope," Avery said heavily, "that Mr. Warren has not overstepped the bounds of propriety."

"He hasn't!" she cried. "He's been a perfect gentleman, I give you my word."

"Who's been a perfect gentleman?" asked Laura from the doorway.

Both Whitney and Avery turned and stared at her in what looked to Laura like startled guilt. Avery recovered smoothly. "We were talking about Ned, Laura."

"Ah, Ned," she said, resuming her seat. "You needn't worry about him, Avery. Apart from his habit of giving unsuitable gifts, he is unquestionably a gentleman."

"What did Nina want?" Avery asked, deftly changing the subject.

"That woman!" Laura said, exasperated. "She saw a photograph of the Brighton Pavilion, and now she wants Christopher to replace the shallow dome on her new house with an onion-shaped dome flanked by four minarets. I told her that at this late date a change of that magnitude is out of the question. As it is, construction has been delayed twice because of her unreasonable demands."

"Unreasonable?" Avery said. "Nina never wanted that house to begin with, Laura."

"That's neither here nor there," she said shortly. "Both Nina and Jeremy have accepted the house. I refuse to permit either one of them to corrupt the integrity of Christopher's design."

"Aren't you overstepping your authority?" Avery asked quietly. "If the Tylers want changes, it's for them to say, not you."

Laura's chin came up defensively. "The Tylers are at liberty to dispense with my services whenever my decisions displease them. Now, I really don't care to talk about it anymore, Avery. To get back to what we were saying, will you dine with us next Saturday?"

Avery glanced at Whitney, whose puzzled gaze was on Laura. "No," he responded, "I'd rather not."

His eyes, Laura noted, were the color of an autumn dusk. Unbidden, the memory of Steven surfaced strong in her thoughts. In his brother's fair face Laura saw her husband's tacit reproach. She felt herself shiver, though the day was quite warm.

Avery did not stay for dinner that evening. He said he was needed at the hospital, and when Laura asked him to return after he attended to his duties, he politely declined. His attitude troubled her. And it obviously troubled Whitney, for the girl had little to say for the remainder of the afternoon, and during dinner she was likewise uncommunicative.

As they partook of a hearty homecoming meal at a table set festively with white damask, fine china, and blazing candles in silver sconces, Laura could only think gloomily that her reunion with her daughter, so sweet at the outset, had insidiously soured. Once more Laura felt a distance between them, the same unbridgeable gap that had yawned between them at the start of the summer. And again, Laura felt, Christopher was at the bottom of it. It was her defense of his design that had changed the pleasant tenor of the afternoon. It was her tortured feelings for him that had caused her to behave in a manner she could only call illogical. Laura had to admit, if only to herself, that Avery had been correct: She had no right to impose her will on the Tylers. It was their house, after all; it wasn't Laura's, it wasn't Christopher's. Christopher, Christopher. Loving him though she did, she could almost begin to hate him. She had to forget him, to put him out of her thoughts once and for all. She had to.

It was easier said than done, putting him out of her thoughts. But with Whitney home, and with several projects to keep her occupied, Laura was at least able to relegate Christopher to the back of her mind. Along with the Tyler house, she was decorating two houses on Gramercy Park. Those she considered quite a coup, for the denizens of Gramercy Park almost exclusively engaged Stanford White to design the interiors of their houses.

The aristocratic White, a tall, restless dynamo with flaming-red hair and mustaches, was New York's current maven of architecture and interior design. His buildings were elegant, his interior designs spectacular. Laura greatly admired his work, though her own taste in interiors was more subdued. She was therefore pleasantly surprised by the Gramercy Park commissions. She assumed that her clients had chosen her because her fee was modest, but in truth, her reputation for distinctive design was beginning to grow.

Laura was not so busy, however, that she could ignore the definite rift that still existed between herself and Whitney. They saw little of each other during the week—Laura was designing and Whitney had volunteered her services at the Bleecker Street Foundling Home—but when they did spend time together, the girl was polite but preoccupied, working constantly on a pretty piece of needlepoint. When Laura talked of the upcoming debut, hoping to stir some excitement in those pensive dark eyes, Whitney only said vaguely, "Mama, that's not until January. We have plenty of time to plan for it later."

When Laura questioned her about her future plans, suggesting the possibility of further schooling, Whitney answered with a shake of her head, "Oh, no, Mama, I don't want to be more educated than . . . than the man I'll someday marry. It wouldn't be fitting."

Laura, thinking of Ned, who was admittedly less than a scholar, could only nod in silent agreement.

Although Whitney had said nothing to indicate that she wished to marry Ned Bailey, Laura, her mind beclouded by other issues, had come to the conclusion that this was the case. Her daughter's choice pleased her. Laura was extremely fond of Ned. He was less ambitious than she would have liked, but he was honorable and kind, and his love for Whitney was indisputably sincere. Steven, too, had liked Ned. "Ned's no ball of fire," he had once said, "but his heart's in the right place." Thus, Laura relaxed a bit about her daughter's remoteness. As soon as Laura made up for her harsh treatment of Ned, Whitney would forgive her, and their relationship would again be as close as it had always been.

On the last Saturday in September, construction on the Tyler house was completed. Laura, with a bursting pride she was hard put to contain, set foot in Christopher's masterpiece for the first time. Only the builder, Leo Cavanaugh, was present at seven that morning when Laura chose to inspect the premises. The Tylers were out of town for the weekend. Some of the furnishings had already been installed. As Cavanaugh showed Laura through room after sun-filled room, as they both gazed with admiration on the Diocletian windows, the octagonal bedrooms, the ceilings and chimney pieces of absolute classicism, it was obvious that his pride equaled hers.

"Mrs. Sheridan," he said, mopping his florid face with a handkerchief when they returned to the circular hall, "I've been building houses for over thirty-five years and never have I worked from plans more painstakingly precise than Mr. Warren's. Even my men said that his calculations were so accurate that they could have constructed this house blindfolded."

"Yes," Laura said softly, her pride increasing a thousandfold. "Mr. Warren knows what he wants."

"That he does!" Cavanaugh agreed. "When one of my workmen accidentally made an architrave an inch smaller than specified, Mr. Warren simply redesigned an entire new cornice and frieze to correct the error. Another architect would have disguised the discrepancy, and no one would have been the wiser. Not Mr. Warren, though. *'Everything,'* he said to me, 'has got to be perfect for this house.' "

Laura looked up at the lofty domed ceiling. "It *is* perfect, isn't it? I almost wish it were mine."

"Mr. Warren's a lot like your late husband," remarked Cavanaugh. "How well I remember Mr. Sheridan's designs. Do you recall the Griffith place on Madison Avenue? Now there was a house! Your husband was an artist, Mrs. Sheridan. And so is that amazing young man."

"Yes," Laura said, "Mr. Warren is like my husband." And to herself she reflected, *But the differences between them is what made me fall in love with him.*

The front door opened, and Christopher walked into the hall. Laura's breath caught in her throat. Despite her resolve to put him out of her thoughts, she was elated beyond description to see him again.

The instant he spotted her, his hat was in his hands. In his eyes, as he approached her, was a curious mixture of surprise, delight, and trepidation.

"Laura, what are you doing here?" His voice was low, vibrant. He nodded briefly to Cavanaugh, but his attention was fixed on only one person.

"I've come to see your house," Laura said with some difficulty. "It's even finer than I had imagined. You've good cause to be proud of it."

"Do you really like it?" His insatiable gaze weakened her knees.

"Yes . . . yes," she said. "I couldn't be more pleased." Unnerved by his presence, she sought help from the builder, who was beaming at Christopher like a proud parent. "Mr. Cavanaugh, too, greatly admires your work."

"Ah, he knows that, Mrs. Sheridan," said Cavanaugh heartily. "I've told him repeatedly how good he is, but it's *your* stamp of approval he's been waiting for."

A pang of conscience further unsettled Laura. She should have visited the house sooner.

"Christopher, I love the house," she reassured him. "There was never a doubt in my mind about how it would turn out."

"I wish I could say the same," he said tersely.

"Mrs. Tyler did her best to try to alter every last detail of my design."

"That's over with," she reminded him. "Nina was troublesome, I grant you, but the house has been built exactly as you conceived it. That's all you need concern yourself with now."

He said nothing, he only looked at her; and in his brilliant dark eyes Laura saw her own twin reflection, an apt representation of the duality of her emotions. How she loved him, how she wanted him, yet how she longed to be free of him. Unintentionally but irreparably, he had altered the design of her serene, harmonious life.

Cavanaugh said, startling her, "I'd best be on my way. I have an appointment downtown, and I'm late for it. Mrs. Sheridan, Mr. Warren . . ." He bowed to Laura and shook Christopher's hand. "I look forward to working again with both of you." Then, lightly, to Christopher: "Stop your brooding now, laddie. Like Mrs. Sheridan said, you got what you wanted. Don't worry your head about anything else."

After Cavanaugh left, Laura said nervously, "I'd better go too."

"No, don't," Christopher said at once. "Stay awhile. Walk through the house with me."

She shook her head, avoiding his gaze. "I've already seen it. I have to go."

"Laura, please." He reached out a hand to her, then quickly withdrew it. "Don't deny me this. Tour the house with me. Let me see it through your eyes. It's all I've been waiting for."

She looked up at him slowly, at the fierce dark

face she loved, at the mouth that looked so hard yet felt so warm to the touch. "Very well," she said softly, allowing him to take her arm. And as they walked through the shining rooms, she thought over and over again, *If only this house were ours, if only we could remain here forever, shutting the door to the rest of the world, ignoring the disapproval of family and friends.*

In Jeremy's study at the rear of the house a luxurious Boucher tapestry covered an entire wall. Christopher said, spotting it, "I haven't seen this. Did you choose it?"

"Yes," Laura said. "It's an Italian hunting scene. Do you like it?"

"It's perfect," he answered with a sincerity that touched her heart. "It lends the exact atmosphere I wished to evoke in this room."

Every room that she saw with him seemed more beautiful in the sharing. The house *was* him: handsome, well ordered, and classically spare. When they returned to the downstairs hall, it was with reluctance that Laura said, "I must go now."

"Please," he said at once. "Don't go yet."

"Christopher . . ."

"Laura, I know you don't want to be alone with me. Let's go somewhere, then, somewhere public. Have breakfast with me at Delmonico's."

She lifted a pleading face to his. "Don't do this to me," she implored him. "It will be difficult enough tonight when you dine at my house with Ned."

"I won't be there tonight," he said bluntly.

"Why not?" She was both relieved and disappointed.

"I . . ." He crushed the brim of his hat with white-knuckled hands. "I wanted to talk to you first . . ."

His hard face was pale. Laura sensed in him an intense inner turmoil that had nothing to do with their immediate problem.

"What's wrong?" she said swiftly, her own distress forgotten as she strove to banish his. "Is it about your work? Tell me. Let me help you if I can."

"You want to help me." He gave a harsh laugh. "I wish I could tell you how funny that is."

His grimness alarmed her. She reached for his hand and was astonished to feel it tremble. Too late she realized she should not have remained with him; indeed, that she should never have touched him.

He stared down at her fiercely, then he dropped his hat and pulled her into his arms. Her purse fell from her grasp. Instinctively she pushed her hands against his chest, but with an ease that disarmed her he took hold of her wrists and pinioned them behind her back.

His mouth came down on hers with a hot, hard, almost brutal intensity. Whatever demon possessed him, it had unleashed in him a fiendish, unholy need. Laura struggled against him, but her effort was no match for the devils that drove him. Beneath his passion she sensed rage; in his kiss she tasted fear. He was so tangibly afraid that she could feel it, she shared it. She was drowning in his fear, engulfed in the tide of her own rising passion. She tore her arms free and reached up to embrace him.

As she returned his bruising kisses, he swept her up in his arms and scaled the marble staircase two steps at a time. He made straight for the master bedroom, pushed open the door with a foot, and deposited his burden on the unsheeted Empire bed. The morning sun was a radiance in Laura's eyes. Through a shimmering haze she watched him shed his clothes, quickly, feverishly. Then with rough, burning hands he undressed her, caressed her, pulled her hard against his body, kissed her cheek, her eyes, her throat, her mouth, then thrust himself inside her, discharging his passion even before he had fully entered her.

She clamped her legs on his as he groaned and stiffened in her embrace, then she took his face in her hands and kissed his hard, shaking mouth. She wanted more of him, all of him; she would never have enough of him. "I love you so much," she whispered fiercely. "I've never loved anyone as I love you."

His mouth stilled her words, his arms crushed the breath from her lungs. Her arms tightened around him, and a hot thrill shot through her as she felt the reawakening of his violent passion. This was what she wanted: to be in his arms, in his power. She was burning with love for him, scorched with desire. She couldn't think, could barely breathe. The very feel of his skin on hers was exquisite torture; the movement of his body was unendurable rapture.

She arched closer against him, her mouth parted pliantly against the deep, probing onslaught of his. She was all heat and passion, straining urgently against him. The more violent his kisses, the more she strained closer; the rougher his caresses, the more erotic her response. Every nerve in her body cried out for release, but at the same time she wished to be part of his flesh forever.

She felt his hands grasp her hips and press her hard against him. His mouth still covered hers, rough and demanding, and she felt at last that dizzying spiral that spun higher and faster, sending hot waves of sensation through her quivering frame. With a moan she arched against him as he released his turbulent passion a second time. A soft sob escaped her lips. She was his now, he was hers. Their hearts, minds, and souls were inextricably linked.

For a long time they lay entwined, silent and still. His weight was crushing her, but she reveled in the encumbrance. This was what she wanted, as much as she fought against it: to be loved by this man and to belong to him wholly. Nothing in her life mattered more.

At last she felt him stir, slowly, heavily, as if rousing from a dream. His hard jaw brushed hers; she felt his mouth on her cheek, near her ear. "I hope," he said in a low, bitter voice, "that I've given you a child."

Her breast ached with fervent longing; she

wished that he had. But she said quietly against his shoulder, "I hope that you have not."

He lifted himself on his elbows and stared down at her darkly. "Is this to be our life?" he demanded. "Stolen moments of passion? Do you find it more socially acceptable to be my mistress than my wife? What a coward you are."

"That's not fair," she protested, but in her heart she agreed with him. "I didn't want to do this, Christopher. You gave me no choice."

He didn't answer, he only looked at her, defying her to sustain the lie. Under his challenging gaze, hers wavered and fell. "Very well," she said in a guilty whisper. "I wanted it to happen. I love you; I can't deny it. But I cannot be your wife, and that's the end of it."

"The end of it," he echoed hotly, wrenching away from her and swinging out of bed. He began to dress in swift, angry motions. "It's not the end of it, and you know it. Whenever we have the opportunity, you'll 'permit' me to make love to you. When we meet in public, you'll play the part of the proper widow, but the moment we're alone, you'll torment me again with your fragmentary love. By Christ, I don't want that. I want *you*; I want all of you!"

"Christopher . . ."

He flung down his shirt and grasped both her arms in a paralyzing grip. "Do you know that when I saw you this morning, I was terrified of facing you? I felt I had done something so reprehensible that you, in your virtuous perfection, could never forgive me for it. But now—" He released her with a sound of disgust and snatched up his shirt from the floor. "You and your class are no better than me. Your money and position are a gilded facade behind which you hide your monumental hypocrisy."

"What have you done?" Laura demanded, ignoring the insult she felt she richly deserved. "What was so reprehensible that you thought I couldn't forgive you?"

"It doesn't matter now," he snapped. "If you should learn what I've done, you may think whatever you please; I don't care anymore." He shrugged into his coat. "How ironic that I should have worried about losing you—as if I ever had a chance of having you."

"Why are you doing this?" she said miserably. "I told you at the outset that what you wanted was impossible."

"So you did," he said bitterly. "Thank you for warning me. From here on in I shall pursue a woman only if I'm certain she will have me."

Something in his eyes frightened Laura more than his words. She reached out a hand to him, to span the lonely breach between them, to revive the love he'd had for her, which she feared was now dead. But he turned coldly away from her, as if he couldn't stand the sight of her; and when she called his name brokenly, he strode rapidly from the room.

Chapter Thirteen

✦✦✦✦✦

MONTHS WENT BY and Laura neither saw him nor heard word of him. Whenever Ned dined at her home, he would say that Christopher was unable to attend because he was busy with a new commission, the design of a two-hundred-suite apartment house on West Seventy-third Street. Laura was pleased by the news, but she doubted that that was the reason for Christopher's absence. When she would tactfully question Ned, attempting to discover the "reprehensible" action that had so disturbed Christopher, Ned's obliging but uninformative answers shed no light on the situation. Otherwise, Ned's only concern was returning to Laura's good graces—and Whitney, of course. Whenever he was with her he would rarely take his eyes off her. Whitney, Laura noticed, would be quieter and more pensive than usual.

Those months without Christopher were as difficult for Laura as the first few months following Steven's death. She experienced the same anguish, the same keen bereavement. And this belief, that she had lost him as irretrievably as she had lost her husband, intensified her pain to insupportable proportions. Even worse than her sense of loss was Christopher's threat to pursue other women. Laura couldn't bear it if he did. The mere thought of his wanting another woman filled her with a rage that physically sickened her.

In October, for a frantic two weeks, she thought she might be pregnant. Her emotions alternated dizzily between trapped terror and ecstatic joy. Now she would have to marry him, she would have no choice. But what would her friends say? And what of Whitney, what of Avery? How could they accept Christopher into their midst when Laura herself hadn't the courage to do so? As it turned out, her torturous questions went unanswered. She hadn't conceived Christopher's child. When she learned this for certain, she broke down and wept.

At the beginning of November she started planning for Whitney's debut. Hopefully, the many preparations for this cheerful event would distract her mind from her troubles. She decided to decorate the ballroom with an appropriate floral theme: pimpernel denoting change; white violets for innocence; hibiscus for beauty; and acacia for friendship and love. The buffet menu would include rissolettes à la Renan, Maryland Club terrapin, mayonnaise de volaille, jellied oranges, and almond cake—all Whitney's favorites, though Laura doubted the honored celebrant would taste a bite.

After many consultations with the dressmaker, Whitney chose to wear for her debut a stunning Paris design of white satin and Valenciennes lace, trimmed at the bodice with tiny satin rosebuds. Laura, at the final fitting, watched her daughter with tears in her eyes. Soon, she imagined, she would be watching Whitney be fitted for her wedding gown. Where had the years gone? How capricious was time.

Was it only two months since she had last seen Christopher? It seemed like a century; it seemed an unendurable eternity.

In December, at the Barneses' annual Christmas gala, Cynthia said to her with her usual tact, "Laura, what's wrong with you? I've never seen you looking so ghastly!"

Laura, who had just been told by Ned that Christopher had declined the Barneses' invitation, said morosely, "Nothing's wrong, Cynthia. I have a slight headache, that's all."

"A *slight* headache? My dear, if I felt the way you look, I'd ask Avery to perform immediate exploratory surgery."

Avery, overhearing his name, turned away from the buffet table and asked Cynthia, "Who needs surgery?"

"Laura does, Avery. Look at her, for heaven's sake! She looks like the last rose of summer!"

"You're the last of the great alarmists," Avery said with a laugh. But there was no laughter in his eyes as he closely appraised his sister-in-law.

Later in the carriage, on the way home, he said to her, "Laura, Cynthia was right, you know. You're not looking well at all. You have very little color, and I believe you've lost weight. You've been doing too much—the decorating, your committee work, preparing for Whitney's debut. It's taking a toll on you. I'm going to prescribe a tonic, and you had better make sure you take it, or I shall be very angry indeed."

"I don't need a tonic," she said listlessly. What she needed, she thought despondently, was beyond Avery's power to supply.

"Laura." His tone was severe. "I insist that you do as I say. You're not as hale as you should be—and neither is your daughter, in case you haven't noticed. I'm going to put you both on a strict regimen of rest, nourishing diet, and a tonic of sweet wine of iron."

This reference to Whitney's health finally roused Laura from her lethargy. In her preoccupation with Christopher she had been totally oblivious to anyone but herself. When she returned home that night, she went straight to her daughter's bedroom and looked at her, for the first time in a while, with eyes undistorted by her own selfish concerns.

Whitney's bedroom was a delightful reproduction of an eighteenth-century French boudoir. The walls were papered in chinoiserie damask in muted shades of pink and rose. A four-poster bed, all delicately turned fruitwood, was covered with a pink damask spread.

At the marquetry desk Whitney sat, like an elegant young dauphine, writing on a sheet of vellum stationery. She was wearing a paisley dressing gown and at her youthful bosom a hint of chemise lace could be seen. Her hair was loose, a froth of dark curls brushing her ivory cheeks. Laura stood for a while at the doorway, astonished as always that this incredibly beautiful creature was her daughter.

"Darling," she said softly, "may I come in for a moment?"

Whitney looked up with a start, then thrust the sheet of paper under the blotter. She stared at her mother with fathomless dark eyes. For just a fraction of an instant Laura had the feeling she was looking at a stranger.

Whitney smiled. The feeling passed. "Of course, Mama. Come in." She rose from the desk, settled on the chaise longue, and picked up the inevitable piece of needlepoint. "How was the party?"

"It was festive, as usual." Laura sat near her daughter on a pretty tufted chair. "I wish you had come, though. Ned was terribly disappointed you weren't there."

Whitney plied her needle with apparent concentration. "Ned came alone?"

Laura smiled at what she interpreted as possessive jealousy. "Of course he was alone. He was hoping against hope that you would change your mind at the last minute and be there, as you had originally planned."

The girl said softly, her eyes on her work, "I just wasn't up to going out tonight, Mama."

"Darling, I wanted to talk to you about that. Uncle Avery is worried about you. And now that I really look at you, I'm a bit worried too. Are you feeling all right?" She reached over to lay a hand against her cheek. "You're a little pale."

"I'm perfectly well," Whitney murmured. "Uncle Avery is a fusspot."

"Whitney, he's not," Laura admonished her. "He's concerned for your health, and rightly so. I fear the preparations for your debut have been too much for you. From now till then you should discontinue all activities and try to get some rest."

"Mama," the girl pointed out, "I've been doing far less than you have."

"Darling, I doubt that," Laura said. "Every afternoon you're running back and forth between Madame Borel's, the florist, and the caterer. At night you stay up until all hours working on your needlepoint. On top of that you're volunteering three or four mornings a week at the foundling home. You're never idle for a moment; you're simply doing too much."

Whitney's soft mouth hardened stubbornly. "I won't give up my work at the foundling home. I'm needed there, Mama. I refuse to turn away from those poor, motherless babies in order to conserve my energies for a mere social event."

"Your dedication is commendable," Laura said gently, "but you do yourself and those children a disservice if you damage your health by overworking. It's only weeks till your debut. Rest now, and then you can return to the foundling home, refreshed and strong."

It was impossible to dispute the soundness of this suggestion. Whitney nodded in grudging agreement. Then she put down her needlework, her gaze turning from Laura's and coming to rest, as if compelled, on the blotter on the desk.

"Whitney," said Laura, following her gaze, "to whom were you writing when I came in? I thought all the invitations had gone out."

Whitney's gaze darted back to hers. She paused before answering. "They have, Mama," she said guardedly. "I was writing to Christopher. Ned told me he's not planning to attend my debut."

"Christopher?" His name aroused in Laura a blend of pleasure and pain. "I don't recall including him on the guest list."

"You didn't," the girl said. "I asked Ned to ask him. Mama, I want him to be here."

"May I see the letter, Whitney?" Laura kept her tone pleasant, but her hands, on her lap, were tightly clenched together.

Whitney hesitated, then rose. "If you wish," she said.

She fetched the letter and handed it to her mother. Laura read:

Dear Christopher, Ned told me you refused the invitation to my debut. I can't say I was surprised, but I am disappointed. Perhaps a debut strikes you as a senseless society extravagance, but it is merely a rite de passage, no different from a school commencement or a birthday celebration; and in that spirit, I'd be pleased if you'd attend. You said to me once that a woman should always speak her mind, which is why I . . .

There was nothing else written. Laura looked up at her daughter and said evenly, "May I ask why you find it necessary to write to this man when he has already refused your invitation?"

Whitney answered resolutely, "Mama, I want him to be at my debut."

"And what about Ned, Whitney?"

"What about him?"

"I was of the impression that you and he had an understanding."

"We don't have an understanding. We're

friends, nothing more. Mama, I know this is going to upset you, but Christopher is the man I care for. I can guess what you're thinking, so you needn't bother saying it. Christopher's *not* too old for me, and I don't care if he's an orphan. I'm eighteen years old, old enough to make my own decisions, and I want him to be at my debut."

"Whitney," Laura said, making a concentrated effort to speak calmly and rationally, "I know you're a woman now, and certainly capable of making your own decisions, but believe me when I say that Christopher Warren is not the man for you."

"Forgive me, Mama." Whitney's hard look belied the soft tone of her voice. "There's no use your telling me what to do in this matter. I love Christopher, I intend to see as much of him as I can, and I want him at my debut. And, with all due respect, there's nothing you can do to stop me."

Whitney's defiance, though quietly spoken, struck Laura as violently as a physical blow. Her stomach contracted; all breath left her lungs. Dimly she thought of Christopher's words: "From here on in I shall pursue a woman only if I know she'll have me."

Laura rose to her feet, unable to think clearly. A maelstrom of emotion raged through her mind. "Listen to me," she said deliberately. "You will not see Christopher again, not ever, do you hear me? If he comes to your debut, I shall ask him to leave the instant I see him. This is my house, Whitney, you're my daughter, and for as long as you reside here, you'll do what I think best, whether you think so or not."

"If that's the case," the girl said hotly, "perhaps I'd better seek lodgings elsewhere. I have the income left me by Grandfather Whitney. It's mine now that I'm eighteen. I can lease an apartment and live comfortably for years. I don't want to leave here, Mama, but I will if you force me to."

Laura's palms tingled. She had never struck Whitney, but she very much wanted to do so now. And yet the anger she felt was exceeded by despair. She felt helpless, trapped, at the mercy of passing time— Time, that merciless captor, who changed loving, obedient daughters into unrecognizable strangers. This wasn't her baby, her darling, the child reared with almost reverential devotion. This woman who stood before her was an entity unknown to her. And what was worse—inconceivable—she wanted Christopher for her own.

"Whitney," she said with a composure that amazed her, "let's not talk anymore tonight. We're both overtired. We can go over this another time, when we're rested."

"Mama, I won't change my mind," the girl said adamantly. "Christopher's the man I love, and I want him at my debut."

Laura said patiently, though her nerves were in knots, "We'll discuss it tomorrow evening."

But first, she thought grimly, there are a few things I need to discuss with Christopher.

* * *

Upon consideration, Laura realized that the last thing she should do was to be alone with Christopher and forbid him to see Whitney. She had done that once before; the result had been disastrous. And yet she couldn't very well ignore the situation. She had to do something. The question was what? If only Steven were alive. He'd know what to do. But, of course, if her husband had been living, Laura would never have found herself in this dilemma.

She and her daughter were enamored of the same man. If it weren't so offensive, it would be laughable. Laura could just imagine her friends' reactions if they should learn of it: "Have you heard the latest gossip? Laura Sheridan is in love with her daughter's beau. Did you ever hear anything so ludicrous?"

It was Cynthia Barnes to whom Laura finally turned for help. Cynthia was Laura's oldest and dearest friend. Her sardonic dark eyes were the window to a soul that saw much and seemed to understand everything. Perhaps that same no-nonsense intuitiveness might see the answer to a problem that, to Laura, was hopelessly insoluble.

They attended the Met one night in January, escorted by John and Avery. As fate would have it, the opera was *La Gioconda*, the story of a man who is loved by two women, one a beautiful noblewoman, the other an equally lovely young street singer. Ironically, the noblewoman's name in the opera was Laura. In the second act, when the two women confronted each other, both declaring their love for the hero, Laura tensed in her seat, stared down at her lap, and gripped her opera glasses so tightly that she nearly snapped them in two.

At the interval, as John and Avery made their way through the crowd to secure refreshments for their ladies, Laura said quickly to Cynthia, "I must speak to you in private—about a personal matter that's been troubling me."

Cynthia idly plied her ivory fan. "That doesn't surprise me, my dear. You haven't been yourself for months. I was wondering how long it would take you to confide in me."

Laura glanced about at the richly dressed crowd—stiff shirtfronts, smooth black broadcloth; butter-yellow satin, peacock moire; emeralds and rubies; long kid gloves, diamond tiaras—the opulence unaccountably bothered her. Her own gown, an ecru silk with seed pearls and embroidered lace, was an extravagance that likewise discomfited her. "We cannot talk here," she said uneasily.

"No, we can't," Cynthia said, taking her arm. "Let's return to the box. We'll have fifteen minutes alone before curtain time."

"But John and Avery—"

"They'll think we've gone to freshen up," Cynthia said. And in her peremptory way she steered Laura back to the seclusion of the Barnes box.

When they were seated on the red plush chairs, Cynthia said briskly, "Come now. What's it all about?"

Laura hesitated, unsure of how to begin and uncertain of how much to reveal. To her utter astonishment Cynthia prompted, "It's Christopher Warren, isn't it?"

Laura's mouth dropped open. Cynthia said impatiently, "Good heavens, Laura, I'm not blind. You've been talking of little else for more than a year. And the way you talk about him! As if the sun rises and sets on that extremely handsome head of his. You think you're in love with him, don't you?"

"Y-yes," Laura stammered, too astonished to lie.

"Well, you're not!" Cynthia declared. "It's Steven you see in him, Steven's looks, Steven's genius, Steven's choice of career; and, moreover, you're looking for an attachment. Now that Whitney's grown up, you feel all at sea, alone and lonely, with no one to care for."

At the mention of Whitney's name Laura choked back a sob and covered her face with her hands.

"My dear!"

Cynthia was all instant regret and solicitude. She moved her chair closer to Laura's and put an arm around her shoulder. "Laura, forgive me for being so blunt. I never dreamed— Laura, please don't cry."

"I'm not crying," Laura whispered and looked up at her bleakly. "Cynthia, you don't know the half of it. Whitney thinks she's in love with him. I don't know what to do."

Cynthia sat bolt upright, taken aback by this unexpected development. "Whitney, too? You *are* in a pickle, aren't you?"

"I'm at my wits' end," Laura said miserably.

"Nothing I say will convince Whitney that the situation is impossible."

"My word!" Cynthia exclaimed. "You haven't told her how you feel about Christopher?"

"No, of course not! I'd never do that. But, don't you see? I must do something to keep them apart. Whitney is dead set on Christopher's being at her debut next week. When she told me that, we had a bitter quarrel. I threatened to banish Christopher from the house. In turn, Whitney threatened to leave home, to get an . . . apartment." Laura choked on the word. "I don't know if Christopher is coming to the debut; Whitney has barely spoken to me for days. But I have to stop him somehow, Cynthia."

"Why don't you speak to him?" Cynthia suggested. "He seems the sensible sort. I'm sure if he knows you disapprove of the situation, he'll make it his business to stay away from your daughter."

Again Laura thought of Christopher's words: *I shall pursue a woman only if I know she'll have me.*

"I can't do that," she mumbled.

"Whyever not?"

Laura looked guiltily away. "I simply can't."

Cynthia gave her a puzzled frown. "Well, if you won't talk to him, Laura, the only other thing to do is to ignore the situation and let it resolve itself."

Laura turned back to her swiftly, her blue eyes ablaze. "Are you mad? This is not a situation that can be ignored."

"Laura, get hold of yourself!" Cynthia commanded. "If you were in possession of your senses, you'd see at once that it's the only thing to do. Stop and think for a moment. Hasn't Whitney been in love with young men of whom you disapproved? What did you do? You merely let nature take its course. The fact that you fancy yourself in love with Christopher has blown this situation out of all proportion for you. Let Whitney alone. She'll soon realize she doesn't love him—as you will, my dear."

"But I do love him!" Laura cried.

"You love him?" Cynthia echoed. "And what do you intend to do about it, Laura. Are you going to marry him, pray tell?"

"I want to," Laura said wretchedly, "more than anything else in the world . . . but I cannot do it."

"Of course you can't marry him," Cynthia agreed. "I'm glad you're aware of that. And as time passes, you'll also see that what you feel for him is simply a girlish infatuation."

"That's not true!" Laura protested. "I love him, I tell you. I'm not eighteen years old, Cynthia; I know my own heart."

"Laura," said Cynthia pointedly, "an infatuated woman knows only what she wants to know. The truth of the matter is: Steven is dead. You and your daughter are both chasing after rainbows."

Chapter Fourteen

❖❖❖❖❖

IN THE LAST decade of the nineteenth century, apartment dwelling in New York City had attained a measure of respectability due largely to the success of the Dakota apartments on the upper West Side. Built in the 1880s, the Dakota was an impressive, completely fireproof, buff-colored brick building. Some of the lavish suites boasted as many as twenty rooms, all paneled and wainscoted in oak or mahogany. On the grounds were croquet lawns, tennis courts, and deliciously fragrant gardens in which the tenants could luxuriate. So innovative was the concept that every one of the Dakota's sixty-five suites was rented before the building was completed.

To surpass such a triumph seemed an impossibility; but Christopher Warren undertook to design a building that would put the Dakota to shame. He was fortunate in that George Winston, who had commissioned the work, owned a picturesque tract of land on West Seventy-third Street, a most desirable location for the Winston Court Apartments, as Winston had already dubbed them. Moreover, Winston, only thirty-three years old, was a dynamic self-made man, a millionaire many times over, and as such he was an inspiration to Christopher.

The Dakota was nine stories high. Winston said to his architect: "I want the Court to be eighteen stories high!"

The Dakota had sixty-five suites and very few

bathrooms. Winston told Christopher, "The Court'll have two hundred suites, and each suite will have two fully equipped bathrooms!"

For the comfort of his tenants (and for his own glorification) Winston intended to provide a choice of electric or gas ranges in the kitchens; a house telephone in every suite; central heating and cooling; and two elegant restaurants on the lower floors for those tenants who wished to socialize in public within an elevator ride of their own abodes.

As to the exterior design of the structure, Winston more or less gave Christopher a free hand.

"I want everyone who sees the Court," he said, "to gasp in awe. This building must be the showpiece of New York. I want a design," he added strongly, "that no one in this city has ever seen before."

Christopher correctly interpreted those suggestions to mean, "Make it different, but not so different that the general public can't appreciate it."

With this thought in mind, Christopher designed Winston Court in the familiar Gothic Revival Style, with a towering single spire that housed the topmost luxury suites. He chose cream-colored terra-cotta for the exterior, adding a confection of tracery that gave the slender structure the look of an icing-swirled wedding cake. So delighted was Winston with Christopher's work that shortly after the New Year, when he reviewed the design, he said, "You've done it, Mr. Warren! Next to this, the Dakota will look like a ramshackle hovel."

Christopher was gratified by this show of approval, but his pleasure was mitigated by the fact that in pandering to popular taste, he had betrayed every standard he held sacred.

"Why have you been avoiding me?" Ned Bailey asked Christopher on the day before Whitney's debut.

They were at work; it was after hours. Christopher had remained to make final modifications on the plans for Winston Court. Ned had stayed specifically to find out what had been bothering Christopher since the end of the summer.

Christopher looked up from his drawing board. Ned lounged against the partition, hands in pockets, one elegantly trousered leg crossed over the other. Beneath his casual pose lay a watchful alertness. His lazy green gaze was as cool as a cat's.

Discomfited by that gaze, Christopher gestured abruptly toward his plans. "I've been rather busy for the past few months . . . or haven't you noticed?"

"I notice more than you think I do," Ned replied. "For example, since I returned from Newport, you've barely looked at me, let alone talked to me. You've refused every invitation I've extended. You won't lunch with me; you no longer go to Madame Beverly's with me. If I've done something to offend you, I'd very much appreciate it if you'd tell me what it is."

Christopher said defensively, "You're imagining things. I've been busy, that's all. This design has been taking up all my energies. I can't go gadding about town as I used to. I just don't have the time for it."

Ned considered this explanation, then ostensibly elected to accept it as truth. "I see," he said. "In that case, I imagine it would be useless to try to persuade you to attend Whitney's debut? You'd see Laura. I know she cares for you, Christopher. Her face is an open book whenever I mention your name."

"No," Christopher answered, his eyes on his design. "It's not a good idea for me to see her right now."

Ned was silent for so long a time that Christopher looked up, thinking he had gone. But he had not. He still stood there, hands in trouser pockets, his amiable face uncharacteristically sober.

Christopher eyed him questioningly. Ned said in a low voice, "I wish you'd change your mind about the debut. I was hoping you'd be there with me tomorrow night. You see, I'm going to ask Whitney to marry me."

Christopher's pulse quickened. Warily he asked, "Have you already discussed marriage with her?"

"Not outright," Ned said. "But she knows how I feel about her. Besides, lately she's had other things on her mind. She's still at odds with her mother, you know. And it's been damned uncomfortable for me. Whenever I'm with them, I can actually feel the tension between them. That's another reason I was hoping you'd come tomorrow. Perhaps you can talk to Whitney and persuade her to drop her unreasonable grudge. She'll listen to you; I'm sure she will. She's enormously fond of you, Christopher. She told me what a grand time the two of you had at Bar Harbor." Ned paused and added earnestly, "She also told me how you praised me to the skies. I've never thanked you for that. I do now—most sincerely."

Christopher shook his head, silently declining Ned's thanks. But as he sat there uncomfortably, pondering what he had done to Whitney in Bar Harbor, a faint feeling of relief began to temper his discomfort. Whitney, it appeared, had said nothing of his conduct of that night. Perhaps, since she hadn't as yet, she never would. Most likely, in fact, she now regretted her declaration of love; indeed, she must wish she could retract it. That was probably the reason she was so anxious to have Christopher at her debut, so that she could tell him it was Ned she really loved.

Impulsively he said, "Look, Ned, if you want me to go with you tomorrow night, I will. I'm sorry I've been such a bastard lately. It hasn't been intentional, I swear it."

Ned's aspect changed dramatically. His green eyes widened; his mobile mouth curved into a Cheshire Cat grin. "Christopher, you're first-rate! Wait'll I tell Whitney I convinced you to come to her debut. She'll accept my proposal on the spot."

Christopher smiled and nodded agreement. Watching Ned's joyous face, it was easy to share his optimism.

*   *   *

The Georgian house on Fifty-fifth Street was ablaze with light and music on the night of Whitney Sheridan's debut. Although outdoors the temperature was below the freezing point, indoors it was springlike, the vast ballroom having been transformed into a bower of flower and fern. The room glittered with life and gaiety, from the highly polished oak floor to the stucco figured ceiling, which depicted Artemis being serenaded by Apollo on his lyre. Beneath these deities stood the evening's young celebrant, more beautiful than the virgin goddess who smiled down on her.

Flanking Whitney on the receiving line were Avery and Laura, who was as lovely as her daughter in a slim gown of ice-blue crepe de Chine. Laura's eyes glowed with pride whenever she glanced at Whitney, poised and self-confident, the quintessence of a society miss as she greeted each guest with a welcoming smile and a warm personal word.

Hostilities between mother and daughter had been suspended for the occasion. Earlier, when Whitney was dressing, Laura had gone to her room and had said appealingly, "Darling, I want this to be a happy night for you. If Christopher has decided to come, I shan't make a fuss. I know you're been worried about that, and I've—"

"Oh, Mama, thank you!" Whitney cried, leaping up and throwing her arms about Laura's neck. "Christopher *is* coming tonight, and I was desperately worried what you might do." She stepped back but still held on to Laura's arms. "Mama," she said urgently, "I didn't mean what I said about leaving home. I was angry and upset. I hate when we quarrel. Let's make a pact: no more disagreements. I want us to be as close as we used to be."

Laura readily agreed; she wanted the same thing. The rift between Whitney and her had been an insupportable agony. Cynthia Barnes was probably right. Laura had only to be patient and Whitney's puppy love for Christopher would die a natural death. As for Laura's feelings for Christopher— She couldn't think of that now; she must only think of Whitney. She embraced her daughter tightly and kissed her flushed cheek. "I promise you, darling," she said fervently, "nothing is ever going to separate us again."

In the ballroom, as the dancing began and Ned and Whitney led the cotillion, Laura, seated with Cynthia on the sidelines, watched Christopher across the room, engaged in conversation with Malcolm MacKenzie. When Christopher had greeted her on the reception line, he had been formal and correct, taking her hand and bowing courteously, as convention decreed. With Whitney he had done the same, but he had smiled at Whitney, a genuine, warm smile. Laura had had to consciously restrain herself from raking her nails across his cheek.

Cynthia, noting the direction of Laura's gaze, said casually, "Have you seen the plans for Malcolm's new summer house?"

"Why, no," Laura said, dragging her attention, with reluctance, from Christopher. "What's it like, Cynthia?"

"It's wonderful!" Cynthia declared. "Mr. Warren quite surprised me with his versatility. After that extraordinarily boring design he did for Nina and Jeremy, he has gone and created a gem for the MacKenzies. Janet showed me the plans last week. The house, she told me, is a copy of some Scottish castle. It has turrets and battlements, and it even has a bell tower. Your young genius, I take it, has finally come to his senses."

This description took Laura aback. *Christopher? Willingly designing such a house?* She couldn't understand it. His work on the Parker School additions had been entirely another matter. There he had had no choice but to adhere to the mode of the existing building. But to have gone against his grain in designing the MacKenzie house was not like him. Why, Laura wondered, had he done it?

"How very curious," she said, looking again toward Christopher and MacKenzie. "He once told me he'd rather dig ditches for a living than design that type of house. How did Malcolm ever persuade him to do it?"

"From what Janet told me," Cynthia explained, "it took no persuasion at all. Mr. Warren couldn't have been more amenable to Malcolm's suggestions. By the way, did you know that John is financing George Winston's new project, an apartment building uptown?"

"No," Laura said, her eyes still on Christopher. "I've heard nothing about that."

"Then you probably don't know that Mr. Warren is George's architect," Cynthia said. "I've seen those plans too, and, my dear, Mr. Warren has outdone himself!"

Cynthia went on to describe the whimsical style of Winston Court, while Laura listened in appalled silence. What had come over Christopher? Why was he designing what he had once called monstrosities? Was he doing it for the money? No, no! Christopher was too gifted and too honorable to be swayed by mere monetary considerations.

Laura rose abruptly from her chair, cutting Cynthia off in midsentence. "Cynthia, excuse me. I must speak with Christopher."

She started to leave, but Cynthia deftly caught her hand. "Is that wise, my dear?" she said pointedly. "If you show too much interest in him, mightn't people get the wrong idea?"

"What do you mean?" Laura demanded, staring down at her fiercely. "I'm worried about him, Cynthia. I'm terribly worried that he's beginning to compromise his principles."

"Come now," Cynthia said impatiently, "you're not fooling anyone. It's not his principles you're concerned with, it's the fact that you fancy yourself in love with him. Laura, forgive me, but I'm going to speak bluntly. Christopher Warren is a man with no background, no money; in short, a relationship between the two of you is simply out of the question. Now, get hold of yourself, please, and try to act your age."

A swift rage swept over Laura. She *was* acting her age. She was thirty-five years old, not fifty or sixty, like most of her friends. Did Cynthia think that life and all its pleasures were open only to eighteen-year-old debutantes? Laura's existence was far from over; her vitality and emotions were surely as alive as Whitney's—and as demanding. Laura loved Christopher. What did it matter that their backgrounds were poles apart? As Christopher had once told her, all that mattered was what they felt for each other. Propriety didn't matter, her friends' opinions didn't matter. Only she and Christopher and the love they shared mattered. Dear God, why had it taken her so long to see that?

She sat down as abruptly as she had risen. She was pale and slightly breathless from her sudden realization.

"Laura!" said Cynthia worriedly, regretting her harshness. "You look faint. Are you all right?"

"I'm fine," Laura said as a great surge of happiness brought some color to her cheeks. "For the first time in a long time I feel perfectly fine. I want to thank you, Cynthia, for helping me to come to my senses. Much of what you've just said is true. But do you know something? It doesn't matter. I love Christopher Warren; that's the only thing that's important. And before this night is over, I'm going to tell him that I've decided to marry him."

To Christopher's surprise, he found himself enjoying Whitney's debut. He had been watching Laura for most of the evening, her lovely face, her graceful form, and he had been thinking that not one woman present was more beautiful than she. Her gown was perfection, a shimmering silky thing of a blue so pale and subtle it seemed the color of an icy winter lake. Her lips and cheeks shone with a springlike tint of rose; her brown hair was glossy with autumn-russet lights. On her soft, curving breast lay a diamond heart pendant, no more radiant than the summer blue of her eyes.

"Christopher." The soft voice startled him. "Why are you standing here alone?"

He turned from his rapt contemplation of Laura to see Whitney, demure and pretty, smiling up at him. Her gloved hands were clasped before her; her white gown enhanced her youthful loveliness. She looked like a girl who had a secret to share. Christopher readily returned her glowing smile.

"I'm taking a solitary moment to enjoy the festivities," he told her. "This has been a grand night for me. You, too, seem to be enjoying yourself," he added meaningfully.

"Oh, I am!" she said. "I'm so glad you decided to come. But I'm sorry I couldn't have had a waltz with you. Christopher, you must give me a dance."

He laughed and shook his head. "If I had been dancing, I couldn't have watched the pretty picture you made with Ned, leading the cotillion. You looked like the queen of France."

"Do you think so?" She blushed charmingly. "The queen of France?"

"Indeed," he assured her. "And Ned made a

perfect king. What an attractive couple you are!''

Her eyes lost some of their fervor, but Christopher, his perception distorted by the glitter of the evening, didn't notice.

"Christopher," she said, looking down at her clasped hands with what appeared to be a sudden attack of shyness, "I need to talk to you."

He was both touched and amused by her maidenly modesty. He almost said, "I already know what you want to talk about." But he said instead, "What is it? Tell me. I'm bursting with curiosity."

"Not here," she said nervously. "It's private. I need to talk to you alone."

"Really?" he said, his amusement increasing. "It must be a matter of gravest importance. Where shall we go so that we won't be overheard?"

"Come with me," she said in a whisper, taking his hand and leading him out of the ballroom with a stealthy swiftness that brought a bubble of laughter to his throat. They crept out the door like two sneak thieves. When they were standing in the empty hall, Christopher asked, suppressing the laughter, "Where to now?"

"My father's study," she said in a conspiratorial low tone.

Still holding his hand, she led him to a room down the hall at the rear of the house. A small lamp burned atop a carved mahogany desk. It was a handsome room, a man's room with paneled walls and deep leather chairs and a practical drugget rug covering the planked oak floor. Christopher barely glanced at his surroundings;

his attention was wholly on Whitney and on her "secret." But when they were in the room, affording them the privacy on which she had insisted, Whitney released his hand, looked up at him uncertainly, then looked down at the floor, and said nothing.

"Well?" he said, smiling down at her encouragingly. "I'm waiting with baited breath for you to make your announcement."

Whitney raised her head and gave him a puzzled look. "It's not exactly what I'd call an 'announcement.' "

"Very well," he conceded, thoroughly charmed by her innocence. "Whatever it is, tell me. I can no longer contain my curiosity."

"Well, you see," she began haltingly, "I had a talk with my mother this evening before the party started . . ."

"Yes?" he urged.

"And she finally gave us a blessing of sorts."

"I'm delighted to hear that," Christopher said. "But I never had any doubts about her feelings on the subject."

"You didn't?" Whitney stared at him in astonishment.

"Of course not," he said. "I know how your mother feels about Ned."

"Ned? Who's talking about Ned?"

"Why, you are." Christopher frowned. "Aren't you?"

"No. I'm talking about you."

"About me?" he echoed suspiciously. "I don't understand."

"Christopher . . ." She paused, disconcerted,

then went on in a rush, "Christopher, my mother has been telling me for months that she disapproves of our relationship. We had the most dreadful quarrel about it last month; she actually threatened to banish you from the house if you came here tonight. But when we talked tonight, she finally relented. She said she wanted me to be happy. Don't you see what that means? It means she has at last come to terms with the fact that we love each other."

Christopher stared at her, horrified. "That we love each other? God Almighty, Whitney, did you tell her that?"

Whitney quailed beneath his violent gaze. "Why are you looking at me like that? I *had* to tell her, don't you see? She had got it into her head that you were too old for me, but the truth is, she couldn't bear the thought that I've grown up. Christopher," she pleaded, "everything is going to be all right now. We can declare our love openly; my mother approves. You don't have to be afraid anymore. I know that you wouldn't admit you loved me in Bar Harbor because you were worried what my mother might think."

"You foolish child!" He grasped her arms with brutal, hurting hands and shook her so hard that she cried out in fear and pain. "I don't love you! What does it take to make you understand that? Tell me exactly what you said to your mother about me. Did you tell her I love you? Whitney, answer me, or by God, I'll—"

"What the devil's going on in here?"

Christopher released the girl and swung

around toward the sound of that voice. Ned stood at the door, looking hard and suspiciously from Whitney's cowering figure to Christopher's face, pale with rage and startled shock.

"Ned . . ." he said quickly.

"What were you doing?" Ned demanded, striding into the room. "What was all the shouting about? And why were you manhandling Whitney?"

Ned's hands were clenched into fists at his sides. Whitney, seeing this, stepped quickly between the two men and took firm hold of Ned's arm. "Ned, it was nothing," she placated. "We were talking, that's all."

"If you please, Whitney," Ned said curtly. "I was speaking to Christopher."

Christopher stared at him in silence, his mind working furiously. Despite his turmoil he couldn't help noticing the protective manner in which Whitney held on to Ned. It was screamingly obvious to Christopher that Ned and Ned alone was the man she loved. Couldn't she see it, that reckless girl? Whatever Whitney thought she felt for Christopher was an illusion, a figment of her childish imagination. And because of her foolish fancy, Christopher was standing here, in the impossible position of having to explain the unexplainable to Ned.

"I'm waiting, Christopher," Ned said heavily. "Will you kindly tell me what you were doing when I came in?"

"Ned, please," Whitney implored, plucking at his sleeve. "It's nothing of importance. Let's go back to the ballroom." She tugged at his arm, but he stood there like a stone.

"Christopher," he said in a deadly low voice, "I'm not leaving this room until I have a full explanation of your actions. You've been behaving strangely ever since you returned from Bar Harbor. If Whitney is somehow at the bottom of this, you'd better tell me right now what it's all about."

"Ned, listen," Christopher tried to explain, "it's nothing that you should be worried about. Whitney and I had a misunderstanding, that's all. It's straightened out now, isn't it, Whitney? Come along, Ned." Christopher took him by the arm. "Let's rejoin the other guests."

Ned drew back from Christopher's touch as if scorched. "I don't know what kind of fool you take me for, Christopher, but no one's going anywhere until you've told me the truth." He turned to Whitney, who was staring at him with fear-filled eyes. "Whitney, what happened here? Did Christopher . . . did he try to take advantage of you?"

"No, no!" the girl cried.

"Don't be afraid, Whitney," Ned said tensely. "If he's done anything to you, you're not in the wrong; it's not your fault. Did he approach you at all in a physical way?"

"Ned, for the love of God—" Christopher began.

"Shut your mouth, Christopher!" Ned hissed. Then, his tone softening: "Whitney, please, dear. You can tell me, you can trust me."

"No!" she cried again. "Stop it, Ned! Don't
make it ugly. It wasn't like that at all. Christopher did kiss me, but it didn't happen here. It
was in Bar Harbor. I've been meaning to tell you
about it—you had to know it sometime—but I
didn't want to hurt or upset you."

"Jesus," Christopher whispered, looking
wretchedly toward Ned.

Ned turned to him, his face red with rage.
"You kissed her?" he uttered. "You *kissed* her?"

"Ned," Christopher said, spreading out his
hands in a gesture of appeal. "Ned, I . . ."

Ned lashed out with a closed fist and struck
Christopher's jaw hard. Christopher reeled back
toward the desk, his head swimming. His hip
struck the edge of the desk with a painful jar.
Dimly he heard Whitney cry out, then he heard
another voice, a woman's voice. His vision
cleared. Stricken with panic, he saw Laura enter
the room. Her eyes swept over the scene: Whitney's trembling form; Ned's fists, still clenched;
the bruise beginning to form on Christopher's
jaw. Peremptorily she said, "What's the meaning of this? Ned, did you strike Christopher?"

"Yes, I struck him," Ned said, moving menacingly toward Christopher. "And by heaven, I
think I'll kill him."

"Ned!" Laura commanded. "Don't take another step. Look at me. Tell me what happened."

Ned stopped in his tracks and swung his murderous gaze toward Laura. "Ask *him* what happened. Ask him where he got the gall to make
advances toward your daughter when he's
known for a year I wanted to marry her."

Christopher froze as Laura drew a sharp breath and turned a stunned face to his. The room rang with silence. In her eyes he saw a torrent of conflicting emotions: shock, reproach, condemnation, and love. The last must have surmounted the rest, for she finally said quietly, "You're surely mistaken, Ned. Christopher would never do anything like that."

"Oh, no?" Ned said hotly. "Ask Whitney if you won't believe me. She's the one who told me that he kissed her."

Laura shook her head impatiently and turned to her daughter. "Whitney, where will this end?" she demanded. "What did you hope to gain by telling such a lie?"

"Mama, it's not a lie," the girl said miserably. "Christopher did kiss me. And I know for a fact he loves me, but he won't admit it because he's afraid of how you'll react. He saw how angry you got with Ned at my commencement. He probably thinks you'd do the same thing or worse if he were to tell you how he feels about me."

"Whitney," Laura sighed, "it is you who have fabricated an entire fantasy in your mind. Christopher doesn't love you. Look how you've hurt him . . ." Laura gestured toward Christopher, who stared at her in dazed silence. Why was she defending him, now of all times, when he was thoroughly guilty of the charges against him?

"And look how you've hurt Ned," she went on, "with your improbable tales."

"Mama—"

"Whitney," she said sternly, "we won't discuss it any further. You've done enough mischief for one night." She looked significantly at Christopher's bruised jaw, then she directed her attention to Ned, who was looking at Whitney in questioning confusion. "Ned," Laura said, "I think you owe your friend an apology."

Ned hesitated, bewildered, obviously wondering why Whitney should have lied about such a thing. And yet, if Laura was so convinced of Christopher's innocence . . .

"Christopher, I'm sorry," Ned mumbled. "I truly am."

Christopher tried to speak and failed. With all his heart he wanted to tell Ned, "Don't apologize. You had every right in the world to hit me. I did kiss Whitney; I did much worse than kiss her." But if he said that, if he admitted his guilt in the face of Laura's trust, he would destroy once and for all any chance of ever having her.

Laura said, interrupting his anguished thoughts, "Ned, would you escort Whitney back to the ballroom? I'd like a word with Christopher before we join you."

"Yes, of course, Laura." Ned went at once to Whitney, apparently anxious to flee the scene of his embarrassment. He took her arm; for a moment she did not move. Her dark gaze turned from Christopher to the woman who had championed him. Then, in stiff, pale-faced silence, she accompanied Ned from the room.

When they were alone, Laura said softly to Christopher, "This was all my fault."

"Your fault?" His voice was strained. "How?"

She shook her head ruefully. "A friend gave me some bad advice, and I was foolish enough to take it. I should have relied on my own judgment rather than seeking help from someone outside the circumstances."

Christopher said, "I don't know what you mean." Nor did he care. This dream of an evening was turning into a nightmare. As much as he didn't want to, he had to tell Laura that Whitney had spoken the truth. He could not sustain a lie; it would catch up to him in the end. It was better, he decided bitterly, that Laura should think him a scoundrel rather than a coward who hadn't the courage to own up to his actions.

But before he could speak, Laura said, "I've known for some time how Whitney feels about you. I ought to have told you about it, warned you, but instead I told a friend, who suggested that I ignore the situation." Laura gave a short laugh. "Ignore the situation. What dangerous advice!"

She moved toward him with a soft rustle of silk. The diamond pendant at her breast caught the light and threw back a blinding brilliance into Christopher's eyes. She stopped just short of touching him, but the effect on him was the same as if she were pressing full length against him.

"Cynthia gave me other advice," Laura went on, "which I choose now to disregard."

"What advice?" he asked blankly, distracted by her nearness.

"She suggested," Laura said, "that I put you

out of my thoughts. But I find it impossible to follow that suggestion. You see, I love you so much that to live my life without you would be no life at all. You were right, Christopher, and I was hopelessly wrong. All that matters is you and me and how we feel about each other. If you still want to marry me, I'd be happy and proud to be your wife."

At first her admission did not penetrate his consciousness. His focus was solely on confessing his sin. But then, suddenly, keenly, her words became clear to him. A great tide of incredulous joy swept all else from his mind.

"Are you serious?" he gasped.

She nodded and smiled.

"Laura!" He could not contain his elation. His arms went hard around her and he crushed her close to him in a suffocating embrace. "Laura, my God, do you know how much I've longed to hear you say that?"

"Christopher, please," she laughed, "I can't breathe!"

He released her at once but still held fast to her arms. "You're certain?" he said intently. "You won't change your mind?"

"I'm certain," she assured him. She reached up to kiss his mouth, then twined her arms about his neck and laid her head against his chest. "What a fool I've been," she said remorsefully. "All these months I've been agonizing over what to do, when the simple solution to my problem was to marry you."

He didn't answer, he couldn't speak. He

would have thought he was dreaming were he not holding the living proof of his dreams in his arms.

"I've caused you no end of needless suffering," Laura went on, castigating herself. "I should have listened to you from the start, but I was too stubborn, too afraid."

"It doesn't matter," he said, his arms tightening possessively around her. "All that matters now is that we'll finally be together." He kissed her brow and cheeks in an excess of emotion. "Laura, this couldn't have happened at a better time. I'm currently working on an important commission, and more offers have come my way than I can handle. You'll never have to be ashamed to be my wife. I'll be as wealthy and successful as any of your friends."

Laura drew back a bit in his embrace and looked up at him, surprised. "Christopher, that was never a consideration. I could never be ashamed of you."

He forbore to contradict her; he was too happy now to debate the issue. The thought of Laura marrying a pauper, however, brought a sardonic smile to his lips. "Of course it wasn't," he said. "I just wanted you to know that your faith in my work has been justified."

A fine line creased her brow. "Christopher, about your work . . ." She moved reluctantly out of his arms, and her gaze fell momentarily on her husband's empty chair. "I heard something tonight that disturbed me."

"What did you hear?"

"Cynthia told me about the MacKenzie house and George Winston's apartments. Why are you doing such designs?"

"Need you ask?" he frowned. "I had two choices in regard to my career. I could either design to please my clients, and succeed; or I could design to please myself, and starve to death."

"That's not true," she said at once. "Look at the Tyler house."

Christopher gestured impatiently. "That was all your doing, and don't deny it. You know as well as I do what people want. If I design to my own taste, I'll never win a commission. Face facts, Laura. If I want to get anywhere with my career, my designs will have to be more vulgar and ostentatious than anyone else's."

"No," she said pleadingly. "That's simply not true. Christopher, please don't compromise your principles. I couldn't bear it if you—"

"Forget my work," he stopped her, pulling her into his arms. "This is a night for celebration, not debate. Name the wedding day; let's make plans."

But before she could respond, his mouth covered hers, and he gave himself up to the glory of the moment. He forgot about his work, he forgot about his principles; he even forgot that he had intended to tell her what he had done to her daughter in Bar Harbor. This perfect woman, who had breathed life into his every impossible dream, had consented to be his wife. That was all that mattered, that and the feel of her body against his, the fragrance of her skin, and the warmth of her lips yielding submissively to his.

As he held her close and kissed her, he felt again that blessed completion, the sense of being whole and entire, at one with the universe and with the woman he loved. He was no longer alone; he belonged to someone, and someone belonged to him. The feeling warmed him, stimulated him, gave his passion new dimensions. His trembling arms crushed the breath from Laura's lungs. He swayed on his feet as if he were standing on the platform of a runaway train, careering blindly through the night under a black, starless sky toward an unknown destination that both frightened and excited him. His emotions were so heightened that he could have taken her, right there, fully clothed, standing up. He didn't, of course; it wouldn't have been proper. Besides, he had years and years ahead of him to make love to her.

Chapter Fifteen

✦ ✦ ✦ ✦

NEVER IN HER life had Laura made so impulsive a decision, and never before had she been so absolutely convinced of the wisdom of her choice. She thought it a curious irony that she had made that decision on the night of Whitney's debut. As Whitney had emerged from the protective

shell of childhood, likewise Laura had shed her
chrysalis of indecision and fear. The occasion,
Laura thought in wonderment, had indeed been
a *rite de passage*, for both mother and daughter.

She woke the next morning with a smile on
her lips. As she lay drowsily beneath the fluffy
quilt, she watched the dancing pattern of light
and shadow that played on the ceiling and listened to the cheerful clanging of the central heating system as it pushed welcome warmth
through the pipes and radiators. Soon, she
thought dreamily, she would be sharing this bed
with the man she loved. She would no longer be
a woman alone, a husbandless wife living a
shadowy half life. She would be part of a whole
again; her existence would have meaning. As
she had shared all with Steven, she would likewise share all with Christopher. Her life would
not change, it would merely continue on its earlier predestined path. How sweetly fortuitous
that the man she now loved embodied all she
had loved in her youth.

A tap at the door brought her back to reality.

"Yes?" she called. "Who is it?"

"It's Rachel, madam," answered her maid.
"It's after ten. Will you be rising now?"

Laura flung back the covers and leaped out of
bed. After ten? She'd slept most of the morning
away!

"Yes, come in, Rachel." Laura drew on a
wrapper as the maid entered. "Why didn't you
wake me sooner?"

"Madam, I knocked at seven and eight, and

then again at nine. You must have been dead
asleep, for I got no response."

Rachel laid the heavy breakfast tray on a table
under the window, then smoothed the front of
the white apron that covered her crisp gray uniform. She was a comely brunette, the same age
as Laura, who had been with her since her marriage to Steven. Their relationship was a close
one, though tempered by the barrier of class
distinction. Laura would have loved to tell Rachel of her coming marriage, but she had cautioned Christopher last night that neither of
them should tell anyone until they had made
definite plans.

Rachel said as she poured Laura's coffee, "I
looked in on the tyke earlier. She was up and
dressed and ready to go out. I asked her where
she was bound, but she wouldn't say. No doubt
she's off to the MacKenzies' to chat about the
party with Miss Marcella."

Laura sat down at the table with a slight
frown. She had wanted to talk to Whitney this
morning. Last night, after the guests had gone,
the girl had vanished upstairs, and when Laura
knocked at her bedroom door, there had been no
answer. Whitney was very probably angry, but
that couldn't be helped. She must understand—
and she must understand it well—that her fan-
ciful fabrications were both dangerous and cruel.

Imagine Whitney's saying that Christopher
had kissed her. What utter nonsense! What was
wrong with the younger generation? Had they
no scruples, no sense of decency? Didn't Whit-

ney realize that such an unconscionable state-
ment might have created an even greater
calamity than it had? As it was, it had caused
Ned to lash out violently against his best friend.
Laura shuddered involuntarily as she pictured
the livid bruise on Christopher's jaw. She had
kissed the injury last night and had said to him
penitently, "I blame myself for this." Christopher, oddly, had quickly turned his face away.
"Don't," he had muttered. "It's nobody's fault
but my own."

What a curious thing to say. How, Laura wondered now, could Christopher blame himself
when he was an innocent victim of a foolish
girl's lie?

She shuddered again as an underlying uneasiness threw a pall upon her earlier happiness.

"Are you cold, madam?" Rachel asked. "Shall
I stir up the fire?"

"No," Laura said, her soft mouth set deci-
sively. "Just draw my bath, Rachel, and lay out
my heliotrope wool. I think I, too, will pay a call
on the MacKenzies."

When she was ready to leave, she went downstairs and was met by Thompson at the foot of
the staircase just as the hall clock struck twelve.

"I'll be back at four, Thompson," she informed
him, pulling on her doeskin gloves. "If Dr. Sheridan should stop by, ask him to stay for tea."

"Very good, madam." Thompson drew an envelope from his inside coat pocket. "Mrs. Sheridan, Miss Whitney asked me to give this to you

at the stroke of noon. She was most insistent about the time."

Laura smiled as she took the envelope. "Thank you, Thompson. Children *must* have their little intrigues, mustn't they?"

"Yes indeed, madam." He returned her smile. "Will there be anything else?"

"Thank you, no," she dismissed him. And as he left, she went to the hall table, picked up the paper knife, and slit open the envelope.

The salutation disconcerted her.

Dear Mother, it read.

Never, *never*, had Whitney called Laura Mother.

With a fast-beating heart she forced herself to read the rest.

It became clear to me last night, Whitney had written, *that you and I can no longer live peaceably under the same roof. You simply refuse to acknowledge that my childhood is behind me. But worse, you publicly impugned my honesty—and for that I cannot forgive you. I've decided to lease an apartment in town. Please don't try to find me or to communicate with me. I have nothing whatever to say to you, and I don't wish to hear anything you might have to say to me.*

The letter was signed, *W. Sheridan*, as to leave no doubt in Laura's mind that Whitney was declaring her independence from parental tyranny.

To Laura's mild surprise she was not as upset as she might have been under the circumstances. She *was* annoyed, though. She was getting rather tired of Whitney's outbursts of rebellious temper. If the girl insisted on considering herself an adult, she ought to first learn to think and act like one.

With an irritated sigh Laura stripped off her gloves, picked up the telephone, and gave Avery's number to Central. His butler answered and informed Laura that he was not at home.

"When do you expect him, Briggs?"

"I couldn't say, Mrs. Sheridan. He left no word as to the hour of his return."

"Briggs," Laura said, "my daughter isn't there, by any chance, is she?"

"Why, no, madam. Should I expect her?"

"No . . . no," she said. "Tell Dr. Sheridan to telephone me the instant he returns home."

She bade Briggs good-bye and hung up the telephone. Her annoyance at Whitney was fast being displaced by an active concern. Where was she? Laura had half suspected that she'd gone running to her uncle as she often did when her desires were thwarted by her mother. If she wasn't with Avery, where in heaven's name was she?

Her concern increasing, Laura picked up the telephone again and tried the MacKenzies. But when she spoke to Marcella, obliquely seeking to ascertain Whitney's whereabouts, the girl only chattered cheerfully about the party, convincing Laura that she knew nothing.

She next considered trying Ned, but quickly vetoed the idea. Ned would be frantic if he learned Whitney had left home. Laura felt he'd had enough of a nerve-shattering experience last night. To add to his guilt—for Laura was sure he'd blame himself—was out of the question.

She sat down on the hall chair and thought for

a moment. Where would she go if she were an eighteen-year-old girl who had just suffered a keen disappointment? Laura was positive that Whitney's threat of permanently leaving home was that: a threat. What did Whitney know of leasing an apartment, of living on her own without a half dozen servants to attend to her every need? Laura's annoyance returned, stronger than before. That thoughtless child! The moment she came home, Laura intended to have a serious talk with her. Whitney's insolent behavior could no longer be permitted. And Laura intended to tell her so in no uncertain terms.

But Whitney didn't come home. The day dragged, the hours crawled. Twice more Laura telephoned Avery, and each time she was told by Briggs that Dr. Sheridan had not yet returned. Exceedingly worried now, she thought of telephoning Christopher, but, as with Ned, she changed her mind. Christopher, like Ned, would surely hold himself responsible for Whitney's leaving. Why burden him with a problem that was none of his doing?

She dined at eight, barely tasting the tempting fare. Just as the last course was being served, Thompson informed her that Avery was on the telephone. Laura leaped from her chair and made for the hall with all haste.

"Avery!" she said without greeting. "Where have you been? I've been trying to reach you all day."

"I've been at the hospital," he said. "Mrs.

Standish took a turn for the worse, and I had to—"

"Whitney's gone," Laura interrupted him, not hearing his explanation. "She left early this morning, and I don't know where she is."

Her words were tinged with panic. Her breathing, rapid and shallow, was audible over the wire. Avery said at once, "What do you mean she's gone? Laura, calm down. Start at the beginning."

His voice, commanding but soothing, brought a halt to her racing thoughts. With a measure of composure she related the events leading up to her daughter's disappearance.

For a time Avery said nothing. Laura pictured his poet's face, imagined his dreamy gray eyes wide with worry and alarm. At last he asked, "Are you so certain Whitney lied? I find it difficult to believe that she would invent such a tale. What did Mr. Warren say to the charge?"

"I wouldn't insult him by questioning him!" Laura exclaimed. "I know Christopher Warren. He's honorable and good. He would never dream of touching Whitney. Avery, you have no idea what I've been going through these past months. Whitney has been impossible. When she hasn't been moody and withdrawn, she's been brazenly rude and rebellious. I don't know her anymore. She's a stranger, a stranger—"

Laura's voice trembled. She drew a deep breath to control herself. "Avery, you must help me find her. Who knows what will happen to her, alone out there in the city?"

"Of course I'll help," Avery said, his low, unruffled voice allaying the worst of Laura's fears. "I'll go around to as many apartment buildings as I can tonight, and if I don't find her, I'll contact the Pinkerton Agency in the morning."

"The Pinkerton Agency? Oh, Avery . . ."

"Laura, don't worry. Their investigations are highly confidential. You needn't fear that the newspapers will get hold of the story."

"Avery, I'm not worried about that. It's just . . . a detective agency! Dear God," she said brokenly. "If Steven were alive—"

"Laura, stop it," Avery said. "I know what you're thinking: If Steven were alive, he'd blame you for what Whitney's done. Well, that's simply not true. Now get hold of yourself. Self-condemnation is not going to solve anything."

Again his untroubled voice acted as a balm on Laura's overwrought nerves. Fleetingly it occurred to her that at the first sign of trouble, she had instinctively turned to Avery for help—instead of to the man she had promised to marry. Despite her distress over her daughter, she clearly recognized the incongruity of her action. With a vague sense of guilt she refused to confront, she deliberately pushed the thought from her mind.

"Yes, you're right," she agreed, grateful for his understanding. "Avery, do what you think best and let me know the moment you hear anything."

"I will," he promised her. "And Laura," he added, "if I were you, I'd make it my business to ask Mr. Warren about his behavior with Whitney."

"Absolutely not!" she burst out. "Avery, I told you before: I won't insult Christopher by questioning him."

"That's odd," Avery said. "You thought nothing of insulting Whitney by calling her a liar."

His words left her defenseless; she could think of no reply. When it became evident that she wasn't going to answer, Avery bade her a quiet good-bye and hung up the telephone.

During the first few days after Whitney left home, Laura, numb with shock, felt little except worry and an occasional wave of anger. But as the days turned into weeks and the reports from the Pinkerton Agency continued to be negative, the shock wore off, paving the path for the most curious of sensations. Laura's daughter had left home—not for school, not for marriage, not for a summer's vacation. Whitney had severed herself from her mother as violently and as irrevocably as the birth process tears infant from womb.

The void Laura felt now was not unlike that brutal disengagement. She felt dazed, depleted, an empty vessel from which all of life's fluids had been drained. Her child, the flesh of her flesh, was no longer a part of her. Whitney had willfully separated herself from the protective womb of her mother's love.

To Laura, who had been an obedient daughter and devoted wife, such an action was incomprehensible. One did not sever one's self from one's roots, no matter the provocation. Despite her despair, despite Avery's charge, she refused to blame herself for Whitney's defection. Whitney *had* lied about Christopher; her own guilt had caused her to leave home. Laura, groping blindly for equilibrium in a world of spinning upheaval, clung to that belief.

The man from the Pinkerton Agency was not at all what Laura had expected. He looked to be in his late thirties, well dressed, soft-spoken, his dark hair neatly groomed, his brown eyes alert and intelligent. His name was Dennis Tierney. Laura had spoken to him many times on the telephone following Whitney's disappearance. When he finally came to the house, a month to the day after Whitney's debut, it was almost like receiving an old family friend.

"Good morning, Mrs. Sheridan," he returned her greeting after Thompson had shown him into the downstairs sitting room. "May I take the liberty of saying that I'm happy to meet you after speaking to you so often on the telephone."

He knew his manners. He did not extend his hand until Laura had extended hers. He shook her hand briefly but firmly, bowing as he did so. His attire was correct and subdued; he smelled pleasantly of starch and shaving soap. Laura was curiously soothed by his immaculate aspect.

She bade him sit down and sat opposite him on the matching Hepplewhite chair in front of the fireplace. He placed on his knees a leather briefcase, from which he extracted a list of names and addresses. Laura watched him and waited in numb, captive silence. It was inconceivable to

her that she should be sitting here with this
nice-looking gentleman, waiting for him to tell
her that he couldn't locate her daughter.

"As you know, Mrs. Sheridan," be began in
his perfectly modulated voice, "I've made inquiries at every major apartment house in the
city, and in the past week and a half I've even
tried . . . the less respectable places." He handed
her the list, which she glanced at and handed
back to him. Returning the list to his briefcase,
Tierney continued, "It occurred to me that your
daughter might not be using her own name, so
I showed the people I spoke to the photograph
your brother-in-law gave me, but no one anywhere has admitted to seeing her."

Laura said nothing; her throat felt hot and dry.
This couldn't be happening to her—not to her
and Whitney. This was something that happened to . . . to other people.

"That's not proof positive," Tierney said further, "that no one has seen her. Your daughter
was very clever and very thorough, Mrs. Sheridan. The morning she left here, she went to the
bank and withdrew a great deal of money. She
knew there might be a problem, so she took the
precaution of writing a letter of approval and
signing your name to it."

"That doesn't matter," Laura said faintly.
"The money is hers, Mr. Tierney. It's not as if
she had stolen it."

"I realize that, Mrs. Sheridan. I'm merely trying to point out that this was not an impulsive
action on your daughter's part. She knew exactly
what she was doing. I wouldn't be surprised if

she *is* at one of the apartment houses I've been
to. I think the reason I haven't found her is that
she's bought someone's silence."

"Bought?" Laura echoed. "Do you mean she
paid someone to say he hadn't seen her? But
how could anyone do that? Whitney's only a
child. Didn't that person realize he had a responsibility to—"

"Forgive me, Mrs. Sheridan," Tierney said
softly. "But some people forget responsibility in
the face of hard cash."

"Mr. Tierney," she said distractedly, "if that's
the case, how on earth will you ever find my
daughter?"

"It will be difficult," he allowed, "but not impossible. Mrs. Sheridan, have you gone through
your daughter's things, as I suggested?"

"Yes." Laura pulled a handkerchief from her
sleeve and began to pleat and unpleat it on her
lap. What a horrible experience that had been,
like ferreting through the effects of a loved one
who had died. "I found nothing helpful, Mr.
Tierney."

"Have you talked to her friends?"

"To some of them, yes." But to Christopher
and to Ned she had said nothing. As far as they
knew, Whitney was in Palm Beach, vacationing.
Laura had been unable to tell either of them a
truth that might only hurt them both.

"Mrs. Sheridan," Tierney said tactfully, "I can
well understand why you'd hesitate to talk to
certain people about what's happened. But
you'd be surprised at how much information
you can gather from the most unexpected

sources. If you find it too distressing to do so,
may I have your permission to question anyone
who knows your daughter?"

"No," she said at once, thinking of Christopher and Ned. "I'd rather you didn't."

Her refusal seemed neither to surprise nor an-
noy him. "Very well," he said pleasantly.
"That's your decision to make." He latched his
briefcase and rose. "Good day, Mrs. Sheridan."

"Good day?" she repeated blankly. "You're
not . . . ? You haven't given up on the case?"

"Certainly not," he said. "A Pinkerton never
gives up. Moreover, I have a few tricks up my
sleeve—if you'll pardon the vulgarity."

"What sort of tricks?" Laura asked hopefully.

"I can't tell you that, Mrs. Sheridan. You see,"
he added with a smile designed to encourage
her, "they're tricks of the trade, and I've sworn
a solemn oath never to reveal them."

Tierney's tricks, whatever they were, brought
no immediate results. Weeks passed with no
word of Whitney's whereabouts. Laura began to
despair of ever finding her. When Avery suggested calling the police in on the matter, Laura
would have none of it. "Have them hunt for my
daughter like a common criminal? Never. I
couldn't bear it. I'll continue to rely on Mr. Tierney."

In the meantime she tried to keep herself occupied. She had almost completed the decoration of the two Gramercy Park houses and she
had promised the MacKenzies that she would

decorate their summer house when it was completed. Malcolm had shown her the plans; she found it difficult to believe that Christopher had done the design. The house reeked of medieval feudalism; it had circular bedchambers, winding staircases, small embrasured windows, and gloomy, narrow reception rooms with vaulted ceilings and rough stone walls. Laura was appalled; Malcolm could not have been more pleased with it.

Laura was also disappointed in Christopher's design for the Winston Court Apartments. Ironically, everyone she knew was singing its praises. Even the newspapers hailed it and were running weekly features on the progress of this "architectural coup."

"George Winston," the *Journal* expounded, "New York's boy genius of real estate, has engaged the services of a new architect, Christopher Warren, to design his Winston Court Apartments, the ground-breaking to take place late this summer. As one can see from the sketches on these pages, Mr. Warren has a true feeling for all that is the spirit of this city. This mighty structure will rise like the Colossus over Rhodes. Its spectacular facade will pay homage to the New York natives who will inhabit its gilded rooms. Mr. Warren is to be congratulated; nay, he is to be lauded! His religious adherence to Gothic design will ensure an honored place for him in the annals of architectural excellence."

Laura, studying the sketches, could hardly believe her eyes. Had Christopher actually designed this whimsical confection? It looked, she thought painfully, like the work of a man who had compromised every last one of his ideals.

Laura had seen little of Christopher since the night of Whitney's debut. It was difficult to speak to him without thinking constantly of Whitney. It was impossible for her to share his unbridled happiness when her heart was breaking over her daughter. So she put off his constant urgings to set a wedding date and she explained her reluctance to see him as often as she would have liked by citing the fact that they were both so busy with their work.

"That's nonsense," he said to her one day in March over the telephone. "I happen to know that you've completed your work on Gramercy Park and that you don't start on the MacKenzie house for another few months. Laura, I insist on seeing you tonight. I've got tickets for the opera. It's Donizetti, your favorite. *Lucia di Lammermoor*. I won't take no for an answer."

Laura's heart throbbed with love and gratitude at his unexpected words. She knew how much he disliked the social scene, yet he had arranged a night at the opera because he remembered her fondness for Donizetti. He was ignoring his own discomfort to please her. And Laura, in the past few weeks, had done exactly the opposite.

She went with him, of course; she could refuse him no longer. Very well, Whitney had left home, and Laura was desperately worried about her; but the choice had been Whitney's, no one else's. Laura's responsibility now lay with the man she had promised to marry.

She dressed with great care that evening. She wanted to look especially lovely for Christopher. Her dress was a vision of midnight blue satin with a daring low bodice, completely unadorned. Her hair, freshly washed, was a fragrant crown above the regal contours of her face. In her ears she wore diamond starbursts; on her snowy breast a shower of diamond stars lent a shimmering luster to the elegant night sky of her gown.

Her effort was successful, for when Christopher called for her, broodingly handsome in his excellent evening clothes, he could not take his eyes from her. When he escorted her to the carriage he had engaged for the evening, he kept a possessively firm hold on her arm. When they were on their way to the opera house, he said with a quiet intensity, "You're so beautiful it makes me ache. You cause me more pain by being with me than you do when we're apart."

His implication was clear; he was obliquely reproaching her for keeping distance between them. Laura was strongly tempted to confess the circumstances that had kept her from him, but she had promised herself she would talk of nothing unpleasant this night.

And yet, as they approached Thirty-ninth Street, she said without thinking, "Is everything all right between you and Ned? There haven't been any repercussions because of—?"

"No, none," he replied, too quickly, too easily. "Everything's fine."

"Are you sure?" she asked, dubious.

"Yes, I'm sure."

His voice now had an edge to it; he stared out the window. The grim set of his mouth convinced Laura that everything was far from all right.

"Christopher," she said, compelled to pursue what she would prefer to put from her mind, "be honest with me. Your friendship with Ned is intact, isn't it? He apologized for striking you. Please don't hold a grudge against him."

Christopher turned to face her, a curious, hard look in his eyes. "If I did bear him a grudge," he said deliberately, "that wouldn't be playing the game, would it?"

"What do you mean?" she asked, disconcerted by his stony gaze.

Christopher said coldly, "This didn't occur to me until days after Ned struck me. Despite our years of friendship he believed what Whitney said without stopping to ask me whether I was guilty or not. He took Whitney at her word because she's a member of his class. I can only conclude then that because I'm an orphan—a bastard—Ned thinks I am lying."

His profanity shocked Laura less than the probable truth of his suspicion. Before she had a chance to defend Ned, Christopher went on: "Understand me, Laura; whether or not I'm guilty is not at issue here. The heart of the matter is this: If Whitney had accused one of her moneyed peers of an impropriety, would Ned have struck first and asked questions later?"

"Christopher—"

"In fact," he continued, "I wonder if you've been avoiding me because you're starting to have doubts of your own. Or perhaps," he said rigidly, "you're simply beginning to regret your decision to marry me."

Just then the carriage stopped in front of the opera house, and their conversation ceased. The coachman sprang down from the box and pulled open the door, saving Laura the necessity of responding immediately to Christopher's charge.

As they joined the crowd entering the lobby, she took his arm, which felt like stone beneath her hand. "Please," she whispered, looking up at his unyielding face. "I don't regret my decision to marry you. I'll explain everything to you after the opera."

He stopped dead in his tracks and stared down at her. "Is this your way of telling me that it's over between us?"

"No!" she said at once. "It's not that at all. Nothing in this world is going to stop me from marrying you."

Lucia di Lammermoor was gloriously sad. The work was an adaptation of Sir Walter Scott's *Bride of Lammermoor*, recounting the ill-fated love of Lucy Ashton for Edgar of Ravenswood. As always, with Donizetti's operas, Laura found herself completely captivated by the primitive passion of the music. When the lovers secretly plighted their troth, Laura, with a lump in her throat, looked over at Christopher and silently renewed her own pledge. In the mad scene, when Lucia hallucinated about the marriage that would never take place, Laura reached for Christopher's hand and held on to it tightly while tears blurred her eyes and traced a trail down her cheeks.

After the final curtain fell and the house lights went on, Laura dabbed at her eyes with a pretty fluff of cambric. Christopher said dryly, "I see you enjoyed yourself."

"Yes, wasn't it wonderful?" she said with a plaintive catch in her voice.

He rose and took her arm. "I would hardly call unrequited love 'wonderful,' Laura. To be perfectly frank, I don't much like opera. The lovers are rarely united, and invariably one or both of them dies."

Laura laughed as they made their way up the aisle. The gay babble of the surrounding crowd buoyed her spirits. "You miss the point, Christopher. Grand opera is supposed to be sad. That's the secret of its appeal."

"Then you'll have to forgive my plebeian aversion to it," he said shortly. "I see nothing appealing about heartbreak and death."

Laura said nothing; she simply slipped her arm through his as they followed the throng into the crowded lobby. It was her fault he was acting this way. She felt fully responsible for making him conscious of class distinction. If she had agreed to marry him at the outset, he would not now be so embittered about the differences between them. And if she had married him months ago, as he had wished, her daughter would be home now, where she belonged.

When they were seated in the carriage, traveling down Broadway, Christopher said, watching her, "I've engaged a table at the Beer Garden. I thought it would be amusing to follow an evening of Italian tragedy with an hour of German *Frivolität*."

The irony in his tone put Laura on the alert. His words were vaguely familiar. She had heard them before, spoken differently by someone else. She thought for a moment, then, with a jolt, she remembered. Jeremy Tyler had made that same suggestion on the night Christopher dined at her house. She remembered it clearly now: the discussion of opera; Christopher's careful replies; the Tylers and herself in casual dress; Christopher in borrowed evening clothes, probably aware that his attempt to conform had merely alienated him more from the company he sought to emulate.

With a sigh that was almost a sob she wound her arms about his neck. "I love you," she whispered fervently. "I love you because you're who you are. If you had been born wealthy and privileged, if you had attended the best schools, if you belonged to the most exclusive clubs, you would be different, another man. I would not love you as I do now."

She felt his arms tighten around her; she felt his love, his desperate need for her. "If I were all those things," he said somberly, "you would love me more. You would have married me before now; you would not have made me wait."

"Christopher . . ." She drew back in his embrace and faced the indictment in his gaze. "My hesitancy to set a wedding date has nothing to

do with you. I should have told you this immediately. I didn't realize you would misunder-
stand my motives. You see, the day after her
debut Whitney left home. I've not seen or heard
from her since. *That* is the only reason I've put
off marrying you."

"Whitney's left home?" Christopher frowned
and released her. "What are you talking about?
You told me she was in Palm Beach."

"I had to explain her absence somehow,"
Laura said. "I didn't want everyone to know that
she had . . . run off."

"But why did she leave?"

Laura paused, reluctant even to touch upon
Whitney's inexcusable accusation. "We've been
having problems for some time," she evaded.
"Whitney may have felt that the only way to
solve them was to run away from them."

"What problems?" Christopher pursued. "Did
they have anything to do with me? Did Whitney
say—?"

"No," Laura stopped him. "She did not repeat
that reprehensible lie. We never talked after that
night. She left early the next morning without
saying a word to me."

"Laura . . ." He was watching her closely, an
odd, restrained look in his eyes. "I think we had
better discuss what Whitney said that night."

"No," she said adamantly. "To discuss it
would give it an importance it doesn't merit. Just
to think of what she said makes my blood boil."

"Laura—"

"I said no, Christopher. I doubted you once,

with almost disastrous results. I'll never do that again as long as I live."

He looked out the window and was silent for a time. Laura watched his moody profile, outlined darkly against the glare of the gaslights that lit the quiet streets. She knew he was blaming himself; this was exactly what she had wanted to avoid. She wished now that she had kept silent, especially when he said, his eyes still averted from hers, "Why didn't you tell me that she'd left home? Why couldn't you have confided in me?"

"I'm sorry," she said sincerely, realizing the insult of her omission. "I shouldn't have lied about her whereabouts. But, Christopher . . ." She paused remorsefully and lowered her gaze. "Sometimes lies are necessary. Sometimes they serve to spare a loved one pain. You do understand, don't you?"

He said nothing for a moment, then quietly he asked, "Tell me, Laura, did you also spare your brother-in-law the pain of the truth?"

She looked up at him abruptly. "What do you mean?"

"Let's stop fencing with each other, shall we?" His tone was hard. "You didn't tell me Whitney left home, but I'm willing to wager my life that your brother-in-law knows it."

"Christopher—"

"You're surely aware," he said, driving on, "that it's been almost two months since you agreed to marry me, but you haven't told anyone and you haven't set a wedding date. Was it a whim that made you agree to marry me that night? Because it's crystal clear to me that you have no intention of going through with it."

"You're being unreasonable," she snapped, stung by his charges. "My daughter has left home, Christopher. I don't know where she is. You haven't the vaguest idea what I've been going through these past months."

"No, I haven't," he said deliberately, "because you so graciously decided to 'spare me the pain' of knowing Whitney left home."

"I admitted I was wrong," she shot back, "but now that you know the truth, you can't really expect me to plan a wedding under those circumstances."

"And if she never comes back," he pressed her, "does that mean that there'll never be a wedding?"

"Yes! No!" she burst out, feeling cornered and trapped. "What's wrong with you? How can you do this to me at a time like this? Have you no feelings for anyone but yourself? Perhaps we should just forget about marrying for the time being. In fact, perhaps it would be wise to spend some time apart for a while."

The silence that greeted her outburst was a din in her ears. She glared at him furiously, yet beneath the shield of her anger was the stabbing suspicion that he was right in his demands.

"If that's what you want," he said coldly at last, "then that's what we'll do."

It's not what I want! she wanted to say. *I love you, I need you, I couldn't bear a life without you.* But when he rapped on the panel and instructed the

coachman to take her home, she found she could
say nothing at all.

Chapter Sixteen
✦ ✦ ✦ ✦

SOUTH OF HOUSTON Street in New York City, toward the close of the nineteenth century, lay a
commercial district with buildings so typical of
the times that Christopher, whenever he saw
them, reflexively gritted his teeth. Although he
approved of the cast-iron construction of the
buildings, wherein the weight was borne by a
skeleton of rolled-iron beams, he abhorred the
corruption of classical design: the scrolled grill-
work, the overly ornate capitals, the indiscrimi-
nate blending of three or four conflicting orders.
How easily attainable, he thought scornfully, was
the key to architectural success. One had only to
set aside every iota of common sense and taste,
and automatically wealth and celebrity were his.

That he had stooped to that practice did not
lessen his contempt for it. When he was offered
a fifty-thousand-dollar commission to design a
silk mill on Greene Street, with mansard roof
and cavorting cupids above curved-arch windows, it was with mingled pride and disgust
that he accepted the work. His design for Winston Court had opened many doors to him,

doors through which he had no wish to travel,
but for Laura's sake he had done so; he had had
no choice in the matter. If the only way to have
her was at the cost of his integrity, so be it. Laura
Sheridan was too great a prize to risk losing.

But after that night at the opera, he knew he
had lost her in spite of everything. Laura didn't
want to forget about marriage for the time being;
she wanted to forget it indefinitely. Whitney's
absence was just another convenient excuse to
put off doing what she had never wanted to do
in the first place. It infuriated Christopher when
he thought of the countless concessions he had
made to try to please her, of the dozens of different ways he had deferred to her. To the devil
with her and her daughter; they were two of a
kind. By Christ, he was well rid of the both of
them!

North of Houston Street, on Bleecker Street,
diametrically opposed to its southern neighbor-
ing precinct, lay a section of the city that seemed
to have sprung intact from the previous century.
A neat row of Federal-style houses looked out on
cobblestone streets. The houses were simple and
dignified. Christopher had often ridden the
streetcar past these pretty dwellings and had
admired them. Whitney Sheridan, too, had admired the houses when passing them on her
way to the foundling home. It was ironic, then,
that she had moved into one of them on the very
morning she left her mother's home.

It was through Ned Bailey's intercession that Whitney had been able to make so smooth a transition. On the night of her debut, when she told Ned in a fury that she could no longer remain beneath her mother's roof, Ned realized at once that she had not lied about Christopher, that Laura's defense of him was unjustified, and that this final discord between mother and daughter had driven Whitney to desperate measures.

As he had escorted her back to the ballroom, she blurted out her intentions in a hot rush of words. Her slim body trembled; her mouth quivered. Ned, much disturbed, urged her to calm herself. "Whitney, you can't leave home," he had said, slipping a supportive arm through hers. "Where could you go? How would you take care of yourself?"

"I *will* leave home!" she had cried, wrenching herself away from him. "I have money. I'll go anywhere rather than stay here with her."

"Whitney—"

"Did you see how she took Christopher's part against mine? Did you see how she looked at him? Haven't you seen how she *always* looks at him? I've been telling myself for months that I'm imagining things. But I'm not, Ned; it's true. My mother has taken a fancy to Christopher, a man *younger* than she is. Did you ever hear anything so revolting? Just to think of it sickens my stomach!"

Ned had ignored what he already knew and endeavored to learn what most concerned him.

"Whitney, you must tell me what Christopher did to you. Did he do anything more than kiss you?"

Whitney had gazed at him steadily, her eyes a dark blaze in a colorless face. "Yes," she said deliberately. "He did much more than kiss me. And his actions proved to me beyond a doubt that he loves me. However, my mother has turned his head with her flattery and her patronage. He's so afraid of alienating her that he won't admit he cares for me. But I'm not a fool. Christopher made his feelings for me crystal clear in Bar Harbor. I can see now that the only way he'll admit the truth is if I separate myself from my mother. I'm leaving this house first thing tomorrow morning, and no one's going to stop me!"

A burning thirst for murder had suddenly parched Ned's throat. What had Christopher done to Whitney that had convinced her he loved her? Had he touched her? Had he taken her? No! Ned refused to believe that. And yet, whatever it was he'd done to her, it had also convinced Whitney that she was in love with him.

Ned suppressed the violent urge to rush back into the study and knock that bastard's teeth down his throat. But Whitney was his first concern. Lest she strike out on her own, courting God knew what manner of danger, he must keep a cool head and think only of her.

With an effort, he had said evenly, "Don't do anything on your own. Meet me tomorrow morning at nine at Saint Mark's on the Bowery. We'll discuss what to do then."

"Ned, you'll help me?" she had said, stunned,

gazing up at him with an emotion they were both too distracted to recognize.

He had nodded silently, too filled with rage to speak. For now, all his thoughts must be centered on protecting Whitney. He would take care of Christopher Warren at a more opportune time.

The house on Bleecker Street was partially furnished. There was a sofa and hassock in the parlor, a bed and a wardrobe in the second-floor bedroom, and a table and four chairs in the spacious, sunny dining room. The kitchen held only a cast-iron sink, a bloated black stove, and an icebox; but before Ned installed Whitney in the charming house, he stocked the cupboard with staples, had a block of ice delivered, and filled the icebox to the brim with butter, eggs, fresh milk, and sundry delectable perishables.

The ease with which Whitney transferred her welfare from her mother's hands into Ned's did not consciously occur to her. Nor did she think it extraordinary that on the same day she left the protection of her mother's home, she moved into a house provided for her by someone else. Ned loved her, and she loved him—as a *friend*, she constantly told herself. One naturally turned to one's friends in time of need. If their roles had been reversed, and if it were in Whitney's power, she would do the same for Ned as he had done for her. She was grateful for his help and deeply regretful if she had hurt him. But it was Christopher, not Ned, she wanted to marry.

Not for a minute, not for an instant, did she doubt she would marry Christopher. In all her eighteen years, nothing she'd ever wanted had been denied her. Some goals she'd attained with a modicum of struggle: her first long dress, putting up her hair, going away to school—but she'd gotten her way in the end. It was with those victories in mind that she viewed her difficulty with Christopher. If she tried long enough and hard enough to win what she wanted, there was no question in her mind that she'd succeed.

When Whitney tried to view the situation with a rational eye (which was extremely difficult), she had to admit that she understood her mother's attraction to Christopher Warren. Was he not as handsome as Papa had been, with his slender height; his curling dark hair; and those fierce, magnetic dark eyes? Was there a finer architect in the city now that Papa was gone? And Christopher's background notwithstanding, there wasn't a man in New York who even equaled, let alone surpassed, his effortless look of distinction and elegance. Yes, it was easy to see why Mama found Christopher appealing. But a woman her age really ought to have better sense.

"I'll never forgive her," Whitney constantly told Ned.

It was Ned's habit to dine with Whitney at night. Her days now were fully occupied. She had applied for and secured a paid position at the Indigents' Hospital on Third Avenue. The salary was low, the work grueling; but never had Whitney felt more useful and rewarded. She was assigned to the women's ward, her duties at first consisting only of making beds, emptying bedpans, and sometimes soothing a frightened patient. As she proved herself equal to greater tasks, her responsibilities were increased (but not her salary). It was a job few people wanted: caring for the poor, washing scabrous bodies, delousing vermin-infested hair, but Whitney did it well and gladly. To her mind, she was justifying her father's faith in her. She was more than just a pampered socialite performing nonoffensive services such as caring for foundlings or, as in her mother's case, arranging charity balls and bazaars. She was doing "real" work for people who desperately needed help. If her mother should ever learn of it, she would most likely cringe in horror.

On the weekends, Whitney refreshed herself with various diversions carefully chosen by Ned. They might drive through Central Park in a closed carriage or roller-skate at the Olympian Rink. When the weather warmed, they cycled on Riverside Drive, careering up and down the street like carefree youngsters. That they never encountered anyone they knew surprised neither of them. As geographically small as New York was, it afforded a "big city" anonymity. There was no better place Whitney knew of to hide in plain sight.

* * *

As the days grew longer and warmer, a fever-ish restlessness took hold of Whitney, a feeling she attributed to her work at the hospital. When she'd come home every night after a day spent with patients whose illnesses often stemmed from their poverty, Whitney could not shake the memory of their misery from her mind.

When Whitney reflected on those women and their condition, it was difficult for her to sum-mon the rage and indignation that had prompted her to leave home. Her differences with her mother seemed childish inconsequences, hardly worth thinking about. And Christopher. . . . Oddly, she was thinking less and less about Christopher and more and more about Ned. Some nights she couldn't sleep for thinking about him.

She did love Ned—not as she loved Christopher—but she loved him all the same. She had known him all her life. One of her ear-liest memories of him was of his lazy green eyes and his firm hands on her waist as he lifted her from the ground and placed her securely on his horse. She had been seven years old; he a tall grown man of seventeen. "Don't be afraid, Whit-ney," he had said in the low voice she loved. "I won't let you fall." And he hadn't let her fall— ever, ever. He had supported and protected her always, especially now, when the person she most trusted had so sorely disappointed her.

On the nights Ned dined with her, she would listen quietly as he filled her in on all the latest gossip. When he spoke, she would watch the vivid color of his eyes, the expressive movement of his hands, the sensuous curve of his mouth, which she had never before noticed. On the nights he didn't call, she thought of him incessantly, of his soothing voice, his warm hands, his gentle good-night kiss.

One evening, on impulse, she telephoned her mother. Thompson answered, and if he was surprised to hear from her after some five months' absence, it wasn't evident. He merely said in his habitual neutral tone, "Madam is out, Miss Whitney. May I give her a number where you can be reached?"

For a moment she hesitated. How tempted she was to give him that information. But her nerves suddenly tightened, and she said with a stammer, "N-no, Thompson, that won't be necessary." Then she hung up the telephone and she didn't call again.

On another occasion, in August, very late at night, she walked to Patchin Place and stood across the street from Christopher's house. Earlier that evening, Ned had said to her, "My cousin Cynthia told me that your mother and Christopher have had some sort of falling out. Your mother no longer talks about him as if he were Palladio reincarnated. I daresay she's finally realized what a bastard he is."

But Whitney thought differently. If Christopher and her mother were at odds with each other, it was no doubt because Christopher's love for her, Whitney, was at the bottom of it.

It was raining lightly as she stood across the street from Christopher's house. She had no umbrella; the rain cooled her cheeks, which were

feverishly hot. Christopher's windows were
dark. Whitney assumed he was asleep. She
stood there for an hour, debating whether or not
to cross the street and knock at his door. She
could imagine his look of surprise if she should
summon the courage to do so. He would most
likely be in nightclothes, his hair would be tousled, and she imagined herself smoothing back
his tumbled locks, then kissing his brow, his
lean cheeks, his hard, handsome mouth . . .

But even as she conjured that hazy fantasy,
the harsh light of reality gave sharp edges to the
scene. What would really happen is that he
would stare at her in shock. The first words out
of his mouth would be, "Whitney, what the devil
are you doing here?"

What, indeed, Whitney asked herself as she
gazed numbly. at Christopher's dark house, was
she doing here? He didn't love her; he never
would. He had told her that more than once,
and in no uncertain terms. And Whitney? Did
she love him? Of course she did; there was no
question in her mind about that. She had left
home because of him, had she not? What more
proof did she need that she loved him? She had
upended her entire life because of her love for
him.

Against her will, but unable to stop herself,
Whitney stepped off the curb and crossed the
street, her footsteps beating a muffled tattoo in
the quiet, muggy night. She rapped on Christopher's door. To her surprise he answered almost
immediately. He hadn't been asleep; he was
fully dressed but for his coat. From a room in the

rear of the house—Whitney assumed it was the kitchen—a light cast eerie shadows at the end of the narrow hall.

"Whitney?" he said in the exact shocked tone she had imagined.

"Yes, it's me," she said quickly, forestalling his next remark. "May I come in for a moment? I want to talk to you."

He hesitated for only the briefest instant. "Of course," he said, recovering, and ushered her into the house.

"I hope I'm not disturbing you," she murmured.

Now that she was here, she felt uncomfortable, embarrassed. Christopher seemed different to her: older, more serious (if that were possible), and disconcertingly remote. Always before when he had greeted her, it had been with an encouraging smile. He wasn't smiling now. He was watching her quietly with a wary expectancy.

"You're not disturbing me," he said. "I just completed some last-minute detail work on an apartment house."

"Winston Court?"

"Yes," he said, astonished. "How did you know that?"

"I've been reading about you in all the newspapers. I . . ." She lowered her gaze, unable to shake her embarrassment. "I always knew you would be a great success one day."

He said nothing; he continued to watch her with those densely dark eyes. Whitney surmised he must be just as uncomfortable as she was.

She fidgeted with her purse, unnerved by his steady gaze. At last she said sheepishly, "Could we sit down somewhere? I want to talk to you."

"Forgive me," he said at once, directing her into the parlor. "You took me somewhat by surprise," he said, turning up the gaslight. "You were the last person I expected to see when I answered the door."

Some of her tension eased as he bade her sit on the sofa, then sat opposite her on the chair. The room was sparsely furnished, but it was charming, much more homey and inviting than her parlor on Bleecker Street. "I know you were shocked," she said ruefully. "You tried to hide it, but you've a very easy face to read."

His brows drew together. He leaned back in the chair and folded his arms over his chest. "Where have you been?" he asked abruptly. "Why did you run off like that?"

The straightforward questions took Whitney aback. And then she remembered Ned's saying that Laura had been telling everyone she was in Palm Beach. "Christopher, how did you know I'd left home?"

"Your mother told me," he said.

"She told you? But why?"

"She didn't want to," he said with an irony that escaped her notice. "But she was so worried about you that it must have just slipped out. Why haven't you contacted her?"

Whitney's hackles rose. Would she ever be free of her mother? "I'm myself!" she wanted to tell Christopher. "I have nothing to do with my mother." But that wasn't true. She was her mother's daughter. As long as she lived, no matter the number of miles that separated them, Whitney would never be free of the woman who had borne her.

"I imagine my mother has been worried about me," she said wearily. "But I've had problems of my own lately. I haven't given her much thought in the past few months."

"Your mother," Christopher suggested, "might be a great help to you in solving your problems." And now there was no irony in his tone, only genuine concern.

Whitney gave him a skeptical look. "I doubt that, Christopher, since she is the one mostly responsible for causing them."

He returned her gaze silently for a moment, then he leaned forward, elbows on knees. "Don't blame your mother for what's happened," he said. "I am at fault for your troubles with her. If I hadn't done what I did to you in Bar Harbor, none of this would have happened. I was wrong, monstrously wrong, to behave with you as I did. And then, to compound my error, I kept silent about what I'd done, causing your mother to think you a liar—which is really the reason you left home, isn't it?"

"In part," she admitted. "But I know why you kept silent. I know you were afraid of losing my mother's patronage."

"Her patronage?" Christopher's low tone was bitter. "No. That's not what I was afraid of losing."

"I don't understand," she said, puzzled. "What could you be afraid of losing, if not my mother's patronage?"

His eyes came ablaze with emotion. Just as quickly, the light died. He shrugged and said tonelessly, "It's not important." Then, after a pause: "What was it you wanted to talk to me about?"

Whitney did not answer at once. Face-to-face with him at last, she felt purposeless and confused. Yet she found herself saying, "Christopher, why did you kiss me that way in Bar Harbor? You said you didn't love me, but a man doesn't kiss a woman like that unless he wants to make love to her. And if you wanted to make love to me, you must have some feeling for me."

Christopher got to his feet and walked restlessly back to the fireplace. Whitney could almost read his thoughts: He was trying to think of still another way to deny that he loved her.

"It's difficult to explain," he said tersely. "I had other things on my mind that night. When you started crying, when you threw your arms around me—" He stopped and shook his head. "Whitney, no amount of explaining can change the fact that I behaved like an unmitigated bastard. You were probably right to believe that I loved you, but the truth is, I didn't." He paused, then added grimly, "I was in love with someone else at the time."

"Someone else?" she said incredulously. "That can't be. You've never talked about anyone; I've never seen you with anyone. Who is it?'' she demanded.

''It doesn't matter who it is,'' he said, starting for the door. ''All that matters now is that your mother should know you're all right. I'm going to telephone her and let her know you're here.''

''Don't!'' Whitney leaped to her feet and detained him with a hand. ''I don't want you to telephone her. That's not why I came here. I want to talk about us.''

Christopher drew a steadying breath. ''Whitney,'' he said as calmly as he could, ''there is no 'us.' You don't love me. It's Ned you love. Don't you know that yet?''

''I don't!'' she cried. But even as she denied it, she envisioned Ned's face and felt the warmth and the love in the touch of his gentle hands. ''It's you I love! And I know you love me. How could you have kissed me and touched me as you did and then expect me to believe that you were in love with someone else?''

With a patience she hadn't known he possessed, he took both her hands and held them firmly in his. ''Whitney, please,'' he said, ''please try to understand me. I did love someone else; I had loved her for a long time, even before I met you. Circumstances prevented my marrying her, but that doesn't change the fact that I never loved *you*.''

No, no, she thought wildly. *This couldn't be happening.* This was merely another of his lies to hide the truth of his feelings. If he loved someone else, then Whitney had humiliated herself by leaving home, by coming here like a shameless shopgirl, asking him, *begging* him to admit that he loved her.

"If that's true," she persisted, grasping at straws, "then tell me who it is."

"I can't," he said. "Just believe me, Whitney. Go home to your mother. Try to work out your problems with her." He paused a moment, and his hands tightened painfully on hers. "If it will be of any help to you, I'll tell your mother the truth about that night in Bar Harbor."

Something in his expression called a sharp, sudden halt to Whitney's reeling thoughts. She had seen the same look in his eyes before; she had heard him use that same tone of voice. Always, when Whitney spoke of her mother, that look was in his eyes. Always, when Christopher spoke of her, his low, restrained voice proclaimed more loudly than words what Whitney, before now, had been too childishly blind to see.

With a gasp of horror she tore her hands from his. "Dear God," she said hoarsely. "It's my mother, isn't it? You were in love with my mother. You still are. And she—"

And then she remembered her mother's voice, her mother's eyes when she spoke of Christopher, when she insisted in that adamant, irrefutable way of hers that Christopher was unacceptable as a suitor for Whitney.

"Whitney, listen—" Christopher said, and now in his voice there was alarm and concern for her. But Whitney saw nothing but the anguish of her revulsion and humiliation.

"Stay away from me!" she cried, stumbling backward on shaking legs.

"Whitney, listen to me," he pleaded. "Go home to your mother. Talk this out with her."

"Go home?" she echoed. "Do you think I'll ever go home now? You and my mother—" She swallowed convulsively. "I should have known," she said sickly and moved blindly toward the door. "I should have known . . ."

"Whitney, wait!"

But she neither saw him nor heard him. She fled the room, hearing only the roar of her own outraged betrayal. She fled from his house—as her mother had once done—seeing only her mother's face, a lovely, saintly facade concealing the ugliest and most despicable treachery.

Chapter Seventeen
✦✦✦✦

THE FOLLOWING SUNDAY, Ned took her to Coney Island, where they walked for an hour on the colorful Concourse, lunched on fresh lobster, took a ride on the terrifying roller coaster, then capped their day by watching the fireworks display that depicted the destruction of Pompeii by the eruption of Mount Vesuvius.

The day had been enjoyable, but hot and exhausting. After the steamboat deposited the weary couple at the Battery, Ned flagged down a hack to take them to Bleecker Street. In the hack, Whitney leaned tiredly against Ned; his arm went at once around her shoulder. He spoke not a word on the entire trip home, for which Whitney was grateful, because for the past several days she had been struggling desperately to suppress both rage and tears.

Whitney had not told Ned that she'd seen Christopher, nor did she intend to do so. To have learned that Christopher was not in love with her was humiliation enough; to learn that he loved Laura was too ghastly a fact to impart to anyone. For days Whitney had performed her duties at the hospital in a silent fury that had festered within her as destructively as a malignant illness. The aura of doom and despair that prevailed at the hospital only added to her helpless rage.

As if that were not enough to plunge her into the depths of desolation, she had run into her uncle at the hospital the day before, and his reception had been anything but cordial. When she tried to explain her reasons for leaving home, he had only said coldly, "I'm afraid I haven't the time to listen to you now. If you wish to discuss why you treated your mother so shabbily, I'll be happy to hear you out later in the physicians' dining room at ten."

She had left the hospital that very morning, determined never to return to it again.

Now, as Ned saw her to her door, Whitney heard the clock at Saint Mark's chime the hour of midnight. The lonely sound in the quiet night intensified her morbid feelings. When Ned unlocked the door, she said in a plaintive voice, "Don't go yet. Come inside for a while. I don't want to be alone now. I—"

"My dear!" Ned said softly, perceiving her troubled state of mind. "Of course I'll stay."

The naked love in his eyes released the tears Whitney had valiantly been holding in check.

"Whitney, don't!" he said, ushering her quickly into the house and closing the door behind them. "I knew this was going to happen. You've been blue for days— Darling, please don't cry."

But the tears wouldn't stop; there was no way she could control them. Ned took her in his arms, and Whitney let herself be held, sobbing openly, helplessly, because she was so miserable and confused. She would never forgive her mother for her contemptible duplicity. And yet, whenever she thought of Laura with Christopher, whenever she tried to hate her for loving him, she could only hate Christopher. *He* was at fault for her mother's unseemly behavior. He must surely have bewitched her, just as vilely and deliberately as he had seduced Whitney into thinking he loved her.

"Please stop crying," Ned said wretchedly, kissing her wet cheeks and mouth. "Dearest, I love you so much. It breaks my heart to see you unhappy."

Whitney's heart, too, was breaking and sending pointed shards of pain through every part of her body. Ned loved her, poor darling Ned. And

Whitney had wasted her love on his perfidious best friend.

"Whitney, stop it now," he said, slipping a firm arm about her waist and leading her into the darkened parlor. "Sit down," he said, then turned up the gaslight. "I'm going to the kitchen to get you some brandy."

Whitney's sobs ebbed, but hot, silent tears continued to fall. Numbly she unpinned her hat and took it off, then stripped off her gloves as Ned returned with two glasses.

"Sip it slowly," he said, sitting beside her and downing his own drink in one swallow.

He put the glass down on the side table, then watched Whitney anxiously as she tasted the brandy and grimaced.

"Darling, I know it tastes nasty to you," he said, "but drink it anyway. It'll do you good."

He steadied her hand as she raised the glass again to her lips. She watched him over the rim; his ginger-colored hair bleached fairer by today's strong sun; his pure-green eyes dark now with worry. She looked at his mouth, that mobile mouth that could smile and laugh with such infectious gaiety. It wasn't smiling now; it was grim, deadly serious, yet tender with loving concern.

She continued to study him as she sipped the brandy, and his steadying hand on hers was at once a soothing balm. Ever since Whitney could remember, she had felt as comfortable with Ned as she did with the members of her own family. She loved him, she always had, and she knew she always would. But she had never known how much until just now.

She finished the brandy, then wearily leaned back against the sofa.

"Do you feel better?" Ned asked, setting aside her glass.

"Yes," she said softly. She felt better than she had in months. She didn't feel happy or cheerful, but she felt strangely at peace. Ned was half turned toward her, watching her closely, his arm on the backrest above her head. She moved her head and rested it on his shoulder. "Yes," she said again, "I feel a hundred times better."

Ned's arms folded about her, and he drew her close. "I knew the brandy would do the trick," he said, relieved. "You've been wound up for days. I knew it was just a matter of time before you came undone. Whitney, please give some thought to contacting your mother. You needn't go back home if you don't want to, but at least let her know you're all right."

"Ned . . ." She didn't want to think about her mother. "Ned, do you remember when my father died? On the night before the funeral, you found me crying in his study, and when I said I wouldn't go to the cemetery the next day to see him buried, you said I didn't have to go if I didn't want to."

"Yes," Ned said, gently stroking her arm. "I remember that, Whitney."

"Do you remember you talked to me then— for hours, it seemed—about everything else but Papa's death and the funeral? And before you left, you said, 'I'll see you tomorrow morning.' And I said, 'Yes, I'll see you then.' And when we got to the cemetery, you came over to me and held my hand. And you never once let it go throughout the service and the burial.''

''Yes,'' Ned said, ''I remember.''

''And do you remember,'' she asked further, bemused by the brandy and by memories long forgotten, ''when Mama and I went to Oyster Bay to celebrate your parents' fortieth wedding anniversary? We walked through the woods, you and I, and you picked roses for me. I got a thorn in my finger and you squeezed it out, then you wrapped the finger in your handkerchief and kissed the bandaged wound. 'There!' you said. 'That's a medal for bravery.' Do you remember that, Ned? I was fifteen years old.''

''I remember that, too,'' Ned said. ''I remember every conversation and every single thing I ever did with you.''

His candor touched her. She turned in his arms and looked up at him searchingly. ''You loved me even then, didn't you?'' she said. ''At Oyster Bay? When I was only fifteen.''

''I've loved you longer than that,'' he said honestly. ''I've loved you ever since I can remember.''

Again Whitney felt the sting of tears in her eyes. How cruel, she thought, were the vagaries of fate. Ned had loved her for untold years, and she had given her heart to a man who cared nothing at all for her.

''I love you, too,'' she said softly. ''You do know that, don't you?''

"Do you?" he said, his voice low and grave, Christopher's unspoken name a ghostly barrier between them.

"I do, Ned," she whispered, reaching up to embrace him. "I love you with all my heart."

Impulsively, repentantly, she kissed his brow and his cheek, then pressed her mouth to his. Her indebtedness to this man was impossible for her to convey. Ned had loved her throughout her childhood and her bumpy adolescence. He had saved her sanity by finding her this house, this temporary haven from emotional havoc. He had done more for her over the years than she could even remember. There was nothing she wouldn't do for him in return.

Her gentle kiss changed, became a fever of love and gratitude. She felt him stiffen in her embrace and try to pull away, but she wouldn't let him go; she held on to him insistently. His arms tightened around her, and with a low groan he kissed her in a way he had never done before. It was almost the way Christopher had kissed her, totally, possessively, as if with his hot, hungry mouth he would wish to devour her.

Whitney felt a dark thrill, a will outside her own, urging her to submit to a force that was unfamiliar yet as natural as breathing. She knew that Ned was going to make love to her; she wasn't the least bit afraid. She returned his ardent kisses, her virginal passion increasing his. It felt so good, it felt so right, to be kissed by Ned and touched by him. It wasn't what she had felt in Bar Harbor with Christopher, but it felt natural and good all the same.

Chapter Eighteen
✦ ✦ ✦ ✦ ✦

THROUGH THE FALL and winter of 1897, all the New York City newspapers, as if by tacit agreement, celebrated the glory of the peaceful and prosperous "Gay Nineties." Their pages were filled with plaudits for worthy Americans: Robert Peary, who had been awarded the American Geographical Society's gold medal for his explorations of Greenland; Theodore Roosevelt, who was appointed assistant secretary of the navy by President McKinley; Christopher Warren, the rising young architect whose design for Winston Court had been followed by even more spectacular designs for commercial buildings, churches, and private residences.

It was an age of self-aggrandizement and of unabashed patriotism. "America First and Best" was the catchphrase of the times. Peace had ruled the country for more than thirty years; but when Pulitzer and Hearst, the archrival publishers of the *World* and the *Journal* began printing accounts of Spanish suppression and atrocities in Cuba, outraged New Yorkers, steeped in the principle of liberty, demanded immediate retribution.

"It's a disgrace!" said Jeremy Tyler one night at Laura Sheridan's home. "That Spanish butcher, Governor Weyler, is burning homes, murdering women and children. We should listen to Navy Secretary Roosevelt and go over to

Cuba at once and put an end to Spain's tyranny."

There was an instantaneous response from the gentlemen at the dinner table. John Barnes exclaimed, "Bully!" in emulation of his good friend Theodore Roosevelt. Malcolm MacKenzie, a descendant of fierce Scottish warriors, said, "Spain is an enemy of freedom and, as such, should be totally annihilated."

"Hear, hear," said Ned Bailey darkly, thinking of an enemy much closer to home.

Henry Carlisle, seated on Laura's right, said meaningfully, "Perhaps we should heed President McKinley, who counsels 'friendly relationships with all nations; foreign entanglements with none.' "

"McKinley's a coward!" cried John.

"And a fool, besides," Malcolm added.

Jeremy, very red in the face, shouted, "We should declare war on Spain, capture the bloody devils, and then burn every last one of them at the stake!"

Avery, presiding as Laura's host, said quietly, "Gentlemen, if you please. There are ladies present."

It was February 10, 1898. Laura, with little or no joy, was celebrating her thirty-seventh birthday. At Avery's express command, she had arranged a dinner party for a small group of her closest friends. She was hardly in the mood for a birthday fete, but Avery, with uncharacteristic severity, had insisted that she have one.

The cuisine, as always at her home, was incomparable: Genoa paste soup, porgies with Chablis, sweetbreads à l'Eugénie, tomatoes Trévise, truffled turkey with black olives, and Condé peaches and coffee mousse ice cream for dessert. The table was set with her finest Limoges porcelain and Baccarat crystal. A cornucopia centerpiece graced the fine Georgian table. Laura's chef, Monsieur Dufond, had spun the lovely creation from pulled sugar and royal icing and had decorated it with gold reliefs. Atop the concoction he had placed a gum-paste Cupid, complete with gold wings and tiny bow and arrow. From the cornucopia's mouth of white nougat flowed a delectable array of candied fruit and chestnuts.

The gaiety of the decor did not extend to the reluctant hostess. Although she was radiantly beautiful in an apricot velvet gown studded with seed pearls, Laura's spirits could not have been lower. Over a year had passed since her daughter had left home, a year of anxiety, disappointments, and ever-increasing regrets. The regrets, of course, concerned Christopher. She still saw him at times, but only at social functions or in areas related to their respective work. On all those occasions when she attempted to start a personal conversation, to mend the wretched abyss that now yawned between them, he would deftly and adamantly change the subject. This birthday fete, a happy celebration, seemed ludicrous under the circumstances.

But Avery, ever concerned for her, had been unyielding on that score. "I insist that you have this party," he had said firmly. "All you've been doing lately is your decorating and charity work. Your social life has dwindled to almost nothing. You can't live like that, Laura; I will not permit it."

Only because Laura sensed the guilt behind his demand, only because she knew that his anguish over Whitney was as great as hers, did she consent to give a party that neither one of them was going to enjoy. She remembered too well the day he had told her of meeting Whitney at Indigents' Hospital. She remembered too vividly the look in his eyes when he recounted their futile conversation.

"She never came to the surgeons' dining room," he had said in a voice filled with angry self-condemnation. "I was too harsh," he accused himself, pacing up and down the length of the family parlor. "I should have been more understanding, less judgmental. Instead, I—" He broke off and fell silent, so disturbed by what he saw as his failure to support his niece that Laura had to conceal her own distress in order to ease his.

"Don't blame yourself," she said bleakly. "If anyone is at fault, it is I, not you. Perhaps I babied Whitney too much. Even now, I cannot believe that my daughter is living away from home, functioning on her own without my . . ." She smiled ironically. "Without my maternal wisdom and guidance."

Avery stopped his frustrated pacing and looked over at her with a frown.

"What's the matter?" she asked.

"It *is* hard to believe," he said, his frown deepening, "that Whitney's been living alone all this time."

"Yes," Laura agreed, unaware of his gist. "Going away to school must have accustomed her to a certain independence."

"I daresay it did," Avery said, his gray eyes hard. "Perhaps I should have thought twice before persuading you to let her go."

A week or so later, disturbed by Avery's words, Laura went to Indigents' Hospital, in hopes of settling once and for all her differences with her daughter. But Whitney no longer worked there. And, "No," the administrator told her, "I don't know where Miss Sheridan can be reached. We posted a draft for her final week's wages to the Brooklyn address she had given us for our records, but the envelope came back marked 'Addressee Unknown.'"

This latest disappointment after a host of shattered hopes was less distressing to Laura than she had thought it might be. A heart can take only so many blows, she reasoned. At some point, it must harden or be destroyed. As she had survived Steven's death, she would survive her daughter's defection. As for mending the breach between herself and Christopher, she would do so, and soon. She would do nothing yet; she must first give herself a little time to recover.

And so, she gave her birthday dinner, in the hope that it might distract both her mind and Avery's from Whitney's refusal to come home. But at the table, as the tumult over "Spanish tyranny" died down, Laura couldn't help wondering if her own parental tyranny was what had prompted her daughter to desert her.

Nina Tyler, plump and pretty in celadon silk, said, to change the subject, "How right you were, Laura, about your talented Mr. Warren. His Winston Court Apartments are the talk of the town. I've also heard that he's been asked to design two cottages in Newport; and for Peter and Helen Corbett he's doing a grand baronial summerhouse in Connecticut, in the style of a medieval cathedral. I feel quite the trendsetter to be living in his very first house. I only wish," she added with a sigh, "that he had not been quite so . . . uninspired about the design."

"Your house is unique," Laura said smoothly. "That is the reason I so much wanted you to choose it."

"Why, yes," Nina said, comforted, "it is unique, isn't it? Laura, why isn't Mr. Warren here tonight, helping you celebrate your birthday?"

Laura was silent for a moment. Then: "I did invite him," she told Nina. "But he was otherwise engaged."

"Oh, what a shame," Nina said. "He's such a nice young man, so courteous and attentive. Although," she qualified, accepting a second helping of truffled turkey, "he can be awfully temperamental at times. I suppose that's because he's such an artistic genius."

"Yes," Laura murmured, "you're probably right."

"Well, temperamental or not," Nina chattered

on, "Mr. Warren is a true gentleman, and I wish he could have been with us tonight." She turned to Henry Carlisle. "Henry, how lucky you are to have such a brilliant and versatile architect in your employ!"

"To be sure," Henry said blandly. "Christopher's brilliant versatility never ceases to amaze me."

Ned Bailey, seated next to his cousin Cynthia, commented idly, "If I didn't know better, I would think Christopher's playing a monumental joke on his clients."

Henry shot him a keen look. "A joke, Ned? How do you mean?"

"Well, sir," Ned answered, toying thoughtfully with his wineglass, "I've seen the plans for the Corbett house, and at first glance I had the impression of a deliberate exaggeration of late-medieval architecture. I'm surely mistaken, though," he added, looking up at his employer with ingenuous green eyes. "Christopher would never do such a thing as make sport of his work—or of the people who so generously provide his livelihood."

Janet MacKenzie, who was very fond of the architect who had given reality to her husband's lifelong dream, said loyally, "Of course you're mistaken, Ned. Mr. Warren has far too much integrity to even think of doing what you've just suggested."

"Janet, understand me!" Ned said quickly, putting a hand to his heart. "I'm suggesting nothing. I'm only relaying a first impression I had on seeing Christopher's design."

Cynthia Barnes, with her habitual blunt candor, said, "I agree with you, Neddy. Helen showed me the preliminary sketches, and as much as I admire medieval architecture, I think Mr. Warren has done a droll caricature of the style."

"He's done nothing of the kind," Laura defended him. Then, turning to Ned: "And for you to imply that he would stoop to such a thing is not like you, Ned. I thought you were his friend."

"My dear Laura, I *am* his friend! His dearest friend. That's why I said I must be wrong in thinking what I did. Good Lord," he said in his most earnest voice, "even if Christopher *were* ridiculing his clients, I'd never go around saying so."

"If that's the case, Ned," Henry Carlisle said heavily, "perhaps we'd best drop the subject."

"By all means," Ned agreed with the correct amount of deference due his employer. "I beg your pardon all." He nodded courteously in the direction of the other guests. "You must forget what I said about Christopher. I know him intimately, and if he were not sincere in his efforts, I'd be the first to know it. And of course," he added gravely, "I'd be the very last person to say it."

Henry Carlisle was worried about Christopher Warren. It wasn't Ned Bailey's implication that Christopher was making mock of his own work—which Henry half suspected might be true. What really worried Henry was the apparent ease and indifference with which his young protégé had disregarded every architectural principle he'd ever held.

Christopher was what Henry had been many years ago: an incorruptible idealist; a fierce young crusader dedicated to preserving the holy grail of architectural purity. Over the years Henry had faltered; he had abandoned his crusade and had joined the heathen horde to ensure his success. In Christopher he had found a path to redemption. Christopher had picked up the standard Henry had dropped. What Henry had betrayed, Christopher would defend to his dying breath. It was not the boy himself but his unshakable integrity that Henry prized above all else. That, at any rate, was what he kept telling himself.

A few days after Laura Sheridan's birthday fete, the United States battleship *Maine,* while on a peaceful visit to Cuba, was mysteriously blown up in the Havana harbor. On the seventeenth of February, the *New York Evening Journal* devoted its entire front page to the incident, declaring that the "accident" was no accident at all; that it was, in fact, a deliberate, heinous attack, sanctioned by the bloodthirsty Spanish government. For weeks afterward, both the *Journal* and the *World* roused the sentiments of their readers with more accounts of Spanish atrocities and with irrefutable "proof" of Spain's treachery in connection with the *Maine's* destruction. So pre-

occupied were all the New York newspapers
with this unfortunate happening that when the
Winston Court Apartments finally opened its
gingerbread doors on March first, it was given
only second-page coverage.

New Yorkers, however, slightly bored with
war news, devoured the glowing accounts of
this latest achievement of two of the city's favorite sons. For days following the opening, George
Winston was praised for his wisdom in choosing
such a gifted architect. Christopher was again
lauded for his "religious adherence to Gothic
design." As the weeks passed, more prospective
clients began to beg Henry Carlisle for the priv-
ilege of having Christopher Warren design their
projects, so much so that Henry said to his
protégé one afternoon in April, "I think it's time
I installed you in an office, Christopher. Why
don't you move your things into the room next
to mine? It's hardly suitable for an architect of
your current stature to continue to work in an
alcove."

They were lunching at Delmonico's on roast
squab, eggplant à la Robertson, and apricots
with cream of almonds. For a change, Henry
was Christopher's guest, a role in which the
older man took keen enjoyment. Christopher, as
always, did more than justice to the meal. He
was on his second helping of apricots when
Henry made his proposal. He glanced up from
his dish with a look of suspicion. "The room
next to yours? That's your conference room."

Henry tasted his coffee, then said casually,
"It's wasted space. My conferences are generally

held at construction sites or in drawing rooms. That room will serve better as an office where you can meet with people in comfortable surroundings. You can't very well have your clients perching on a stool or sitting like ramrods on a straightback chair. In your present position, Christopher, you're going to have to start giving some thought to salesmanship tactics. A successful architect wears more than one hat, you know."

"Very well." Christopher shrugged and went on eating. "I'll move my things tonight, after hours."

Christopher's lack of enthusiasm was not surprising to Henry. Lately, nothing about Christopher surprised him. He said in the same casual tone, "Now that your work is in demand, I suppose you'll go back to designing in the classical order."

"No," Christopher said. "I won't."

"Why not?"

"Why should I?" He shrugged once more. "You've always told me that my first responsibility is to my client. Well, I finally took your advice, and it paid off handsomely. I have no intention of tampering with so effective a formula."

"Years ago," Henry reminded him, "you would have scoffed at such an idea."

"I've changed," Christopher said sardonically. "Aren't you proud of me?"

Henry's eyes narrowed. He started to reply, then clamped his mouth shut and signaled for the waiter.

The waiter hastened to the table and inquired solicitously, "More coffee, Mr. Carlisle?"

"A whiskey and soda, Charles."

"At once, Mr. Carlisle."

The waiter left. Henry pushed aside his cup and saucer and said bluntly to Christopher, "You *have* changed—considerably—but I can't say it's for the better. You've replaced your hatred of compromise with contempt for your own success. You have no one but yourself to blame for the turn of events. If you despise what you're doing, stop doing it. It's as simple as that."

Henry's arrow had found its mark. Christopher flushed angrily. "Nothing is that simple, and you know it," he shot back. "I made a choice; I don't regret it."

"Every line you draw," Henry said, "every flèche and triforium you design, is an outcry of regret. Lie to yourself, if you must, but don't lie to me."

"I'm lying to no one," Christopher said hotly. "I'm doing what I want to do."

The waiter returned with the whiskey and soda. Henry took a generous swallow, then set the glass down with a thump. "No one," he charged Christopher, "enrages me the way you do. I've never seen a man battle so ferociously against obstacles he himself has erected."

Christopher threw down his napkin and started to rise. "This conversation is pointless."

"Sit down," Henry said, his tone steely. "Grant me the courtesy of hearing me out. You owe me that at least."

Christopher stopped in midmotion and stared

at him, unable to deny the inestimable debt he owed this man. At last, grudgingly, he resumed his seat.

"Now tell me what's at the bottom of this," Henry said brusquely. "Why are you doing designs that so obviously make you unhappy?"

Before Christopher could respond, there was a hubbub in the restaurant. Several gentlemen had entered, waving newspapers and shouting, "War, war! Congress has finally declared war on Spain!"

"The blasted fools," Henry said disgustedly. "Now we're in for it."

An excited buzz sprang up among the diners. Some ladies anxiously clutched the hands of their escorts; others gaped, thunderstruck, at husbands or sons. One of the gentlemen waving a newspaper was Ned Bailey, who, spotting Christopher, quickly turned the other way.

Henry, noting this, asked Christopher, "What the devil's going on between Ned and you?"

A veil descended on Christopher's eyes. Again he said, "I don't know what you mean."

"You know goddamned well what I mean, Christopher. You two have been barely speaking to each other for months. If you've quarreled, that's your business, and I don't want to know about it. But when one of you starts undermining the other's work in public, then it becomes my business."

"What are you talking about?" Christopher demanded. "Who's been undermining whose work?"

Henry recounted what Ned had said at Laura's house, then asked, "What happened between you that prompted him to make those accusations?"

Christopher stared at him, astounded, then he looked toward Ned, who was at the far end of the room, talking to a trio of architects from Carlisle & Hastings. "Do you believe what he said?" he asked, still looking at Ned.

"Is what he said true?" Henry asked in response.

Christopher's eyes, hard and dark, darted back to his employer. "No," he said flatly. "Whatever I may think of the work I'm now doing, I would never further debase myself by making a mockery of it."

Henry leaned back in his chair; his relief was more than obvious. "I'm glad to hear that," he said.

"Why haven't you spoken to Ned about this?" Christopher asked angrily. "How could you let him get away with saying such things?"

"I almost believed him," Henry said quietly. "That's why I said nothing."

"Christ," Christopher uttered. "Many thanks for your faith in me."

"I deserve that," Henry said. "And I apologize for doubting you. Under the circumstances I shall certainly speak to Ned. And if I were you, Christopher, I'd have a word with him also."

"Don't worry," Christopher said grimly. "I intend to."

Chapter Nineteen

✦ ✦ ✦ ✦ ✦

IT RAINED LATER that day, a cold, driving rain that reminded Christopher vividly of the day he had first met Laura Sheridan. How different he was now from that scruffy vagabond who had stood at the Tylers' door with his heart in his throat. He was successful now, a celebrity; he had a steadily mounting bank balance. He was working continuously, actually turning down commissions because he had no time for them. He led an active social life, attending teas, dinners, and soirees at the homes of wealthy clients. He had everything in life that a man could ever want—except Laura—whom he *had* wanted most of all.

He didn't want her anymore, or so he kept telling himself. Yet as he stood at the window in Henry's conference room, watching the rain hurl itself against the tombstones in Trinity Churchyard, he could think of nothing else but her.

What was she doing? What was she feeling? Did it mean nothing to her that they saw each other now only in passing? Did she know how much he still loved her—as much as he fought against it? Did she care?

He would lie awake some nights, unable to stop thinking of her. His thoughts always alternated between the most bloodthirsty acts of violence and the most erotic visions of physical love. He would imagine his hands around her slender white throat. Like a vengeful Othello, he would kiss the breath of life from his faithless love. So vivid was the imagery that he could feel the rapid racing of the pulse at her throat, the terrified trembling of her mouth beneath his. Unmoved, unmerciful, he would press her down on her bed. She would struggle desperately, writhe beneath him, but his rage, his violent thirst for vengeance would subdue her. And then, just at the point where she surrendered her will to his, he would become intensely aware of the feel of her skin and the fragrance of her hair. He would raise his mouth from hers and look down at her perfect face. She would open her eyes, those celestially beautiful eyes, and whisper his name over and over again. His breath would catch in his throat. The need for revenge would be displaced by a surge of the most exquisite desire. His mouth would cover hers again, in passion, not in rage. His hands would slide from her throat to her shoulders to her quivering breasts . . .

Laura, Laura. Loving her so much, he could almost begin to hate her. She loved him, he was sure of it, but she loved propriety more. If his name had been Vanderbilt, she would have married him in an instant. To preserve the conventions that had ruled her all her life, she was destroying both her life and his.

The door to the conference room opened. Christopher turned from the window. Ned Bailey entered, wearing the same guarded, almost hostile expression he had been directing toward Christopher for more than a year.

"Henry said you wanted to see me," Ned said distantly.

It was almost eight o'clock; everyone else had left the offices. Ned's attitude was not surprising to Christopher. Since the night of Whitney's debut, Ned had had little or nothing to say to him. Christopher suspected that despite his apology that night, Ned was nonetheless convinced of Christopher's guilt.

"Come in and close the door," Christopher said, establishing, by his command, the tone he wished to set for this interview.

Aware of the ploy, Ned complied with a mocking smile and sauntered lazily to a chair. "I see you've made a change," he commented, glancing at Christopher's drawing board and stool, set off in a corner. He sat down at the oval conference table, tilted back his chair, and hooked his thumbs in his vest. "Are congratulations in order, Christopher? Shall I soon be saying I work for the firm of Carlisle, Hastings, and Warren?"

"If you don't learn to separate your private life from your professional life," Christopher said pointedly, "you may soon be working for McKim, Mead, and White, or for George B. Post."

Ned's mocking smile widened. "Methinks a threat lurks beneath that remark. Pray tell me what you mean."

"Drop the Exeter-Harvard jargon," Christopher said shortly. "You know precisely what I mean. What did you hope to accomplish by criticizing my work in public?"

"I see the Widow Sheridan has dutifully reported to her lover—or should I say *former* lover?"

Christopher, still at the window, made a sudden move toward Ned, then stopped dead in his tracks. "Let's leave Laura out of this," he said tightly. "Someone else told me what you said. And I have a pretty good idea of your motives."

"If you know my motives," Ned said with an air of boredom, "why are we having this tiresome discussion?"

Christopher uttered a particularly foul profanity.

"Tut, tut," Ned said. "There you go again, betraying your background. What would your aristocratic clients think if they heard *that*, Christopher?"

If there was a threat in anyone's voice, it was in Ned's quiet drawl. Christopher stared at him a moment, his suspicions confirmed, then he sat down at the opposite end of the table. "So that's it," he said coldly. "You've learned what happened between Whitney and me in Bar Harbor, and you've decided to extract your revenge."

"Yes," Ned said.

Ned's answer was not surprising. The depth of his contempt for Christopher, his naked loathing, was. And yet, Christopher felt oddly relieved. It was done with, out in the open. Christopher was glad Ned knew the truth; he wished he had had the courage to speak of it sooner.

He scowled as a sudden thought occurred to him. "You've talked to Whitney, haven't you? You know where she is."

"That's none of your business."

"It may not be my business, but it's certainly Laura's. If you know Whitney's whereabouts, why haven't you told her mother? You have no right to keep that information to yourself."

"Don't speak to me of rights," Ned flung back at him. "You violated Whitney's rights by treating her like a common whore. You're no better than a satyr, for God's sake. You couldn't be satisfied with Laura; you had to inflict your disgusting lusts on her daughter as well. I wonder what Laura would think if she knew the truth."

A thrill of alarm darted through Christopher, but he said in a steady voice, "If you're so curious about her reaction, why don't you tell her?"

"That would accomplish nothing," Ned retorted. "I want a just repayment for what you did to Whitney. And believe me, I'm going to get it."

Ned suddenly rose to his feet and moved toward the door, as if disgusted by his lack of control.

"Hold on there," Christopher said, his hands clenched, out of sight, beneath the table. "Don't leave yet, if you please. I'd like to say one more thing to you. Your anger with me may be justified, but telling lies about my work is not going to solve anything."

"Lies?" Ned echoed. He went to the drawing board and gestured sharply toward Christopher's latest design, the Corbett house in Connecticut, which was an exact replica of an Italian medieval cathedral. "Norman towers," he jeered, "three apses, dwarf galleries, and a campanile, for Christ's sake. Is that what you call serious work? It's a farce, Christopher; you know it as well as I do."

"It's what the Corbetts want," Christopher said, his dark eyes hard.

"The Corbetts, yes," Ned conceded. "But you always said you would never design for people like them. You vowed you'd starve before you prostituted your talent, that you'd wait all eternity, if necessary, for clients whose preferences paralleled yours. What's happened to your pride, your ideals, your scruples? Oh, forgive me; I forgot. A nameless bastard from nowhere couldn't possibly know the meaning of those words."

Rage and shame raised a splash of color in Christopher's pale cheeks. He leaped to his feet, upsetting the chair as he did so. "Listen here," he said roughly. "I'm telling you once and for all, and for your own sake, to shut your mouth about my work. Henry knows what you're doing and he's not going to tolerate it. If you value your job—"

"This job," Ned stopped him, "is no longer of concern to me. Teddy Roosevelt is going to lead a cavalry regiment against the Spaniards in Cuba, and I've decided to sign on and go with him. If I come back and my job is still available, all well and good. If I don't come back . . ." He smiled coldly. "Then you no longer have to worry about your precious reputation."

"Ned, for God's sake!" Christopher said, forgetting for a moment the animosity between them, remembering only the affection and respect they had shared in the past. "Why should you risk your neck in Cuba? The United States has no call to interfere in foreign matters."

"What the devil's wrong with you?" Ned blazed. "It's our duty to help a nation in need. Have you no courage, no sense of honor?" He broke off abruptly and looked down at the drawing board. "No, of course you don't." He gestured derisively toward Christopher's plans. "I should have known better than to ask *you* such a question."

Ned turned on his heel and left the room. Christopher listened to his retreating footsteps, to the sound of the outer door being slammed shut, then he, too, looked down at the plans on his drawing board.

The piers and engaged shafts, the capitals and canopied arches were a silently screaming testament to Ned's accusations. The choir and transepts were a blasphemy; the pinnacles crowned with statues were, to Christopher's eyes, the final crowning betrayal of his professional integrity. He looked at each view with a revulsion so profound that his stomach lurched sickeningly, and he actually gagged. Then, one by one, he picked up the drawings and with deadly precision tore every piece of work into tiny, indistinguishable shreds.

At that same moment, on Gramercy Park, Laura Sheridan and Cynthia Barnes were dining at the home of Stanford White. White alone presided at the sumptuous dinner table. His wife, Bessie, was, as always, at the palatial White estate on Long Island with her son, Lawrence.

It was said about town that Stanford White

was a voluptuary. One rumor had it that he invited chorus girls to his home for dinner and placed a twenty-dollar gold piece under a candy box on each plate. The girls who kept the gold pieces understood what was expected of them and happily complied. Those who refused the offering were expected to take leave of the gracious house on Gramercy Park before dinner was served.

These rumors, however, did nothing to harm White's career. In fact, the more scandalous his reputation became, the more clients clamored for his architectural services. There was nothing New Yorkers liked better than a daring iconoclast—provided he was as wealthy, talented, and aristocratic as the incorrigible Stanford White.

Laura Sheridan had heard all the rumors and had immediately discounted them. She had known Stanny White since her childhood. He'd been a good friend to both Steven and her father. White's father had been a poet and a scholar; his mother, still living, was an antebellum aristocrat from South Carolina. Stanny himself was an ultimate gentleman: He was a devout Episcopalian, a patron of the arts, a generous philanthropist. Laura categorically disbelieved every lurid tale heard about him. Nevertheless, when he invited her to dine with him to discuss the decoration of the Capital Club, a clubhouse for women, she decided to ask Cynthia to accompany her.

Cynthia Barnes, unlike Laura, fervently believed every scandalous exploit attributed to the theatrically glamorous architect. Moreover, she loved a delicious tidbit of gossip. "Stanny," she said to him over the soup, "I recently read in *Town Topics* that one of our most distinguished citizens gave a dinner at the Hoffman House last week, which culminated in a nubile maiden's popping out of a cake, wearing only a very pretty blush."

White's eyes crinkled mischievously at the corners. "How titillating that must have been, Cynthia, but, alas, I was not there. I was in Long Island last week, snug and warm in . . ." He paused and directed his gaze to her charming, ample breast. "In the bosom of my family."

Cynthia raised a silky eyebrow. "Ah, yes," she said, "how is dear Bessie? I haven't seen her in an age. What a possessive husband you are, Stanny, to sequester your lovely wife from all other admiring eyes."

"Cynthia, stop your nonsense," Laura admonished her. "The Whites' domestic arrangements are their own concern, no one else's." She turned with a smile to her host. "Stanny, tell me all about the Capital Club. I've never known you to be so mysterious about a project."

White readily returned her smile, appreciative as ever of her timeless classic beauty.

"If I've been mysterious," White answered, "I've had good reason, Laura. This clubhouse may cause a furor among the more puritanical of New Yorkers. You see, it's going to be a feminine counterpart of the Metropolitan Club and the Century Association. It will have guest

rooms for out-of-towners, or"—he grinned—
"for irate wives who have quarreled with their
husbands. It will also have a fully equipped gymnasium, Turkish baths, a billiard room, a card
room, and even a cocktail bar for refreshing one-
self at the end of a hectic day."

"Stanny," she said, stunned, "I had no idea. I
thought we were talking about decorating a few
offices and rooms for charity functions."

"Not at all!" White said exuberantly. "The
Capital Club will be the first true haven for ladies, where children are strictly forbidden and
where gentlemen may not set foot above the first
floor. And the marvelous part of it, Laura, is that
you'll be given an absolutely free hand in the
decorating. The planning committee is peopled
by quite a few of your admirers. They've seen
your work and want the same airy, uncluttered
look in the clubhouse."

Laura was silent for a time, reflecting eagerly
on this most exciting of challenges. A club for
women—what a daring concept! And what a
stimulating prospect: devoting herself wholeheartedly to a project that would demand the
most skillful of her talents while imposing no
bans on her creativity.

"Will you do it?" White pressed her. "It will
be a lengthy and time-consuming job, but I
wouldn't want anyone else but you to decorate
one of my buildings."

"Stanny, why aren't *you* doing the decorating?" she asked, puzzled.

"I'd love to do it," he admitted, "but frankly,

Laura, I haven't the time. Will you do it for me?"

She gave him a radiant smile. "With the greatest pleasure!"

White's butler entered the room. "Mr. White," he said, "your pardon, sir. There's an urgent telephone call for Mrs. Sheridan."

Laura's smile vanished; she felt herself turn pale. *Whitney,* she thought with a stab of alarm. *Something's happened to her.*

"Who is it, Randolph?" she asked, rising.

"It's Thompson, your man, Mrs. Sheridan."

"Thompson?" she said with a frown. "Stanny, Cynthia, excuse me, please."

She followed Randolph to the hall and picked up the telephone with great trepidation. After Randolph withdrew, she asked urgently into the mouthpiece, "Thompson, what is it? Have you had news of my daughter?"

"Of Miss Whitney?" Thompson was taken aback by the question. "No, madam, I haven't. I apologize for interrupting your dinner, but I've just had the most peculiar telephone call from Mr. Warren."

Laura's heart leaped. Christopher? Calling her? "What did he want?" she asked, eagerly.

"He wanted to speak to you, Mrs. Sheridan. And when I told him you were out for the evening, he demanded to know where you were."

"Demanded?" A frown creased her brow.

"Yes, madam, demanded. Most emphatically, I might add. As you know, Mrs. Sheridan, I am not in the habit of giving out that information to mere acquaintances. When I refused to say where you were, Mr. Warren became quite . . . agitated. He said he would give me one hour to contact you and ask you to telephone him at his offices. He said if he didn't hear from you by half past nine . . ."

"Yes, Thompson?" Her hands gripped the telephone.

"Well, madam . . ." Thompson's voice bristled with injured pride. "He slammed down the receiver in my ear."

Laura's reaction was a mixture of amusement and indignation. Poor Thompson; at times he was much too sensitive. But she was extremely annoyed with Christopher. What in heaven's name had gotten into him? Didn't he know better than to behave in that manner, to create a situation that might lead to conjecture, or even to gossip?

"Thompson," she soothed, "you did exactly the right thing. I'm going to call Mr. Warren just as soon as you ring off. I daresay he's having some difficulty with the Corbetts. They've been as bothersome with their new house as the Tylers were with theirs. Good night, now. Don't wait up for me; I have my latchkey."

She didn't wait for his good-bye but clicked the switch hook several times until Central came on the line.

"What number, please?"

"Broadway five-three-nine," Laura said, then tapped her foot impatiently while the connection was being made.

Christopher answered on the first ring. Laura sensed trouble in his rigid hello.

"Christopher? It's Laura."

"Where are you?"

She didn't answer at once. Initially she had been glad that he telephoned her, eager to talk to him. But they hadn't seen each other in months, and here he was, acting as if he owned her. She deeply resented his attitude. Coolly she said, "I'm on Gramercy Park; I'm dining with Stanford White. What was so important that it necessitated your being rude to my servant?"

"If Thompson had told me what I wanted to know," Christopher said bluntly, "I would not have had to be rude to him. Now I want you to—"

"There's never an excuse for rudeness," Laura maintained, "especially toward servants."

"Listen to me," he said roughly. "I'm not interested in an etiquette lesson. I want to see you, at once, at my house."

"That's impossible," she said flatly.

"I want to see you," he repeated. "If you won't come to me, I'll come to Gramercy Park and fetch you."

"You're being unreasonable," she said, trying hard to keep her temper. "I said I can't see you now. If you like, I'll try to meet with you sometime tomorrow. I'll have to check my appointments first to see if—"

"It's about Whitney," he said.

"Whitney?" she said, stunned. "What about her?"

"I've seen her."

All the breath left her lungs. "Where? When?" she gasped.

"Come to my house and I'll tell you all about it."

"Christopher, please. You must tell me now. Is she all right? Did she say if she—?"

"My house," Christopher said. "I'll wait for you there." Then he deliberately hung up the receiver.

On the carriage ride to Patchin Place, as the horses' hooves beat a clattering cadence on the rain-slicked streets, Laura kept thinking, *Don't go, don't go, don't go.*

She was both anxious to hear about Whitney from Christopher and inexplicably afraid of what he might say. When and where had he met with her? Under what circumstances? Had it been at the Indigents' Hospital? No, that was unlikely; Whitney no longer worked there. Where, then? Where had Christopher seen her? Or *had* he seen her? Perhaps he had lied; perhaps he'd only mentioned Whitney's name because he knew that that was the only way to get Laura to come to his house. No, no, she thought in the very next instant. He could not be so cruel. He would not stoop that low to achieve his own ends.

Her abrupt departure from Gramercy Park had added fuel to her distress. She'd made a lame excuse: "The telephone call? Oh, it was nothing, some minor emergency with the central heating system. But all of a sudden I have the most dreadful headache. No, Stanny, don't trouble yourself; I can get home on my own. Cynthia traveled here in my carriage, though. Would you be good enough to escort her home?"

She knew they hadn't believed her; she didn't care. Her only concern now was her daughter and Christopher.

After what seemed an interminable time, the carriage drew up to Christopher's house. Laura alighted, unassisted, the instant the horses were reined in. She instructed her coachman to wait for her, then she walked swiftly to Christopher's door, unmindful of the rain that struck like icy needles across her burning cheeks and lips.

She knocked on the door. There was no answer. A shiver went through her; she drew her cloak more tightly about her. She knocked a second time, and he opened the door. The look on his face, grave and unreadable, heightened her nameless fears.

"Come in," he said, stepping aside to let her enter.

She complied with a pounding heart. Her throat was dry; her hands were numb with cold. Christopher walked, without a word, into the parlor. Laura nervously followed, half expecting to see Whitney when she stepped into the room.

She wasn't there, of course; the parlor was empty. There was a good fire on the grate, but Laura felt chilled to the bone. She shivered again. Christopher, noting this, took her wet cloak from her shoulders and laid it on the arm of the sofa.

"May I get you something? Some coffee, wine?"

Laura said faintly, "Something stronger if you have it."

"Of course," he said as politely as if this were a simple social call.

He went to a corner cabinet and extracted a bottle and one small glass.

"Aren't you having any?" Laura asked as he filled the glass and handed it to her.

"No," he said. "I rarely drink whiskey. The schoolmasters at Saint Peter's used to say that spirits dull the mind and destroy a man's will. It is one of the few things I was taught in my youth to which I still give credence."

Something was wrong with him, terribly wrong. Laura had never seen him like this: as courteous as a stranger, aloof and composed, yet exuding an unmistakable aura of tightly restrained violence.

She took a generous swallow of the whiskey and was glad of the bracing jolt that steeled her nerves. "Christopher." Her voice was stronger now, commanding. "About Whitney . . ."

"In a moment," he said, picking up a leather briefcase that lay on the armchair. "I want to show you something first. Won't you sit down?"

"Christopher, please! I don't want to look at anything. I just want to know about my daughter."

"All in good time, Laura."

His voice was calm; he took her arm and steered her gently but firmly to the chair. Laura sat down in frustration, quickly finished the whiskey, then put the glass on the side table.

She felt hot now, stiflingly hot; but Christopher's curious conduct was bone chilling.

"I thought this might interest you," he said, taking a handful of torn bits of paper from the briefcase and dropping them on the floor.

"What . . . what is that?" she asked, bewildered.

"It's the Corbett house." He continued to extract the torn papers, dropping them on the floor like so many pieces of confetti.

"The Corbett house? Why have you torn up the plans? Christopher, stop doing that! Answer me."

He turned the briefcase upside down and emptied the remainder of the contents. Tossing the briefcase aside, he sat opposite Laura on the sofa and leaned forward, elbows on knees. "I didn't like it," he said simply.

Laura's overwrought nerves snapped. She jumped to her feet and glared down at him in a rage. "What in heaven's name is wrong with you? Why did you coerce me into coming here tonight? Did you see Whitney or didn't you? I demand that you answer me."

"I did see her," he replied, still disturbingly serene. "And I intend to tell you all about it—in my own way. You see, I've learned something very important from my association with you, Laura, and that is not to rush into things, to take my time when doing something I may later regret, to take a long, long time."

"You're being childish and cruel," she said angrily. "I know exactly what you're implying, but I refuse to discuss that now. I want to know about Whitney. If you've seen her—which I'm beginning to doubt—I want you to tell me this minute what you talked about."

"Laura, you wound me," he said lightly, but his eyes were dark as pitch. "I thought you were interested in my work."

"Of course I'm interested in your work," she said impatiently. "But I'm more interested in what my daughter had to say to you."

"How extraordinary." He leaned back on the sofa and folded his arms across his chest.

"What's extraordinary?" she snapped.

"The fact that you said, 'I'm interested in what my daughter had to say to you,' as opposed to, 'I'm worried about my daughter's safety and welfare.' "

"Christopher . . ." She was strangling on her rage. "You're making me extremely angry. I don't know what you're driving at, and I don't want to know. I want—"

"Forgive me," he said at once, straightening on the sofa. "I *am* being cruel. You want to know about Whitney. Let me set your mind at rest, then. She came to my house last August, and as far as I could tell she was perfectly all right. She looked fit and well-cared-for; her clothes were clean, her complexion was clear. She wouldn't tell me where she was living, though, and unfortunately she did say she had no intention of ever going home."

Laura stared at him blankly, unprepared for the information he had so unexpectedly imparted to her. She groped for the arm of the chair, then sat down abruptly, as if her legs could no longer support her.

"Whitney came . . . here?" she whispered, looking numbly at the tattered bits of paper on the floor. "But . . ." She raised her head suddenly. "She was here last *August* and you're just telling me now? Why did you keep it to yourself all this time? Why didn't you—?"

"Laura, you won't be so confused, you won't have so many questions, if you allow me to tell you what I want to say to you in my own way."

His tone was warm and solicitous, but there was that odd, unnatural look in his eyes, which gave frightening validation to Laura's vague fears.

"Then tell me," she said, but she didn't want to hear it. She knew with deadly certainty that what Christopher had to say to her was going to alter once again the design of her already precarious future.

"Would you like another whiskey?" he asked.

"Yes . . . please," she said dully.

He rose and filled her glass, then threw more coal on the fire. Laura watched him numbly, sipping at her drink, attempting to gather a strength that she feared she would shortly need.

"I had a talk with Ned tonight," Christopher said, resuming his seat and brushing a cinder from the knee of his trousers. "He made a rather helpful suggestion about my work, a suggestion that threw an interesting light on our relationship—yours and mine, I mean."

"Christopher—"

"I beg you to indulge me, Laura."

Again his voice was faultlessly courteous, but the look he gave her was of naked intimidation. Laura longed to get up and leave this house, yet a dread fascination kept her rooted to her chair.

"Very well," she said with a shudder. "Go on."

"It can't have escaped your notice," he began, "that my work in the past two years or so has undergone a drastic change."

"Yes," she said, her hands clenched tightly about her glass, "I know that."

"I think I've partly been blaming you for the change, Laura, but I realized tonight, when Ned spoke to me, that I've been grossly unfair to you. No outside forces ought to influence a man's standards, and, indeed, I understand now that it was my own cowardice and greed that accounted for the change."

Sensing his gist, Laura started to comment, but Christopher cut her off. "To be more specific," he explained, "this all started when I mistakenly allowed myself to believe you were going to marry me. But my—"

"Christopher, I *am* going to marry you!"

"Not in this lifetime, Laura. But that's neither here nor there. Please let me continue. My error was not in aspiring to marry you, it was in trying to make myself worthy of having you, in other words, to become as much like a member of your class as I could. But in doing so, I became everything I despise: rapacious, expedient, hypocritical, dishonest."

Laura bristled with resentment and set aside

her glass. "Is that what you think of my family and friends?" she asked stiffly. "Then you must necessarily think the same of me."

"Hardly," he said. "Don't you know how I've idealized you? To me you are perfection, totally without flaw."

Impatient with the direction of the conversation, Laura said shortly, "Christopher, about Whitney . . ."

"I'm just coming to that, Laura. My greed ruined my work, and my dishonesty, I've no doubt, will bring an end once and for all to my hopes of ever marrying you. You see, Whitney didn't lie to you on the night of her debut. I did kiss her . . . and I suppose I did give her good reason to believe I loved her. I *don't* love her; it's important that you know that. But I was wrong to do what I did, and I was even more wrong to keep it from you."

"You . . . you kissed her?" she echoed blankly, once again thrown off balance by his lightning-swift change of topic. "When?" she demanded, her senses reeling. *"Why?"*

"It happened two years ago. And to be truthful, Laura, I didn't know why at the time. I think I do now, though. I kissed her because I knew she loved me, unreservedly, unashamedly, because if I had asked her to, she would have married me in a minute. But most of all, I think I kissed her because, deep in my heart, I knew that I would never have *you.*"

"What are you saying?" she cried, gripping the arms of the chair with both hands. "I *told* you I would marry you. How could you have kissed her when you knew, *you knew*, I would marry you?"

He smiled grimly and shook his head. "No, Laura. Take my word for it when I tell you that that is something I never quite fully believed would happen. Even before that night at the opera I doubt you ever had any intention of marrying me. In any case, the incident with Whitney happened long before that."

"At school?" Laura accused him, so filled with rage that she could barely speak. "You kissed her then? When you promised on oath that you had not? What else did you do to her? Did you make love to her?"

"No," he said, "it didn't happen at school. And I didn't make love to her; I swear it."

"Where, then?" she demanded. "When were you ever alone with her?"

"It was at Bar Harbor," he said. "Whitney was spending the summer with the MacKenzies. I had gone up there to speak to Malcolm about his new house. If you will recall," he added, watching her, "that was a few months after I first made love to you—after which you enumerated the many reasons why it was impossible for you to marry me."

Laura stared at him fiercely, trying to make sense of the chaos in her mind. He had touched Whitney, kissed her. He had committed the very outrage of which Laura had always suspected him. For two years he had deceived her. And like the fool that she was she had trusted him, believed his facile lies. And worse, she had given herself to him, had promised to marry him. Marry him! Dear God, what a joke! What a vile, contemptible joke.

She rose to her feet on trembling legs. "You're revolting," she said hoarsely, "despicable, totally without honor. I loved and trusted you, and you repaid me by trying to seduce my daughter."

Christopher rose also, his expression resigned and defenseless.

"I could probably have you arrested," she went on in a blinding fury, "but I won't condescend to drag myself through the mud of your lowborn immorality."

"Ah," Christopher said quietly. "Now at last we have the truth."

"Don't speak to me of truth!" she raged. "You don't know the meaning of the word."

She turned away from him abruptly, went for her cloak, and snatched it up from the sofa. She wanted to strike him, to kill him; she wanted to rake the flesh from his bones with her fingernails. She wanted to shatter him, destroy him, as he had done to her. She wanted to inflict on him the same savage pain and shameful humiliation he had so brutally inflicted on her.

At the parlor door, she stopped and turned back to him. "If you ever come near me again," she said in a deadly low voice, "if ever I hear that you've been near my daughter, I *will* have you arrested; I shall name you for the ill-bred, vulgar seducer that you are."

"You needn't worry about that," he said bitterly, coldly. "I've had enough of the Sheridan women to last me a lifetime."

Chapter Twenty
✦✦✦✦

THANK GOD FOR her work, Laura often thought in the weeks that followed. If she hadn't had her decorating to keep her occupied a good part of every day, she truly feared that her mind would not have been able to stand the strain. Try as she might to put it out of her thoughts, Christopher's appalling confession rose constantly to plague her. In her mind's eye she would see him with Whitney, holding her, kissing her, as he had held and kissed Laura. A killing rage would sweep over her, a rage that blinded her eyes, paralyzed her limbs, so that she couldn't see, couldn't move, could only think over and over again that he had shamed her, betrayed her, he who had sworn to love her. At the first opportunity he had been swayed by the charms of another. He never had been—nor ever would be—a gentleman.

And then she would think of Whitney—whom *she* had betrayed. Laura had taken Christopher's part against her precious flesh and blood. She had doubted Whitney's word, had trusted a man who was a stranger to both honor and truth. No wonder Whitney had left home, no wonder she'd told Christopher she was never coming back. Laura would think of her own disloyalty with a shudder of self-loathing. Thank God her mother had not lived to see her make a mockery of the sacred duty she owed her daughter.

As if she hadn't enough to cope with, several days after her meeting with Christopher, Laura learned that Avery, despite his demanding medical responsibilities in New York, had decided to go to Cuba with Theodore Roosevelt's volunteer group, the Rough Riders.

"They're going to need physicians badly," Avery had said in response to Laura's shocked protests. "Teddy's volunteers are an untrained conglomeration of cowboys and gamblers from the West, and college boys and polo players from the East, who think this war is a great adventure planned solely for their entertainment."

"But, Avery, why must *you* go? There are other doctors, younger men, who are just as qualified as you to take care of the sick and wounded."

"Why, Laura," he had said with a grin, "are you implying that I'm too old for such vigorous duties? I deeply resent that."

"Avery, this is no joking matter! What if something should happen to you? I couldn't bear losing you too; I couldn't bear it!"

"My dear girl," he had said softly, surprised and touched by the intensity of her concern, "I give you my word nothing will happen to me." And when she had stared at him silently, as if her heart would break if he should leave her, he took her face in his hands and looked deep into her eyes. "Laura . . ." He was seeking an answer to a question he dared not ask a second time. "Laura, will you . . . write to me?"

"Yes," she had whispered wretchedly, "I'll write you every day, and I'll pray for your speedy return. Avery, what will I do without you, my brother, my dearest friend?"

Brother. Dearest friend. He released her and stepped back from her, enraged by her response, though he had fully expected it. "You'll manage somehow, my dear," he had said, keeping the bitterness from his tone. Then, with a brotherly kiss on her brow, he had bidden farewell to his grief-stricken sister-in-law.

In this desolate state of mind Laura began to design the interiors for the newly constructed Capital Club on Madison Avenue. The club was her most extensive and challenging project to date, yet never had she felt less disposed to practice the art she so loved. Fortunately, Stanford White had designed the club in the classical style Laura favored. When she saw the finished product—the graceful Corinthian columns, the flawlessly proportioned rooms, the great floor-to-ceiling windows in the grand salon—her spirits lifted somewhat, and her creativity soared.

Initially, when first informed of the project, Laura had envisioned a formal, almost academic decor, much in the manner of a gentleman's study. Instead, when she saw White's sunlit creation, she chose a different tone, the look of an English country house—all soft, pastel walls and light-colored wood, and gay chintz prints for the upholstery and draperies.

Laura's designs for the guest rooms were simple but feminine: pollard oak bedframes, pretty cretonne spreads, and wash pitchers of the finest porcelain. For the library she chose cinnamon-colored chairs, an ivory Aubusson rug, and bookcases of sunny-hued sycamore. The cocktail bar was a triumph: Willow-green tiles covered the floor; white wicker chairs surrounded glass-topped tables; and for the walls Laura designed a crisscross of white garden trellises hung with ivy, giving the room the look of perpetual springtime.

Her preliminary watercolor sketches were enthusiastically approved by the planning committee. Laura anticipated that more than a year's work faced her; so instead of retiring to Newport for most of the summer as she normally did, she remained in the city and immediately plunged into the job. Truth be told, she much preferred to be busy than to be lolling at the seashore with time on her hands. There were issues on her mind she would rather not think about, issues too painful to confront. Moreover, with the country at war, and Avery in service, Laura could not in good conscience take a holiday.

Avery Sheridan was not the only gentleman of his set who felt it his patriotic duty to serve his country. Ned Bailey and several of his co-workers had volunteered. John Barnes had left his Wall Street bank in the hands of his two brothers and his partners. Jeremy Tyler had been refused a commission as a fighting man because of a murmur at his heart (a holdover from a childhood bout with scarlet fever), but he had signed on nevertheless as a war correspondent, reporting to *Harper's* magazine. Even Malcolm MacKenzie, whose first love was his native Scotland, considered it a duty and an honor to protect the interests of his beloved adopted country.

"There's a telephone call for you, Mrs. Sheridan," said Thompson one morning in July.

Laura was in Steven's study, matching drapery and carpet samples for the Capital Club guest rooms. She glanced up impatiently from her work. "Who is it, Thompson?"

"It's Mr. Tierney, madam. The Pinkerton agent," he reminded her. As if she needed reminding.

Laura sighed, set aside her materials, and followed Thompson out of the room. Dennis Tierney had been telephoning her once a month for over a year. Their conversations were invariable: "Mr. Tierney, have you anything to report?" "I'm afraid not, Mrs. Sheridan. But you may rest assured that I will eventually find your daughter."

As she picked up the telephone now, Laura decided to alter their routine.

"Good morning, Mr. Tierney," she said cordially. "How are you? Isn't it delightfully cool today for July?"

Her slight deviation obviously caught Tierney

unprepared. He said nothing for a moment.
Then, recovering smoothly, he replied, "Good
morning, Mrs. Sheridan. I'm very well, thank
you. And it is cool for July, but I hear we're in for
a torrid August."

"Oh dear," she said. "I'm afraid I shall be
spending a very unhappy month, then. I'm not
planning on being in Newport this season."

"If I may be permitted to contradict you,"
Tierney said in his pleasantly modulated voice.
"I think you'll be having an extremely happy
summer. You see, Mrs. Sheridan, it gives me
great pleasure to report to you that I have finally
located your daughter."

Laura's breath caught in her throat. The words
she had been longing to hear for more than a year
had at last been spoken. She said, barely audibly,
"Where, Mr. Tierney? How did you find her?"

"It was a relatively easy matter once you told
me she'd been working at Indigents' Hospital,"
he explained. "I assumed that if your daughter
looked again for work, it would be more or less
in the same line. I then remembered your saying
that she had done volunteer work at the Bleecker
Street Foundling Home, so I began checking all
the hospitals and orphanages in the city. I located her yesterday at the Lying-In Hospital on
Broadway. When she left work, I followed her to
a house nearby. To make sure it was where she
lived, I made some inquiries earlier this morning
at City Hall. The lease was signed 'Amelia Dev-
ereaux,' but the handwriting is identical to your
daughter's."

"That's my mother's name," Laura told him,

her heart beating rapidly. "Where is my daughter living, Mr. Tierney?" And when he gave her the Bleecker Street address, she said faintly, "Dear God. Right under our noses."

"That's often the case, Mrs. Sheridan. It's been my experience that when young people leave home, they don't go very far. My guess is your daughter was hoping to be found. I daresay when she sees you, she'll be most anxious to go home with you."

Laura did not respond. Too many thoughts were crowding her mind, too many emotions.

Comprehending the reason for her silence, Tierney said gently, "Your daughter should be home this evening at half past six or so. I know you're eager to see her."

"Yes," Laura answered, her voice tremulous and soft. "Yes, I am."

"If you like," Tierney suggested, "I'll accompany you to Bleecker Street."

"Thank you, no," Laura said, wondering uneasily if her desire for a reconciliation with Whitney was still one-sided. "I appreciate your offer, Mr. Tierney, but this is something I must do on my own."

She was waiting on Bleecker Street, across the street from Whitney's house, at six o'clock sharp. In preparation for the meeting, she had tried on and discarded at least seven different outfits. She finally chose a two-piece pale-peach walking dress with jaunty epaulets decorating the shoulders. The skirt was straight and narrow; apricot

braid encircled the bodice and sleeves. Her hat
was a perky straw boater banded in velvet. She
looked quite a bit more festive than she felt.

For thirty minutes she sat tensely in the closed
carriage, searching the street for the first sight of
her daughter. Had Whitney changed? she wondered nervously. More important, had her feelings changed toward Laura? Mr. Tierney had
said he believed Whitney wished to be found.
But if that were the case, wouldn't she simply
have come home on her own?

At half past six, Laura heard the clock chime
from Saint Mark's on the Bowery. Impatiently,
she checked the time against the watch at her
lapel. When she looked back out on the street,
she saw a young woman in black turn the corner
onto Bleecker Street. Her head was down, her
face hidden by the brim of her hat, but Laura
knew in an instant it was her daughter.

Laura pushed open the door and stepped
down from the carriage in one swift, eager motion. Whitney, her eyes on the sidewalk, did not
see her. Laura crossed the street hurriedly, nar-
rowly missing collision with a horseless carriage
driven at an alarming rate of speed by a young
rake wearing dustcoat and goggles. She reached
the house first and stood there, quivering with
anticipation, until Whitney came abreast of her
and looked up with a gasp of recognition.

"Mama?" The word conveyed shocked disbelief combined with genuine joy. "Mama, is it
really you?"

Tears stung Laura's eyes; it was difficult to

speak. "Yes, darling," she whispered, "it's really your mother."

Whitney's eyes, too, were bright with tears, and they reflected a multitude of conflicting emotions. Laura saw happiness mixed with pain, eagerness with apprehension. She saw resentment struggling with shame. But stronger than the rest, she saw a love that neither time, distance, nor dissension had had the power to diminish even an iota.

"My dearest child . . ." She held out her arms. "Won't you embrace me?"

"Oh, Mama." Whitney's voice broke. She stumbled forward and threw her arms about her mother, holding on to her so hard that Laura could scarcely breathe. A policeman passing by looked at the couple oddly, but both Laura and Whitney were oblivious to all but the bittersweet bliss of their reunion.

Finally, Laura drew back and held her daughter at arm's length to get a good look at her. "You look older," she said with a shaky smile, "and prettier."

"You look younger," Whitney countered softly, "and more beautiful than ever."

Laura hugged her briefly and turned her toward the house. "Let's go inside," she said in a brisk tone that belied her desire to succumb to maudlin tears. "I'm perishing for a cup of tea."

Whitney unlocked the front door with an unsteady hand and ushered her mother into the house. A narrow foyer branched out into a parlor and dining room. At the rear of the house was a cheery kitchen, very much like Christopher's, with large double windows admitting the rays of a red-gold setting sun. There, however, the resemblance ended. Where Christopher's house had been neat as a pin, Whitney's, Laura noted with parental disappointment, was dusty, untidy, and in places downright grimy.

"Whitney," she said tactfully, stripping off her gloves, "I'll just clear these dishes out of the sink while you put the kettle on."

"No, Mama." Whitney flushed with embarrassment as she filled the teakettle with water. "I'll do them later."

"Nonsense," Laura said kindly. "You've been working all day; you're probably tired to the bone. I'll do them now while you set the table. And then we can sit and chat."

With a look of chagrin, Whitney struck a match and lit the gas as Laura attacked the pile of dirty dishes. "Mama, I'm sorry," she said ruefully, taking cups and saucers from the cupboard and placing them on the table. "The house isn't usually such a mess."

"Darling, don't apologize." Laura glanced back at her with a smile. "I can imagine how exhausted you must be at the end of the day."

Whitney removed her hat and gloves and laid them on a chair, then looked dolefully about the kitchen as if seeing it through her mother's eyes. Laura, sensing her discomfiture, said easily, "Is that a ribbon cake on the sideboard? It looks delicious."

Whitney's countenance brightened. "It is delicious! I made it last night and had a slice for breakfast."

"For breakfast?" Laura's stern tone was negated by her dancing blue eyes. "Honestly, darling. Wouldn't a bowl of hot oatmeal have been better?"

"Ugh!" Whitney grimaced. "I loathe oatmeal."

"I see nothing's changed," Laura laughed, drying her hands on a towel.

"Nothing of importance," Whitney agreed, impulsively planting a kiss on her delighted mother's cheek.

When they were seated at the kitchen table over steaming cups of tea and generous slices of cake, they regarded each other solemnly, each facing at last her own moment of truth. With the first joy of meeting past, Laura noted with some concern that Whitney looked paler and wearier than she should.

"Darling, eat your cake," she coaxed. Her tone and manner were utterly composed, but inside she was still quivering with uncontrollable excitement. It was difficult to believe that she was sitting in the same room with her daughter, looking at her, speaking with her. If she wished, she could easily reach out and touch her hand, hold it in hers, raise it to her lips and kiss each slender finger, as she used to do when Whitney was a baby. "You've lost some weight, haven't you?"

Whitney lowered her gaze and poked with her fork at the confection. "A little," she allowed.

"I think more than a little," Laura said gently. "Whitney, it can't have been easy for you, living on your own all this time. How did you manage?"

Whitney looked up at her mother through the veil of her dark lashes. "It wasn't too difficult, Mama. I had my work to keep me busy, and I had Grandfather's money whenever I ran short."

"But weren't you lonely, darling? Did you ever think of coming home?"

"Yes, sometimes," the girl said honestly. "But I was . . . afraid."

"Afraid of what, Whitney?"

"That you'd still be angry with me. That we'd still quarrel, as we did constantly before I left home. I telephoned you once, but you weren't home."

"Yes. Thompson told me."

"And then, when I saw Uncle Avery at the hospital—did he tell you, Mama?"

"Yes, darling, he did."

"Well, when I talked to him, he was so different, so . . . cold. I was afraid that you felt the same way he did. I was afraid that you both didn't love me anymore."

"Whitney, Whitney," Laura said softly. "Uncle Avery was hurt, that's all. And as for not loving you— Darling, when you have a daughter of your own, you'll learn that there's very little she can do to ever make you stop loving her."

Whitney's eyes grew bright again, and her hand crept cautiously across the table to Laura's. "I never stopped loving you, Mama, even when

I was angry with you. I kept hoping you'd never find me, and then, in the next moment, I'd want to see you so much that I'd hurt all over.''

Laura squeezed her daughter's hand, too moved to respond.

''Mama, how *did* you find me?'' Whitney asked suddenly.

Laura explained about Dennis Tierney.

Whitney was surprised. ''He's been looking for me all this time?''

''Yes, Whitney.'' Laura tasted her tea. ''I'm extremely grateful to Mr. Tierney. He could have given up long ago, but he was determined to find you.''

Whitney smiled wryly. ''You mean *you* were determined to find me.''

''Yes, I was,'' Laura admitted. ''I drove you away, so it was my responsibility to bring you back.''

''Mama . . .'' Whitney's voice was pained. ''It wasn't entirely your fault. I used to think it was, but now I realize there were other reasons—''

''Christopher Warren, for one.''

For a moment Whitney looked startled. Then her dark gaze hardened. ''Yes, Christopher,'' she said as if the name were a vile taste on her tongue. ''Mostly Christopher.''

''Whitney—''

''Mama,'' she said abruptly, ''you're in love with him, aren't you?''

Now Laura was startled. But recovering quickly, she gave an answer that she believed to be the truth. ''Not anymore, darling.''

Whitney nodded grimly. ''Good,'' she said.

"He's a scoundrel, you know. I don't know how I could ever have thought myself in love with him. He's base and unprincipled; he hasn't the least sense of honor. We're both well rid of him, Mama. I detest him with all my heart."

Laura was stunned and alarmed by the depth of her daughter's bitterness. "Whitney," she said swiftly, "did he . . . ? Did Christopher . . .?"

Whitney's pale face flushed scarlet. Laura's heart leaped with fear.

"No, Mama," the girl murmured.

But Laura was unconvinced. "Whitney, dear God," she urged, "if he did, you must tell me."

"Mama, I swear to you, he never . . . I mean, he didn't actually . . . He wanted to, I know he did. But he—I—stopped him. It was at Bar Harbor."

"I know." Laura shut her eyes tightly to blot out her thoughts, but she saw Christopher and her daughter as clearly and as obscenely as if she had witnessed the scene. "He told me."

"He told you?" Whitney's voice rang with guilt and shame. "What did he say? What else did he tell you?"

Laura opened her eyes and took Whitney's hand firmly in hers. What had that devil done to her, her beautiful, innocent daughter? The rage that swept through her was mercifully tempered by maternal protectiveness. She said in a soothing voice, "Whitney, you mustn't blame yourself for what happened between you and Christopher. You were only a baby; he took shameful advantage of you. He at least had the decency to admit he did wrong." She paused, then added carefully, "He also told me you went to his house to see him. Darling, why did you go there?"

A fresh wave of guilty color tinted Whitney's pale cheeks. "I . . . I don't know," she stammered. "I couldn't sleep one night. I went for a walk and found myself on Patchin Place. Then . . . then . . ." she groped, "I saw him walking down the street. When he saw me, he asked me to come in, said he wanted to talk to me, to explain about that night in Bar Harbor."

"And then?" Laura prompted, her voice not quite steady.

Whitney pulled her hand from her mother's crushing grip. "I don't want to discuss it," she said hoarsely. "I don't even want to think about him. He's a cad and a liar. I feel dirty when I think of him."

"Whitney, listen to me," Laura said urgently. "You mustn't feel guilty or dirty in the least. You are the innocent victim of a man without scruples. Your only error was in trusting him—as I did. The fault here is entirely Christopher's."

"Oh, Mama." Whitney rose blindly, stumbled around the table, knelt at Laura's feet, and threw her arms about her waist. "Can you ever forgive me?"

Laura's throat ached, her heart throbbed. She pressed Whitney's head to her breast and kissed her tumbled curls. "Whitney, I do forgive you for leaving home, but as for what happened in Bar Harbor, you did absolutely nothing wrong. You must remember that, darling. Only Christopher is to blame for that incident."

Whitney was crying, quietly, bitterly. Laura said painfully, "My precious girl, it's over, it's done with. You'll come home now, and everything will be just as it was before he came into our lives."

"Will it?" Whitney said, her words muffled against Laura's breast. "Can anything ever be the same as it was once it's spoiled?"

"Yes, yes!" Laura said fiercely. "It *will* be the same."

But despite her insistence, she knew that it wouldn't.

Chapter Twenty-one
✦✦✦✦

ON JULY SEVENTEENTH, one week after Whitney's return home, the Spanish army surrendered to American forces in Cuba, and the war that had begun only three months before was officially ended. Shortly thereafter, Laura received a jubilant letter from Avery expressing his joy over Whitney's return; assuring Laura that he had come through the conflict unharmed, as promised; and informing her that the troops were expected to be mustered out of the service some time in September. There were letters, too, for Whitney, from Avery and Ned. Whitney willingly shared her uncle's letter with Laura, laughing with tears in her eyes because his words were so like him, so loving. Ned's letter she didn't open. "I want to read it," she said with a warmth and a shy blush that brought a smile to Laura's lips, "in private."

Laura's own joy during this period ought certainly to have paralleled Avery's, and, to a degree, it did. Her daughter had been restored to her; her beloved brother-in-law had come through the war unscathed; her work on the Capital Club was the best she had ever done. Every day, from sunup to sundown, she fairly vibrated with exhilaration, with an awed incredulity of the sudden turn of events. She rarely thought of Christopher. In her present fortuitous circumstances, it was easy to ignore that part of her life. She had made a grievous error, but it was behind her now, finished, dead. Yet she wasn't happy—not when she stopped to think about it. Beneath her surface euphoria she felt depressed and vaguely guilty. She didn't know why. Nor did she wish to search her conscience to determine the reasons for this peculiar state of mind.

To divert her uneasy feelings, she buried herself in her work, much like an ostrich, she would think fleetingly, who buries his head in the sand. Whitney, over Laura's mild objections, retained her position at the Lying-In Hospital, and she resumed her volunteer services at the Bleecker Street Foundling Home, working three nights a week, from seven to ten o'clock. Laura was wor-

ried about her. Whitney was constantly pale and
far too slender; there was a driven yet fragile
aura about her that pierced Laura's heart. It occurred to Laura that Whitney, too, might be
overworking in order to ignore other issues.
Laura never broached the subject, though. She
had made the mistake once of interfering in her
daughter's life. She was determined not to do so
again.

   With both of them so busy, they saw little of
each other during the week, but Laura devoted
the weekends exclusively to her daughter. What
a priceless luxury to spend time with her precious darling again! They'd have dinner *à deux*,
dressed as if for a ball: Laura in royal-blue satin,
wearing the sapphire dog collar Steven had
given her on their tenth anniversary; and Whitney in virginal white, her perfect pink ears
graced by Avery's lustrous pearls. They'd have
their coffee formally in the drawing room, es-
chewing the electric lights in favor of softly glim-
mering candles in tall silver sconces. In this
enchanted light they would talk well into the
wee hours, remembering happy times with Steven, winter skating parties in Central Park, summer boating outings on Newport Bay. Their
entire life together was reviewed during these
lovely recollective periods. Their separation,
though, was never discussed; it was as if it had
never existed. They were as close as they had
ever been—closer—because in the back of both
their minds they cherished more deeply the relationship that had almost been destroyed. The
destroyer of that relationship was likewise never

mentioned. It was as if Christopher Warren, also, had never existed.

During these intimate evenings together, Laura often found herself thinking of Avery and of how pleasant it would be if he were once again a part of the Sheridan family circle. More and more she entertained the thought of marrying him. She was tired of being by herself. It was unnatural and pathetic for a woman to be alone. She was not in love with Avery, but she knew she would make him a good wife. She knew, too, that Whitney would heartily approve the match, as would every last one of her friends. Moreover, if she married Avery, she would be secure and safe—secure in the haven of her own ordered world and safe from the treachery of unscrupulous strangers.

She never mentioned these thoughts to Whitney. There would be time enough to do so, she reasoned, when Avery returned from Cuba. She did, however, talk often to her of Ned Bailey, which invariably brought a flustered blush from the girl.

Laura said to her one morning in late July, "Another letter from Ned? Good heavens, Whitney, he'll be home in a month or so. If he tells you all his news now, what will the two of you have to talk about when he comes home?"

They were at the breakfast table, prior to starting their workday. Whitney was dressed in a white shirtwaist and navy blue skirt, similar to the Parker School uniform. Laura, too, wore businesslike garb: a charcoal-gray walking suit and a dove-gray silk blouse.

"Mama, you know what a chatterbox Ned is,"
Whitney said, folding the letter and returning it
to the envelope. "No matter what he tells me
now, when he comes home, he'll still have
plenty to say to me."

"You're anxious to see him, aren't you,
darling?"

The invariable blush; a stammered reply.

Laura smiled, satisfied, and envisioned a
church filled with flowers, Whitney in white
satin, Ned beaming with happiness as he
watched her float down the aisle. She saw a
champagne breakfast reception for all their
friends, a long honeymoon abroad, sun-
drenched days touring Italy, moonlit nights at
the Acropolis. She shared the pride in their first
home, felt the bliss of their first child, a beautiful
dark-haired, dark-eyed son. She saw clearly his
rosebud mouth, his petal cheeks; she felt vividly
the satin smoothness of his baby-soft skin. She
longed to kiss his brow, to cradle his dear head
to her breast . . .

"Mama, what are you thinking about?"

Laura came to herself with a jolt. She had
almost forgotten her daughter was there.

"Why, I wasn't thinking of anything, darling.
My mind was a blank just then."

With an oddly aching heart, she patted Whitney's hand and then forced herself to talk of
something else.

On the nights she was in an expansive mood,
Laura would invite friends in for a spur-
of-the-moment buffet. These parties were largely
"ladies only" affairs, as most of the gentlemen

were still at Guantánamo or Santiago, awaiting
orders to return home. The parties were no less
enjoyable for the absence of male company.
Tasty impromptu meals of Scotch woodcock,
black bean soup, chicken croquettes, and Jenny
Lind cake were followed by an evening of music,
with Whitney at the piano, Marcella MacKenzie
on the harp, and Nina Tyler a virtuoso on the
flute. Other nights were spent more whimsically:
cards or charades, a game of Pilgrim's Progress;
and, on one appropriately foggy evening in early
August, a reading of Tarot cards by a mysterious
"seeress" by the name of Madame Fatima, discovered by Cynthia Barnes.

She was tall and austere, perhaps sixty years
old, clad in a black dress reminiscent of Ros-
setti's Pre-Raphaelites. Her hair was covered by
a black silk turban; her face was dark and inscrutable, made more so by the lusterless glow of her
cryptic black eyes. She was a formidable presence, imposing, almost ominous. Laura, upon
first sight of her, took an instant dislike to her.

"Where did you find her?" she asked Cynthia
while Madame Fatima read Nina's cards in a
corner of the drawing room.

Cynthia sipped at her coffee as delicately as a
cat at a brimming bowl of cream. "She was at
Frances Morgan's house this past spring, reading Tarot for the Whist Club. I engaged her at
once, but I had to wait all this time for her first
free evening."

"I wish you hadn't brought her." Laura passed
a cup to Janet MacKenzie, then glanced across the
room where Whitney and Marcella were seated

on the window seat, heads together, whispering a mile a minute, watching the seeress in rapt fascination. "She's undoubtedly a charlatan."

Cynthia put down her coffee cup with an offended sniff. "On the contrary," she protested. "The woman is frighteningly accurate. She predicted Marcella's betrothal to Jamie Olmsted. She told me that I would temporarily lose a loved one, and two weeks later, John left for Cuba. She told Edith Roosevelt that Teddy would distinguish himself on foreign soil at a place named San Juan Hill—except she called it Mount Saint John. Her most amazing prediction was that the war would last less than four months. And wasn't the peace protocol signed just last week? Laura, I tell you, she's uncanny!"

"Bosh," Laura said with a frown. "It's only guesswork and intuition, coupled with observation and common sense. I daresay *I* could go into a crowd of strangers and predict incidents in their lives with a fair degree of accuracy."

"That may be so," Janet MacKenzie interspersed. "But 'there are more things in heaven and earth than are dreamt of in your philosophy,' Laura. When I was a girl in Scotland, everyone knew of Coinneach Odhar, who prophesied that the lochs in the Great Glen would one day be linked. His prediction proved true more than one hundred years later, when the Caledonian Canal was built. And then there was Thomas of Ercildoune. He lived in the thirteenth century, and his prophesies in rhyme are still coming true today."

"Coincidence," Laura maintained. "I disbelieve in precognition. No one can truly predict the future or know what's buried in another's heart. It's all mumbo jumbo. Madame Fatima is a fake."

"Why don't you put her to the test?" Cynthia suggested. "Have her read for you, and then let me know what you think of her authenticity."

An inexplicable dart of alarm raised the hairs on Laura's arms. "I certainly will not," she said. "That would be pandering to chicanery."

Cynthia said with a taunting smile, "Of course, if you're afraid . . ."

"Don't be ridiculous, Cynthia. I'm not afraid." But she was, she suddenly realized, and her foolish fear disgusted her. "Very well," she conceded. "I'll have her read for me just to prove she's a humbug."

"Good," Cynthia drawled. "Now's your chance. Nina's finished."

Laura looked up to see Nina coming swiftly toward the group, her pink taffeta rustling, an astounded smile on her rosy face. "Ladies," she said breathlessly, "Madame Fatima is a wonder! Wait till I tell you what she revealed to me."

"Have your coffee first," Cynthia said with a sardonic look at Laura. "Our hostess has decided to consult the cards herself."

"Oh, how grand!" Nina said. "Laura, you're in for quite an experience. That astonishing woman knew secrets about me that I have never confessed to anyone."

Laura smiled bleakly, rose from her chair, and

looked across the room toward Madame Fatima. The woman's eyes, black and fathomless, serenely returned her reluctant gaze.

"Mama, you're going to be read?" said Whitney, surprised, as Laura passed by her.

"Yes, darling," she said. "But I don't intend to take it seriously."

Then why, Laura wondered as she took a seat across from the disturbingly watchful seeress, was her mouth and her throat parchment dry?

For a long, uncomfortable moment, the woman regarded Laura in silence, idly shuffling a deck of cards in her ringless hands. Then, in a faint accent of indiscernible origin, she said quietly, "You dislike that I am here."

The unequivocal tone of her voice set Laura's teeth on edge. "I do," she answered frankly. "I think you and your Tarot are a sham."

Madame Fatima smiled and continued shuffling the cards. "The women of your race are passionate in their judgments."

"My race?" Laura echoed.

"Your ancestry is French, is it not?"

This second accuracy further irritated Laura. "My mother was French," she said shortly. "But anyone who reads the *Social Register* would know that."

"Yes, naturally," the woman agreed, and now her smile was faintly sad. "Shall we begin?"

"As you wish."

Laura's face was stony; she drummed her fingers nervously on the table as Madame Fatima drew the Queen of Swords from the deck and

placed it faceup on the table. Laura very much
wanted to get up and leave this odious woman,
but to succumb to that desire would be a cowardly admission of her childish fear.

"Please mix the cards thoroughly," the seeress
said, handing the deck to Laura. "And then,
with your left hand, divide the pack into three
piles."

Laura complied, with both resentment and
contempt. *What do I fear?* she asked herself impatiently as Madame Fatima picked up the piles
and began to lay out the cards in the ancient
Celtic mode. *The woman is nothing but a trickster
and a fraud.*

Ten cards, along with the Queen of Swords,
now lay before the seeress in the form of a cross.
She picked up the first card, the nine of Penta-
cles, without surprise. "You are engaged in artful pursuits," she said, "and are currently
enjoying a great success in your endeavors."

"How perceptive," Laura said scornfully.
"What else do you divine from the cards that is
common knowledge to anyone with the price of
a newspaper?"

Unperturbed by Laura's rudeness, the woman
picked up a second card. "At present, you are
very much involved with your daughter."

"Again I salute your perceptiveness, Madame
Fatima. A mother involved with her daughter. It
takes a person of exceptional powers to recognize such a relationship."

"This is an excessive involvement," the
woman continued serenely. "I believe there was

a rift, a serious conflict, between you and your daughter."

"You've been talking to Mrs. Barnes," Laura accused her.

"Not about you," the seeress said. "All I need to know about you is plainly visible in the cards."

Laura sighed irritably. "Let's get on with it, if you please. I am not enjoying this."

The woman picked up a third card, the Hierophant, then gave Laura a long, appraising look. "How closely you cling to the restrictive bonds of social conformity. You believe it gives you comfort, but, on the contrary, it accounts for a good deal of the unease I sense in you."

"If I am uneasy," Laura said tightly, "it is because I am enduring this reading as a courtesy to my friend."

Madame Fatima said nothing.

Laura, with a surge of anger, realized that she had inadvertently confirmed the woman's assertion. "Congratulations," she muttered. "You have just observed the obvious."

"Sometimes, Mrs. Sheridan, what seems obvious and simple conceals a matter more obscurely complex. I also see controversy in your life, much indecision, an unwillingness to confront that which begs to be resolved. As a result, an upheaval will occur that will bring either tragedy or joy in its wake."

Laura laughed shortly at this apparent ambiguity. "Thank you, Madame Fatima. I shall consider myself forewarned."

The seeress picked up the fourth card, the Knight of Wands. "There is a young man . . ."

Laura's hands, on her lap, clenched convulsively together.

"The rift between you and your daughter was caused by this man. No, wait." The woman paused, evidently confused, and picked up the fifth card, the three of Swords. "There has been much unpleasantness in the recent past: jealousy, pain, disillusionment, deception . . ." She paused again; her brow wrinkled quizzically, then smoothed as the situation was made clear to her. She looked up at Laura with understanding and a trace of pity. "Mrs. Sheridan, this young man is not the cause of the rift; he is a victim of the conflict between you and your daughter."

Laura rose like a shot, jiggling the table and upsetting the configuration of cards. Christopher a victim? Was the woman insane? And yet, beneath the surface of the rage that swept through her, Laura realized at last the source of her peculiar sense of depression and guilt. "This is intolerable." Her voice shook. "I will not listen to another word."

"That is another characteristic I have observed in you," the woman said quietly. "You prize the truth highly, but you often turn a deaf ear to it."

"I turn a deaf ear to impertinent imposters who gather snippets of gossip and try to pass them off as pearls of prophecy."

Laura's voice had risen sharply. Cynthia, hearing the angry tone, started across the room to her, as did Whitney, followed closely by the puzzled guests.

"Mama, what's the matter?" Whitney asked. Laura ignored her daughter and turned sharply on Cynthia. "I want this woman out of my house. I don't know what you hoped to prove by divulging certain details of my private life to her, but I—"

"Laura, I never did any such thing!"

"I won't debate the issue, Cynthia! I want her out of here now!"

Laura's guests openly gaped at her. Madame Fatima rose and collected her deck of Tarot. "Calm yourself, Mrs. Sheridan," she said, apparently unaffected by Laura's outburst. "I'm leaving at once."

She walked around the table, waved aside Cynthia's embarrassed attempt at an apology, then stopped for a moment in front of Whitney. "Young woman," she said softly, so that only Whitney could hear, "tell your mother the truth."

"The truth?" the girl echoed, startled. "The truth about what?"

"Don't ask me that question," Madame Fatima said. "Ask your heart, and then do as it bids you."

Chapter Twenty-two

✦✦✦✦✦

I WISH YOU were home, Whitney wrote longingly to Ned. *September is only a month away, but it seems like an eon until I'll see you again. There is so much I need to tell you in person, things I cannot commit to paper. I can tell you this, though. It feels so odd being home again, but you were absolutely right. I should have come home long ago. Mama has been so understanding about everything. She took the blame for my leaving home; she never once said, "I told you so." She dislikes the idea that I'm still working, but she doesn't say anything about it. She's as nice as she can be. I feel twice as guilty about causing her so much worry.*

The strangest thing happened last week. Your cousin Cynthia brought a fortune-teller to the house who upset Mama terribly. I don't know what she said to her; Mama wouldn't discuss it with anyone. The woman was eerie, dreadful. She rather upset me too—

Whitney stopped writing, reread the last sentence, then crumpled the sheet of paper and tossed it in the wastebasket. It was impossible to explain to Ned how Madame Fatima had made her feel—like a little girl, like a very selfish and bad little girl. And, too, if she were to be honest, she would have to admit to Ned that she had shaded the truth about Christopher when she'd talked to Mama. She didn't want to do that—especially not in a letter. The spoken word, Whitney felt, can easily be denied, but the written word stands as irrefutable testimony and can sometimes embarrass or condemn the writer.

She took another sheet of paper and started anew:

My dearest Ned, she wrote, *I can't tell you how much I wish you were home—*

She stopped writing again, unconsciously put a hand to her abdomen, and nibbled on the end of her pen. She missed Ned so much, much more than she would have ever thought possible. It was exactly three months and a week since she last saw him. She was not likely to forget the day he had come to the house on Bleecker Street in full uniform: blue cravenette blouse and trousers; lieutenant's shoulder straps proclaiming his rank; the insignia of the cavalry, crossed sabers, decorating his campaign hat. He looked slimmer, taller, handsomer, his sober countenance in perfect keeping with his erect military bearing. Whitney stared at him wordlessly, awed by his magnificence. And then, realizing the significance of his dashing attire, she choked back a sob and threw herself into his strong, protective arms.

"You mustn't go," she implored him, embracing him, kissing him, terrified of losing him. "What if you're wounded or . . . captured? The *World* said those Spaniards are depraved monsters. God knows what they'd do to you, what hideous tortures they'd— Oh, Ned!" She clutched him even tighter. "You mustn't go. I beg you to change your mind; I beseech you to—"

"Stop it now," he said, gently but firmly. "I have to go, Whitney; resign yourself." He directed her to the sofa, sat beside her, and slipped an arm about her tensely hunched shoulders. "What would you think of me if I shirked my duty and remained at home while others did the fighting for me?"

"I'd think you were smart!" she blurted out. "Why must you fight for something that doesn't concern us? Let the Cubans defend themselves against the Spaniards."

He withdrew his arm from her so abruptly that she fell back against the cushions. "Don't say that!" he said sharply. "That cowardly bastard said almost the same thing to me."

His vehemence startled her. She straightened and asked warily, "Who did?"

"Christopher Warren." Ned spat the name. "He said the United States had no call to interfere in foreign matters. But if we ignore what's happening in Cuba, what's to stop those bloody Spaniards from coming here and trying the same thing with us?"

She was both silenced and convinced by his argument. She remembered well the ancient history lessons drummed into her by the formidable Parker sisters. If the Etruscans had resisted Rome, if the Medes had stood up to the Persians, if the Phoenicians had withstood the armies of Greece, their excellent civilizations might still be flourishing today. Moreover, any moral stand taken by Christopher Warren *had* to be wrong.

But still she said plaintively, laying her head on Ned's shoulder, "I don't want you to go. I don't want you to die."

Ned laughed shortly and kissed her furrowed brow. "I won't die," he assured her. "All the Baileys have tough hides. My ancestors fought in more wars than I can remember, and their progeny are living proof of their invincibility."

Now, as Whitney sat in her pretty bedroom at home, nibbling on her pen, she thought of those words and reflected worriedly about Ned's inadvertently prophetic accuracy.

She was going to have his child; she had suspected it for weeks. Her hospital work had been an invaluable education in that respect. She knew too well the early signs of pregnancy: the absence of menses; the subtle bodily changes; the bouts of nausea, which she'd been explaining away to her mother as "indigestion." At first, she had blamed the symptoms on a nervous reaction to Ned's going to war and to her being home again. But last week, when that frightful woman said, "Tell your mother the truth," Whitney had to accept at last what she'd been denying to herself all along.

She rose suddenly from her chair and walked restlessly about the room, drawing a modicum of comfort from the familiar surroundings. The cherub clock on the mantel chimed the hour in light, cheery notes, bringing a brief smile to her lips. She was glad she had come home—where she belonged—and yet, as she had written to Ned, it felt odd, almost unnatural, to be here again. She had been on her own too long, perhaps. Her independence, her work, her rift with her mother, had effected an irrevocable change in her. Certainly, her relationship with Ned had changed her. She was no longer a girl, no longer a virgin; more to the point, she was soon to become a mother. It was difficult for her to grasp that momentous fact, but she knew she must. In a few more months it would no longer be possible to hide her condition. She must tell her mother soon; it was the honorable thing to do. But she couldn't, not yet, not when the two of them were getting along so well.

She trudged back to the marquetry desk, sat down with a sigh, and picked up her pen.

"Whitney, aren't you ready yet?"

Laura stood at the open door, wearing a lovely seafoam-green frock that Whitney had never seen before.

"Darling," Laura lightly reproached her, "another letter to Ned? Couldn't it have waited until tomorrow? It's after eight. If you don't hurry and dress, we'll be late for Marcella's birthday fete."

"Oh, my goodness!" Whitney dropped the pen and jumped up. "Is it that late already?" She went to the bed, where her yellow silk lay in readiness. "Mama, help me, please." She shed her dressing gown and handed the dress to Laura, then raised her arms as Laura carefully slipped the heavy silk over her head. She turned to the pier mirror; Laura fastened the tiny buttons that ran from nape to waist.

"How is your indigestion, darling? Are you feeling better? You hardly touched your breakfast this morning."

"I'm fine, Mama," she murmured. "I just wasn't hungry."

Laura turned her daughter to face her and

looked searchingly into her eyes. "What's happened to that gargantuan appetite of yours?" Her smile was teasing, but her tone was concerned. "When your beloved comes home from Cuba, I'm sure he'll be after you to gain some weight."

"He's not my beloved," Whitney answered without thinking, then she flushed with chagrin at her duplicity and disloyalty. If Ned was not her beloved, why had she conceived his child? Why had she allowed him, time and time again, to make love to her?

Laura's teasing gaze grew serious. "Isn't he, Whitney?" she asked softly. "Then why do you find it necessary to write him every night without fail?"

Whitney's gaze flickered away from her mother's scrutiny. "I don't know, Mama."

"Can it be you love him?" Laura suggested.

"I do love him," Whitney said honestly, her gaze still averted. "But I—"

"But what, darling?"

"Mama, I'm not sure I want to marry him."

"Why?" Laura asked gently. "Is it his age?"

"No." Whitney shook her head. "It's . . . I feel trapped when I think about it."

"Trapped?" Laura lifted her chin with a finger. "Darling, no one's forcing you to marry Ned. I admit I'd be happy if you did so, but the choice of husband is yours alone."

Whitney didn't answer. Her mother's concern and trust filled her with a guilt she found impossible to dispel.

"Darling," Laura said softly, "put all thought

of marriage out of your head for now. After Ned comes home, you'll have all the time in the world to make a decision."

"Yes, Mama," Whitney murmured as Laura gave her a hug and directed her toward the door. But as she descended the staircase, smoothing the folds of her dress over her still-slim waist, she thought dismally, *Time is precisely what I don't have.*

Marcella MacKenzie, the third of Malcolm's daughters, was nineteen years old. The elder girls, Jane and Delia, were twenty-two and twenty-one and had been married the previous year within six months of each other. Marcella, recently betrothed to Jamie Olmsted, had chosen a February wedding date and had asked Whitney Sheridan to attend her. The birthday fete tonight, her last as an unmarried woman, was to be the gayest and most festive her parents had ever held for her. It was, in fact, a dual celebration, extending a grateful welcome home to her father, who had recently returned from his service in Cuba.

In the immense ballroom, a twenty-five-piece orchestra played waltzes and polkas and lilting schottisches. Roses, hyacinths, and goldband lilies permeated the room with scent and color. The buffet table was artistically arranged in a symmetrical landscape of fresh summer fruit, hot and cold delicacies, and iced drinks topped with tropical flowers. The ladies present were gowned in their prettiest pastel finery, rivaling the beauty of the floral decorations. The gentlemen, sleekly soigné in black broadcloth and white linen, were reduced in number due to the absence of those still waiting to be mustered out of service, but the party promised to be nonetheless convivial.

By half past eight, almost all of the one hundred fifty invited guests had arrived. Some were milling about the buffet table, appreciatively inspecting the mouth-watering array of delectables; most of the others were dancing. One of the guests, Christopher Warren, stood with his host near the open French doors that led to the garden. Christopher was drinking a potent concoction of pineapple juice and Jamaica rum. Malcolm had selected a less exotic drink of Scotch whiskey and water.

"If I were you," Malcolm warned, gesturing toward Christopher's drink, "I wouldn't have too many of those. I made the mistake of drinking five or six of them the night before I left Guantánamo, and my fingertips and toes are still numb."

Christopher laughed. "I thought the Scots had a good head for liquor."

"For whiskey, yes," Malcolm said. "Not for those dangerously deceptive fruit drinks."

"This is my first," Christopher said, placing his empty glass on a tray held by a passing servant, "and my last. Whoever my people were, they did not bequeath to me a tolerance for hard liquor."

Malcolm tasted his whiskey and eyed Christopher thoughtfully. "I think," he said carefully, "that you are well past the stage of resenting your background, Christopher. If I had spent all my time bemoaning the fact that I was an illiterate fisherman's son who for the first sixteen years of his life ate nothing but tattie scones and seaweed soup and who never wore a stitch of clothing that hadn't been worn threadbare by three older brothers, I wouldn't be hosting this party tonight—which cost me more than my father ever earned in his lifetime."

Christopher looked at him in genuine astonishment, then laughed again. "I *am* past that stage, Malcolm; honestly. There was a time I blamed everything in my life on an absence of traceable lineage, but the more intimate I become with so-called society, the less I am impressed with their specious pedigrees."

A gleam of approval warmed Malcolm's blue eyes. "Is that why you've been refusing certain commissions of late?"

Christopher paused for just an instant. Then: "No," he said. "I've simply decided to be more select about my work."

Malcolm sensed more beneath his answer than he had admitted. He asked bluntly, "You *are* still getting offers, aren't you? This has nothing to do with your decision to remain out of the war?"

"Not at all," Christopher said. "In fact, the offers are so numerous that I'm contemplating opening up my own firm."

"Good," Malcolm said. "I'm glad to hear that. And let me say, Christopher—because I think this may be troubling you—that you made the right decision in not kowtowing to the crowd by volunteering to go to Cuba. It wasn't our quarrel, you know; we had no business being there. To this day no one's proved that the Spaniards had anything to do with blowing up the _Maine_. Moreover, I have it on good authority that while the revolutionaries welcomed our financial support, they were vigorously opposed to American troops setting foot on their territory."

"Then why did you go?"

Malcolm shrugged and looked grim. "Who knows? Bugles and banners; the call to glory. There's no fool like an old fool, Christopher. I should have stayed home, awaiting the birth of my grandchildren, instead of donning a uniform, buckling on a saber, and watching boys young enough to be my sons be cut to ribbons, fertilizing foreign soil with their blood."

"But still you went," Christopher said.

"If I had it to do over again," Malcolm answered with a scowl, "I'd have said, to hell with the glory!"

"You're right, of course," Christopher said, glancing over toward the carefree crowd. "But some of the men at Carlisle and Hastings who've already come home from Cuba have been looking at me with more than their usual scorn. I know exactly what they're thinking: The yellow-belly stayed home to further his career while we risked our necks to ensure his safety."

"Bah!" Malcolm said. "If they risked their necks, it was for their own aggrandizement and nothing else. Besides, what do you care what other people think of you? There's only one opinion that should matter to a man, and that's his own."

At that moment, Laura Sheridan and her daughter entered the ballroom and were welcomed with embraces by Janet MacKenzie and Marcella, the radiant birthday celebrant.

Christopher, his eyes on the new arrivals, said to his host, "You're right again, Malcolm. I don't give a good goddamn what anyone thinks of me."

Across the room, Marcella and Whitney greeted each other as if a year, instead of a week, had gone by since their last meeting.

"Marcella, you look grand!" Whitney said, admiring her white mousseline de soie and the creamy magnolia tucked into her bodice. "Many happy returns of the day."

"Thank you, Whitney." Marcella beamed. "Just think," she said excitedly, "the invitations to my next birthday party will be signed, 'Mrs. James Stewart Olmsted the Second.' Aren't you looking forward to the wedding, Whitney? It's the first time you'll be attending a bride!"

Whitney, who had calculated her child would be born about the time of Marcella's wedding day, smiled bleakly. "I can't wait," she said.

"Where is the happy groom?" Laura asked Marcella.

"He's in the study, sneaking a smoke," Marcella said crossly. "How I loathe those smelly cigars! After we're married, I'm going to see to it that he cuts out the habit entirely."

Janet commented wryly, "The way I saw to it

that your father stop smoking? Good luck to you, Marcie. I hope you're getting a more tractable husband than I have." She turned to Laura and slipped a hand through her arm. "Come and say hello to Malcolm. He's been twice as unmanageable since he came home. In fact, he's been issuing orders left and right, as if the girls and I were green recruits under his command."

Marcella took Whitney's arm and followed Janet's lead. "That's because you don't know how to handle him, Mother," she said tartly. "When I get married, *I'm* going to be the boss. I've already discussed it with Jamie, and he said I could be."

Laura, looking back over her shoulder at Marcella, did not see Christopher as the group approached Malcolm. She said with a laugh, "How clever you are, Marcella, to have wrung such a concession from your intended. But if I were you, I'd have him put it in writing."

Whitney stopped dead in her tracks as she caught sight of Christopher talking to Malcolm.

"What's the matter?" Marcella asked as Whitney hung back and stared at Christopher. "Whitney, you're pale as a ghost! Are you going to faint?"

Laura turned back abruptly. "Whitney, what's wrong? Are you feeling ill again?"

Whitney's stomach contracted; it was impossible to speak. She couldn't see him, she couldn't face him; she would die if she did. She could still feel the horror of her shameless self-debasement: *It's you I love. And I know you love me.* She could still hear the echo of his humiliating reply: *I don't love you Whitney. I never did, I never will.*

"Whitney, what is it?" Laura demanded, for her daughter looked wretched and she was staring across the room at someone whom Laura had not yet seen.

"Mama . . ." Whitney swallowed her nausea, looking helplessly toward the source of her discomfort. She had to get out of here, she couldn't stay. If he saw her, if he spoke to her . . . "Mama, I want to go home."

Laura followed Whitney's gaze and saw Christopher at last. For a moment she froze, then she grasped her daughter's hands in hers. "Janet, quickly," she said urgently, "let me have your vinaigrette. Whitney, don't look at him; look at me!"

Laura's face, both stern and frightened, began to swim before Whitney's eyes. She was going to be sick. The dread, familiar nausea churned violently inside her. She pulled free of her mother's hold and, unmindful of the guests who turned to stare at her, picked up her skirts and ran from the room.

Out in the hall she collided full-force with Jamie Olmsted. She staggered backward, as did he.

"What the devil?" he sputtered, regaining his footing. He looked down at her ashen face; his indignant scowl vanished. "I say, Whitney, are you all right?"

She swayed dizzily on her feet. Jamie reached out a hand to support her. The smell of cigar smoke that enveloped him wreaked further havoc on her assaulted senses. She clapped a hand over her mouth, brushed by him with a groan, stumbled blindly up the stairs, and reached the lavatory just in time to be violently ill in the sink.

Later, as Whitney lay on a chaise longue, a cold cloth on her forehead, Laura said, "I think you should tell me what you've been keeping to yourself since you came home."

They were alone in the MacKenzies' bedroom. Earlier, when Janet and Marcella had fluttered worriedly around Whitney, Laura had shooed them out of the room, saying, "It's nothing serious. Whitney's been suffering from indigestion lately, that's all. I thought it could wait until Avery came home, but perhaps I'd better call Dr. Weber in the morning to have a look at her."

Now, as Laura sat rigidly on a straight chair next to the chaise, Whitney lifted evasive eyes to hers and mumbled, "I'm not keeping anything to myself."

She felt drained to her very soul; it was an effort just to breathe. Was this the price women paid for motherhood? It wasn't worth it. No treasure on God's earth was worth this sickening, humiliating torture.

"Whitney . . ." Laura's tone was low but hard. "I will not play cat-and-mouse with you. Since the day you came home, I've known there was something you weren't telling me. I didn't want to pry; I've done enough of that to last us both a lifetime. But I'm asking you now, and I'll keep asking until you answer me. What's troubling you so much that it's making you ill?"

With effort, Whitney raised herself up to a sitting position, took the cloth from her forehead, and put it on the table next to the chaise. *Why not tell her?* she thought wearily. The secret would be out soon enough. But as she looked into Laura's eyes, as she imagined the shock and disappointment that would appear in those eyes immediately following her disclosure, she elected to take the coward's way out.

"I can't talk about it now." She lowered her gaze. "Mama, forgive me. I don't mean to distress you, but I simply can't discuss it—not now, not tonight."

Whitney heard her mother sigh, an angry, impatient sigh. "Whitney, I don't think you understand me. We *will* talk about it—now, tonight, before we leave this room."

Reluctantly Whitney faced her, feeling miserable and trapped. Was there no way out of this web she had so intricately woven to spare her mother? If she told her now, the shock was sure to be severe. If she said nothing—even if she married Ned the instant he came home—the early birth of the child would be a knife in her mother's breast. Whitney shuddered to think of the pain she would cause the person she most loved in the world. Their relationship, so newly mended, was doomed to destruction, and there wasn't a thing she could do to prevent it.

"Whitney, I'm waiting," Laura said adamantly.

"I . . . I'm pregnant," she finally whispered, wincing when Laura gasped.

It was all there in Laura's eyes: the shock, the disillusionment, the incredulity and pain.

"Mama, please!" Whitney blurted out. "I beg you not to be angry with me. I never meant to hurt you. I'm sorry; please forgive me."

"It's not true," Laura said faintly. "I refuse to believe it."

"It is true," Whitney said wretchedly. "I didn't mean for it to happen. I kept if from you because I knew how horrified you'd be. I'd give anything in the world if I hadn't had to tell you— Oh, don't look at me like that. Mama, speak to me, please!"

"It's not true," Laura repeated in that faint, stricken voice. "I asked him point-blank, and he swore he hadn't made love to you."

"Y-you asked him?" Whitney stammered, wondering when Laura could have talked to Ned. "But when? Why?"

"A few months ago." Laura's words were barely audible. She stared past Whitney into a void of black despair. "It was when he told me you had gone to his house. I demanded to know the truth. He admitted that he'd kissed you; he said he'd only done it because he . . . couldn't have me. He swore on his oath that he'd done nothing else. On his oath." Her soft voice shook. "And I believed him, I believed him . . ."

Whitney opened her mouth to speak, then immediately clamped it shut. Laura's eyes were no longer censorious; they were laden with the burden of guilt and self-reproach. Whitney had only to speak a word to lift that burden from her mother. She had only to indict herself to free her mother of guilt. She wanted to tell the truth, it was the honorable thing to do. But she couldn't, she simply couldn't. So she didn't.

Chapter Twenty-three
✦✦✦✦

DESPITE THE BREVITY of the Spanish-American War—the actual fighting lasted only twenty-three days—it still managed to claim two hundred sixty-nine American lives and more than a thousand casualties. The war, when it ended, did not end the decrement of the men who had fought in it. Many died of their wounds afterward; thousands more sickened or died at home of complications arising from tropical diseases contracted in Cuba. One casualty of the conflict was Lieutenant Edward Bailey, stricken with malaria en route back to the United States. Upon his arrival in New York, Ned, instead of enjoying his long-awaited reunion with the woman he loved, was transported on a stretcher from the ship to a waiting ambulance. At the direction of Captain Avery Sheridan, who was attending Ned, the driver whipped up his horses to a full gallop. The ambulance sped through the city streets toward Saint Luke's Hospital uptown, bells clanging furiously, frightening other horses, scattering angry pedestrians, who neither knew nor cared that within that careering vehicle one of their gallant war heroes was fighting for his life.

Ned's condition was serious. Even at the hospital, with the best medical facilities available, his disease stubbornly refused to yield to Avery's treatment of quinine, strychnine sulphate, and arsenious acid. Chills and fever gave way to pain in the head and limbs, especially the lower legs. Ned's liver and spleen swelled; jaundice appeared. He lost weight at an alarming rate and lapsed into fitful deliriums, with only occasional periods of lucidity. The prognosis was uncertain; Avery could only hope for the best. As difficult as it was to do so, he permitted no visitors, despite Whitney's entreaties and the pleas of Ned's anguished parents. If they saw him in his present state—jaundiced, emaciated, delirious— it would only serve to anguish them the more.

Thanks to Avery's excellent skills, Ned's condition was eventually stabilized—that is to say, the disease did not worsen, but neither did it show much improvement. Avery, during that period, had spent much time at Ned's bedside; but finally, realizing that the outcome was in God's hands, he resumed full-time duty as chief of staff at Saint Luke's Hospital and reopened his private practice.

Though he had been away from his work for less than four months, there was much for Avery to do. The hospital was overflowing with convalescents from the war. Avery had thought that coming home would call an end to the horrors he had witnessed in Cuba; but everywhere he turned, he saw men on crutches or in wheelchairs, men with missing limbs, shattered faces, blinded eyes. At his offices it was little better; young veterans came to him, obviously whole, apparently undamaged by the war, yet their vacant stares, their listless complaints of loss of appetite and an inability to sleep told Avery that the mental wounds he must treat would be every bit as difficult to heal as the physical.

Avery's own lessened appetite and sleepless nights indicated a need for treatment, but he ignored his own symptoms; there were patients who needed him. Since coming home, Avery had been doing the work of four men. He had not even taken the time to pay calls on Laura and Whitney. Had they not come to the hospital in hopes of visiting Ned, he would not have seen them at all. Laura had said to him firmly the first time she saw him, "Avery, you must take some ease! Your nurse told me you divide your time between the hospital and your offices, with hardly a moment to yourself. Come dine at my house tonight—come *every* night, for I doubt you've had a decent meal since you went off to Cuba."

Despite his weariness, despite the crushing burden of his never-ending caseload, Avery smiled at his beautiful sister-in-law. Although she had refused his proposal of marriage, her love and concern for him were indisputable. He captured her chin with a hand and planted a brief kiss on her charmingly determined mouth.

"I shall dine with you at the first opportunity," he promised her. But almost a full month went by before he was able to keep his promise.

At the end of September, when he was finally free to take some leisure, Avery donned his evening clothes—the first time he had done so in months—and set off for his sister-in-law's fine house. So delighted was he to see her in familiar surroundings at last that he didn't immediately notice that her daughter was not present.

Laura looked extraordinarily beautiful in a formal gown of black lace over white silk. When she greeted Avery at the door, she kissed him warmly and clung to his arm as they went to the music room for an aperitif before dinner. Avery settled at the piano, touching the ivory keys with a wave of nostalgia, but he did not play. Laura, watching him from the Carlin settee, said in a quiet voice, "I can't tell you how good it is to have you home."

Avery tasted his sherry appreciatively. The rum he had drunk while in Cuba had forever soured his taste for that drink. "It's good to be home," he said. "I doubt I shall ever voluntarily leave the United States again."

"Was it very bad?" Laura asked softly.

Avery looked about at the pink and ivory splendor of the music room. A painting of the nine muses graced the ceiling; a Feraghan carpet covered the floor. About the room were scattered the most exquisite objets d'art: a Ming Dynasty bowl, a Barye bronze, a Sèvres potpourri vase on a base of gilt bronze. But he saw nothing of his elegant surroundings. In his mind's eye he saw only a blood-drenched medical tent, he heard only the young men moaning in malarial delirium or screaming in agony when he amputated a gangrenous limb. "No, it wasn't too bad," he said. "How did you fare while I was gone?"

"I worried about you constantly," she said frankly.

"You needn't have, Laura. I saw no action— only its aftermath." He drank again, then suddenly became aware of his niece's absence. "Where's Whitney? I hope she hasn't gone out. I've been looking forward to seeing her away from the hospital." He smiled fondly, remembering Whitney's touching concern for Ned. "I'm glad to see she's finally come to her senses about Ned Bailey." And then his smile faded as he remembered the gravity of Ned's condition. "I only hope it's not too late."

"Avery, you're not saying—?"

"I don't know, Laura. I honestly don't know."

"Has there been any change?" she asked. "Is he at least lucid?"

Avery shook his head. "Most of the time, no. He thinks he's still on the battlefield. He keeps saying, 'I'll kill him, I'll kill him; he doesn't deserve to live.' "

He rose suddenly, anxious to rid his mind of death and illness. "Where's Whitney?" he asked again, looking restlessly toward the door. "When is she coming down?"

Laura paused, then answered in a curiously dull tone, "Whitney won't be joining us tonight."

"Why not?"

"She's . . . not feeling well."

"Not feeling well?" Avery frowned. "What ails her? I'll go up and have a look at her."

"No!" Laura's voice rose, then dropped to a whisper. "I'd rather you didn't."

Avery looked at her closely. He had not done so before. He had been so relieved to be away from the hospital, away from anguished suffering, returned to the beauty and sanity of peaceful family life, that he had only glanced at his sister-in-law. If he had done more, if he had gazed at any length on the face and form he so loved, he doubted he could have contented himself with a brotherly kiss and embrace. But now he saw what earlier had escaped his notice. Now, in Laura's eyes, he saw a torment she could not hide.

"What's wrong?" he asked, alarmed, joining her on the settee.

She shook her head; she would not look at him.

"Laura, answer me!"

"Avery . . ." With great reluctance she faced him. "I didn't want to tell you until after we'd dined. I didn't want to tell you at all, but I know I must."

"Yes, go on," he urged.

"Whitney," she said in a hushed, halting voice, "is pregnant."

All the breath left Avery's lungs; he clenched his hand on the back of the settee. "Did you say—?"

"Yes, pregnant."

Her words were a choked sound, but to Avery
they rang as keenly as the report of a rifleshot. A
sudden surge of rage displaced his shock.
"Who's the father?" he demanded. But even as
he fired the question, he knew the answer. Even
as Laura's startled gaze darted to his, he knew
with deadly certainty whose name she was going to speak.

"She says . . ." Laura faltered, then tried
again. "She told me it's Christopher Warren, but
I can't, I simply cannot believe it."

"You can't?" Avery said harshly. "You mean
you *won't*." He rose to his feet and glared down
at her accusingly. "How could you have let this
happen?" were the words he flung at her.

"That's not fair!" she burst out. "How could I
have prevented it?"

"How, Laura? By not involving yourself with
that man in the first place. I knew from the start
he'd bring nothing but trouble to this family. I
tried to warn you in a dozen different ways, but
no—you *had* to see him, you *had* to encourage
him. Because of your misguided need for a devoted admirer, you yourself paved the path for
your daughter's destruction."

"That's not fair!" she repeated. But beneath
her quick protest Avery detected a latent guilt.
"My relationship with Christopher had nothing
to do with Whitney's actions."

"Whitney's actions?" he echoed hotly.
"You're blaming *her*, are you?"

"No, no! I only meant—"

"And as for your relationship with that black-
guard, he was your lover, wasn't he? Don't

bother denying it, Laura; I know you better than you think I do. That's why you can't believe he made love to Whitney. How naive you are to think that such a trifling circumstance would stop a man of his caliber. If seducing you was easy—as I daresay it was—how much easier it must have been for him to seduce your daughter."

Laura leaped to her feet. "That's enough!" she said, furious. "If I'm in some way responsible for what happened to Whitney, I'll willingly accept blame. But whatever existed between Christopher and me has nothing to do with her. Nor is it any of your business."

"Nothing to do with her? Laura, for the love of God Almighty, it has everything to do with her. You knew how she felt about him. You could have stopped this before it began."

"Don't you think I tried?" she defended herself. "Nothing I said to Whitney made any difference. When all else failed, I forbade her to see him. What did that accomplish? She left home. If she was so determined to do as she wished, how can you even think of saying it's my fault?"

"She's pregnant by your *lover*," Avery snapped. "Whose fault is that?"

Laura stared at him, silenced, trembling with rage. Avery, despite his own anger, wanted very much to take her in his arms, to hold her and comfort her, to show his love and support, to assure her that no burden was so great that together they couldn't bear it—and at the same time he wanted to seize her by the shoulders and shake her until her teeth rattled.

A few moments went by; Avery drew a steady-ing breath. "Laura, let's stop this," he said with a composure that belied the wild disorder of his emotions. "I'm sorry I shouted at you. Instead of quarreling, why don't we discuss what must be done about Whitney?"

"What do you suggest?" she asked stiffly. And Avery saw that his apology had gone for naught.

"First," he said, slipping his hands into his trouser pockets, "I think I should have a talk with Mr. Warren. As much as I dislike doing this, I'm afraid I'm going to have to insist that he marry her."

"No!" Laura gasped. "I won't have it."

His eyes narrowed. "Why not, Laura?"

"I couldn't," she said faintly. "To have him as a member of my family . . . It's impossible; I couldn't."

"Then, what do *you* suggest?" he pressed her.

She took a moment to answer; he easily guessed her thoughts. "Avery, could you possi-bly . . . Would you—?"

"Terminate the pregnancy?" His tone was deadly. "Absolutely not."

"Avery—"

"I said no; I will not do it. That baby will be born—in or out of wedlock. The choice is yours, Laura. Do you want Christopher Warren for a son-in-law, or would you rather your daughter give birth to an illegitimate child?"

He knew his question was cruel, but at the moment he wasn't feeling very charitable. He knew, too, what Laura was feeling; her anguish was undisguised. As incredible as it seemed, whether she realized it or not, she was still in love with that scoundrel. For just a fraction of an instant Avery hated her.

"Well?" he said coldly. "What's your decision? I'll not interfere, I won't speak to him, if that's what you want."

She said nothing for the longest time; she gazed desolately at the floor. Finally she said in a voice barely audible, "Do whatever you think best."

Chapter Twenty-four

✦✦✦✦

IT WAS A momentous day for Christopher Warren, a day he had thought he would never see. On October 3, 1898, despite Henry Carlisle's tactful advice to "think twice before making a decision," Christopher opened the doors of his own architectural firm, C. Warren and Company. He could not have picked a better time to go out on his own. On the heels of the Spanish defeat in Cuba, New York City became the mecca of celebration and spending. Victory parties abounded throughout the city. Fifth Avenue ballrooms were decorated with red, white, and blue bunting and with flowers of those colors, proclaiming national pride. In residences less grand, front parlors sported small celluloid

American flags and tintypes of Teddy Roosevelt, bearing the legend HERO OF SAN JUAN HILL.

The variety halls on Longacre Square featured patriotic reviews with pretty girls in brief costumes kicking up their heels to the rousing strains of Sousa's marches. War-end sales prompted customers to buy a new Belter bedroom suite, "marked down to one hundred dollars especially for veterans"; or Spanish lace, "appropriated from the enemy at great risk by our brave boys." Now that the country was at peace again, people wanted to spend money extravagantly, to celebrate life in the aftermath of death. For the common man, a few inexpensive trinkets satisfied that need. For the rich, only a new townhouse or country house would do. The firm of C. Warren and Company was more than willing to fill the bill.

To assist him in his new enterprise, Christopher had engaged the services of an apprentice architect, two experienced draftsmen, and a fledgling engineer, whose duties ranged from reviewing specifications to keeping the work areas in a state of general tidiness. The second-floor offices on Madison Avenue were small, only one-quarter the size of Carlisle & Hastings, but Christopher, with confident optimism, had already discussed with his landlord the possibility of leasing additional offices on the third floor should the need arise.

On the day he opened for business, more than an hour before his staff was scheduled to arrive, Christopher was in his private office, looking out the window, a freshly brewed cup of coffee in his hands. He had arrived at six, and with an odd blend of pride and superstitious fear that it would all soon vanish, he had inspected every nook and cranny of his new operation. He was especially proud of the northern-lit drafting room with its soldierly row of tables and cabinets. The austere efficiency of that room fit it well, as did the casual comfort of the clients' reception area, with its deep leather chairs and wood-paneled walls handsomely decorated with watercolor renderings of the Acropolis and the Roman Forum.

His favorite room was his own private office, facing on Madison Avenue. Tall double windows admitted a sunshower of dancing light onto polished oak floors. One entire wall was covered with Christopher's technical tomes, and beneath the windows stood a fine antique Carel desk of tulipwood and kingwood, with gilt-bronze mounts. Every item in the offices belonged to Christopher outright. He had debated buying on credit the drafting tables, file cabinets, furnishings, and supplies and had decided against it. The cash purchases had bit deeply into his bank balance, but he didn't care. He needed to own what was his, not lease or finance it. If he was eventually beggared by the extravagance, so be it. He was done with living the life of a second-class citizen.

The telephone on his desk rang. With a start of expectant pleasure Christopher turned from the window, put down his coffee cup and picked up the receiver. His first official telephone call, and he wasn't even open for business yet! The decision to go out on his own—which had caused him many a sleepless night—was already proving to have been the correct one.

"Good morning," he said eagerly. "Christopher Warren here."

"Mr. Warren," said a vaguely familiar voice, "I hope I haven't caught you at a bad time. I passed by your offices just now on the way to mine, and I thought I saw someone at the window—which is why I'm telephoning so early."

"No," Christopher said, trying to place the voice and failing. "It's not a bad time. How may I help you?"

"This is Avery Sheridan," said the caller, "Laura Sheridan's brother-in-law."

Christopher tensed at the mention of her name. For months he had been trying to erase her from his thoughts. Every day without surcease he struggled unsuccessfully to forget her, the struggle itself ensuring that her memory become indelibly etched on his brain. The more he tried to forget her, the more he could hear her soft voice, feel the touch of her skin, smell the fragrance of her hair. The more he thought of her, the more he wanted her; the more he wanted her, the more he came to despise her for tormenting him with the hypocrisy of her half-hearted love for him. She was a blight on his life; she haunted his every waking hour. His violent love for her had crossed the fine line over to hatred, and yet, even when he despised her the most, even while in his mind he called her hypocrite, manipulator, treacherous Circe, he knew he would never want any woman but her.

"Dr. Sheridan," he said stiffly, "how are you?"

"I'm very well, thank you," Avery replied in that neutral well-bred tone that always, to Christopher, had smacked of condescension. "I was wondering if we could meet, Mr. Warren. There's a matter of some importance I'd like to discuss with you."

"Are you in need of an architect?" Christopher asked, somehow knowing that he wasn't.

"No," Avery said. "It's a personal matter. Perhaps you could stop by my offices late this afternoon. I'm just down the avenue from you, at the corner of Madison and Twenty-fifth. If you could be here at, let's say five or five-thirty, I'd very much appreciate it."

The courteous request sounded to Christopher like a command. His teeth clenched. "I'm sorry," he said. "That would be most inconvenient for me."

"Oh." The word expressed mild disappointment. "Well then, when do you think we could meet, Mr. Warren? I'm rather anxious to talk with you."

Christopher thought for a moment. What the devil did he want? It couldn't be about Laura; Christopher hadn't talked with her since April. In fact, it couldn't be about anything at all that was of interest to Christopher. He said in cool dismissal, "This is an extremely busy time for me, Dr. Sheridan. I really couldn't say when I'd have a free moment. Unless," he suggested sardonically, "you'd care to come to my offices right now. I could spare you a quarter hour or so."

To Christopher's annoyance, Avery said at once, "That's very good of you, Mr. Warren. I'll be there in ten minutes." And before Christopher could even think of retracting the invitation, Avery rang off.

Christopher glanced at the mantel clock; it was just past seven. Irritated by Avery's unexpected request, he returned to the windows and gazed restlessly out over the avenue toward Madison Square Garden. Atop the Garden's tower stood Augustus Saint Gaudens's nude *Diana*, the gilded copper statue that had raised a storm of public protest while eliciting titillated admiration from private quarters. Christopher had met the brilliant sculptor recently at Carlisle & Hastings and had been awed by his genius and by the scope of his artistry, which was as flawless in delicate cameo as it was in massive bronze. Saint Gaudens, like his good friend Stanford White, was married but had an eye for the pretty ladies. His *Diana*, in fact, had been modeled on his current mistress, Davida Clark, by whom he had fathered a son. Again like White, Saint Gaudens's rakish private life only enhanced his public image. Christopher marveled bitterly at the double-edged morality of the gentry.

The mantel clock chimed. Christopher heard the outer door open and close. His irritation increasing, he left his office and walked to the reception area, where Avery awaited him, hat and gloves in hand.

"Good morning, Mr. Warren," Avery said pleasantly. "Thank you for taking the time to see me. Ordinarily I would not have imposed on you this way, but, you see, it's extremely important that I speak with you."

Again Christopher's teeth clenched. Why did that man's every utterance sound like an imperial decree?

"Won't you sit down?" Christopher said, then added with none too good grace, "I'm rather pressed for time, Dr. Sheridan. If you could state your business . . ."

"Very well," Avery said, taking a seat while Christopher remained on his feet. "I'll come straight to the point. I don't know if you're aware of it, Mr. Warren, but my niece is going to have a child—in February, my sister-in-law tells me."

Christopher stared at him blankly. *Whitney pregnant?*

"I see you're not aware of it," Avery said, noting his genuine shock. "Well, that's sometimes the case. But, naturally, now that I've brought the matter to your attention, I've no doubt that as a gentleman you're more than willing to do the right thing."

Avery stressed the word "gentleman"; Christopher sensed it rather than heard it. At the same time he grasped the situation with a jolt. It was Ned Bailey, indisputably, who had gotten Whitney pregnant, and now this arrogant aristocrat was blaming Christopher for her condition.

"Dr. Sheridan," he said deliberately, "despite

your belief to the contrary, I *am* a gentleman. Had I fathered Whitney's child, I wouldn't need you to tell me what I ought to do about it. As it is, I did not get her pregnant and I have no intention of marrying her. If I were you, I'd look closer to home for the culprit in this case."

"There's no need for me to do that," Avery said with infuriating calm. "My niece has already named you as the father."

For the second time, Christopher stared at him in stunned silence—until he remembered that Ned was in the hospital, mortally ill. "Your niece is lying," he grated.

"As she lied about Bar Harbor?" There was an edge now to Avery's voice, and his gray eyes were steely. "Whitney told me about that summer, about how you made clear to her your . . . intentions. She didn't go into detail, but from what little I know of you, I can surmise what went on. In view of your behavior then, there's no question in my mind who fathered her child. Do you still say she's lying, Mr. Warren? Do you still refuse to accept a responsibility that is clearly yours?"

"She may have told the truth about Bar Harbor," Christopher said frankly, "but she's lying now. I have never had intimate relations with your niece."

"I don't believe you," Avery said.

"Believe what you like," Christopher retorted. "The people of your class always do." He strode to the door and swung it open. "Would you mind leaving now, Dr. Sheridan? I have a busy day ahead of me, and I imagine you do, too. Let's neither of us waste any more of each other's time."

Avery's face was expressionless, but his steady gaze was murderous. For a moment he didn't move, then he rose and went toward the door, stopping a few feet short of Christopher. "Your attitude doesn't surprise me," he said coldly, "but it does disgust me. I should have known that anyone who refused to defend his country would certainly shirk all other duties incumbent on him. It's useless for me to try to convince you to do what any man of honor would do of his own accord, but I want you to know this: In one way or another, you're going to pay for what you did. If I were you, Mr. Warren, I'd dig myself a comfortable grave and crawl into it. Whether you know it or not, you're as good as dead in this city."

"I've already been threatened in that manner," Christopher said with contempt. "Ironically, by the man who *did* father Whitney's child."

"And who might that be?" Avery shot back. "Not that I'd believe you."

"Nor would I tell you, Dr. Sheridan. If the 'gentleman' in question wishes to deny his own child, that's his and Whitney's business, not mine."

Chapter Twenty-five
✦ ✦ ✦ ✦ ✦

NED BAILEY'S CHILD was born on February 20, in
Newport, Rhode Island, two months to the day
after Whitney's twentieth birthday. A violent
snowstorm accompanied the lying-in. While
Whitney labored for hours, holding desperately
to her mother's hands, snow laced with sleet
hurled itself against the house, and a turbulent
wind blew in from the Atlantic Ocean, creating
mountainous snowdrifts, rattling windows and
doors, and echoing through Whitney's bedroom
like a monotonous dirge.

Avery and a local nurse were in attendance,
but the principal physician was Dr. Stanley Maddox, a semiretired Newport practitioner, who
had been chosen to preside at the birth because
of his utmost discretion. He was a vigorous man,
with cheerful brown eyes, luxuriant brown hair,
and muttonchop whiskers that belied his almost
seventy years. Whitney had known him since
her toddler days, and the fatherly warmth with
which he had treated her during her two-and-a-
half month stay in Newport had been a welcome
gleam of light in a darkly trying time.

Never once did he admonish her for being an
unmarried mother-to-be. For that matter, during
the last months of her pregnancy, neither did
Laura or Avery. Avery, in fact, didn't in any way
allude to Whitney's condition. He had only said,
when she and Laura left for Newport in November, "I'll join you in February and remain there

for the month." He had pointedly refrained from saying why.

To their friends Laura explained the trip as sea-air therapy prescribed by Avery for "mild lung infection" contracted by Whitney. She told the Capital Club planning committee that due to her daughter's health her work would have to be suspended until the spring. Everyone believed her. The Tylers and the Barneses sent flowers and candy. Janet MacKenzie sent a lovely imported shawl, and Marcella, on the telephone, wept with disappointment that her most beloved friend would not be attending her at her wedding.

In Newport Laura was exceptionally attentive to Whitney's needs, and so were the few trusted servants Laura brought with her from home. Thompson was there; and Brownie, the senior coachman; and Rachel, Laura's maid, who was making herself useful to both mother and daughter. But it was almost as if the coming child didn't exist. None of the servants mentioned Whitney's pregnancy, and Laura only did so when absolutely necessary. They might have all been there on winter holiday instead of awaiting the birth of an illegitimate child. Whitney should have been relieved that they ignored her shameful condition, but to the contrary, their kindness and collective silence gave her the willies.

More than shame or uneasiness, Whitney felt guilty about Christopher. More than guilt, however, she feared the possibility of being caught in a lie. Once or twice she attempted to speak of him with Laura—to see how the land lay—but Laura seemed oddly unwilling to take up the gauntlet.

"Don't upset yourself," Laura said, deliberately changing the subject on one occasion when Whitney mentioned his name. "What's done is done. We shall deal with the situation as best we can."

"But, Mama," the girl said, "how are we going to deal with the appearance of a child?"

"You needn't worry about that." Laura's gaze did not quite meet hers. "Uncle Avery knows this lovely couple who've been longing for a child—"

"We're giving the baby away?" Whitney said, stunned.

"Yes," Laura said, and now she faced her daughter squarely. "What else can we do? I know Ned would marry you in a minute if he were able, but would it be fair, Whitney, to ask him to accept a responsibility that isn't his? Thank goodness he's on the road to recovery. When this is all over, I daresay he *will* ask you to marry him. But you'll be starting afresh with him—unencumbered—which is really the only honorable thing to do."

The honorable thing to do; Whitney cringed inwardly at the term. Too cowardly to own up to an offense that was exclusively hers, she had committed a double dishonor. She had condemned an innocent man and she had also betrayed the coming child's true father. Was that what her mother had been trying to say to her?

Did she know that Whitney had lied, and was she tactfully prompting her to own up to the deceit?

Now, as Whitney writhed on her bed struggling painfully to give birth, her guilt and confusion were almost as agonizing as her labor.

"It won't be long now, my dear," Dr. Maddox soothed as her contractions intensified.

But it had already been too long, eleven torturous hours. Whitney could bear it no longer; she was certain she was going to die.

"Mama," she rambled feverishly when the pain abated for just an instant, "I'm sorry for putting everyone through this. I never meant to cause so much trouble. I've hurt so many people, so many innocent . . ." Her words became a groan as the contractions attacked her once more.

"Darling, don't talk," Laura whispered, her throat aching as she helplessly witnessed her daughter's suffering. "Save your strength. It will soon be over."

"Mama, say you forgive me," Whitney begged, crushing her hands. "I must have your forgiveness before I die."

"You're not going to die!" Laura said fiercely. "Don't even think such a thing."

"I am, I am," the girl moaned as the pain tightened with a viselike grip. "Mama, say you forgive me."

"Say it!" Avery said sharply to Laura. His face was very white. He stood at the foot of the bed, watching his niece with the same anguished helplessness as Laura.

"Yes, I forgive you," Laura said rapidly, looking questioningly at Avery. *Will* she die? her eyes asked him. But his, instead of answering, remained intently on Whitney.

For Laura, the past eleven hours had been a torment straight from hell. She knew firsthand what her daughter was suffering; she, too, had thought she was at death's door when Whitney was born. But to watch her own child in the throes of the same relentless agony was even worse than the birth pangs she had experienced herself.

And to what end was Whitney suffering if the child she bore was to be given away? Avery had said there was no other alternative. Against his adamant arguments Laura had strongly protested. Avery was a man; he had no conception of what it meant for a mother to give up her own flesh and blood. Moreover, the child was part of Laura, too. He was a link in the glorious chain of which her mother had been so proud: Du Guesclin; Joan of Arc; the fearless Plantagenet men-at-arms. If Christopher was his father—which Laura still could not fully believe—he was the son of an artist truly touched by God with genius. The child was not an "unfortunate accident," which was what Avery kept calling him. He was a blessed continuation of a magnificent heritage.

But Avery had hammered away at her:

"If Whitney keeps the child, her chances for marriage are as good as over."

"But—"

"If you're thinking of telling everyone that

you've adopted a foundling, forget it. Who will believe you?''

"Avery—"

"If you don't care a jot for Whitney's reputation, think of the child. Will you have it live its life bearing the stigma of being a bastard?''

In the end Laura relented, but not without pain. Everything Avery said was true, and yet why must it be so? Why should the dictates of society forever separate a child from his natural family? Was that how it had been with Christopher's mother? Had she given him up to spare him future humiliation? But what good had it done? Christopher was still stigmatized by the circumstances of his birth. Whitney said he had fathered her child, and Avery never for a moment doubted that he had, despite Christopher's claim of innocence. And what was the source of those ugly rumors surrounding Christopher that Laura had been hearing? Who had started them? Were they true? Or were they simply another legacy of Christopher's illegitimate birth?

"It's time," said Dr. Maddox, gesturing to the nurse, who waited alertly at his side.

Laura's hand tightened on Whitney's. "It's almost over, darling," she encouraged her. "Be brave just a little while longer."

Whitney did not respond. Her entire concentration was bent on delivering her child. In a feverish daze she obeyed her doctor's commands, pushing, groaning, gasping desperately for breath. Laura's own breathing was labored; her eyes stung with unshed tears. Avery, still at the foot of the bed, thrust his fine surgeon's hands impotently into his pockets. Outside, snow and sleet and a tornadolike wind buffeted the house as if the wrath of God Himself were making known its fury. Finally, in a last convulsive burst of violence, Whitney brought Ned Bailey's son into the world.

He was a tiny scrap of humanity with a wisp of dark hair, a dot of a nose, and a small bud of a mouth, charmingly upturned at the corners. He looked far too fragile to have survived his laborious ordeal, but survive it he had, like the stalwart soldier's son he was. He yelped when the doctor slapped him, he howled as the nurse bathed him, but when he was fresh and clean and blanketed and placed in his mother's arms, he quieted down instantaneously, as if he knew he was where he belonged.

Whitney looked down at her masterpiece with weary but awe-filled eyes. The long months of carrying him, the suffering in bearing him, faded from memory as she beheld the magnificent outcome. Oh, it was worth it, more than worth it, to feel this blessed warmth against her breast, to touch his smooth silken skin, to trace the line of his small perfect mouth. "Mama," she said in a hushed voice, "isn't he the most beautiful baby you've ever seen?"

Laura gave a tremulous smile and gently caressed her daughter's cheek. "Almost," she said softly, "but not quite."

*   *   *

Later, while the new mother slept, while the
nurse tended the infant, Laura, near a state of
complete emotional exhaustion, sat huddled in
an armchair in Steven's study downstairs. An
untouched cup of coffee cooled on the table by her
side. Avery, seated opposite her, stared silently
into the fire. The wind had died down, and only
occasional snowflakes slapped wetly against the
windows. It seemed that Nature herself had been
exhausted by the twelve-hour ordeal.

Laura's entire body ached as if she and not her
daughter had just delivered a child. She felt
spent to her very bones, numb, almost paralyzed. She kept thinking of the child, of his kit-
tenlike mewling, of his sweet, tiny features, so
like Whitney's as an infant . . .

"Why don't you go to bed?" Avery's soft voice
startled her. "It's almost midnight."

She looked up at him without really seeing
him. His face was haggard, his eyes heavily
shadowed, but Laura was so deeply immersed
in her own inner turmoil that for once she was
insensitive to his. "I wouldn't be able to sleep,"
she said listlessly.

"At least you could rest," he persisted.

She shook her head and straightened in her
chair. "I want to talk to you about the child."

"Yes, go on," he said warily.

"I won't give him up." And with those reso-
lute words sudden strength flowed into her
limbs, and a rush of color tinted her cheeks.
"I've made up my mind, Avery. There's no use
your trying to convince me otherwise."

To her surprise, he didn't protest; he merely sighed and leaned back in his chair.

"Have you nothing to say?" she asked, deflated, for in the space of a second she had mentally girded herself to do battle to the death. It was the thought of losing the child that had drained her of all vitality. The decision to keep him had infused her with new life.

"What is there to say?" Avery said with a shrug. "I rather expected you'd feel this way once you saw him." He turned apathetic eyes back to the fire. "And to be truthful, Laura, I'm too tired to debate the issue."

Laura studied his averted face. The hard set of his jaw was more revealing than his words.

"If you're angered by my decision," she said straight out, "why don't you say so."

He shrugged again. "You know my feelings on the subject. What's the point in restating them?"

"The point," Laura said, "might be to clarify your motives for wanting to dispose of the child."

"Dispose of him?" he snapped. "You, Laura, are the one who pleaded with me to abort him."

Her face flushed deep red. She shifted uncomfortably. "I deserve that," she said in a low voice. "And I shall regret that plea to my dying day. I think I was trying to sweep my troubles under the carpet—which is what I suspect you're trying to do now." She paused, then asked outright the question that had been plaguing her. "Or is there another reason, Avery? Perhaps it's not the child you wish to bury in obscurity, but his father."

"That's nonsense," he said dismissively.

"Is it?" she pressed on. "I know how you feel about Christopher, how you've always felt about him, even before Whitney's accusation. I daresay you'd love to see him discredited, ruined. What I'm wondering is if you would go so far as to do something about it."

His eyes narrowed. "Kindly tell me what you're talking about, Laura."

Did he sound guilty? She couldn't be sure.

"I've heard rumors," she said deliberately.

"What rumors?"

"About Christopher. Cynthia's been writing to me. It's being said about town that he's in collusion with certain contractors, their object being to erect structures cheaply and ultimately dangerously. Oddly, no one knows who the contractors are, but Christopher's involvement in the scheme seems to be common knowledge. None of our friends believe it. Malcolm and Jeremy were up in arms when they heard it, and John has assured his colleagues on Wall Street that the rumor is unfounded. Still and all, Cynthia said that Christopher has recently lost several important commissions. I wonder, Avery, how such a scurrilous lie could have gotten started."

"What makes you think it's a lie?" he asked coldly. "And how can you defend him after what he's done?"

"That's not what we're talking about," she

said stubbornly. "In any case, I'm still not that certain that Christopher fathered Whitney's child."

"How can you doubt it?" Avery shot back. "What more proof do you need?"

"Christopher's own admission, for one thing. If he confessed the truth about Bar Harbor, why should he lie about . . . the other thing?"

"Christ Almighty!" Avery leaped from his chair, dragged Laura up from hers, and gave her a violent shake. "Is that why you're so determined to keep his child, because you can't have *him?* To what depths are you prepared to sink for him? Whose life will you destroy next because of your disgusting obsession with that man?"

"Let me go!" she cried and twisted out of his grasp. "You're the one who's obsessed with him; you're the only one bent on destruction!" But even as she glared at him in indignation, she wondered why she was defending a man who had brought her nothing but anguish since almost the first day she met him.

She didn't love him anymore, she couldn't possibly love him after all that had happened between them. And yet, why did she refuse to believe that he had fathered Whitney's child when the evidence against him was almost irrefutable? Almost. That was the key word. Despite the overwhelming circumstances that pointed to his guilt, despite Laura's initial assumption of his guilt, she knew now, from the practical perspective of logic and hindsight, that he was innocent.

"Avery, come quickly!" said Dr. Maddox from the doorway.

Laura started at the unexpected intrusion. Avery, with a sudden dart of foreboding, went at once to his colleague. "What's wrong?" he said. "Is it Whitney?"

"No," Maddox said heavily. "It's the child. He's cyanotic."

Laura wasn't sure what "cyanotic" meant, but from the look that crossed Avery's face, she suspected it was critical. Forgetting the unpleasantness that had just passed between them, she hurried to his side. "Avery, what is it? What's wrong with him?"

Too worried himself to spare her, he said, "He's not breathing properly."

"But why? What's causing it?"

"I don't know," he said impatiently, anxious to see to the child. "I have to examine him before I can say what's wrong with him."

He turned to go, but she detained him with a hand. "Avery, let me come with you."

"Absolutely not. Wait here," he commanded. "I'll be down as soon as I can. Now let me go, Laura; we're wasting time."

He left the room with Maddox. Laura stared after him numbly. Her arms throbbed where he had grasped her in anger, but she was oblivious to all sensation save a paralyzing dread. *Dear God*, she prayed, fearing the worst, *don't let him die. He's an innocent baby. The sin isn't his. It's not fair for you to punish him . . .*

She called a halt to her racing thoughts, moved

distractedly to the fire, and stared blindly into the flames. Even as she had begged God's mercy, she had realized dimly that if the child died, it would not be a punishment but only another of life's inexplicable tragedies. Her mother had once said to her, "It is futile to rail against the things we cannot change. It is more productive if we learn and gain strength from them." But what did one learn from the death of an infant? Whatever the lesson, it could only be a bitter one.

An hour went by; Laura never moved a muscle. She stood in front of the fire, eyes closed, hands clasped before her in an attitude of supplication, but she had long ceased to pray; she only waited and hoped.

When Avery returned, she sensed rather than heard him enter. Her eyes flew open. She turned from the fire and froze when she saw his face.

"Is he all right?" she asked swiftly, although the answer was evident.

"No," Avery said, and in that one hoarse word was all the impotent rage of his failure. "I did what I could to save him, but it wasn't enough."

Chapter Twenty-six

✦✦✦✦✦

THEY LAID HIM to rest in Newport, in a small corner of the ancient burying ground behind Trinity Church. Snow had been cleared from the gravesite. Mounds of it were heaped near the wrought-iron gate that encircled the premises, and a whining wind blew icy flakes against Laura's veiled ashen face. Under a slate-gray sky that promised more foul weather, the Right Reverend Samuel Kendall, an acquaintance of the Sheridans and a man of great discretion, conducted the brief but moving service. Whitney had begged to be allowed to attend the funeral, but because of her weakened condition Avery had forbidden it. Only he and Laura and two solemn-eyed gravediggers, shivering against the frigid wind, witnessed the lowering of the tiny coffin into its place of eternal repose.

On the carriage ride home, as the coachman skillfully guided the horses down Bellevue Avenue, Avery looked out at the ice-slicked street and said in a strained voice, "I did try to save him, you know. I wouldn't have let him die, no matter what you may think."

Laura looked over at him with a start, perceiving for the first time the extent of his suffering. His, she saw, was even worse than hers, for all of his medical skill and knowledge had been unable to save the life that had barely begun.

"I know you did your best," she said softly, aching for his despair. "Those things I said to

you the other night . . . they were cruel, unfair.
You mustn't blame yourself, Avery. It's God's
will that he died."

"God's will?" he said bitterly, who had seen
more than his share of death. "To what purpose,
I wonder."

Laura said nothing. To what purpose, indeed?
She had been thinking of nothing else from the
moment the child died.

Why, she wondered constantly in the days
and weeks that followed the funeral, had God
given the infant life only to snatch it away in a
matter of hours? And whenever she asked herself that unanswerable question, she would
think of that dreadful woman, Madame Fatima.
"An upheaval will occur in your life," the seeress had said, "because of your unwillingness to
confront that which begs to be resolved." Laura
could no longer deny the truth of those words. If
she had been honest with Whitney from the
start, if she had faced their problem squarely and
tried to resolve it, this devastating, senseless
tragedy might never have happened.

She longed to confront Whitney now, to bring
out into the open all that lay unspoken between
them. Had Christopher fathered her child or had
it been someone else, a young man with whom
Whitney had worked at the hospital, perhaps?
That it might have been Ned Bailey never entered Laura's mind. The gentlemen of her set
didn't do things like that.

At any rate, she couldn't broach the subject
now; the time wasn't right. Whitney had been
through too much, and the experience had left

its mark on her. She was pale and thin; she rarely spoke, she hardly ate. Avery had reluctantly left Newport, loath to leave his niece in that condition but no longer able to ignore his duties in New York. Laura did what she could, but ever since the morning of the funeral when she had backed Avery's command that Whitney must not leave her bed, a change had come over the girl; it was almost as if she blamed her mother for the child's death. Despite every effort on Laura's part to lift Whitney's spirits, she still rarely spoke, she still hardly ate. She only stared out the window with dark, dull, disinterested eyes, as if her own life had ended with her son's.

They returned to New York at the end of March, to a glorious early spring that saw a premature greening of the city's parks, which prompted daily promenades of chic ladies in flowered bonnets escorted by dapper young blades playing truant from their work. The newly built Conservatory Garden in Central Park promised a dazzling display of lilies to be exhibited at Eastertime. Already, concerts were being held on Jacob Mould's polychromed bandstand, and awning-covered rowboats and "gondolas" were filled with carefree sun worshippers, who enlivened the lake with color and laughter.

The fine weather was also responsible for a burst of new construction in every quarter of the city. Andrew Carnegie's stately Georgian house was to have fifty rooms and a miniature golf course. The University Club, in the style of an Italian Renaissance palazzo, boasted murals by Harry Mowbray in the council room and library. On Gramercy Park, Stanford White was redesigning Alexander Lawrence's residence with his usual innovative éclat. And eight blocks north of Laura's house, facing Central Park, was a new Palladian-style beauty that could only have been designed by one man.

"Whose house is that on the corner of Sixty-third and Fifth?" Laura asked Cynthia Barnes on her first night back in the city.

They were dining alone in Cynthia's fussy rococo dining room. John was out for the evening. Whitney had remained at home, pleading weariness from the long trip back to New York. Laura, too, was fatigued, but she had needed a night of diversion. The trying months in Newport had almost done her in.

Dinner with Cynthia had been the ideal prescription for mending Laura's wounded psyche. After the first few awkward moments over the aperitif, when Laura had had to answer questions about Whitney's "illness," the two women had done nothing but chatter and chuckle over five months of frivolous gossip. It was not until dessert was served that Laura asked about the house on Sixty-third Street. She already knew the answer—no other architect could have created such perfection—but another thing she needed this night, though she couldn't think why, was to speak of him, to hear of him, to savor the sound of his name.

"It's Christopher Warren's," Cynthia said, sampling her French cream meringue. "Isn't this confection delicious, Laura? I first tasted it at the Ocean Hotel in Long Branch, and I *had* to have the recipe; but the chef, a truly unpleasant Parisian, refused to share his secret—until John produced some greenbacks, that is. Frenchmen are so venal, don't you agree?"

"Some of them, yes," Laura qualified. "But then, so are some Americans. And I know Christopher designed that house, Cynthia. I want to know who owns it."

"Why, he does," Cynthia said. "Didn't you get my last letter? John was there several weeks ago on a business matter, and he said he couldn't believe the elegance of the place. There were cut-glass chandeliers, Fragonard panels on the walls, Boulle cabinets, and fresh flowers everywhere in porcelain vases and doré bronze urns. Mr. Warren decorated the house himself, and John said if he didn't know better, he'd have thought Stanny White did the interiors, that's how flawless they are."

A warm glow of pride raised the color in Laura's cheeks. Disconcerted by the feeling, she lowered her gaze and poked at her dessert.

"Not that he'll get to enjoy it much longer," Cynthia continued her train of thought. "Mr. Warren's in desperate trouble, John said. He's probably going to lose his firm—and the house too, I imagine."

"But why?" Laura looked up abruptly and was amazed at the dart of alarm that tightened her nerves. "Is it those rumors you wrote me about? Is he still losing commissions?"

"My dear, his commissions are practically nonexistent. No one can prove he's designing inferior structures, but everyone's afraid to take a chance on him. Just last week his membership in the New York Council of Architects was terminated. You know that Henry Carlisle is on the board. Henry put up a ferocious fight to retain Mr. Warren's standing, but he was outvoted nine to one."

"The Council expelled him?" Laura said, astounded. "Without proof of any kind?"

"Laura, you know the people in this city as well as I do. Inference is synonymous with guilt, as far as they're concerned. It's a good thing you changed your mind about marrying that man. I'm sure he's innocent of the charges against him, but what does innocence matter if no one wants to believe it? You're well out of it, my dear."

Well out of it? Laura wanted to say. *How can I be out of it when I'm probably the cause of it?*

Cynthia finished her dessert and rose with a signal to her butler. "Laura, let's have our coffee in the drawing room."

As they left the room, Laura felt compelled to ask, "Do you know when the rumors started, Cynthia? Was it after the war, when the men came home? Please try to remember. It's important."

Cynthia shook her head as they crossed the marble-paved entry hall. "I'm not sure, Laura. It might have been when—"

The front door opened. John entered the house followed by Christopher Warren. Christopher had his hat in his hand, his dark hair was ruffled, and he was laughing, apparently at some remark made by John.

Laura's heart leaped when she saw him. Her first instinct was to bolt from the room, but she stood rooted to the spot, unable to tear her eyes from him. A torrent of conflicting emotions flooded her brain: She wanted to flee from him, to be near him, to strike him, to embrace him. When he spotted her, his laughter ceased. He returned her numb gaze with a long, steady, penetrating look that seemed to see to the core of her thoughts.

"Laura!" John boomed, his brown eyes beaming from behind his sparkling pince-nez. "I didn't know you were back in town. Welcome home, my dear!"

He went to her and favored her with one of his bone-crushing bear hugs. Laura was grateful for the diversion; it gave her time to compose herself. When John let her go, she was quite in control. She looked again at Christopher, prepared now to face his scrutiny, but he was looking at his hostess, who had gone forward to greet him.

"Why, Christopher Warren," said Cynthia, extending her hand, "what a pleasant surprise." She glanced at Laura as if to assure her that his presence was indeed unexpected.

"Good evening, Mrs. Barnes." He shook her hand and bowed. "I found myself stranded on Wall Street tonight, and your husband was kind enough to taxi me uptown. He then insisted I come in for a drink, but I see you have company, so if you'll excuse me—"

"By no means!" John broke in. "We're not strangers here, are we, Christopher? You and Laura know each other. You'll stay and have that brandy, and the ladies will join us."

"Yes, do stay, Mr. Warren," Cynthia said courteously. "John, why don't you and Mr. Warren have your drinks in the study? Laura and I were just about to have coffee in the drawing room. We've been gossiping all evening. I'm sure you gentlemen would be bored by our chattering."

"On the contrary," John said, dropping a kiss on the tip of her nose. "I've been closeted all evening with a group of stuffy bankers. There's nothing I'd like more than to look at and listen to two of the most charming ladies I know."

The hall telephone rang. John picked it up and raised his eyes heavenward when he found himself talking to one of the bankers he had just left. At the same moment, the butler appeared. As Cynthia turned to him to give him instructions, Christopher moved toward Laura and said so that only she could hear, "If you'd prefer, I'll leave."

He was standing so close that she could see a vein throbbing faintly at his temple, so close that she could detect the light, pleasant aroma of his shaving soap. She remembered the scent vividly, clean and fresh like the sun on new-mown grass. She remembered other things about him, things she would rather forget, memories that made her legs go weak and her breath catch painfully in her throat. She remembered touching him, holding him, tracing her finger against the line of his mouth, the mouth that looked so hard yet felt so warm to the touch. She remembered wanting him so much, loving him so fiercely, that nothing else in life had any substance or meaning. She remembered all those emotions as if she were feeling them now. But no, it was only a memory. She didn't love him anymore.

"Stay or leave at your own convenience," she said coldly. "It makes no odds to me."

She saw the hurt leap into his eyes—why did that hurt her? She immediately wanted to apologize, to say, "No, don't go! There's so much I need to say to you."

But before she could speak, Christopher said in a hard, low voice, "My regards to your family." Then he turned on his heel and left.

Laura found it difficult to sleep that night, and the next morning, when she went to the Capital Club to take up her duties there, she found it even more difficult to concentrate on her work. Despite her distraction, she was amazed at the progress that had been made in her absence: The billiard room and gymnasium were fully appointed; the Turkish bath had been started. But as she talked to the crew boss about tile and grout, her thoughts were a million miles away.

"Inference," she kept thinking, "is synonymous with guilt." "What does innocence matter if no one wants to believe it?'' Was Laura herself guilty of the same blind injustice? Was she ignoring another truth too distressful to confront? Why hadn't she simply asked Christopher if he had fathered Whitney's child? Because if he had denied it and Laura believed him, it would have exposed her faith in Whitney as a self-deluding sham?

At noon, no longer able to keep up a pretext of industry, she left the Capital Club and went home with the intention of having some lunch. Perhaps food would revive her; she felt empty and drained. But when she sat down to yet another solitary meal, she rose from the table, leaving her roast beef untouched, went directly to Whitney's bedroom, and found her lying on the chaise longue, still in nightgown and robe.

''Hello,'' Whitney said listlessly. ''I thought you were working today.''

''I came home for lunch,'' Laura said, regretting the impulse that had sent her up here. The room was dark and stuffy; it felt like a crypt. And Whitney, on the chaise, looked as lifeless as a corpse.

Shaking off that ghastly thought, Laura began to fuss about the room, straightening the mantel clock, realigning the Yung Chêng jars. When she went to draw back the rose-colored draperies, Whitney protested, ''Mama, don't open the curtains. The light hurts my eyes.''

''Nonsense!'' Laura said brusquely. ''You can't bury yourself in the dark like a little mole, Whitney. It's a wonderful day.'' She raised the window wide and breathed deeply of the balmy air.

"Get dressed, why don't you? We'll call on Ned. Cynthia told me that he's recovering nicely. He's not back to work yet, but he's up and about. I'm sure he's most anxious to see you."

Whitney lowered her gaze and plucked at the folds of her dressing gown. "You go without me, Mama. I'm not up to going out today."

Laura turned from the window and studied Whitney's downcast face. She looked fourteen years old curled up against the cushions with her dark hair atumble about her fair cheeks and brow. How tempted Laura was to say, "I understand, my baby. Stay home if you wish." But Whitney wasn't a baby; she was a woman full grown. And it was time, Laura decided, that she act like one.

"Whitney, listen to me," she said reasonably. "I know things are difficult for you right now, but as unappealing as it may seem, you should get out of the house, be active. It's the only way you're going to forget."

"Some things," Whitney mumbled, "are impossible to forget."

"I know that," Laura said gently. "But time heals, darling, it really does—as long as you don't shut yourself off from the people who care for you. Don't you know how difficult it was for me to get over Papa's death? But I did it, Whitney; I went on with my life."

"Yes, I know you did," Whitney said. And the look she gave her mother, suddenly cool and adult, was an outright indictment to which Laura felt bound to respond.

"You're angry with me," Laura said candidly. "You've been angry for some time."

"Yes," Whitney said, though the admission did not come easily. "I am."

"And you blame me for everything that's happened," Laura said further, "including the baby's death."

Whitney did not answer at once. Laura could sense her mind working, sorting out her feelings. "I think so. Yes," Whitney finally said. "All of it might have been averted if . . ."

"Go on," Laura urged, both expectant and oddly sad.

Whitney's dark eyes looked inward as if evaluating her theory before giving it voice. "I've been blaming myself for so much of what's happened," she said slowly, "but since the baby died, I've come to feel that you, Mama, because you're older, more experienced, ought to have had the wisdom and maturity to stop it all before it began."

"It's odd you should say that," Laura said agreeably. "For the longest time I've been thinking more or less the same thing. And yet whenever I asked myself how I could have stopped matters from getting out of hand, the only answer I could think of was that I should have forbidden you to see Christopher, which, if you will recall, Whitney"—her voice was not so agreeable now—"is exactly what I tried to do."

"Perhaps," Whitney responded, her own voice an accusation, "you forbade the wrong person to see him."

"Meaning myself, I suppose."

"Yes, meaning you," Whitney shot back. "*I* am not the one who forgot Papa, who found a new love a scant four years after his death, completely forgetting he ever existed."

"I see," Laura said gently and wondered why she hadn't seen it all sooner. "Could that possibly be the reason you allowed yourself to get pregnant? To teach me a lesson."

"That's absurd!" Whitney's lassitude was totally gone now. She sat bolt upright, both hands clutching the arms of the chaise.

"Is it, Whitney? Then why did you get pregnant? Your work at Indigents' Hospital must have been an education in more ways than one. While you were there, I daresay you learned certain methods of preventing conception. Why didn't you use one of them?"

"I didn't think," the girl said hotly. "Conceiving a child was not something I *wanted* to happen."

"Did Christopher want it to happen?" Laura pressed on intransigently. "Did *he* want a child?"

"I don't know," Whitney snapped. "We never discussed such a thing."

"You didn't? How very curious. During the course of your affair, did the subject never come up? And after you learned you were pregnant, didn't you tell him?"

"It wasn't an affair," Whitney said without thinking. "It only happened one time."

"Oh, I see. When was that, Whitney?"

"I-I can't recall," Whitney faltered, caught off guard by the question. Then, recovering quickly:

"Oh, yes. It was the night I went to his house."

"That was the only time?" Laura asked. "It never happened again?"

An odd note in Laura's tone put Whitney on the alert. She regarded her mother silently with wary, dark eyes.

"Whitney, come now," Laura said with a trace of impatience. "I know it distresses you to talk about him, but try to be brave about it, just this one time."

Whitney rose abruptly and strode to the window, averting her eyes from her mother's steady gaze.

"Whitney?" Laura prompted.

"Mama, I don't see what all this discussion is going to accomplish," she said obstinately. "It's a dead issue. Why don't we just forget about it?"

"That's precisely what I want to do," Laura assured her. "Just answer my question and that will be the end of it. Did Christopher make love to you again after that night you went to his house?"

"No, he didn't!" Whitney cried. "Why do you care? What does it matter?"

"Because if he didn't," Laura said calmly while her pulse raced with exhilaration, "he couldn't possibly have gotten you pregnant."

"What are you saying?" Whitney insisted. "Of course he did. I just told you—"

"Be still!" Laura said strongly. "Don't insult my intelligence any further. Christopher told me about your visit to his house. It was months before a probable date of conception. Even if you continue to insist he made love to you on that night, someone else and not he fathered your child."

Whitney's face, already pale, turned the color of ashes. Her shoulders slumped; she moved back to the chaise like a very old woman and sank down against the cushions with a defeated shudder. She aged before Laura's eyes; she looked haggard and ill. When at last she responded, the words, low and muffled, seemed to come from the depths of a tomb. "You're right; he isn't the father. And he never made love to me. I'm glad you finally know. I'm sick and tired of living a lie."

Laura's joy on learning of Christopher's innocence was superseded by her rage at her daughter's duplicity. But as angry as she was with Whitney, Laura was even more angry with herself. Why hadn't she questioned the girl months ago, a year ago? All this precious time wasted thinking that Christopher . . . Oh, what a fool she'd been, what a blind, prideful fool. How ready she had been to believe the worst about him, because it was impossible, inconceivable, that "one of her own kind," her own flesh and blood, could have behaved in so dishonorable a manner.

"Whitney, why?" she demanded. "How could you have done such a thing?"

"I don't know," the girl mumbled, plucking listlessly at the skirt of her robe. "Or maybe I do." She raised her gaze unwillingly to her mother. "It was easier for me, I think, to have been the victim in the matter, instead of an accomplice."

"What do you mean, an accomplice?"

Whitney took a moment to answer. The truth did not come easily when deception had been the norm for so long a time. "I think," she said slowly, dragging the words from the deepest recess of her conscience, "that what happened in Bar Harbor was as much my fault as it was Christopher's. He told me repeatedly he didn't love me, but my vanity refused to believe him. I loved him, therefore he had to love me in return. If I'd had an ounce of perception, I'd have known from the start that it was you he loved—"

"Did he tell you that?" Laura asked swiftly.

"He didn't have to, Mama. A blind man would have seen it, and yet I, with perfect vision, saw nothing but what I wanted—or what I thought I wanted. It wasn't until the baby was born that I knew whom I really loved. But, unfortunately, it may be too late for us."

"Who is he?" Laura said, fearing another unacceptable situation. "Who fathered the child?"

"Ned," Whitney said softly.

"Ned?" Laura gasped. "*Ned?* Do you mean to say he got you pregnant and then refused to—"

"No! He never knew about the child. That's why I say it may be too late. I have to tell him the truth, I can't lie anymore. And I must tell him everything, that I led you to believe that Christopher was the father. I don't see how he can ever understand my doing such a thing. And now that the baby is dead— Oh, Mama," she said with a sudden desolate sob, "nothing is ever going to be the same between us again."

Laura's throat tightened. She had never been

able to bear the sight of her daughter in tears. She wanted very much to embrace her, to say *There, there, my baby; everything's going to be all right*. But hurt and shock and anger were stronger at the moment than any compassion she might be feeling.

"Stop your crying," she said more sternly than she intended. "It's too late for that now. You're right about telling Ned the truth; it's the only decent thing to do. And if he can't forgive what you've done, you'll simply have to accept it and learn to live with it."

"But, Mama, I love him, I want to marry him! Oh, why didn't I know it sooner?"

"Yes, why?" Laura echoed, her voice low and grim. But she was questioning herself, not her daughter.

Chapter Twenty-seven
✦ ✦ ✦ ✦ ✦

"WHITNEY, WHY?" ASKED Ned Bailey the following morning when the woman he loved finally called on him. "Why didn't you visit me sooner? Don't you know how much I've been longing to see you?"

They were alone in the garden, sitting together on the swingseat. Laura and Mrs. Bailey had tactfully left them to themselves. It was another fine day with gentle, balmy breezes. The scent of hyacinths and spider lilies mingled sweetly in the air, and a great golden sun raised sparklets of light on the young blades of grass that were still touched with dew.

"I wanted to come, Ned, but I . . ." Whitney's voice was barely audible; it was an effort to speak. Her confrontation with her mother had completely sapped her strength. She felt an enormous relief that the deception was over at last, but she couldn't forget the look in Laura's eyes when she heard the truth, nor could she stop thinking of something Laura had once said to her: "There's very little a daughter can do to make a mother stop loving her." Whitney wondered despondently if Laura still believed that was true.

"Are you recovered?" Ned asked, searching her pallid face. "Your mother said you're fine, but you look like the very devil— I'm sorry, Whitney." He lifted her hand and pressed it ardently to his lips. "You look wonderful, exquisite. It's just that you're a little pale."

"You're the one who's looking wonderful," she said, trying to rouse herself from her doldrums. Ned was thin but tanned and healthy. His eyes, clear and brilliant, rivaled the green of the new spring grass. Whitney, conversely, looked tired and drawn. The cheery pink of her frock lent no color to her ashen cheeks. "You're much too slender," she scolded lightly, "but I imagine your mother will soon remedy that."

"Good Lord, I hope not!" he exclaimed, relieved to hear her bantering tone. "Now that I'm this svelte, I intend to remain so for the rest of my days."

Whitney rested her head on his chest. His arm went at once around her shoulder. "I like you better with some meat on your bones," she murmured, toying with a button on his vest. "You were more comfortable to lean on then."

"In that case," he promised her, "I shall regain the thirty pounds I lost just as quickly as I can."

She was silent for a time. The day was so beautiful. How ugly it might turn when she made her confession.

"Ned," she said, putting off the inevitable, "was it awful in Cuba?"

"It was a bloody, stinking cesspool," he muttered. "I wish I'd never—" Her startled look stopped him. He laughed shortly and squeezed her arm. "Forgive the vulgarity, Whitney; it just slipped out. Going to war wasn't at all what I thought it would be. You know, it's ironic . . ." He withdrew his arm from around her and leaned forward, elbows on knees. "I called Christopher a coward because he didn't want to enlist, but he was right; it wasn't our fight. All those men who died there did so for nothing." He closed his eyes, remembering, and his voice went very low. "My God, what a waste of young lives."

"Ned . . ." She touched his arm. When he turned and looked up at her, it frightened her. "Ned, don't think about it. It's over, you're home, you're safe. Don't torture yourself by remembering."

He smiled, albeit bleakly, and reached over to kiss her cheek. "You're right," he said. "Let's talk of something else. Have you heard from Marcella? Are she and Jamie back from Europe yet?"

His return to pleasant subjects relaxed her. "They won't be back until next month. I had a letter from her just before I left Newport. She . . ." Whitney paused, then went on. "She's going to have a baby."

"Already?" Ned grinned. "They didn't waste any time, did they?"

"No . . ." She paused again and took his hand as if to draw strength from his touch. "Ned, I have something to tell you. It's . . . I'm a little afraid to say it."

"You want to propose," he teased her. "Very well, I accept."

"Yes, that's part of it," she said. "But I—"

He drew back and stared at her. "Are you joking?"

"Of course not. I wouldn't joke about such a thing. Why does that surprise you?"

He frowned and shook his head as if to clear it. "I must be hallucinating again. You're saying, as calmly as you please, that you want to marry me, when for more than a year you kept telling me over and over again that you'd never marry anyone. And you ask me if that surprises me?"

"I didn't know what I wanted then," she said defensively. "I was confused; there was so much I had to come to terms with. But I always loved you. I do want to marry you, and I hope you want it too."

"Whitney, you know that's what I want!"

"Yes, but listen to me, Ned. I have to tell you . . ."

It took her a moment to summon her courage, but then, knowing she could put it off no longer, she told him the whole sordid story from beginning to end. She omitted nothing. She confessed the half-truths, the outright lies, her shame, her fears, her sense of helplessness and despair. With dread she watched his face change, saw him pale beneath the tan, saw puzzlement turn to shock, shock to disillusionment. Anguished, she witnessed the death of his once-unshakable trust in her. It was like watching her son die again, in the depths of his father's eyes.

"He was so beautiful," she whispered when Ned's stricken silence persisted. "He looked exactly like you. I loved him so much. Even though I only had him for a few hours, I loved him more than I've ever loved anyone. I would never have given him up, no matter what Mama and Uncle Avery said. He was mine, *ours*, and I was going to keep him. But then he died." Her voice broke. "Then he died."

"Christ!" Ned erupted, rising abruptly from the swingseat. "Why didn't you tell me? Why did you let all this time go by without saying a word to me?"

"I-I wanted to," she stammered, looking up at him in a panic. "But first you were in Cuba; I didn't want to tell you in a letter. And then you were ill. And then, then . . . I was trapped in my lies. I didn't know what to do."

"Did it never occur to you to tell the truth?" he flung back at her.

Whitney cringed at his tone, contemptuous and hard, but to herself she conceded that it was no more than she deserved. "I couldn't," she said wretchedly. "It had gone too far, I didn't know how to stop it. It was hateful of me, I know, but . . ." She couldn't go on; she had no defense. She had been wrong from the start, and there was nothing she could say to exonerate herself.

"My God," Ned uttered, pacing up and down in front of the swingseat, "what must your mother think of me? And your uncle—" He stopped in midstride and stared down at her fiercely. "He saved my life, Whitney! When he learns the truth, he's going to think I engineered the entire scheme. Jesus! As if I'd ever deny my own child."

"Ned," she whispered helplessly, "Ned . . ."

"Is there anything else you haven't told me?" he demanded. "Did you lie about Bar Harbor too? Was that another 'trap' you couldn't get out of?"

"I didn't exactly lie," she faltered, "but perhaps . . . I may have led Christopher on."

"Whitney, for the love of—!"

"I know, I know!" she cried, leaping to her feet. "I'm despicable, loathsome, dishonorable. There isn't a name you can call me that I haven't called myself. But it can't be undone, no matter how much you shout at me. So if you want nothing more to do with me, just say so and let it end!"

She faced him defiantly, suppressing bitter tears. She would not cry; she would not further insult him by trying to melt him with feminine wiles. If he hated her now, rejected her, so be it; she must accept it. But to live her life without him would be no life at all.

"You do want to marry me?" he said with a suddenness that startled her. "You weren't lying about that?"

"God, no," she choked. "I'd never lie about that. I want to marry you more than anything in the world."

"And Christopher?" he charged her. "Is that finished with you or not?"

"Finished?" she echoed painfully. "It never even started. He never cared for me; it was always my mother. And I . . . I . . ." She groped for a truth she had too long avoided facing. "I thought I loved him, but I suppose now I never did. When the baby was born, I realized it was you I loved, you I wanted to marry . . ."

She trailed off despairingly, unable to speak further. Ned stood motionless, watching her; she was afraid to guess his thoughts. She knew only that she loved him, that she had never loved anyone else. And with that knowledge came the dread fear that she had lost him forever.

But then, to her intense joy and gratitude, he said gruffly, "I want to marry you too. I don't want it to end. I love you."

"You do?" She could no longer contain the

tears. They flowed freely now, scorching her cheeks. "After everything I've done? Aren't you angry with me?"

"Of course I'm angry," he said with a scowl, "but I haven't stopped loving you."

Whitney drew a sharp breath. Her heart began an ecstatic pounding against her ribs. "You still love me," she said with a kind of wondering awe and dared to hope that her mother's love, too, had transcended all else.

"Whitney, what the devil do you think love is?" Ned said impatiently. "A plaything that can be discarded when it no longer amuses you?"

She didn't answer at once. What could she say? *Yes, that's probably what I had thought it was?* With the clarity of hindsight she saw that her "love" for Christopher had been merely the greedy need of an acquisitive adolescent. Like a spoiled, thwarted child she had craved the unattainable, ignoring the treasure already in her grasp. When she thought of how dangerously close she had come to losing what she really wanted, she could easily have wept again—but she was done with babyish weeping and with childish uncertainty. She looked up at her future husband and brushed away the last of her tears. "No, I don't think that," she answered, reaching up to embrace him. "Not anymore."

"I think Whitney has grown up at last," Laura said to her brother-in-law later that same morning. She had dropped her daughter off at home and had gone to Avery's Madison Avenue of-

fices. As luck would have it, he had been between patients, and his nurse had immediately
ushered Laura into his comfortable consultation
room. With barely a greeting, Laura had related
the stunning turn of events while Avery listened
silently with what appeared to be a curious indifference.

The consultation room was dim. The day had
darkened and grown humid. Thunder rumbled
ominously in the distance, but neither the threat-
ening weather nor Avery's odd attitude had the
power to dampen Laura's spirits. All was right
with the world; a sun shone within her. Christopher's innocence had finally been proven beyond a shadow of a doubt.

"We had a good talk after we left Ned," she
concluded, barely able to control her exhilaration, "an *honest* talk. I wish a less tragic experience had been responsible for maturing her, but,
unfortunately, we cannot change the past."

"No, we can't," Avery agreed, toying idly
with a tin of arnica salve on his desk.

"What's the matter with you?" she frowned.
"Why are you behaving so strangely? Aren't you
relieved that this ghastly nightmare is over at
last?"

He looked up at her with an expression she
could not identify. A flash of lightning illumi-
nated a thin line of perspiration on his brow. It
was hot in the room and unbearably close.
Laura's giddy excitement began to waver and
fade. "Yes, I'm relieved," Avery said with little
conviction. "I'm disappointed in Ned, though."

"But he didn't know about the child."

"No, but he conceived it, Laura. He also lied to you about knowing Whitney's whereabouts for more than a year. It astonishes me how quick you are to forgive him for that."

A crack of thunder made her jump, and then a torrent of rain erupted from the skies and beat against the windows like a ceaseless barrage of gunshots. Now Laura was able to read Avery's expression: It was frankly reproachful, and, at the same time, it hurt and annoyed her.

"Whitney was the one who initiated the physical relationship," she said more sharply than she intended. "And as for Ned's not telling me her whereabouts, he was only being loyal to the one he loved. In those circumstances, I don't see why I shouldn't forgive him—or why I should presume to forgive him at all. I prefer not to set myself up as a judge of other people's actions. I'll leave that to God."

Avery dropped the tin of salve and uttered a sound of contempt. "Why don't you stop it, Laura? You damned well do judge others when it suits your purposes."

"I do not!" she said vehemently, but from the depths of her memory disturbing thoughts began to surface.

"Don't you?" he persisted. "I seem to recall an incident involving an unsuitable gift Ned presented to Whitney. From the scene you created, one would have thought he had given her a chemise and a pair of drawers instead of a simple piece of jewelry. And yet now, when you

discover that he deflowered your daughter, all
you can say is, 'I cannot presume to judge him.'
Come now, Laura," he said harshly. "Lie to
yourself, if you must, but don't bother lying to
me. The reason you're feeling so almighty be-
nevolent is because of your enormous relief that
someone other than Christopher Warren fathered Whitney's child."

Christopher's name, spoken with such hostil-
ity, raised the fiercest of Laura's defenses. "That
may be part of it," she said hotly, "but let's both
be honest, Avery. You weren't half as angry
when you thought Christopher fathered the
child as you are now, knowing he didn't."

"Whether he fathered the child or not, Laura,
I still dislike him."

"I think you more than dislike him," she accused him. "I'd say you despise him. I also think
you're the one who started the rumors about his
work."

"What if I did?" he said acidly. "It's no more
than he deserves."

"How can you say such a thing?" she gasped.

"With great ease," he retorted. "Look what
he's done to us: He divided our family; he took
advantage of Whitney. And as for you, Laura,
did you fondly imagine he was in love with you?
It was your money and connections he found so
eminently desirable. Did you expect me to let
him get away with all that? I did start the rumors
about his work. And what's more, I don't regret
it!"

She was silenced and shocked by the depth of
his animosity. For a moment she stared at him,

while the sound of the pounding rain echoed loudly in her ears. This wasn't Avery, the brother and companion who had seen her through the worst of life's tragedies. This man was an alien with his violent white face and the violent hatred that had stripped him of all integrity.

"Avery," she said faintly, "you can't mean what you just said. Christopher—"

"Shut up about Christopher!" he shouted. "I'm sick to death of the sound of his name. Don't you have the slightest awareness of what a fool you've made of yourself over that man? If it was a bed partner you wanted, you should have come to me—or to any of the men we know—instead of behaving like a common shop-girl with that nameless vagrant from nowhere."

"My God," she said hoarsely, sick and breath-less from his attack, "I don't know you anymore. All those years I had thought you were like Ste-ven, but you're nothing like him. Nothing."

"You know even less than you think you do," Avery said coldly. "You don't know me, you don't know your precious Christopher. Since my brother died, your one aim in life has been to remake some other man in his image. When I failed to meet your standards, you turned to—"

"Don't spout alienist gibberish to me!" she cried in a rage. "You may have ruined Christo-pher's career with your irrational hatred."

"At least I hate him honestly, Laura. Your love for him has been a mockery of hypocrisy and self-delusion."

She rose to her feet and looked down at the

stranger before her. How, she wondered, could she ever have thought he was like his brother? Why, for that matter, had she tried to cast any man in Steven's mold? Steven was dead; there was no resurrecting him.

"You may be right," she said heavily. "I've deluded myself in more ways than one. My love for Christopher has been almost as destructive as your hatred for him, but by heaven, I'm going to do everything in my power to right that wrong."

"You're going to marry him, I suppose," Avery said scornfully.

"If he'll have me," Laura replied.

"And in your effort to clear his name, you'll blacken mine."

"No," she said, pitying him. "You needn't worry about that. What you did to him, Avery, is between you and your conscience."

When she left Avery's offices, it was still raining hard. She stood in the doorway, trembling with emotion, momentarily confused as to what to do next. Her coachman, spotting her, seized an umbrella and jumped down from the carriage box.

"Come along, Mrs. Sheridan," he said, raising the umbrella above her head. "I'll have you home and dry in a jiffy."

"No, Brown," she said, feeling sick and disoriented. "I don't want to go home yet. Take me to Twenty-eighth Street, to Mr. Warren's offices."

"Very good, madam," he said and assisted her into the carriage, then he climbed back onto the box and turned the horses uptown.

It was a three-block ride to Christopher's offices. Laura stared out the window at the deserted, wet streets, trying not to think of Avery's violent tirade, unable to think of anything else. The more she thought of his brutal assessment of the situation, the more she came to see that it was not far from the truth. She *had* been hypocritical in her relationship with Christopher. Her love for him was real—there was no denying that—but she had never fully committed herself to him. His lack of background had stood between them from the beginning. As much as she loved him, the thought of having him for a husband had frightened her. In her heart of hearts she had always wanted to have back again the security and social acceptance of her marriage with Steven. If she had married Christopher it would have meant leaving her fragile sand castles of habit and dependency and erecting a substantial house of unselfish love and sharing.

"We're here, Mrs. Sheridan."

Brown was holding open the carriage door. Laura hadn't even been aware that they had stopped. She stepped down to the sidewalk with some reluctance. She doubted that Christopher was going to welcome her with open arms.

His reception room, when she entered it, was empty. Laura waited a moment. Then, when no one appeared to greet her, she went through an open doorway into the next room. A lone figure sat hunched over one of the three drafting tables under the windows. He looked up at the sound of footsteps. Laura was surprised to see that it was one of the talented draftsmen who used to work for Steven.

"Why, Sam," she said, drawing closer to shake his hand, "how wonderful to see you."

"Laura!" he exclaimed, dropping his pencil and rising. "This is an unexpected pleasure."

He shook her hand warmly, and Laura remembered that Sam Mitchell had been one of Steven's favorite, most conscientious employees. He had a mop of red hair and a friendly freckled face. Laura had always liked him; it somewhat soothed her now to see him.

"Gosh, how long has it been?" he said with the boyish enthusiasm he hadn't lost. "Two years? Three?"

"It's more like four or five," Laura said. "It was at the dedication ceremony of Stanny White's Washington Arch."

"Good grief, was it that long ago? Where does the time go? Laura, you haven't changed a bit."

Oh, but I have, she said to herself; then aloud she said, "I didn't know you were working for Christopher."

Sam's cheery countenance sobered. "I won't be for much longer. He's letting me go at the end of the week. As you can see"—he gestured at the empty room—"everyone else is already gone. You've heard the stories about him, I suppose. They're a pack of lies, you know."

"I know," she said softly. "Sam, is he in? I'd like to see him if he's not busy."

"I'm sure he's not too busy to see *you*, Laura. Have a seat in the reception room. I'll tell him you're here."

She returned to the outer room and nervously pulled off her gloves. What should she say to him? How should she start? There was no use saying she had been unforgivably unfair to him; he already knew that. There was even less use saying that she was largely responsible for his present dilemma. Why state the obvious? And if she told him she loved him, would he believe her after all she'd done? More to the point, did he still care whether she loved him or not?

"Laura."

She whirled around at the sound of her name, but it was Sam who had entered the room, and the look on his face needed no explanation.

"He won't see me," Laura said, dejected.

"He . . ." Sam was clearly uncomfortable. "Christopher has a lot on his mind lately. He hasn't been himself since—"

"Sam, tell me what he said," she interrupted him. "Be truthful, please; it's important."

"Laura—"

"Please, Sam."

"He said . . ." Sam shook his head apologetically. "He said, 'There's nothing she has to say to me that I care to hear.'"

"Anything else?"

Sam's freckled face reddened. "He told me to show you to the door and lock it behind you."

Laura gave a mirthless smile. "I'll wager his phrasing was not as courteous as yours."

"You're right; it wasn't. Laura, why is he behaving like that? I thought the two of you were friends."

"We were," she said quietly, "a long time ago."

"But what happened?" Sam asked.

"When he most needed a friend," Laura said bleakly, "I failed him."

She spent the next several days trying to reach him, but he never took her calls when she telephoned him at his offices, nor did he return the many messages she left for him. She finally got hold of him one night at his house. She had not wanted to telephone him there, but she was penitent enough—and desperate enough—to intrude on the privacy of his home.

"Don't ring off," she said as soon as she identified herself. "It's important that we talk."

"I have nothing to say to you," he said icily.

"Then just hear me out," she begged. "I want to help you; I want—"

"You've helped me quite enough," he said in a cutting tone that slashed at her heart. "My house is on the market; my firm is a hair's-breadth away from bankruptcy. I had thought that only your brother-in-law was trying to bury me, but after I talked to you at the Barneses' house, I realized he had a cohort."

"No, you're wrong," she said in a rush. "I had nothing to do with that. Christopher, you must listen to me. I know you have every right in the world to despise me, but I do want to help you. Please meet with me so I can explain—"

"Thank you, no," he cut her off, then he slammed down the receiver so hard it made her jump.

His bitterness anguished her, but it in no way defeated her. She spent the next few weeks talking to every person of influence she knew in the architectural community. Very well; Christopher wanted nothing more to do with her. But if she was responsible for ruining his career, then it was up to her to try to reverse the tide of scandal that was drowning his good name.

It wasn't easy. Too many of Laura's peers were uninterested in the fate of an "outsider," an "upstart." One of the men she called on, Lewis Stallings, a board member of the New York Council of Architects, said, "I won't vote to reinstate him, Laura. We just can't have that sort of man in our organization."

"What do you mean 'that sort'?" Laura probed.

"I mean," he said smoothly, "that a charge has been made against him—"

"An unsubstantiated charge, Lewis."

"—and the Council," he went on, undeterred, "has a duty to disassociate itself from anyone suspected of professional misconduct."

"I thought a man was considered innocent until proven guilty," Laura said testily.

"In a court of law, perhaps," he agreed. "But the laws of the Council are not as lenient. In any case, my dear . . ." He smiled haughtily and his voice dropped to a conspiratorial whisper. "I never wanted him as a member in the first place. Laura, let's be frank: he's cut from a different cloth, isn't he? Why waste your time trying to help him?"

She was less shocked than revolted by his unconscionable bigotry. In the days that followed, when she called on other men with similar attitudes, she wondered how she could have shut her eyes for so many years to a caste system as grossly intolerant as existed anywhere on the globe. That it existed—nay, flourished—in the most democratic country in the world was even more incredible. And yet, when she thought more about it, she had to admit that she had been guilty of the same hidebound prejudices— by passive acceptance if not by commission.

Fortunately, not everyone she knew was as priggishly insular as Lewis Stallings and his ilk. Stanny White and his partners, Charles McKim and William Mead, were outraged when she told them of Christopher's predicament and promised vigorous support of their colleague. John Carrère and George Brown Post likewise vowed to be of assistance in any way they could. Henry Carlisle, of course, needed no persuasion to champion his former protégé; he had been doing so for months—with little or no success.

When Laura called on Arthur Brisbane, the editor of the *New York Evening Journal*, a man who was rabid on the subject of social injustice, he was incensed upon hearing of the situation.

"But who started such a vicious story?" he demanded, raising his voice above the clamor in the newsroom.

"Arthur, it doesn't matter who started it," Laura said. "The important thing now is to stop it. Would you consider doing a series of features on Christopher in your Sunday supplements? It might be a good idea to get a cross-section of support. You could talk to builders who've worked with him—Leo Cavanaugh, for one—who would vouch for his character. You could interview building inspectors, carpenters, electricians; tenants of the Winston Court Apartments; Nina and Jeremy Tyler; Janet and Malcolm MacKenzie—"

"Hold on there, Laura!" Brisbane said with a laugh. "What are you trying to do, usurp my job? I know very well how to sell a product to the public."

Sell a product to the public. The phrase didn't exactly sit well with Laura. But if that was what it took to restore Christopher's good name, then by heaven she'd be the most convincing crackerjack saleswoman in the city!

Throughout April and May, Laura's every waking moment was filled with activity. The Capital Club was nearing completion; she was planning Whitney's wedding; and while she carried on a daily campaign to exonerate Christopher, nearly every newspaper in town had jumped on the *Journal*'s bandwagon and had taken up her cause. Joseph Pulitzer of the *World*, for whom Christopher had designed a splendid weekend retreat in the Hudson Valley, wrote many editorials in his defense. In one he said in his inimitable melodramatic style: "Certain dastardly charges have been made against this profoundly talented and honorable architect. If his accusers can come up with even a shred of evidence attesting to his guilt, I will personally pay them fifty thousand dollars, so convinced am I of Christopher Warren's incorruptible integrity.''

Whitney, upon reading this, said one morning to Laura, ''Mama, did you have anything to do with this?''

She handed the paper across the breakfast table. Laura glanced at the editorial, then gave Whitney a playful look. ''I did have a chat with Mr. Pulitzer about Christopher.''

''You must have chatted with every journalist in town,'' Whitney said wryly. ''I can't open a newspaper without seeing his name.''

''I owe him this, Whitney.'' Laura's expression turned suddenly serious. ''Do you remember that woman who read my fortune last summer? She told me that Christopher was the victim, not the cause, of the dissension between you and me. How furious I was when she said it! But she was right, of course. You and I both did as much to harm him as the person who started those rumors about him.''

Whitney lowered her gaze self-consciously. ''Yes,'' she said softly, ''I suppose we did.'' She looked up as a thought occurred to her. ''Mama, who started the rumors? Did you ever find out?''

''No. I haven't any idea who did it.''

A hard note in Laura's tone suggested that she had her suspicions. Whitney said at once, ''Mama, you don't think that I—?''

''Good heavens, no, Whitney!''

''Because despite what I did to him, I would never, never—''

''I know that,'' Laura said gently, really looking

at her daughter for the first time in months. Whitney's dark eyes were searching; her slender hands, clenched around her coffee cup, were a suppliant plea for understanding and forgiveness. "Whitney, you think I'm still angry with you, don't you? Or that I'll never trust you again. But that's simply not true. I know we haven't talked much lately; I've been so busy with the Capital Club and with your wedding plans. But I've learned some things about myself lately—and about you too, I think. What you did to Christopher can neither be minimized nor ignored, but I doubt that you did it deliberately or maliciously. It was something that got out of hand—how well I know how that can happen!—and I understand now the torture you must have endured when you felt you couldn't tell me the truth."

"Oh, Mama," Whitney whispered. Her eyes were very bright. "I *was* worried that you were still angry, even though you seemed to have gotten over it. When I kept seeing Christopher's name in the newspapers, I wanted to ask you about it, but I thought that if I mentioned his name, it would revive all the unpleasantness."

"Whitney," Laura said with a frown, "I thought we'd made a pact to be open with each other."

"Yes, I know. But—"

"No buts," Laura said sternly. "I want you to promise me that you'll always trust me enough to confide in me."

"I do promise," the girl said shakily. "Mama, I love you so much."

Laura gave her a tender smile and reached over to squeeze her hand. "I love you too, Whitney. I always have."

"Oh, Mama," Whitney whispered, but now her eyes shone with love, "I only wish . . ."

"What do you wish, darling?"

"I only wish you were marrying the man you love, too."

Laura did not respond; her aching heart kept her mute. She looked down at the newspaper, and while Whitney watched compassionately, she traced the letters of Christopher Warren's name.

Chapter Twenty-eight

◆◆◆◆

WHITNEY SHERIDAN WAS married on October 8, 1899. A lovelier bride had never walked down the aisle of Saint Thomas's Episcopal Church. Her gown was by Worth, a fairy-tale creation of white satin with seed-pearl embroidery. The skirt fell in godet pleats with a ten-foot train, also studded with seed pearls. Her veil, crowned with a coronet of orange blossoms, covered a sweet ivory face and radiant dark eyes, which never left her future husband's face as she approached him on her uncle's arm.

In the front pew, Laura, beautiful in turquoise

moire, watched her daughter walk gracefully toward the altar. More than twenty years of memories kept crowding Laura's mind and bringing
tears to her eyes. She saw Whitney as an infant,
nursing contentedly at her breast; Whitney as a
toddler, taking her first steps, clutching Laura's
hand for dear life. She saw a long vista of laughter and tears stretching behind her, yet she could
feel each day, each hour, each moment as vividly now as when she had experienced them for
the first time. How quickly the years passed! Too
quickly, Laura felt. Her daughter was being married, and it seemed only yesterday that Laura
had walked down the aisle on Laurence Whitney's arm.

Ned, in morning coat and gray trousers,
looked the perfect picture of an expectant bride-
groom. Avery, also in formal clothes, looked
handsome and proud. Laura's glance met his as
he and Whitney neared the altar. He smiled at
her; she smiled back. She was still deeply angry
with him, but for this blessed occasion she had
called a truce. Avery was Whitney's uncle, after
all. Laura would never completely forgive him
for trying to ruin Christopher's career, but by the
same token, she would never forgive herself either for the havoc she had wreaked with Christopher's life.

Thinking of Christopher brought fresh tears to
her eyes. She was grateful at least that his firm
was once again flourishing and that he hadn't
lost his house, but any hopes she'd had of marrying him were now out of the question. In a last
desperate attempt to reach him, Laura had sent

him an invitation to the wedding. *"Please* come," she had written. "Don't let the past distort your view of the present and the future." Christopher hadn't responded—which didn't surprise her. He was most likely thinking he was well rid of the Sheridan women.

The ceremony was solemn and moving. As Ned and Whitney exchanged their vows, Laura couldn't help wishing that it were she and Christopher who stood before the altar, promising to love and cherish each other until death parted them. *Till death do us part.* She remembered how much those words had unsettled her when she had first spoken them to Steven. She had been barely seventeen then; death had seemed the most fearsome of tragedies. Now she could only think that there were tragedies other than death that just as irrevocably separated a woman from the man she loved.

"Will you stop crying?" hissed Cynthia, who was seated on Laura's left. "You're going to look awful at the reception. This is a happy day, for goodness' sake!"

"Yes, it is," Laura whispered. "The happiest day of my life." But try as she might, it was impossible to stem the flow of her bittersweet tears.

The Sheridan ballroom had been decorated to resemble a gay autumn garden. Spiky clematis and brilliant bougainvillea vied for first place in beauty amid a showy profusion of nasturtium and bouvardia. A tempting buffet, including crab croquettes, veal française, chicken zampino, and eggplant à la Duperret, was aesthetically arranged on four corner tables. The finest of wines quenched aristocratic thirsts. For dessert there was a delectable variety of fruit and confection, all artistically arranged by Laura's excellent French chef.

On the reception line, Laura and Avery were on one side of the bridal couple, the Baileys on the other, greeting guests. The guests looked quite as festive as the colorful autumn flowers: Cynthia in leaf-green satin; Nina in burnt-orange faille; Janet in golden-hued surah; and Marcella, pregnant but pretty in chrysanthemum-yellow silk. Laura, on Ned's left, felt better now than she had in church. Whitney looked radiant; her happiness was contagious. She kept reaching across Ned and squeezing Laura's hand, as if the ceremony had been only a preliminary and the best were yet to come.

"Darling, calm down," Laura said with a delighted laugh. "You haven't even had a glass of champagne yet, but you're behaving as though you were tipsy."

"I *feel* tipsy!" Whitney said. "I feel wonderful, marvelous!" She winked at Ned. "Don't you, my love?"

"Yes." Ned grinned and stole a kiss from his bride. "I feel absolutely smashing." He turned to his new mother-in-law. "And so will you, dearest Mama, before the day is over."

"What are you two scamps up to?" Laura

asked suspiciously. "Are you planning some devilment?"

"Really, Laura," Ned said indignantly. "What do you take me for? I'm a sedate married man now. I couldn't plan devilment if my life depended on it."

"What's all the chattering about?" Avery asked after he had greeted the last arrivals and Ned's family drifted off toward the buffet.

"It's a surprise," Whitney said. "A surprise for Mama on my wedding day."

"What is it?" Avery smiled, pinching his niece's cheek.

"I can't tell you, Uncle. That would spoil the surprise."

Avery turned his smile on Laura. "Have you any clues, my dear?"

"Not a one," she said, and the smile she gave him in return did not quite reach her eyes.

Avery, clearly discomfited, tucked Whitney's hand under his arm. "Let me get you a glass of champagne, Mrs. Bailey. Perhaps then you'll divulge this mysterious secret."

"I'd love a glass of champagne, Dr. Sheridan," Whitney said grandly. "But my lips are sealed. Wild horses couldn't drag the secret out of me."

When Whitney and Avery were out of earshot, Ned's jocular look sobered and he said quietly to Laura, "I thought I'd never see this day."

"Oh, Ned," Laura said, moved, "she always loved you, you know. It just took her some time to see the truth."

Ned nodded gravely and looked across the

room toward his bride. "That happens to all of us, I think," he said. "Sometimes the truth stares us in the face, but we're too close to see it. Time and distance are what finally clear our vision, and if we're lucky, as I was, it comes out all right in the end."

"And sometimes it doesn't," Laura said bleakly, thinking of all the truths she had seen too late.

"Don't despair," Ned said gently. "Your life isn't over, Laura, despite what you may think now."

"Ned, you're such a good man," she said with a catch in her voice. "I can't tell you how happy I am that you're a member of my family. And I know my life's not over. Whitney and I are closer than we've ever been. I have a new son." She smiled and caressed his cheek. "The finest son a woman could ever wish for."

Ned took her hand in his and raised it briefly to his lips. "And if you could have one more wish granted today, what would it be, Laura?"

Laura's throat began to ache. "Don't ask me that," she whispered. "Don't spoil a perfect day."

"It's not perfect yet," Ned said. "But it will be."

It was early evening before all the guests departed and Whitney and Ned left to spend the night at the Waldorf-Astoria Hotel. Tomorrow they'd be boarding the Cunard ship *Campania*, bound for Liverpool, England. When Laura kissed her daughter good-bye, she couldn't resist saying, "Aren't you glad you're going to Europe with your new husband, instead of with friends?"

"Yes, Mama," the new bride said. "You were right as usual. And I'm so happy right now that I don't even mind your saying 'I told you so.' "

Laura said her farewells with a minimum of emotion, but later, after changing into a comfortable blue cashmere, she went into Steven's study, curled up in his armchair, and there in the gathering darkness she succumbed to her loneliness. Whitney had been gone only a little more than an hour, and already Laura missed her. She tried to console herself with the fact that when the newlyweds returned from abroad, they'd be living with her until they found a house of their own; but she found little comfort in that. She felt more alone now than she ever had before. Whitney was gone; Christopher was gone . . . Christopher, Christopher; she had to stop thinking of him.

A light tap at the door brought her out of her self-indulgence. "Yes?" She straightened on the chair, switched on the table lamp, then dabbed hastily at her eyes, and smoothed the folds of her skirt. "Come in."

Thompson entered, looking totally done in from the festivities. "There's someone here to see you, Mrs. Sheridan." He sounded annoyed.

"Another well-wisher?" Laura groaned. "Thompson, I'm too weary to receive anyone now. Say that I've retired for the evening."

"He says he has an appointment, madam."

"An appointment? That's absurd. I would not have made an appointment for tonight."

"I rather thought not, madam," Thompson concurred, "and I told him so. But he says the appointment was made by Miss Whitney and Mr. Ned."

A smile curved Laura's lips. *It's a surprise for Mama on my wedding day.* "Who is it, Thompson?"

"It's Mr. Warren, madam."

"Mr. Warren?" She rose with a soft gasp. Her heart began a furious pounding. Unconsciously she smoothed her hair and adjusted the drape of her bodice. "Show him in at once, Thompson!"

"Yes, madam." He turned to leave.

"And, Thompson . . ." She took a flustered look around the room, making sure everything was in order. Her legs were shaking; she could hardly stand erect. "Bring some coffee and pastries."

"Yes, madam. Will there be anything else?"

"I don't know; let me think." She hurried to the desk and switched on the small lamp, then she glanced at the darkened fireplace. "Is it too warm for a fire?"

"Much too warm, Mrs. Sheridan."

"Would you bring some whiskey too? No, never mind; he doesn't drink. Thompson, go on, go on! Show Mr. Warren in."

"Very good," he said at once, then hastily made his escape before his mistress could think of another nuisance of a chore.

Laura tried to calm herself, to slow the rapid beat of her wildly racing heart, but both were impossible; she felt charged with electricity. Why was he here? What possible feat of magic could Ned and Whitney have performed to induce Christopher to see her?

"Mr. Warren!" announced Thompson, then made another hasty departure.

"Christopher, how nice to see you." Was that her voice, steady, controlled, without the least hint of the turmoil that tripled the tempo of her pulse?

He was carrying under his arm what looked like a roll of architectural plans. Laura went to him and extended her hand, thinking how wonderful he looked with those broody dark eyes and that hard, handsome, sensuous mouth. He was wearing dark blue, with a blue silk tie that fell in perfect folds on his immaculate white shirt. He looked older, more solid, self-possessed, as if his past tribulations had served to strengthen, not defeat him. Laura had the strongest urge to go into his arms, to brush the hair from his brow, to press slow, ardent kisses to his dear face and mouth. She didn't of course; a lady does not do such things. Moreover, the look in his eyes, dark and unreadable, seemed a barrier she would be wiser not to cross at just this moment.

"Laura." He shook her hand briefly. The sound of his voice and the touch of his skin made her knees go weak. "You're looking well."

"You, too, look fine," she said serenely while her mind danced with chaos. "Won't you sit down, Christopher? Ah, Thompson," she said as the servant entered and placed a tray on the table. "Thank you; that will be all."

Thompson left. Christopher seated himself in

the armchair, placing the plans beside him on the floor. Laura sat opposite him on the leather sofa and picked up the coffeepot with a surprisingly steady hand. She kept glancing up at him as she poured coffee and filled a dish with delicacies. He was watching her too, but his expression told her nothing. Hers, she feared, was much easier to read.

"Isn't it—?"

"I want to—"

They spoke simultaneously. Laura laughed shakily and said, "You go first."

"I want to apologize," Christopher said, "and to thank you."

Laura frowned uncomprehendingly. "To thank me?"

"For your help in clearing my name," he reminded her. "Henry Carlisle and several other people made it a point to tell me that it was your efforts almost exclusively that brought about the change in public opinion."

Her spirits soared. Was it possible? Had he finally forgiven her for her unforgivable cruelty? "Christopher," she said with a rising excitement, "there's no need for you to thank me. I felt it my duty to—"

"The apology," he interrupted, "is for not responding to the wedding invitation. I ought to have done so; it was rude of me not to. But I think you know the reasons I preferred not to attend."

So exhilarated was she by his mere presence that she didn't notice the coolness of his gaze or the underlying bitterness in his faultlessly courteous voice. "No, don't apologize," she said, the words tumbling out breathlessly. "I know I placed you in an awkward position when I sent the invitation. I suspected you wouldn't want to come, but I had to try. You see, I so much wanted to talk to you. And now that you're here, I can finally tell you how wrong I was about so many things, and . . ." Her mouth trembled. "And how dreadfully I've missed you."

"I don't want to talk about that," he said with an abruptness that startled her.

"But why not?" she said, caught off balance. "I want to tell you; I *need* to tell you—"

"No," he said inflexibly.

"I-I don't understand." His attitude confused her. "Why are you here if not to—?"

"I'm here about the house."

"What house?"

"Ned and Whitney's house, of course. They asked me to design it, and they've told me that you're to decorate it. Surely you know about it?" He noticed her bewilderment, and his brows drew together. "Or is this some very unfunny joke of Ned's?"

With a jolt she grasped the situation. Her spirits plummeted. So that was how Ned and Whitney had convinced him to come here. "No," she said, crestfallen, "it's not a joke, Christopher. I just thought . . . Well, it doesn't matter what I thought."

He stared at her, still frowning, fully aware of her confusion and distress. "You *didn't* know about it," he said bluntly. "Tell me what's going on."

She paused before answering, so close to tears that it took a superhuman effort to draw breath. "It was a surprise," she managed to say, lowering her gaze. "Ned and Whitney must have thought that if they could get us together—" She looked up suddenly as a thought occurred to her, infusing her with new hope. "Why did you agree to design their house, Christopher? I should think you're as angry with them as you are with me."

His mouth hardened in that closed, defensive way she remembered so well. "I never let personal considerations interfere with business," he said shortly. "The house is costly; it will bring in a good commission. More important," he added, "Ned and Whitney have given me carte blanche on the design."

She didn't believe him. She knew him too well to fully accept his pat reasoning. He *did* have some feeling left for her, she was sure of it, else he would not be sitting here now, trying to convince her that his motives were purely professional.

She decided to play his game.

"I see," she said, and although it was difficult to do, she adopted a businesslike tone of voice. "Well, whatever your reasons, Christopher, I'm delighted that you've decided to do it. Despite everything that's happened, I'm sure you know how I feel about your work."

"Yes, I do," he said pointedly. "That's one thing, at least, about which you have never vacillated."

Ignoring his irony, she rose, gesturing toward

the plans. "I'm anxious to see your design," she said, and the echo of those words, spoken years before, sent her hurtling back in time to the day when she had first met this very gifted—and stubborn—man.

She smiled when she saw his expression. It was obvious from the hard set of his jaw that he, too, recalled the day. "Do you realize," she said softly, "that I said those exact same words to you when you brought me the plans for the Tyler house?"

"Did you?" he said, picking up the plans and rising. "You have the advantage of me, Laura. I'm afraid I remember very little of that day."

His choice of words was telling. Laura *knew* he was afraid to unbend; she knew he was afraid of opening his heart again to the woman who had so callously taken advantage of his love.

"Come," she said gently, directing him to the desk. "Let's look at the plans and discuss only that. Perhaps it's wiser if we both forget the past."

He gave her a long look that set her heart once more to racing. She returned his steady gaze, her face an open book. Her love, her life, her very being were his for the asking; he had only to speak a word, and she would be in his arms forever. But abruptly he moved away from her and spread the plans out on the desk. His hands, she noticed, aching, were trembling.

He held her chair for her as she sat, then pulled a straight chair next to her so they could view the design together. His nearness filled her with both pleasure and pain. She could barely refrain from reaching out and touching him, from pressing his head to her breast and telling him how much she loved him, how much she had always loved him—but she knew he was not yet ready to listen.

With a great deal of effort she directed her attention to the matter at hand. When she looked at his work, she was not disappointed. He had designed a house of such classic beauty, a house so stunning in its simplicity, that her eyes stung with tears, and she said in a shaking voice, "You have surpassed yourself."

He leaned back in his chair, and his formidable look softened. "It is good, isn't it?" he said gently.

"It's better than good." Her eyes shone with pride. "I can't wait to start decorating it! In the entry hall we'll have marble floors and a great chandelier wired for electricity. In the center of the hall we'll have a round tulipwood table holding a beautiful brass urn filled with seasonal flowers. The drawing room should be done in muted pastels: pale green and yellow perhaps, with Gainsborough and Reynolds paintings above the twin fireplaces. And the dining room, Christopher; I have the most splendid idea! We'll put niches in the walls to hold statues between the pilasters. What do you think?" she stopped to ask, as excited as if she were decorating the house in which she would live as Christopher's wife.

"What I think," he said, watching her with

amusement, "is that it's going to be quite an experience working with you again."

He was smiling at her now, his eyes unguarded. Encouraged, Laura laid a hand on his, but the instant her flesh touched his, he stood up and moved away from her, thrusting his hands into his trouser pockets.

"We can begin construction in a week or two," he said, not looking at her. "I've already talked to Leo Cavanaugh, and he's agreed to do the job."

"Christopher . . ." Spurred by the excitement that still bubbled within her, she rose and went to him, no longer able to ignore what was uppermost in both their minds. "Christopher, please, we must talk about it. We cannot work together and pretend that nothing ever happened between us."

"I don't want to talk about it," he said tersely. "No amount of talking is going to change what happened."

"No," she agreed sadly. "Nothing can ever change what I did to you. But I think it's important that you know I love you, that I always loved you—even when I was hurting you the most."

"I don't care what you think I should know!" he snapped. "Nor am I interested in your here-again, there-again love. Did you expect I would come running back to you because you so graciously decided that I'm now worthy of you?"

"Christopher, no! It isn't like that."

"Oh, no?" he said harshly. "Didn't this latest turnabout of yours occur at the same time you learned Ned had fathered Whitney's child? Yes, I know about it; don't look so surprised. Ned and Whitney told me everything. They felt guilty, you see, for 'treating me so shabbily,' as Ned put it, and they wanted to 'square things' with me, to let me know that they were 'mortally sorry' for having caused me 'unnecessary anguish.' Christ!" he said contemptuously. "You people make me sick. You think you have the right to go about smashing someone's life on a mere suspicion, and then when you learn you've been unjust, you think that a flowery apology is going to set things right again."

"I know I was unjust," she said wretchedly. "But even at my worst, I loved you—"

"Goddamn you, stop saying that!"

"But it's true!" she cried. "I love you; I've always loved you."

"Have you?" he grated. "Then where have you been for the past year and a half?"

"Christopher, please. If you'll only listen—"

"Listen to what? More of your lies? More of your hypocrisy?"

"No!" she said. "That's all over with. I'll never lie to you again—or to myself. Can't you see that I've changed? Can't you see how much I want your love?"

"My love?" He reached out and grasped her wrist with a hard, hurting hand. "Or my services? Now that your daughter is married, are you looking for someone to occupy your time again?"

"Dear God, no," she said miserably, her wrist growing numb in his crushing hold. "I want to *marry* you. That's what I've been trying to tell you."

He released her abruptly as if her very touch disgusted him. "I doubt that," he said roughly. "I think that what you want from me is a lot more exciting to you, and a lot less permanent than marriage. I may be too ill-bred for a husband, but breeding isn't important when it comes to a lover, is it, Laura?"

"Christopher," she whispered, her eyes smarting with tears, "I love you, I want you. I want your name, your love, your children. I want to live with you, work with you. I want to sleep every night in your arms, wake up every morning and see you lying next to me—"

"Shut up!" he cried and grasped her brutally by the arms. "Stop telling me what you think I want to hear. It won't work. I don't love you anymore!" But Laura knew that he did. And when he stared at her violently, then pulled her hard into his arms, she knew he'd never stop loving her for as long as he lived.

His mouth came down on hers with all the pain and rage and love he could no longer restrain. His arms were hurting her, crushing her, but she reveled in his nearness. She felt him tremble in her arms; she felt the years of despair in his hard, hungry kisses. She returned those feverish kisses with a hunger of her own, a hunger that could be sated by no other man but him.

His arms tightened around her; his fierce kisses deepened. She was intensely aware of his physical arousal. She wanted him too; she had never in her life wanted anything more. Helpless with wanting him, she sagged heavily against him, and her mouth parted pliantly against the sensual aggession of his.

With a low groan he picked her up in his arms and carried her to the sofa. Her heart pounded as he put her down, then pulled off his coat and tore loose his tie. She held out her arms to him; she wanted him so much. When he covered her body with his, she received him eagerly, and a wild thrill went through her as he swept aside her clothing and pushed deep inside her with a love, rage, and need that was beyond his control.

She kissed him deeply, possessively; she could not have enough of him. She was utterly his as she had never been before. He was her love, her life, her spirit; she belonged to him fully. And when at long last he filled her with the essence of his passion, she knew that now, as never before, he was utterly hers.

For a long moment afterward they neither stirred nor spoke. His head was on her breast, her hand stroked his brow. Her nerves hummed with pleasure at just the mere touch of his skin. She was where she belonged at last—in his arms, in his heart—for his violent passion had told her that he had never for a moment stopped loving her.

As if sensing her victorious thoughts, he raised his head and looked down at her. "I'd like to throttle you," he said, but his warm hands on her body contradicted his threat. "You probably goaded me into making love to you, because you knew that once I did—"

She touched his hard mouth and gave him a tremulous smile. "I knew only that you still loved me, Christopher. I knew it most strongly when you told me you didn't."

He moved away from her, sat up, and straightened his clothing. A line, fine as a wisp, creased the smoothness of his brow.

"Christopher." She sat up quickly beside him. "You're not angry? You don't really think I tricked you into—?"

"Angry?" His dark eyes scanned the seduction of her half-undressed form. "Not when you've just given me what I've been wanting for more than a year."

She sighed and rearranged her disordered attire. "We've wasted so much time," she said in a low voice, "so much precious time that could have been spent together."

"Perhaps," he said, staring moodily at the darkened fireplace, "we're not meant to be together."

"You can't believe that!" Her heart leaped painfully. "I know what's behind us, I know it's probably impossible for you to ever completely forgive me, but we *are* meant to be together. We love each other, Christopher. Don't you remember telling me that our love is all that matters?"

"I remember," he said quietly. "But it didn't prove true, did it? We've lied to each other, hurt each other—yes, I've hurt you too, so don't worry about my 'forgiving' you. After I told you about Bar Harbor, it was only natural that you should have believed Whitney when she said I fathered her child. How I hated you for believing her! And then, when those rumors began circulating, I was convinced that you were the one who had started them. So you see, Laura, I've been as unjust with you as you say you've been with me."

"Christopher," she said urgently, "that only goes to prove that our love has been strong enough to survive the worst."

"No." His voice was somber. "It proves only what I have feared from the inception of our relationship: that the gap between our worlds is incapable of being bridged. I used to think that once I was rich and successful, nothing would stand in the way of your love for me. But you were right when you told me years ago that your life was immutably fixed and you couldn't change it. The fact is, you don't want to change it. You want a quality of security that I can never give you . . . and that's unfortunate," he added quietly. "Because there's so much else I have to give to you."

"Don't you think I know that now?" she cried softly. "What you're saying used to be true, but it isn't anymore. My life was almost destroyed by propriety and convention. Even though I once told you that a man's worth shouldn't be judged by his ancestors' accomplishments, I was afraid to marry you for fear of what people would think. It never occurred to me that by not marrying you I was giving up what mattered most in the world to me. Is that what you want to do now? Will you give me up because of my misguided obsession with heritage?"

He got to his feet abruptly and walked restlessly to the desk. He looked down at the plans, at the clean, spare lines, at the graceful, airy spaces, at the floor-to-ceiling windows that would allow blazes of brilliant sunlight to illuminate every corner of the house. *That* was his heritage: his work and his talent. He had always known it. Did Laura finally know it, too?

He looked up at her presently with inscrutable dark eyes. Alarmed by his silence, Laura rose and went to him. "What is it?" she asked swiftly. "What are you thinking? Why do you look at me like that?"

He didn't answer at once, which further alarmed her. But then he gave her a slow smile and cupped her chin with a hand. "I'm looking at my future wife," he said, "and trying to decide on a wedding date."

"Oh, Christopher!" She flung her arms around his neck and kissed him until she was breathless. "Let's make it soon," she said joyously. "Next month, next week, tomorrow!"

His expression sobered suddenly; he held her a little away from him. "Yes, we'd better make it soon," he said, concerned. "There's always the possibility that I've given you a child tonight."

"I hope you have!" she said delightedly. "I want a dozen at least."

"A dozen?" he laughed. "And where do you propose to keep them all?"

Laura kissed his warm mouth, then she reached up to embrace him. "In houses designed by their genius of a father," she said ardently, "and decorated by his proud and loving wife."

A Message To Our Readers...

As a person who reads books, you have access to countless possibilities for information and delight.

The world at your fingertips.

Millions of kids don't.

They don't because they can't read. Or won't. They've never found out how much fun reading can be. Many young people never open a book outside of school, much less finish one.

Think of what they're missing—all the books you loved as a child, all those you've enjoyed and learned from as an adult.

That's why there's RIF. For twenty years, Reading is Fundamental (RIF) has been helping community organizations help kids discover the fun of reading.

RIF's nationwide program of local projects makes it possible for young people to choose books that become theirs to keep. And, RIF activities motivate kids, so that they *want* to read.

To find out how RIF can help in your community or even in your own home, write to:

RIF
Dept. BK-2
Box 23444
Washington, D.C.
20026

Founded in 1966, RIF is a national nonprofit organization with local projects run by volunteers in every state of the union.

A HISTORICAL ROMANCE
TO CAPTURE YOUR HEART!

KAT MARTIN
MAGNIFICENT PASSAGE

Mandy Ashton is fleeing her stifling existence at
Fort Laramie and is heading toward Califor-
nia. Travis Langley, a white man raised by the
Cheyenne, is hired to escort her, although he
mistakenly believes she is the rebellious daughter
of the governor. This dangerous deception becomes
even more perilous when the two discover they've
become captives of a passion as untamed as the
wilderness of the American West! Will they be able
to overcome their contest of wills and let true love
reign?

ISBN: 0-517-00620-0   Price: $3.95